DÌLEAS SECURITY AGENCY

near
MISS

C.S. Smith

Near Miss By: C.S. Smith

Published by: Jug End Media, LLC

This book is an original publication of C.S. Smith.

Editor: Liana Brooks

Editor: April Bennett, The Editing Soprano

Cover Design: Deranged Doctor Design

Publisher's Cataloging-in-Publication Data

Names: Smith, C.S. (Cynthia S.)., author.

Title: Near miss / C. S. Smith.

Description: [Charlotte, North Carolina] : Jug End Media, LLC, [2023]. | Series: Dìleas Security Agency ; book 1.

Identifiers: ISBN: 979-8-9858549-0-9 (print) | 979-8-9858549-1-6 (eBook)

Subjects: LCSH: Afghanistan--Fiction. | Afghan War, 2001-2021--Veterans--Fiction. | Warlordism-- Afghanistan--Fiction. | Private security services--Afghanistan--Fiction. | Security consultants--Afghanistan--Fiction. | Afghanistan--Politics and government--2001-2021--Fiction. | Illegal arms transfers--Afghanistan--Fiction. | International crimes--Fiction. | Sex in the workplace--Fiction. | Suspense fiction. | LCGFT: Action and adventure fiction. | Military fiction. | Detective and mystery fiction. | Romance fiction. | Thrillers (Fiction) | BISAC: FICTION / General. | FICTION / Action & Adventure. | FICTION / Mystery & Detective / International Crime & Mystery. | FICTION / Romance / General. | FICTION / Romance / Action & Adventure. | FICTION / Romance / Contemporary. | FICTION / Romance / Military. | FICTION / Romance / Suspense. | FICTION / Romance / Workplace.

Classification: LCC: PS3619.M55397 N43 2023 | DDC: 813/.6--23

Ebook ISBN: 979-8-9858549-1-6

Print ISBN: 979-8-9858549-0-9

CHAPTER ONE

SOMEWHERE OVER THE ATLANTIC

Blood, propellant, and death clung to the insides of Lachlan Mackay's nostrils, burned into his olfactory memory as surely as the images of war were engraved inside his mind.

The barren browns and grays of the Hindu Kush dissolved into mist, banished from his internal gaze by the dimmed main cabin lighting and throbbing, ever-present hum of the triple seven's engines. His heart pounded out a furious rhythm.

Some days, two years felt as close to his skin as two minutes.

The sensation of being watched prickled the back of his neck. The middle-aged Arab businessman in the window seat to Lachlan's left regarded him anxiously from beneath his white *kaffiyeh*. His rigid posture told Lachlan he hadn't succeeded in keeping his nightmare private.

"Sorry, pal, bad dream." Lachlan brushed to one side the unruly strands of black hair that had fallen across his forehead and made a mental note to get a trim when he returned to the States. He gave his seatmate a smile meant to reassure, although it felt more like an awkward twist of his lips.

After a hesitant nod, the man slumped back against his neck pillow and closed his eyes, dismissing Lachlan.

Lachlan stared down the aisle toward the galley next to the lavatories and caught the eye of one of the flight attendants. She gave him a sultry smile and navigated the aisle like a runway model in the distinctive uniform of her airline—tan suit, red cap, and white scarf, a slash of matching crimson adorning her lips. Her attire was fashionable but, he suspected, no more comfortable than his British Army dress uniform had been the few times he'd been required to don it.

He gave her a polite smile. "Scotch, please, and a bottle of water."

"Glenfiddich again?" Her brown-eyed gaze roamed his face and dropped to measure the width of his shoulders.

"Aye, thank you." He ignored her obvious interest. Women had found him pleasing to look at since he'd hit puberty and shot to six feet four.

There'd been a time when he would have returned her admiration, maybe made plans to share a meal and a bed on her layover. Now, he couldn't look at a woman without wondering if everything he saw was a lie.

When she left to get his drinks, he took measured breaths to calm his rapid pulse that hadn't yet distinguished between reality and memory. His singular nightmare never changed. In it, he rendered a crisp salute neither seen nor returned. He brushed his glove over his staff sergeant's empty blue stare and zipped the black body bag. It was the last time he'd seen Thom, unless you counted the many times his staff sergeant had shown up in his head.

The flight attendant returned with his whisky, a bottle of water, and a cup of ice. Ignoring the cup, Lachlan twisted the cap off the small plastic bottle of Glenfiddich, drank the contents in one long pull, and then took a sip of the tepid water. The whisky burned his throat, and the ghosts receded from his consciousness but didn't disappear completely. They lingered in his tense muscles and the headache forming behind his eyes.

The seatback screen showed the progress of his flight from Dulles to Dubai, where he'd board another flight to Kabul to meet with the security teams he oversaw as head of global security for Landry Associates International. According to the monitor, the plane was somewhere over the northern Atlantic, only four hours into the thirteen-hour flight. It was a grueling journey, made worse by the fact LAI's US government contracts didn't offer him the option of flying business class. He was jammed into a seat with no leg room and even less elbow room.

A slight smile lifted one corner of his lips. Some would say it was posh compared to his previous transports to Afghanistan. His memories fresh, he pulled his phone out of the seatback pocket, tapped out his unlock code, and opened the photos app, scrolling until he came to the photo he was looking for.

Sixteen men smiled into the camera behind the gates of the SAS compound inside Bagram Airfield, located an hour north of Kabul in the Parwan Province. His men had wanted a picture taken kitted out in full combat gear on the day they arrived for what ended up being Lachlan's final deployment. The temperature already had been this side of Hell in the mid-morning hour.

The noobs on their first deployment looked confident and cocky, and why not? They were part of A Squadron in the 22nd British Special Air Service regiment. Blades. Those like himself on their second or third tour projected confidence as well, but the brutal realities of war had knocked out the cockiness. As his troop's company officer, it had been Lachlan's job to keep them safe and execute the mission. He'd trusted them with his life, just as they'd trusted him with theirs.

Almost without thought, his fingers strayed to the chain around his neck, hidden beneath his dark gray, long-sleeved Henley.

But he hadn't kept them safe. He'd trusted the wrong person.

The wrong woman.

A familiar tightness gripped the back of his neck, and he lifted his hand to massage the constricted muscles. He'd find a way to avenge Thom, Fitzy, and the others, no matter how long it took. Even if it wouldn't bring them back, maybe they could finally rest, and he could figure out how to move from beneath the constant shadow of his failure.

He pulled out the ID disc from beneath his shirt—what American soldiers called dog tags—and rubbed a thumb over the round piece of metal etched with blood type, serial number, name, and religious affiliation. *O POS, 25068743, BARNWELL, T, CE.* The hard edges dug into his palm. His other hand fisted and swept down to massage the round, puckered scar midway up his left thigh, hidden beneath his jeans.

I'm sorry.

Today would be a bloody long day.

Fifteen hours later, Lachlan descended the mobile boarding stairs off his flight and onto the tarmac at Hamid Karzai International Airport. The milder temperatures of mid-March were notably absent today as a frigid wind swept down from the jagged brown mountains ringing Kabul to seep through his olive field jacket. Snow had receded from the majority of the mountainous terrain but still capped the highest peaks in this section of the Hindu Kush.

He rubbed gritty eyes and slung his black duffel over one shoulder, stifling a yawn before he headed across the tarmac to the arrivals terminal. Sleep had never been a problem in the stripped-down military transports that had ferried him across this landlocked, mountainous country, despite the deep-throated thump of Chinook rotor blades and the pervasive smell of diesel fuel that had clung to his gear long after he'd exited his ride.

But that was a long time ago. Before betrayal colored his days and the dead invaded his nights.

He scanned the area as he made his way to the terminal, always on alert for anything or anyone that felt out of place. Although no longer subject to daily shelling from the Taliban, IEDs and suicide bomb attacks on the airport and in Kabul were ever-present threats that Lachlan understood better than most, given his time in country with UK special forces.

The men who made up his civilian security teams in Kabul were all former military and well-trained. It was his job to guarantee they had the procedures, weapons, and protective gear to ensure their safety and the safety of the contractors working on LAI's development projects.

He bloody well intended to make sure no one died on his watch again.

Once inside the terminal, he set his watch for fourteen forty-three local time, checked his mobile for service, and tapped out a series of numbers.

"You made it." Ryder Montague's proper English accent came over the line.

Lachlan's shoulders loosened a fraction at the sound of his security team leader's voice. Ryder had been part of his SAS troop, a corporal with an aristocratic background who'd fought hard to earn the respect of his teammates. Lachlan had jumped to hire him as soon as he'd learned Ryder planned to leave the British Army. "Aye, you here?"

"I'm ten minutes out. We need to talk. Alone."

Lachlan's grip on his phone tightened at the uncharacteristic note of tension in Ryder's voice. He glanced around at the other arriving passengers as they milled around him. "We'll talk on the way to the compound."

Thirty minutes later, he'd made it through customs. The headache spawned on his first flight from Dulles to Dubai returned to pound behind his eyes. He dry-swallowed some ibuprofen and exited the terminal into the diplomatic area. The bright afternoon sun made him squint and aggravated his headache. He donned his polarized glecks and scanned his surroundings, spying Ryder's tall, broad-shouldered figure and chestnut brown hair heading toward him in jeans and a black hooded jacket.

The other man acknowledged Lachlan with a brief tilt of his head. Nicknamed "Clark Kent" by the men of A squadron for his resemblance to the British actor who'd played Superman, Ryder had a quiet reserve and understated strength Lachlan found reassuring.

He clapped his team leader on the shoulder. "Mate."

Ryder's brilliant blue eyes met his. The Englishman hadn't liked his nickname in the SAS, and Lachlan made sure never to use it. Still, it beat the derogatory names Ryder suffered through during selection because of his posh background. He'd earned the respect of his teammates with his sheer tenacity, closed mouth, and skills in combat.

Those skills had been tested in the crosshairs of Nadia Haider's AK-47 when she'd chosen to die rather than surrender. Ryder had almost become another death on Lachlan's conscience.

Ryder lifted his hand, wordlessly offering to carry Lachlan's duffel. "How was your trip?"

Lachlan declined with a polite shake of his head. "Same as always—long."

He followed his team leader to the NATO-controlled section of the airport, where guards protected vehicles used by foreign military and civilian contractors. When they reached Ryder's modified black Chevy Tahoe, Lachlan tossed his bag in the back and settled into the passenger seat. He opened the glove box and took out the Glock 19 Ryder kept handy. The polymer frame warmed in his palm as he balanced the weapon on his thigh.

The five-kilometer drive from the airport to the city center—and the secure compound that housed LAI personnel in Kabul—consisted of a multilane highway partitioned by trees and low, concrete barriers. As they drew closer to the city center, the traffic increased, as did the density of buildings lining the road. Pedestrians crowded the sidewalks.

Lachlan scrutinized their surroundings for anything that looked out of place or caused a blip on his internal radar. He'd learned from experience to recognize the signs of an impending Taliban attack—a sudden traffic jam, where someone on foot or a motorbike could attach a sticky bomb to a stopped vehicle. A pickup or sedan driven by a lone, visibly nervous male near a target building or convoy.

Given the rise of attacks by Afghan soldiers on allied soldiers in so-called *green-on-blue* incidents, he wasn't even sure he trusted the men in Afghan military uniforms sporting assault rifles who cruised the streets in pickups mounted with fifty-caliber machine guns.

"What do you need to tell me?" he asked Ryder, referring back to their conversation on the phone shortly after his arrival.

"Josh has been leaving the compound when he's off duty. Alone. He leaves no itinerary of his whereabouts and doesn't bring his work-issued mobile with him."

"Burkette's a fucking team leader," Lachlan growled, "he should know better than to violate security protocols. It's a bad example to set for the rest of the men when he could be abducted or killed."

"His men don't care for him, but no one's accused him of not doing his job." Ryder's shoulders lifted in a faint shrug. "We don't socialize in our downtime. He keeps to himself."

"And you don't find that odd?" Lachlan had worked with soldiers of all types, from the loud and fun-loving to the quiet, keep-to-themselves ones, like Ryder. But in an environment like Kabul, where the only safe place to relax was within the compound walls, even the most antisocial men tended to seek the company of others for a drink or conversation.

Ryder gave another shrug. "There's something else." He passed through their compound's security checkpoint, pulled into the Tahoe's designated space, and killed the motor. "I spoke with Gilly yesterday. He heard a rumor about Khan."

Lachlan's pulse ticked up at the news. Mohammed Razul Khan was unfinished business. Khan played whatever side of the war benefited him personally at any given moment. He'd had access to government intelligence that allowed his son, Razul Sharif, and Nadia to bait the trap Lachlan had willingly led his men into, but the warlord's deep connections to members of the national government made him untouchable.

For now.

If Khan's status ever changed, Lachlan would volunteer for the mission to take the warlord out himself. Like he had the bastard's Taliban son.

"Arrange a meeting with Gilly." If he were to ferret out any credible information on Khan's activities, his former SAS teammate, currently stationed in Kabul with his detachment training Afghan special forces, would be the one to point him in the right direction.

"I already did. He'll be here tomorrow, around twelve hundred. I've notified security to let him in." Ryder's gaze stayed fixed on the Tahoe's dashboard.

The temperature outside continued to drop, leaching residual heat from the SUV. Traces of snow drifted in the air. When Ryder made no move to exit the vehicle, Lachlan tensed, then steeled himself.

"You've something to say, then say it."

Ryder exhaled long and slow. "It wasn't your fault, mate. You've got to let it go, move on with your life."

Lachlan's throat constricted. Ryder, of all people, knew why that was impossible. "I was in command. I trusted Nadia, and good people died."

Beneath his shirt, the ID disc branded his flesh.

CHAPTER TWO

OLD TOWN ALEXANDRIA, VIRGINIA, a suburb of Washington, DC

Sophia Russo opened the door to her Old Town condo to find none other than her best friend Emily's father, Admiral Porter Dane, on the other side.

"Admiral Dane. I didn't know you were in town." She turned her cheek automatically for his fatherly peck. "Sal didn't call up to tell me you were here."

Tall, with regulation-length salt and pepper hair and a trim mustache, the recently retired four-star admiral radiated intelligence and the kind of authority that made people—her included—instinctively stand straighter in his presence. It was an aura his casual ensemble of khaki trousers and neatly tucked blue button-down couldn't disguise.

The admiral wrapped her in a hug. "Sal knows me."

Sophia suppressed a grin. Of course the security guard downstairs knew Admiral Dane and would let him pass. He left an impression. And he'd been here before, when his daughter Emily shared the condo with Sophia before she'd been assigned to her embassy position in Paris. "Back in DC so soon?"

"I had a meeting. It's not too early, is it? I know you were taking this week off before you start your new job."

If he'd been fifteen minutes earlier, he would have caught her in her pajamas, her shoulder-length auburn hair a rat's nest of tangles. She let out a subtle sigh of relief that she had things to get accomplished today and decided on an early start. "It's fine. I just made coffee, want some?"

"Love some." He followed her to her galley kitchen, where she poured two mugs of the coffee she'd brewed. Leaving his black as he preferred, she added a splash of half and half to hers.

"Muffin? I have blueberry." When he shook his head and demurred, she handed him his mug and led him into her living room.

Her open floorplan, combined with light oak floors, white walls, and the sliding glass doors to her fifth-floor balcony, gave the room a bright and airy feel, with plenty of natural sunlight. She sat on her white couch, tucking one of the oversized floral pillows behind her back, and set her mug on the glass and chrome coffee table. The admiral took a seat in one of the club chairs upholstered in narrow pinstripes of lavender and pastel pink.

The aesthetic was clean but feminine and welcoming rather than sterile—a sharp contrast to her childhood home in Cincinnati, filled with heavy, traditional décor and dark stained hardwoods.

"To what do I owe the honor of this visit?" She curled her jean-clad legs and bare feet beneath her on the cushion.

He cocked a brow to match the slight tilt of his lips. "You're starting an exciting new job on Monday. Director of Legislative Affairs for Landry Associates International. I thought I'd congratulate you in person."

A genuine smile raised her cheeks. "I really appreciate your glowing recommendation."

A small company with a big footprint, LAI oversaw several US Government-funded development projects in Afghanistan. Her former job as a legislative aide for Congressman Kellerman had given her a sense of purpose, a way to make a difference in the world. But she'd been a worker bee, one of many. LAI was her chance to prove her worth and make the legislation she'd helped craft come to fruition through real, tangible projects. New schools, health clinics, the creation of a civic and judicial framework that fostered opportunities for the women and children in Afghanistan's largely conservative, tribal society.

The admiral waved away her thanks. "I know you can do the work. LAI's opening was the perfect fit." He took a sip of his coffee, his gunmetal blue eyes gazing at her with a directness that tightened her shoulders. "And I trust you."

Sophia picked up her mug, cradling its warmth in her suddenly cold palms. Her mind raced at the wealth of meaning behind those simple words. The admiral's faith in her meant more than he realized and warmed a neglected part of her soul. But the way he'd said *I trust you* had her instincts on alert. "Trust me to do what?"

Admiral Dane set down his coffee and leaned forward, forearms braced on his thighs, hands loosely clasped in front of his knees. "A friend of mine believes an Afghan warlord may be obtaining brand new weapons and materiel directly from a US source and selling them to the Taliban and ISIS."

She frowned. By "friend," he meant someone in one of the alphabet agencies—CIA, DIA, NSA, DOJ, FBI. The admiral had connections everywhere. "That's terrible, but I don't understand what that has to do with my new job lobbying Congress for LAI's development projects."

His commanding stare held her hostage. "I want you to keep your eyes and ears open at LAI and report directly to me if you discover anything out of the ordinary."

Her eyes flew wide, a knot forming in her stomach that didn't sit well with the coffee. "Are you telling me LAI is selling weapons illegally?" Why hadn't he told her this before she accepted the job?

Her heart sank. The father figure had taken a backseat to the Navy SEAL who'd worked his way into the rarified air of senior flag officer using both leadership skills and political savvy. Emily often complained her father was a master strategist who considered everyone a potential pawn on his grand chessboard. "You're asking me to spy on my new colleagues."

She must have gone paper white because the admiral placed his mug on the coffee table and reached for her icy fingers. "It might not be someone at LAI. No one has to know."

No one *could* know, or she'd be out of a job and her career in tatters like a confetti bomb at a gender reveal.

"Sophia." Admiral Dane squeezed her hand. "If someone is funneling US weapons to the Taliban and ISIS, they're not only endangering Afghan and Coalition troops, they're threatening the progress Afghanistan has made. We need to stop them."

Sophia's mind raced at the implications. She'd gone after the job at LAI to have a more direct impact on improving the lives of Afghanistan's women and children.

Something that wouldn't happen if the Taliban regained power.

If someone at LAI was dirty and she helped expose them, her new boss would be grateful, not angry.

Wouldn't he? The company bore his name, after all. His reputation was on the line.

The admiral stood and picked up his mug, signaling the end of his visit. "Promise me you'll think about it."

No one has to know.

"I'll do it."

"Good." The admiral nodded as if he hadn't expected her to answer any differently. "Start by looking into the global security division and its director, Lachlan Mackay." He handed her a thumb drive. "Take a look at this when you have the chance."

She escorted him to her door and said goodbye. The thumb drive she held felt like a grenade. Viewing the information it contained would be pulling the pin. If she read its contents, she'd committed to be Admiral Dane's inside man—or woman in her case—at LAI.

Her laptop sat on the dining room table encased in its Lily Pulitzer sleeve. Sophia stood in the foyer, staring across the room at it, willing her feet to move. Curiosity finally won out.

Who was Lachlan Mackay?

She opened her laptop, plugged in the USB drive, and clicked on the single electronic file stored on the drive.

Lachlan Mackay's bio was brief. Born in Scotland and educated at the University of Edinburgh, he'd served as a captain in the British Army's 22nd Special Air Service regiment before getting out of the military and coming to work at LAI. Her respect for the man rose a notch. The SAS was considered one of the world's most elite special forces units.

There was a list of military commendations she was unfamiliar with, and the dates of his deployments. He'd served in both Iraq and Afghanistan. The file also contained the names of individuals who currently made up his security teams in Kabul, their prior military affiliations, and the dates Lachlan had traveled to Afghanistan in the past year.

But it was his photo that grabbed her attention and held it. He had a model's chiseled cheeks and jaw, a straight nose, and black hair that looked thick and carried a touch of wave that she bet would be more pronounced if he let it grow.

The Hot Scot. That would be her nickname for him. In secret, of course.

The color of his eyes was hard to distinguish from the photo, but the cold stare he'd directed at the camera spoke volumes. It wasn't hard to believe he'd been a highly trained, dangerous soldier.

An involuntary shiver skittered across the back of her neck. She had no idea how to handle a man like him. She'd been the shy, geeky girl in high school, overlooked by most of the boys in favor of the prettier, more adventurous girls. There'd been a couple of boys in college, including the one she'd lost her virginity to, but those relationships hadn't lasted, and she wasn't the type to engage in casual sex. Since then, she'd been too busy trying to prove herself in her career, and no one had come along who piqued her interest enough to try.

Of course, maybe she'd set the bar too high, expecting a Prince Charming to sweep her off her feet and make her feel like she was the only one in the world that mattered.

It'd be nice to matter.

She sighed, her gaze returning to the face on the screen. This guy was way out of her league. And possibly a cold-blooded criminal.

Monday was her first day of work at LAI. She'd know soon enough if the flesh and blood man was anything like his photograph.

CHAPTER THREE

LACHLAN WAS STILL FIGHTING jet lag the morning after his arrival as he sat across the table from his other team leader, Josh Burkette. Street maps and drone photos of Kabul and LAI's project sites adorned the whitewashed walls of the windowless first-floor conference room. Unlike LAI's headquarters in Alexandria, Virginia, the décor in the Kabul offices was strictly government-issue metal desks, file cabinets, and veneer-covered particle board furniture.

Burkette slouched in a metal folding chair in his form-fitting rip-stop t-shirt and khaki cargo pants, his full brown beard not enough to mask an insolent expression. Burkette had been a Ranger in Jared Landry's rifle platoon, hired before Lachlan had come on board. The bloke had weapons skills and native intelligence, but that was about it.

"Where were you yesterday afternoon?" Lachlan kept his tone level.

"It was my day off." Josh's flat black stare had Lachlan's fingers curling into fists beneath the table.

"And you know there are rules about leaving the compound when off duty. Rules you neglected to follow. As a team leader, you must set an example for the men under your command."

"Got it. We done here?" Burkette ran the tip of a silver mechanical pencil beneath his short nails, one at a time, inspecting them as he went along. "I've got to be on-site in an hour."

Lachlan suppressed the exasperated huff in his chest and gave a curt nod, staring at Burkette's broad back as he sauntered out of the room. He'd sack the man tomorrow if he thought Landry would allow it. There was something off about the former soldier.

Ryder stuck his head in the door. "Gilly's arrived. Meet in here or the canteen?"

"The canteen," said a voice from the hall. A wiry ginger-haired man with blue eyes poked his head around Ryder to peer in at Lachlan. "Least you could do is buy me a proper meal, ya bloody Rupert." The words tumbled out end over end in a South Yorkshire accent.

Lachlan grinned, setting aside his concern about Burkette to shake hands with Squadron Sergeant Major Michael Gill. "Gilly, how are ya, pal?"

"Eh, not so bad. You know how it is." Gilly wore a short-sleeved, collared black shirt and khaki trousers rather than his MTP combat uniform. He scratched an ear as he contemplated Lachlan. "Looks like you've done all right. Landed on your feet. Working for the Yanks now, are you?" He gestured toward Ryder. "Both of you. Better pay, I'd expect."

"Come on." Lachlan slapped Gilly on the back. "Let me buy you an alcohol-free beer."

Gilly snorted. "I'd rather drink piss."

"Aye," Lachlan agreed with a laugh. He led the way across the compound's open courtyard to an orange-painted shipping container modified into a kitchen serving authentic Afghan street food to the compound's Western inhabitants. After receiving their trays, the men stepped into another shipping container that served as indoor seating when it was too cold to eat at the picnic tables outside.

Once they were all seated with their meals in a quiet corner away from other diners, Lachlan got to why he'd asked Gilly for a meeting. "What's the word on Khan?"

Gilly took a bite of his chicken sandwich, eyeing Lachlan thoughtfully. "It's not your fight anymore, mate."

Lachlan bristled. "It will always be my fight. I owe it to Thom and Fitzy. And the others." He held Gilly's stare until the other man pinched the bridge of his nose with a resigned sigh.

"There's been some chatter about a recent raid the SEALs and Afghans executed on an ISIS stronghold in the Nangarhar Province," Gilly said. "Got into a firefight and leveled the place, but word is, they got photographs of some of the weapons and equipment at the compound before they blew it."

Gilly dropped his forearms on the table and leaned closer to Lachlan, speaking in a hushed tone. "They found M16 and M4 rifles, Glock pistols, tactical gear, NVGs, and drones—them fucking lightweight, small surveillance drones. All new equipment, mind you, not Afghan Army issue."

Jesus.

Lachlan's lunch dropped from his nerveless fingers, bits of lamb, cucumber, and onion escaping the confines of the naan bread. The Taliban were an ever-present threat, and now ISIS was growing its presence in Afghanistan. Insurgents kitted out with the same high-tech weapons and equipment his teams used was a security nightmare.

"There's more," Gilly added. "Rumor is Khan is holding a private weapons auction sometime in the next few weeks, and he's not choosy about his buyers. We already know he maintains ties to the Taliban, and I wouldn't put it past the cagey bastard to also have ISIS connections."

Lachlan frowned. "Where are these weapons coming from?"

"Some of his inventory undoubtedly comes from corrupt Afghan military leaders and soldiers looking to make some coin given their dismal salaries," Gilly replied, "but the Afghans we're training say Khan may have a source in the US. Can you bloody believe it? You know those weapons will be used against Coalition troops and our Afghan counterparts."

Gilly's last bit of information had Lachlan's heart thumping against his chest like a war drum, the adrenaline surge drowning out extraneous background noise. "If we could prove Khan's bringing weapons and materiel into the country illegally and selling them, it might be enough to pressure the Afghan government into sanctioning action against him."

Gilly shrugged. "Maybe. More bloody likely they'll overlook this auction like they do his opium business if it isn't enough to destabilize the national government. But you can be sure if the rumors are true, the Americans are tapping into their resources to track down his supplier."

Lachlan massaged the ache in his thigh, a souvenir from that day in Hell, and cursed the cold moisture sweeping through Kabul. "The US government won't move fast enough to stop the auction if it's happening so soon."

If it was true, and some bastard in the States was funneling weapons to Khan, Lachlan would track down the traitor personally. He purchased and shipped weapons and equipment to Afghanistan for his security teams and knew the suppliers, the shippers, and the other companies engaged in the same business.

Then he'd find a way to use the information to bring down Khan.

He whipped out his mobile and opened his airline app.

"What are you planning?" Ryder asked.

Lachlan caught the hint of wariness in Ryder's tone. "Talk to the other security teams here in Kabul, see if anyone else has heard these rumors and has information or is acting cagey about it. I'm heading back to the States to find Khan's supplier."

Chapter Four

THE EARLY SPRING MORNING brought a chill that Sophia shook off as she made her way through the glass and marble lobby of her new office building to the bank of elevators. When the electronic ding announced the next car's arrival, she let the other people waiting board first, then stepped in and gingerly pressed the button for the eighth floor with the hand holding her travel coffee mug. Her other hand clutched the leather handles of her new briefcase.

She gave her reflection in the shiny brass doors an approving nod. Her hair was swept up in a loose bun, small gold hoops adorned her ears, and her khaki trench coat, paired with a lavender cashmere scarf, covered a suitably conservative navy suit, the skirt ending a couple of inches above her knees. Matching navy pumps with four-inch heels lent stature to her five-foot-two frame.

"I am so ready."

One of the men in the car gave her a sidelong glance, and a woman's lips tilted upward.

Heat suffused Sophia's cheeks. "First day at my new job." The combination of nervous energy and excitement fizzed in her veins like her favorite diet pop.

Emily texted this morning to wish her luck from Paris, and Admiral Dane and his wife Carla sent her flowers with a sweet note.

Her parents hadn't called or sent a text. Sophia's enthusiasm dimmed. Maybe they forgot.

Or it wasn't important enough for them to remember.

She gave her reflection a firm look to banish the sudden, hollow ache in her chest. *It doesn't matter.*

"Congratulations and good luck," said the man who'd given her the side-eye before he stepped out on his floor.

"Thanks." She pushed away the negative thoughts trying to dampen her mood.

The doors opened on the eighth floor. She gave a brief nod to her fellow riders and stepped out, turning right toward a set of glass doors with the name *Landry Associates International* stenciled in a dark, metallic silver across the glass.

Sophia pulled open the door and stepped inside.

LAI's office manager, Penny Turner, sat behind a mahogany-paneled reception desk detailed with silver laminate and flanked by potted dracaenas. The fluorescent lights in the overhead ceiling glinted off her chic white bob, diamond stud earrings, and bright fuchsia blouse.

She stopped typing and greeted Sophia with a welcoming, maternal smile that instantly put her at ease. "Good morning, dear."

Sophia returned the smile. "Good morning, Mrs. Turner, it's nice to see you again."

The woman waved off Sophia's formality. "Oh, please, call me Penny. Jared's waiting for you in his office."

Several feet behind Penny, blue-gray color dominated the back wall, broken up by a small, glass-fronted conference room on the left and a varnished wood-stained door on the right that sported a stylish silver nameplate.

"Thank you, um, Penny." Sophia's heels sunk into the blue and gray patterned carpet as she made her way past Penny to the ornate wooden door. After a tentative knock, she pushed the door open just enough to peer around the edge. "You asked to see me?"

Her new boss, Jared Landry, stood from behind his cherry executive desk. She couldn't help but admire the subtle authority he wore as naturally as his dark gray tailored suit and blue and silver silk tie. He was in his mid-thirties, tall and lean, with light brown hair and a short, neatly trimmed beard.

She'd researched him when she applied for the job. He'd grown up in California, gone to UC Santa Barbara, and served as an Army Ranger for several years before leaving to start LAI. He seemed to be incredibly well-connected in government circles. Congressman Kellerman had joked to her before she left that LAI was as successful as it was because Jared Landry knew where all the bodies in town were buried.

"Come in, Sophia." He waved her to a brown leather settee in the far corner. "Have a seat."

Morning sunlight streamed into the spacious office courtesy of the wall of windows behind Jared's desk. Behind the seating area he'd indicated, the walls were decorated with photographs of Jared with politicians, a celebrity or two, and even a former president. Her gaze lingered on the shadowbox center stage that held his military badges and medals—what her new boss had called his *chest candy* when he'd first interviewed her.

When she'd asked him why he left the military to become a government contractor, he'd smiled cryptically and simply answered, "The pay is better."

"Welcome aboard." Jared took a seat opposite the low coffee table in a wingback leather chair while she set her briefcase and mug down, smoothed her coat beneath her, and sat on the sofa.

"I'm excited to be here." She moderated her giddiness and nerves into a practiced smile. At twenty-seven, she was a bit young for her new position, and the last thing she wanted to do was sow any doubt in her boss's mind that she wasn't mature enough to handle the job.

"Good." Jared gave her an approving nod. "Because I'm throwing you in the deep end. The executive committee meeting is in three hours. I'd like you to give a presentation to the rest of the team on upcoming legislation that may impact our funding."

She met his look with a wide-eyed one of her own. "This morning?"

"Is that a problem?" His gray eyes narrowed. "I assumed you'd already be up to speed on the legislation."

She reached down deep and pulled a façade of confidence from her bag of tricks. "No, not a problem at all. I'll be ready."

Jared clapped his palms together and stood. "Excellent. Penny will set you up in your new office so you can get started."

She stood as well and gathered her belongings. "Thank you, Mr. Landry."

He smiled. "Call me Jared." He walked her to the door, then shut it behind her with a firm click.

Sophia leaned against the wall, her stomach flip-flopping all over the place like a fish out of water. Her presentation had to be perfect. This job was important to her, and she was determined to impress her new colleagues.

Then there was her other task—the one from Admiral Dane.

Lachlan Mackay.

Did Jared Landry know he might have a traitor in his midst?

No one has to know.

Sophia's nerves settled after Penny showed her to her new office. It was a significant step up from the cramped, windowless government cubicle she'd had for the past few years. The glass behind her desk took up most of the exterior wall, and she reveled in the glorious natural light. She'd hang her bachelor's and master's diplomas on the wall to her left and her framed poster of Monet's *The Artist's Garden at Giverny,* with its purple brushstroke flowers, on the wall by the door. She made a mental note to bring in a small potted palm for the corner and another plant for the top of her credenza.

Taking a seat at her desk, she placed her favorite photo of her and Emily at their college graduation, tucked away in her briefcase this morning.

The executive committee meeting was at eleven o'clock. She logged into her office computer with her new security credentials and got to work. After two hours, she gave her presentation one last critical eye, then clicked the print icon. Penny had warned her some of her new colleagues were still old school and would want to see handouts. Once her presentation registered in the network's print queue, she hurried down the hall to the central copy room, scanning her speaker notes on her tablet one last time.

Rounding the corner, she bounced off an unexpected wall of fabric and muscle. The tablet flew from her grasp. She staggered back, and her ankle gave way. A pair of large male hands shot out to wrap around her upper arms, steadying her so she didn't tumble to the floor in an embarrassing heap.

She peered up at her tall savior. The reflexive thank you forming in her mouth died. Her hormones, on the other hand, sprang to life. Her blood heated, sparks of arousal arrowing straight to her center.

Emerald eyes with traces of gold around the irises swept her in a bold perusal. His face was marred only by a thin white scar on his chin and a shadow of ruthlessness around his mouth and eyes. A few strands of neatly trimmed ebony hair had rebelled at his attempts to sweep them back and hung defiantly across his forehead. For some reason, her fingers itched to brush the wayward locks into place and feel their silky strands against her skin.

He let her go to crouch and pick up her tablet. Her attention snagged on his grimace when he straightened and handed her the device.

"Lachlan Mackay." His name slipped out, and she froze. They hadn't met yet; she shouldn't know who he was. Her secret agent skills needed work.

One arrogant black brow arched as he looked down his perfectly straight nose at her. "Aye, and you are?"

She straightened to her full height, barely reaching his shoulder even in heels, ignored her runaway pulse, and thrust out her hand. "Sophia Russo, the new director of legislative affairs."

The body she had slammed into under the dark navy suit was rock hard, with no soft parts whatsoever. He really was a Hot Scot.

Her traitorous cheeks heated. *Great.* The curse of fair skin. She probably looked like a neon sign.

His large hand engulfed hers briefly, then let go as if he didn't care to waste time on such niceties. "You might want to pay attention when you're walking." His melodic Scottish accent and deep voice poured like finely aged whisky over her senses. He smelled good, too, a clean, woodsy, masculine scent that made her want to lean into him and take a deeper sniff.

Until his words and the irritated tone he'd wrapped them in finally registered. Sophia's eyes widened, then narrowed. She'd nearly ended up on the floor, not him. It was on the tip of her tongue to tell him he was the one who needed to watch where he was going.

"I'm sorry." She apologized instead. The firm, assured tone of voice she'd been aiming for came out breathless as if he'd stolen all the air from her lungs. The flames heating her cheeks leaped to singe her ears. This was not the impression she'd hoped to make on LAI's head of global security, especially as she would need to find a reason to stick her nose in his business.

He glanced at the military-style watch adorning his wrist. "I assume you'll be at the executive team meeting in thirty minutes, then?"

"Yes." She waved her arm in the general direction of the copy room. "I'm making copies. Of my presentation. For the meeting." *Great.* Now she was rambling.

Judging by the scowl on the Hot Scot's face, he was not impressed. "Then I'll leave you to it." With a nod, he brushed past her and strode down the corridor. The barest hitch in his gait didn't diminish the aura of power and hint of danger surrounding him.

She rubbed her shoulder where it still tingled from the heat of his touch. Admiral Dane wanted her to spy on this guy? Her stomach gave a nervous flutter.

Lachlan Mackay might be drool-worthy, but he gave off an unfriendly vibe.

Had his military experience so jaded him that he could sell weapons to the enemy and not care about the people whose lives would be ruined by his actions? There was only one way to find out.

She had to get him to trust her.

Chapter Five

Lachlan studied LAI's newest employee as she stood next to the video monitor mounted on the conference room wall at the far end of the long rectangular table. The can lights in the ceiling highlighted strands of copper threaded through the deeper red of Sophia Russo's hair.

She was a wee thing, bonnie in a fresh, wholesome way, her body made of soft curves he'd registered when she'd bounced off him in the hall. Her eyes were a light brown embedded with flecks of green and gold, her oval-shaped face ending in a slightly squared chin with just the suggestion of a dimple in the center. She'd make a terrible poker player, her expressive features mirroring her every thought. He guessed she was in her mid-to-late twenties—a bit young for her new position.

She'd been tentative at the beginning of her presentation, her voice strengthening as she grew more comfortable speaking. It was well-modulated with a soothing cadence that reminded him of American TV newsreaders and gave him no hint of where in the States she might be from.

He glanced at the handout she'd provided, then let his gaze wander around the table to the other executive team members. Christian Meier, head of global development, scribbled notes, his blond head bobbing between Sophia and the papers in front of him. Rob Salas from IT ran his fingers through his short, dark brown hair and eased into the back of his chair. Rob usually looked bored at these meetings, his only interest being LAI's computer network and not its core business, but his attention stayed on Sophia.

Fred Biller, LAI's government contracts manager, sat next to Lachlan, his coffee-stained tie resting on his protruding stomach. Lachlan's nose itched at the odor of burnt tobacco from the cigarettes Fred smoked outside the building whenever he took a break. Penny Turner, the woman who kept them all organized and the company running smoothly, sat on Fred's other side. At the head of the table was Jared Landry, their boss.

Sophia had everyone's attention—even Fred's, the old codger. She spoke with a keen intelligence and innocent charm that was...*intriguing*.

Lachlan stiffened. Beads of perspiration dotted his forehead.

He knew better than to trust a woman simply because she made a good first impression. He wiped his forehead and brushed his fingers against his trousers, silently cursing the slight tremor that ran through them.

Lack of sleep must have weakened his defenses. He'd gotten back from Kabul yesterday afternoon, his mind racing with the news of Khan's upcoming weapons auction. The last thing he needed was to lose his shit at work because his new colleague triggered old memories. Not for the first time, he regretted his decision not to keep a bottle of Scotch in his desk drawer. He could use a wee dram.

Sophia finished her presentation to murmurs of approval. "Excellent job." Jared clapped his hands. "I told you I'd throw you into the deep end right away, and you performed beautifully."

The appreciation in Jared's eyes hinted at more than a professional interest.

Or maybe that was Lachlan's admittedly jaded view. Not everyone made the same mistakes he had.

Sophia's cheeks flushed a pretty shade of pink, something else he'd noticed about her earlier. She blushed easily.

"If Sophia gets us more funding, maybe we can hire additional help here instead of overseas," Fred grumbled. "We've got the annual compliance report to the government coming up, and I can't do it all on my own."

Jared gave Fred a placating smile. "You know each division head is responsible for submitting their information for the report, Fred. It won't be left only to you."

"Is it something I can help with?" Sophia's expression faltered when all eyes turned to her. "I mean, if it's appropriate. It sounds like a good opportunity to learn more about LAI's activities."

Lachlan narrowed his gaze on her. She was a bit too eager to be of help. What was her end game? As if she could sense his stare, her head turned, and their eyes met. He felt an unexpected and unwelcome jolt of awareness. A pink tide swept up her neck to her face. She looked away.

Christ. She might not be that much younger than him in years but in life experience? He had a feeling they were miles apart.

Unless it was all an act.

"Perfect." Jared favored Sophia with an ingratiating smile that set Lachlan's teeth on edge, although he wasn't sure why. "You and Fred can work out the details later."

After everyone finished providing their updates, the meeting adjourned.

"Jared, a moment?" Lachlan spoke to his boss, but his gaze followed the gentle sway of Sophia's hips as she left, chatting away with Christian about the construction of the co-ed primary school he oversaw in a rural village outside of Kabul.

The sound of a throat clearing brought Lachlan's attention back to the only other person in the room.

"Is this something you couldn't bring up in the meeting?" Jared's chilly tone matched the frost in his eyes.

Lachlan schooled his expression so his irritation wouldn't show. He and Jared were too much alike in some ways to truly get on. They were both leaders who valued control. When Jared contacted him to offer him the job at LAI, he'd taken it for one purpose—to return to Afghanistan and have a freedom of movement not afforded him in the military.

"Aye. It's important." He needed to discuss Josh Burkette's behavior and, more importantly, what he'd learned from Gilly.

"Let's go into my office. We'll be more comfortable there." Jared strode from the conference room, leaving Lachlan to follow. When Lachlan shut Jared's office door behind him, the other man gestured toward a crystal decanter filled with expensive whisky, a wordless question in his raised brows. "You look like you need one."

Lachlan shook his head. "Not at noon when I have a lot of work to catch up on." He settled into one of the two navy and silver striped armchairs in front of Jared's desk while Jared sat on the opposite side in his high-backed black leather executive chair, making the power dynamic between the two men clear.

"You got pale in the meeting earlier, during Sophia's presentation. Did something she said bother you?" To Lachlan's ear, Jared's question sounded more mocking than genuinely concerned.

He dismissed the thought. The situation in Afghanistan had his nerves on edge. "No, she's very accomplished." He wasn't sure what it was about Sophia Russo that annoyed him. "The problem is in Kabul. Josh ignores security protocols—disappears from the compound during his downtime without letting anyone know where he's going."

Jared frowned. "Is he getting the job done?"

"Aye." Lachlan already knew bringing up concerns about Jared's former Ranger teammate was likely to be a waste of time, but he had to try for the sake of his men. He wasn't sure he trusted Burkette and didn't know why Jared did.

"Then why are we having this conversation? I let you bring your SAS buddy on board as the other team leader. I trust Josh to carry out his responsibilities."

"I don't want Josh ending up dead. An American wandering around alone is a tempting target." Lachlan swallowed the rest of what he wanted to say. Unless Burkette did something that endangered LAI's contracts, Lachlan's hands were tied. "There's more. Mohammad Razul Khan has stockpiled weapons and equipment, possibly with the help of a US contractor, that he intends to auction off very soon."

"How does this involve LAI?"

Lachlan frowned at the question. It should be evident to the former Ranger why it mattered. "We don't need the Taliban or ISIS attacking LAI's projects with the same first-rate firepower and protective gear my teams have. And if the warlord is getting those weapons directly from an American contractor, we need to find the source before this auction takes place."

Jared's cool gray gaze assessed him across the desk. He picked up the black and silver Montblanc pen lying on his desk blotter and spun it around his fingers, never taking his eyes off Lachlan. Jared was skilled at keeping his thoughts hidden when he chose to, and Lachlan couldn't get a clear read on the other man. "That's not your job."

A slow, steading pounding took up residence in Lachlan's temple. "I'm only suggesting I make a few phone calls and do some digging. If that weapons auction takes place, my security teams' ability to keep our development partners safe in Afghanistan becomes exponentially more difficult."

Jared shook his head. "I get it, but your job isn't to track down illegal arms trafficking, nor is it to get involved in the business of an Afghan warlord,"—he pointed the pen at Lachlan—"one, I might add, that enjoys the protection of the Afghan government." Jared let the Montblanc drop to his desk. He swiveled to face his computer, signaling that the conversation was over as far as he was concerned. "Let the US and Afghan governments work the problem."

Lachlan stood, frustration making his movements stilted. He may not have Landry's support, but he wouldn't let this drop. Khan's supplier needed to be unmasked and the full extent of Khan's terrorist activities exposed so the US and Afghan governments would have no choice but to sanction action against him. He gave Jared a curt nod and headed for the door.

"Lachlan."

At the sound of his name, Lachlan glanced over his shoulder to meet Jared's flinty gaze.

"Your job is to protect our contractors. Stick to that."

Jared's parting words from earlier in the day still rang in Lachlan's head as he took his frustration out on the paper target silhouette in front of him. The indoor shooting range he and Nathan Long frequented was a favorite of local law enforcement and the military. It was busy for a weekday evening. The room they were in was one of three at the range, each divided into five lanes surrounded by eight-inch block concrete-filled walls. Behind the shooters, ballistic glass windows provided a view into the main lobby and lounge area.

Double-tap to the chest, one to the head, he recited in his head despite the routine being as automatic as breathing. His ear protection muffled each bullet's sharp report as it left his Sig Sauer on its way to the paper target. The acrid odor of propellant was strangely comforting in its familiarity, as was the din of other weapons discharging around him. He reloaded the magazine, settled back into his ready stance, and fired in the same pattern as before until he ran out of ammo. Pointing his weapon downrange, he placed it on the platform in front of him and flipped the switch to reel in his target.

A concise grouping of holes with tattered paper borders had obliterated the X in the center of the silhouette. He scowled at three shots that barely nicked the target's head.

Nathan leaned around the partition, glancing at Lachlan's target, then at Lachlan. The six-foot-six former Navy SEAL turned white hat hacker removed his ear protection before swiping a hand over his spiky dirty-blond hair.

"What's eating you, amigo?" His central Texas drawl conjured up images of a guy in a cowboy hat and boots. He looked more like a member of a biker gang in his worn jeans, tactical boots, and black metal band t-shirt that exposed the tattoos on his muscular upper arms. Despite his rough-edged appearance, Nathan generally was a relaxed, uncomplicated bloke—unless you got on his bad side.

He was one of the few people in the world Lachlan trusted with his life.

Lachlan stepped closer to his mate to be heard over the noise as he tried to figure out what to say.

The upcoming weapons auction festered like a splinter beneath his skin. He had to find a way to bring down Khan, even if, as everyone continued to remind him, it wasn't his responsibility.

Then there was his new colleague, Sophia Russo.

He rubbed his chest to try to loosen the bands that were suddenly squeezing his lungs. One day in her presence and he was restless and edgy. She distracted him, which made her dangerous. He had let down his guard with a woman before, and people he was supposed to protect died because of it.

"We both trusted Nadia, you know. We both lost good men."

Lachlan recoiled, his gaze colliding with Nathan's icy blue one. Nathan knew where his mind had gone. They had a bond forged in blood and death, cemented by Nadia Haider's betrayal. They'd led their men into an ambush.

He'd led them.

He'd been the designated mission leader and the one who had pushed Command to greenlight the hostage rescue mission after his beautiful Afghan-born British translator insisted the information she'd gotten on three kidnapped Western aid workers was authentic.

"Mohammad Razul Khan is holding a weapons auction sometime in the next couple of weeks, supposedly with brand new weapons and equipment from a US supplier," he told Nathan.

The former SEAL's low whistle conveyed his sentiment. "Shit." He shook his head. "That guy makes money doing business with his government's enemy, and they still won't let the Coalition sanction an operation on him."

"If I can track down his source, I may be able to disrupt the auction and provide concrete proof of his treachery to both the US and Afghan governments. Maybe they'll act then."

Nathan's answering look was studiously blank.

The back of Lachlan's neck tightened. "You're going to tell me it's not my responsibility like everyone else has."

His best mate threw his head back and laughed. When his gaze met Lachlan's again, amusement warmed his icy eyes. "I know you. I'd be wasting my breath." Nathan grinned. "Need any help? Of course, if we went in, took out Khan, and actually made it out alive, our governments would throw us in the hoosegow."

Lachlan had been around Nathan long enough to know "hoosegow" was his friend's peculiar Texas slang for prison. He allowed himself a brief smile. "Aye, but if we still were active duty, it could be a sanctioned mission."

Nathan sobered. "But we aren't active duty anymore, are we."

The reminder of why had them both going quiet for a moment.

Nathan cleared his throat. "How's your boy working out?"

"Ryder? It was a stroke of luck he let me know he was getting out of the military right after you turned down my very generous offer of employment."

Nathan's massive shoulders lifted and fell in a shrug that Lachlan recognized as an attempt to deflect deeper feelings. "I think I'll stick to protecting information."

Lachlan had no response. The two stood there without speaking amidst the din of discharging weapons until the range monitor signaled their time was up.

Nathan nodded in acknowledgment to the trim, middle-aged woman before turning back to Lachlan. "Seriously, let me know how I can help."

The bands around Lachlan's lungs constricted again, this time for a different reason. As alone as he felt most of the time, he knew Nathan and Ryder had his back. "I need information on munitions cargo to Afghanistan in the past year. They have to be shipped by air, but, depending upon the size of the shipment, they may travel by sea to a Persian Gulf port before being flown in. We also can't discount the idea that someone is diverting weapons brought in directly by the Coalition to arm the Afghan military and police—that might be harder to track."

"I'll see what I can dig up." Nathan stowed his gun in its case and shoved it into his backpack along with his ear and eye protection.

"That will solve one of my problems at least," Lachlan muttered.

His friend's brows flew up. "You got another problem?"

"No," he snapped and immediately realized his mistake.

Nathan's grin widened. "Now you gotta spill."

Lachlan heaved a sigh. Nathan was like a dog with a bone when his curiosity was triggered. He'd pester Lachlan until he gave in.

"I have a new colleague," Lachlan gritted out. "She annoys me, and I'm not sure she can be trusted. She seems a wee bit too good to be true."

Nathan stared at him long enough for his neck to itch. "She annoys you or intrigues you, and that's what annoys you?"

The former SEAL was too perceptive for his own good. Lachlan snapped his gun case shut with a violent thud. "She's a distraction I don't need and don't want."

He and Nathan pushed through the double set of doors separating the range from the lobby area and headed for the parking lot. The temperature had gone down with the sun, and a cool breeze ruffled Lachlan's hair. They'd grabbed dinner before heading to the range and flipped a coin to see who would drive. Nathan lost. They climbed into the cab of Nathan's black Ford F-150 pickup, and he headed south toward his Fairfax Station home, where Lachlan had left his car.

"Not every woman is like Nadia." Nathan's voice was quiet. He kept his gaze on the road.

"Maybe not," Lachlan finally allowed, "but I don't trust myself to know the difference."

CHAPTER SIX

TIME IS OF THE essence.

Sophia bit her lip, shoulders knotting at the cryptic text from Admiral Dane she'd received on the way into work this morning. She needed to step up her efforts to find evidence—if there was any—that Lachlan Mackay was selling weapons to the Taliban. The thought of it made her queasy.

Sweeping into her office, she came to an abrupt halt, staring over the peace lily in her hands at the sight of a small brown paper bag and Styrofoam cup sitting on her desk. Next to the cup were two single-serving containers of creamer. A warm fizz of delight stretched her cheeks, Admiral Dane's buzzkill reminder shoved to the back of her brain.

She placed her new plant on the credenza, along with her purse and briefcase, hung up her coat, then turned back to examine the unexpected bounty. When she pried the lid off the cup, steam tendrils drifted upward, the aroma of hot, black coffee a good morning wake-up call. She added one of the creamers and took a cautious sip. The toasty burnt caramel of her favorite dark roast bathed her tongue.

Diving into the bag, she withdrew a warm, paper-wrapped bagel, plain, toasted, with cream cheese. Just the way she liked. Her stomach gurgled at the yeasty smell and her mouth watered. She took a bite and savored the creamy, chewy goodness.

"That's what you like, right?" Fred's voice from the threshold of her open door made her jump.

He stepped further into her office. His gaze moved over her new décor, resting briefly on her diplomas before returning to meet her face. "That's what Penny said, at least."

Holding the bagel aloft, she eyeballed her unexpected visitor. "This from you?"

He shrugged, then hitched the trousers of his gray suit over his stomach. The acrid smell of tobacco wafted her way, Fred's de facto cologne. "You did a good job on your presentation. I guess you know your stuff, even if you seem kind of young." He glanced at her before taking an excessive interest in an old water stain on her ceiling.

"Thank you." How sweet, even if it felt a bit like a backhanded compliment. She gave him a bright smile. "This was a very nice gesture."

His stubby fingers toyed with the tip of one ear. "I, ah, could use your help on the government report I mentioned. It's due at the end of the month. You might have noticed we don't have a lot of administrative help here. Jared runs a lean operation."

"I'd be happy to help. What do you need me to do?" Her offer at the executive team meeting may have made her look a bit like a suck-up, but the more she learned about LAI's operation, the better she could do her job promoting the success of LAI's projects to Congress so they stayed funded.

Fred tossed a substantial-looking document on her desk. "Here's a copy of last year's annual compliance report. Look it over. Each division is supposed to provide project summaries and financials, but Meier and Mackay travel often, and I always have to harp on them for the documentation I need."

Sophia kept her expression neutral even as her insides buzzed with nervous energy. "I can start with their divisions if you'd like." Fred had just given her the perfect opportunity to peek into Lachlan Mackay's files.

Fred snorted. "Good luck, and uh, thanks." He flashed her a brief but genuine smile that reached his weary brown eyes, shoved his hands into his pockets, and shuffled off without another word.

She picked up her bagel and took another bite, chewing slowly. Her brief interactions with LAI's head of global security so far had been unnerving. Lachlan did more than make her jumpy. When he was nearby, he generated some kind of magnetic current to which her feminine senses were particularly attuned. Unfortunately, he didn't seem to like her. And why was that? She hadn't done anything to earn his disapproval.

Yet.

Her appetite disappeared beneath a twinge of guilt. If Lachlan Mackay was involved in activities that undermined all the good LAI and other companies were trying to do to help the people of Afghanistan, he deserved to be exposed.

With a last lingering glance at the remainder of her bagel, she tossed it into the trash. Time to strap on mental armor and beard the Scottish lion in his den.

Her heart gave a strange flutter. Nerves. It had to be nerves.

She took her time walking down the hall until she came to the door with the nameplate that read, *Lachlan Mackay, Director, Global Security*. What was it about the man that had her so off-balance? It could be that he was a bit hostile and, possibly, a criminal. It had nothing to do with his model face and hard, masculine body wrapped in wicked temptation that a girl like her only read about in steamy novels.

A Billy Joel song about a good Catholic girl and a bad boy popped into her head. She rolled her eyes at the fanciful left turn her brain had just taken and raised her fist to deliver two firm knocks on his door. Her pulse pounded hard enough to feel at the base of her throat.

"Come in." The deep voice that answered was infused with the lilting melody of the Highlands.

Taking a deep breath, she squared her shoulders, pasted a polite smile on her face, and opened the door.

Lachlan's office was larger than hers. Tall glass windows also lined his back wall, but his blinds were closed, denying the space the benefit of natural light from the sunny afternoon. His desk was the size of Jared's but darker—espresso rather than cherry. In place of a credenza, two tall, four-drawer filing cabinets sat against the side wall. Three canvas panels, each showing a section of a rocky seashore, hung between the filing cabinets and a small round table and chairs near the windows.

Great. She glanced down at her plum skirt and jacket with a wince. She matched the fabric covering his chairs.

He was seated behind his desk, minus his suit coat. The crisp white fabric of his dress shirt stretched across broad shoulders and muscular biceps. His sleeves were rolled up, exposing the black hair on his forearms, his face a mask of grim concentration as his fingers pecked at the computer keyboard. The sight of a ballpoint pen lodged behind his ear was oddly comforting. It made him look friendlier.

He looked up, and a flicker of irritation crossed his face.

She bit back a sigh. *So much for friendly.*

"What can I do for you?" From his dismissive tone, she could tell there was nothing he'd like to do for her, which stung.

She raised her chin and held eye contact. "Fred asked for my help with the government report. Starting with your division."

He sat back with an irritated huff and flicked the pen behind his ear onto the desk. It bounced and skidded along the smooth wood surface before being stopped by a large cream envelope and matching cardstock.

Her shoulders hunched at the display of temper before she could control her reaction, drawing his gaze. His lips pursed, and a brief flash of what looked like regret darkened his emerald eyes to a deep jade.

Nothing escaped this man.

He ran his fingers through his hair, dislodging the neatly groomed locks at his forehead. "I don't have time for this right now. I've been out of country and have other work to catch up on."

Now she knew why the wayward strands were out of place and, once again, found herself wanting to smooth them back. Her cheeks warmed.

Work. She was here to do a job. "I understand."

"Good. Is there anything else?" His attention had already returned to his computer screen, dismissing her.

Temper straightened her spine. If he thought he could simply brush her off, he had another think coming. She didn't know why he found her so objectionable, but his attitude offended her, which was rich, given that she was attempting to spy on him and uncover any secrets he might be keeping. She shouldn't care what he thought of her.

"When can we meet? Fred asked for my help, and I honor my commitments. This report is due to the government at the end of the month."

He muttered something she didn't catch under his breath and gave his computer screen a longing glance before he stood and gestured to the table by the window. "Have a seat."

She stalked past him, close enough to catch a subtle hint of his clean, woodsy scent. Whatever cologne or aftershave he used wreaked havoc on her hormones. She needed to find out what it was so she could buy a bottle and indulge in some exposure therapy—sniff it until she was desensitized to its magic.

Once she'd seated herself at the table, she pointed at his wall art to break the ice with some neutral conversation. "Is that someplace in Scotland? I like it."

Lachlan glanced at the canvas pieces, brows furrowed. "I don't know. Penny picked them out."

Okaaay. She looked around for family photos, a personalized coffee mug, or other knickknacks that might give her some insight into his personal life and found nothing.

He opened the top drawer of his filing cabinet, rifled through it, and pulled out several folders before bringing them to the table. "I hope you have a few hours to spare." He rubbed the back of his neck. Restless energy poured off him in waves.

She remembered the feel of those fingers wrapped around her arms to keep her from falling and wondered what they'd feel like on other parts of her body.

No. No. No. Her brain was hiking off the main trail and about to fall off the edge of a cliff. He was pouting when she was doing him a favor, collecting the data Fred needed for the report.

That annoying twinge of guilt returned and sat like lead in her stomach. Of course, she was also looking for information that might put him in jail.

He handed her one of the folders. "Start here."

Admiral Dane had given her an idea of what to look for. Hopefully, she wouldn't come across anything that confirmed the man sitting next to her valued money more than innocent people's lives.

Sometime during the morning, Lachlan excused himself. When he returned, he placed a mug in front of her, then set another cup in front of his space at the table. "I brought you caffeine."

She glanced down and sucked in her lips at the dark brown liquid. "Uh, thanks."

His gaze narrowed. "You don't drink coffee?" When she hesitated, understanding lit his face. "You don't drink it black."

Plenty of people didn't drink black coffee. It was his fault for not asking. Still, she gave him an apologetic smile. "I add a touch of half and half to mellow the bitterness—not a lot. I weaned myself off sugar because I don't need the calories." Her cheeks warmed. He hadn't asked for a complete accounting of her beverage preferences.

"I should have asked." His hand wrapped around the mug. He pushed to his feet.

"Oh, you don't have to—"

"Yes, I do. It was rude of me to assume."

When he returned, the dark brown liquid was now a dusky brown, just the right color.

"Perfect." She beamed at him, absurdly pleased that he'd even bothered to bring her the drink, let alone make sure it was to her liking.

Her smile had the opposite effect from what she'd intended. Instead of relaxing, he stiffened, his gaze shuttering. When he sat back down, the invisible wall separating them at the beginning of the morning was back.

She gnawed on her lip and peered at him through her lashes. What had just happened?

The unspoken tension dissipated as they continued poring over files. She took copious notes as she read over each paper, trying to soak up all the information. Protecting contractors as they worked on projects in Afghanistan was far more complex than she'd realized.

"Sophia."

Her head snapped up at Lachlan's commanding tone. "Did you say something?"

His striking green eyes hinted at amusement, as did the slight purse of his lips. He was even more attractive when he wasn't scowling.

Imagine if he actually smiled, with teeth.

A rush of warm heat pooled between her thighs. She clamped them together and stared at the tabletop until her hormone surge abated.

"I said, I think we should take a break for lunch. There's a shop downstairs where we can grab a piece."

She blinked. "A piece of what."

The edges of his mouth curled up. "Sorry. A sandwich."

"Oh." She blinked again. "Sure." Was he suggesting a lunch date where they could sit down and get to know each other better, or was he planning on grabbing something and bringing it back to his office? She wanted to learn more about Lachlan Mackay than what she'd read about in the file from Admiral Dane.

He stood, and his lips twisted, a soft grunt escaping.

Her gaze dropped to where he massaged his left thigh. "Are you okay?"

"I'm fine," he answered in a sharp tone that indicated otherwise.

He gestured for her to go in front of him. His fingers grazed the small of her back, sending a bolt of lightning through the fabric of her suit straight to her womb.

She wobbled at the impact.

"Careful." His long fingers shot out to steady her. "Maybe you should try shorter heels."

He grabbed his suit coat off the back of his door before rolling down his shirt sleeves and slipping into the jacket.

"It's not the shoes," she mumbled. She kept her head down, her gaze slanting to try and read the fancy invite perched on the corner of his desk. *The Reston Gallery of Art cordially invites you to—*

"Ready?"

She gave a guilty start, her gaze jerking to meet his before she preceded him out of his office.

If he'd noticed her snooping, it didn't show. Contained power radiated from him, even as he shortened his stride to match hers. His limp smoothed out as they kept walking.

Maybe she was a snob, but Lachlan hardly seemed the art patron type. He had a rough-around-the-edges aura clothed in a custom suit—a Daniel Craig as the urbane James Bond vibe.

The doors closed on one of the elevators before they could reach it. She pressed the button to summon another car. The next elevator that arrived was empty. They stepped in, and Lachlan pressed the button for the ground floor. As if on cue, they retreated to opposite corners.

She stared at the digital floor indicator above the doors to keep from staring at the man. The floors ticked downward—seven, six, five.

The elevator shuddered to a stop with a bounce. The green digits on the floor indicator disappeared. Lachlan frowned and pressed the open door button. Nothing happened.

She opened her mouth to speak when the overhead lights in the ceiling panels went dark.

"Bollocks," Lachlan swore.

"Is the elevator stuck?" Sophia turned her wide-eyed gaze on him in the dim light.

"We'll be fine." He pressed the alarm button. Nothing happened. He punched the call button, his neck muscles tightening. The scent of moon-kissed flowers, lush and sweet with a dusky edge, permeated the small space. Sophia's scent. He'd been breathing her in all morning, willing his body not to react as they worked together. He needed fresh air that didn't smell like her.

"Hello?" A disembodied male voice responded.

"Elevator number three is malfunctioning." Lachlan gave the man the building address.

"Hang tight. We're sending a technician."

Sophia had moved to stand next to him. She bit her lip, and he zeroed in on dainty white teeth gripping a generous lower lip.

A wave of lust hit him square in the chest. "How long?" he snapped at the faceless man on the other end of the line.

"Please try to stay calm, sir. We'll get you out as quickly as we can."

"Are you claustrophobic?" Sophia's delicate, pink-tipped nails clutched his sleeve. The concern in her eyes would have made him laugh if a strange warmth wasn't spreading through his chest.

"Not hardly. I've been in situations much worse than this." No one was trying to shoot him or blow him up, and, unlike the movies, the lift cables weren't going to snap and send them plummeting to the basement.

If anything threatened his well-being right now, it was this wee woman.

She took a deep breath, and his gaze was drawn to the gentle swell of her breasts, generous enough to fill his palms, over her flat midriff to her smooth, toned legs and black heels. She had nice legs. And those shoes...She had to be in shape to walk in them. Barefoot, she'd probably stand no taller than mid-chest on him.

"You should take self-defense classes," he heard himself say.

Where did that come from? Had he gone daft?

Her startled laugh was a light, musical sound that went straight to his groin. "I took a couple of classes in college." A teasing look crossed her face, but he could read the anxiety lurking behind her eyes. She took a step back. "Why do you say that? Do I need to defend myself against you?"

Yes. "Never. But men without honor might view you as prey because of your size."

The thought filled him with an unexpected rage that must have been reflected in his eyes because Sophia's head reared back, wariness shadowing her gaze.

She retreated to the opposite side of the car. "You certainly think the worst of humanity, don't you."

"I think the worst because I've seen the worst," he snapped.

The apprehension in her eyes deepened. Her fingers crept to her purse.

He inhaled a calming breath, shame burning a hole in his stomach. He'd frightened her. *Christ.* He was a shite bastard. She was probably ready to mace him or stab him with a shiv.

He threw up his hands in surrender. "I didn't mean to upset you. I'm sorry. Let's change the subject." His brain scrambled for a general, non-threatening question normal people would ask. "How old are you?"

She gave him a startled look but eventually answered. "I'm twenty-seven," her chin lifted, "but I have a master's degree in Global Development and experience drafting legislation as a Congressional aide. I assure you I am qualified for this position."

He'd done a crap job changing the subject if the tilt of Sophia's head and her frosty tone were anything to go by. At least she no longer looked at him like he was a bloody axe murderer. "I was just curious about your age and meant nothing by it. I know you're qualified. The presentation you gave to the executive team proved that."

Her skin pinkened. "Sorry. And thank you." She peered at him. The curiosity in her eyes had his entire body tensing. "What about you?"

"Thirty-four. But in terms of what I've experienced in life, decades older." His ghosts stirred, threatening his equilibrium. *Not here, not in front of Sophia.*

She stepped toward him again, too close, the green flecks in her eyes brimming with an emotion that made his jaw clench. "I'm sorry for whatever put that pain in your eyes, and,"—she gestured toward his left leg—"hurt you physically as well."

He stared down at her, his lungs so tight he could barely draw in enough air. Sweat dotted his forehead. *Fuck.* Maybe he was claustrophobic after all because he needed out of this bloody box before he did something stupid.

Like kiss Sophia.

He looked at his watch. *Twenty minutes. That was all?* It felt like they'd been stuck in the lift for hours. He eyed the ceiling. Chances were there was an emergency hatch above the panels, but it was likely bolted from the outside. Maybe he could get an idea of where the lift had stopped. He moved to the doors, got a finger hold on each panel where they met, and tried to pry the doors open, grunting as his shoulder and back muscles screamed from the strain.

"What are you doing?" Sophia's voice rose in pitch. "We need to wait for the elevator repairman or the Fire Department. I read that the safest thing to do when stuck in an elevator is to do nothing."

Shite piece of crap lift. He gave up his efforts, his breath ragged from exertion. He should have known modern buildings such as this one would have lifts equipped with door resisters designed to keep people from doing precisely what he'd tried to do.

"I thought I'd see where we were." He wasn't good at waiting for someone else to rescue him. He was the one who usually did the rescuing.

Without warning, his ghosts took control.

"Get down!" he screamed to be heard over the din. "Get down!"

The female hostage's head rose, eyes peeled back in terror as she searched the darkness in the direction of his voice. Relief poured over her face. She stretched out her hand. He took a palm off his rifle and reached out. The tips of his glove had barely brushed her fingers when her body jerked, and she crumpled to the ground like a rag doll.

"Lachlan!"

He blinked and refocused. Soft hands cradled his jaw. Wide, hazel eyes stared up at him.

He drank in Sophia's face and breathed in her scent to ground himself. His hands lifted to cover hers, pull them off, but instead, he held her to him until his ragged breathing slowed. "I'm sorry. I'm sorry." He wasn't sure who he was apologizing to, Sophia or Katherine, the woman he hadn't been able to save.

Sophia's thumbs moved across his cheeks in a gentle caress. He dropped his gaze to her pink lips. His muscles tightened. His heart pounded, sending blood south to his awakening cock.

He needed to taste her.

"You have nothing to apologize for," she whispered.

Guilt rose in the back of his throat, bitter as acid, dousing his arousal. He stepped back, breaking from her hold and the spell she'd woven around him.

She had no idea of the amends he had to make.

He needed to focus on bringing down Khan and his supplier, not indulging himself in a stolen moment of pleasure. With a colleague, no less.

The lift jolted, the overhead lights flashed on, and the car began to move.

Lachlan cleared his throat, carefully avoiding the questions in Sophia's eyes. "I've got to take care of something. We'll need to continue working on the report another time."

When the car opened to the lobby, he headed for the revolving glass doors that spit him out into the cool spring afternoon, leaving Sophia in his wake.

His leg didn't feel up for a long walk, but exercising his Mercedes's high-performance engine on the Beltway before traffic piled up might clear his head.

He strode to the surface lot next door. He'd handed over his car this morning to Jeremy Powell. The lad probably made more money detailing cars than he would if he had stayed at uni and finished his studies. With Jeremy's brains and motivation, he'd be franchising his business before his twenty-fifth birthday.

He spied Jeremy buffing a white SUV. "Jeremy."

Jeremy lifted a hand in greeting. "Hey, Mr. Mackay, I was just about to get to yours." A light breeze ruffled Jeremy's shaggy, dark brown hair. He swiped the strands out of his eyes with his forearm.

Lachlan hesitated. His skin itched with the need to escape, and he had meetings this afternoon. "I need to take the car, pal. Any chance you can clean it tomorrow?"

Jeremy dropped the rag he'd been using to buff the SUV and pulled his phone out of the back pocket of his jeans. "I'm pretty booked this week. How about next week? I can do it on Monday."

Lachlan nodded. He kept his car clean enough. It could wait another week. He accepted his key fob from Jeremy and gave him a friendly pat on the back. "You're a hard worker, lad. Keep it up, and soon you'll have people working for you whilst you build your empire."

Jeremy grinned, his brown eyes lighting up. "That's the plan, Mr. M. That's the plan."

Lachlan headed for his Mercedes, his mood darkening again. His ghosts mocked him as he drove out of the surface lot to the street, determined to leave them behind.

CHAPTER SEVEN

THE TOYOTA HILUX PICKUP Roshan Haider rode in smelled like a rubbish bin. He stared at the sheer cliff face on his right as the truck careened around another curve and avoided looking to his left. The low stone guardrails on this mountainous stretch of Afghanistan's AH1 highway reminded him of the stone fences found in rural Great Britain and appeared a flimsy barrier separating the winding, narrow road from the Kabul River some three hundred meters below.

One mistake and not even the grace of Allah would prevent them from plunging to their deaths. The air conditioning from the truck's vents barely reached him and did little to cool the sweat beading his forehead.

He leaned forward as far as his seatbelt would allow. "Perhaps you could slow down?"

The driver sent to pick him up at the Kabul airport met his gaze in the rearview mirror with a smirk but said nothing, nor did he decrease his speed. He was transporting Roshan to Mohammad Razul Khan's home outside Jalalabad, three hours away.

Roshan slumped further into the backseat and sent up a prayer.

He replayed in his head the message from his contact two days ago. *Khan knows the name of the man who murdered your sister.*

The warlord was a dangerous man, well-connected and feared by many, including Afghanistan's current leaders. He managed to deftly play all sides of the conflict between the Afghan government, the Western governments, and the Taliban.

Khan's son, Razul Sharif, had joined the Taliban and had been the one who'd filled Nadia's head with the misbeliefs that led to her death. After the video of Nadia taking credit for an operation killing Coalition soldiers circulated on the Internet, it hadn't taken the British press long to brand his sister a traitor.

When she came home in a coffin three months later, the official story the UK government had given to Roshan and his parents was that Nadia tragically had been caught in the crossfire during a Coalition assault on a Taliban stronghold.

It was a lie. Two British Army soldiers had been buried in Hereford at the SAS cemetery shortly after the video's release. The operation that killed Nadia and Khan's son had been a joint operation between Afghan and allied special forces. Afghanistan's president had been furious that the son of a powerful warlord was killed and leaked the information that he died at the hands of British special forces, not the Afghans.

Roshan didn't care for Khan. Frankly, he was glad Khan's son was dead for his part in corrupting Nadia.

But what he and the warlord shared in common was a desire for money and a man—the British soldier who'd gunned down Khan's son and Roshan's sister in an act of revenge.

The rest of the message had instructed him to fly from his home in London to Kabul and purchase a local prepaid phone once he arrived. He'd been given a number to call. So he'd taken the mid-afternoon flight to Dubai, then secured a flight to Kabul.

His dual Afghan-British citizenship and numerous business dealings in the Middle East and Asia through his import-export business gave him cover for his sudden travel and, hopefully, kept him off the radar of the UK government. He didn't tell his parents where he'd gone. They would worry and plead with him to let Nadia's death rest.

That, he wouldn't do. His family's reputation was at stake.

Eventually, the road flattened out as they reached the outskirts of Jalalabad. Colorful mid-rise buildings loomed over older, squat two-story shops, their goods piled on outdoor tables whilst Toyotas, yellow motorized rickshaws, and pedestrians mingled in crowded streets.

The driver continued to the outskirts of the city. As they neared Khan's home, men with automatic weapons appeared—two near the gated entrance and another two patrolling the top of the compound's concrete barrier walls. Roshan had no doubt there were more armed men than the ones he could see.

The driver stopped and spoke to one of the men before driving through the gates. Roshan's brows rose. The mansion inside rivaled many of the posh country homes in England in grandeur. Clearly, Khan had managed to leverage his power and connections into financial gain.

An older man in his late sixties stood in front of the glass-paneled wood doors to the spacious home, his head wrapped in a black *lungee*, his full beard more white than black. Oval-shaped frames sat atop his bladed nose. He wore an ivory-colored tunic and trousers beneath a brown embroidered vest. Two more men wearing army green fatigues flanked him, pistols strapped to their hips.

Roshan didn't need to be told this was the warlord he'd come to see. He stepped from the car and placed his right hand over his heart, lowering his head. "*Salam alaikum*," he said, bowing. "Peace be upon you."

"*Salam alaikum*." Mohammad Razul Khan shook his hand. "Welcome. Come, let us have tea."

Roshan followed Kahn and his escorts into the home, removing his shoes at the door, then discretely placed a gift-wrapped box of Swiss chocolates on the table at the entrance, ones he'd picked up in the duty-free zone in Dubai International Airport before catching his flight to Kabul. As was Afghan custom, he did not present the gift but instead left it to be opened at the host's choosing.

They made their way into a salon where cushions garbed in red and yellow silk were arranged around a low, square dark wood table.

"Please." Khan waved him to one of the cushions and took a seat across the table on another cushion. Khan's two bodyguards flanked the warlord.

Two women bustled in, dressed in flowing robes and hijabs. They brought a large bowl of water for each man to wash his hands, then removed it and returned with glass cups. The older woman poured *kahwah*—a green tea mixed with cardamom, cinnamon, saffron, and other spices, into each cup from an ornate porcelain teapot and added copious amounts of sugar. Their second cup of tea would be unsweetened. Roshan's mother followed the same custom when his parents received guests in their London home.

The younger woman placed a bowl of sugar cubes, a plate of sugared almonds, and another plate of pastries on the table. Then the women disappeared as swiftly and as silently as they had arrived.

While they sipped their tea, Khan quizzed him on his father, a doctor who'd taken the family and fled from Kabul to London when the Taliban first came to power. They discussed the idea of a business partnership—a subject Roshan navigated as carefully as possible to avoid offending the warlord. Western governments had forbidden their companies from doing business with Khan and other warlords in the country, despite the warlords' relationships with Afghan government leaders.

He had suspicions that he was already doing business with Khan in a roundabout way, facilitating the import of certain items his contact wanted to be shipped into Afghanistan as discretely as possible. He was happy to be a step removed from the contents of the cargo so he could claim ignorance if needed.

After two hours, the sweets pained his stomach, and his bladder was about to burst from the amount of tea he'd consumed. All he wanted was to demand that Khan relinquish the identity of the man who killed his sister, but he knew better than to commit such a breach of etiquette.

"An Afghan-owned trucking company in Nangarhar Province has a contract with the US to transport fuel and other goods to the military bases." Khan's dark eyes assessed Roshan. "Someone such as yourself, an Afghan expatriate who wishes to support the development of his homeland, would be wise to consider investing in such a business."

Roshan understood the unspoken subtext. The information he wanted from Khan would come with a price. "This is an excellent idea, Khan Sahib. What kind of investment would you recommend?"

Khan waved his hand as if it was of no consequence. "It is not for me to say, but fifty thousand euros would be a most generous sum."

The amount made Roshan swallow. Hard. But worth it if he could expose Nadia's killer and restore his family's honor. "I'm sure it will be a beneficial arrangement."

The warlord stood, signaling their meeting was over. "You are welcome to stay as a guest in my home, but if you wish to return to Kabul today, you will need to leave before it grows dark. The road is quite dangerous at night."

Roshan rose from his cushion, his movements clumsy. A rising tide of heat burned his face to the tips of his ears. "Khan Sahib, I came all this way. Our mutual friend assured me you had knowledge of the man who killed your son and my sister."

A dangerous tension filled the room, freezing the air in Roshan's lungs.

Khan's bodyguards stepped closer to the warlord, hands resting on their weapons.

Khan raised his palm. The warlord's gentle smile contrasted the ice glazing his dark eyes. "Haider Sahib, I share your pain. But as an ally of the Afghan National Government, I cannot condone retaliation against Western soldiers." He placed his hand over his heart and gave his head a slight tilt. "*Khudaa hafiz.*"

Roshan's heart beat as fast as a swift's wings. He knew better than to push the warlord. Squelching his disappointment, he returned the farewell gesture. "Goodbye. I am grateful for your hospitality."

He followed the guards out of the home and climbed into the backseat of the waiting pickup. Frustration clogged his throat, making it hard to breathe. All this way for nothing.

The same driver as before sped his way through the city and began the climb into the mountains.

Nadia had been a British citizen. The SAS killed his sister instead of letting her return home alive. He'd vowed to make the soldier who'd shot her pay, even as his father urged him to stop making waves in the media.

He would find another way to unmask the identity of his sister's killer.

An hour into the trip back to Kabul, the phone he'd procured upon arriving in the country rang. The number was local but one he didn't recognize. "Hello?"

An unfamiliar male voice answered in Pashto. "The man you seek is Lachlan Mackay."

CHAPTER EIGHT

LACHLAN SAT HUNCHED OVER his office computer and studied the files Nathan sent him listing munition shipments flown into Kabul in the last year. A cup of coffee sat cooling on his desk next to the new security contract Jared had asked him to review.

From what he knew of the other firms operating in the same region as his teams, none of the shipments seemed excessive, although he'd flagged two that were possibilities. He'd reach out to his suppliers to see if he could glean any information, although they were likely to be tight-lipped about their sales to other clients. Frustration settled around him like a Bergen kitted out for a mission, weighing down his shoulders. He rubbed the back of his neck to try to loosen the tension.

There was a soft rap before his door opened to reveal Penny, dressed in an ivory blouse and navy skirt, a plant with shiny, dark green leaves in her hands. "Sophia said you need some nature in your office." Her lips pursed as she held back a laugh. "She asked me to give this to you." Penny placed the plant on his table, taking care not to disturb the stack of files he and Sophia had been working on the day before.

Lachlan frowned. "Why didn't she bring it to my office herself?" And why did he need a plant? Was he supposed to take care of the shite thing?

"Probably because she was afraid you'd growl at her." Penny sent Lachlan a knowing look, conveying a gentle admonishment that reminded him of his mam and made him avert his gaze. "She's a sweet young woman, and I know you'll make an effort to welcome her to LAI."

He grunted, then sent Penny a brief nod and a weak attempt at a smile because his mam wouldn't approve of his surly attitude either. When his door closed behind LAI's office manager, he glanced over his shoulder at the files and his new greenery.

Sophia had emailed him earlier, asking when they could pick up where they'd left off with the government report. Before they'd gotten stuck in the elevator.

Before he'd behaved like a twat.

Before he'd fled the building so he could rebuild his defenses.

He clicked on her email to reply. His fingers hovered over the keyboard, waiting for his brain to direct them.

His mobile rang, Ryder's name lighting the screen.

The government report could wait.

"Any news?"

"I heard from Gilly." Ryder's voice crackled over the long-distance connection.

Lachlan stilled. "Tell me."

"Khan is hosting a wedding for the son of the mayor of Jalalabad at his compound. Rumor is, he's using the celebration as cover for his weapons auction. No one will launch an assault at a wedding where several prominent members of Afghan society will be present."

Fuck. Tension coiled at the base of Lachlan's spine. "When is the wedding."

"In two weeks."

Two weeks to try and disrupt Khan's plans. Lachlan stood, pacing back and forth between his desk and the table to work his leg muscles. Sophia's plant waved gently in the breeze generated by the supply vent in the ceiling directly overhead. "Do you still have your contact at customs?" He fingered the broad, glossy leaves.

"Sayed? Yes."

"See what he knows. Don't tell me what you need to do to get the information."

"Right." Ryder paused. "There's something else you need to know."

"Burkette again?" Lachlan's hand left the plant to curl into a fist. His other team leader's antics were the last thing he needed to deal with at the moment.

"No. Nadia Haider's brother was in Afghanistan. He met with Khan."

Surprise rooted Lachlan in place. "How the hell did he pull that off? And why?" He returned to his desk, easing onto his chair with a faint grimace as his left quad protested.

Roshan Haider was in the import-export business. Khan was bringing weapons into Afghanistan to sell to the highest bidder.

Was it possible Gilly's information had been dodgy about the source of the weapons?

"Could Haider be the one supplying Khan?" Although honestly, Lachlan didn't think the little prick had it in him. Haider led a posh life, and unlike Ryder, who'd also grown up in the elite circles of British society, the only weapons Roshan had ever wielded were his money and his mouth.

"I don't know." Ryder's voice lowered as if he were trying to keep from being overheard. "It's possible, I suppose. But I think we should assume they also discussed Nadia and Razul Sharif. Khan knows they died at the hands of the SAS. With his connections, it's possible he's unearthed our identities."

Lachlan let out a harsh exhale. "If Khan does know, watch your six. What does that bastard Haider think he's going to do with the information? Leak it to the British media? The government will file charges against him." Roshan had spent the last two years trying to convince anyone who would listen that British special forces murdered his sister.

"There's more. Haider left Afghanistan yesterday. I checked his flights."

"And?" Lachlan prompted.

"He's headed to Washington."

Lachlan let that piece of news sink in. "You think he discovered my identity and is coming to confront me."

"It could be a coincidence, but my gut tells me otherwise."

Ryder had solid instincts that had served him and their troop on the battlefield more than once. Still, Lachlan didn't consider Haider much of a threat. "I have bigger issues than Nadia's petulant older brother. Let me know if Gilly learns anything more about Khan's plans."

He hung up with Ryder and assessed his options. Two weeks wasn't enough time to identify Khan's weapons supplier and stop the shipments. Even with Nathan's hacking prowess and Ryder's local contacts, he might be unable to put the pieces of the puzzle together in time.

His jaw tightened. As much as he hated to make this next move, it had to be done. He scrolled to a phone number he hadn't called since he'd accepted the job at LAI and relocated to the States.

A low, gruff voice answered on the third ring. "You've been in town for a year. Nice of you to touch base finally."

Lucas Caldwell, former US Army colonel, now FBI Assistant Director for International Operations, had put his own career with Joint Special Operations Command on the line defending Lachlan and

Nathan after the hostage rescue mission disaster. Katherine Purcell's death and Nadia's triumphant video released by the Taliban had dominated the news worldwide and left officials in both the US and UK with egg on their faces. Not to mention the deaths of a Navy SEAL, two SAS soldiers, and an American Apache helicopter crew. It hadn't taken long for enterprising reporters to piece together details of the classified mission and tie everything together in a proper bow.

As the junior officers in charge, Lachlan and Nathan were the easy targets. Lucas defended them, arguing the failure was an intelligence one, combined with sloppy vetting of translators. Ultimately, the US admiral who served as head of JSOC at the time agreed.

Lachlan would always be grateful, even if he'd kept his distance from Lucas since. He had enough reminders of those days. While they'd been spared an official reprimand on their service records and their names had been kept out of the press, Lachlan and Nathan hadn't escaped the unofficial consequences that led both men to separate from active duty.

He shook off the past and focused on his current problem. "I need to meet with you. It's urgent."

The rustle of cellophane and click of a lighter on the other end of the line told Lachlan that Lucas hadn't kicked his nicotine habit from his active-duty days. The Assistant Director took an audible drag on his cigarette before responding. "Something you can tell me over the phone?"

"I'd prefer not to." He didn't want to be seen cozying up to the FBI in case Jared found out and rightly assumed he hadn't let the matter of Khan's weapons auction drop. He started to suggest a discrete bar in McLean when his gaze fell on the embossed invitation still perched on the far corner of his desk.

The reception for the visiting Scottish artists. He'd agreed to be a sponsor and was now obligated to attend.

He fingered the envelope. "Can you be at the Reston Art Gallery tomorrow evening, nineteen hundred?"

"I'm assuming you want me to come alone."

"Aye."

"I'll be there." Lucas hung up.

It was a gamble, getting Lucas involved. But what if they managed to stop the weapons auction, unmask the supplier, and Coalition and Afghan leaders still didn't go after Khan?

Lachlan massaged the headache forming at his temple. He owed it to the dead to try.

Moon-kissed flowers tickled his nose. *Sophia*. He dropped his hands. He had on the same suit coat he'd worn when she barreled into him on her first day at LAI. A trace of her perfume lingered on his jacket.

Lifting his sleeve, he breathed her in, his body hardening instantly. *Dammit.* The woman had been at LAI less than a week, and she was decorating his office and messing with his head. What was it about her? She was hardly his type, a colleague to boot, and he wasn't even sure he could trust her.

He'd drop the suit off at the cleaners tomorrow.

Sophia read the same paragraph on her computer for the fourth time before giving up. Penny had delivered the peace lily to Lachlan this morning. She'd been hesitant to deliver it herself, unsure how he'd react given that he'd been determined to put distance between them yesterday after they'd gotten unstuck from the elevator.

Her mind kept returning to the moment when he'd gone somewhere deep and dark so fast she'd acted on instinct, grabbing his face, calling his name until his gaze refocused, and she knew he'd returned from whatever bad memory held him in its thrall. The torment in his eyes and his whispered words of apology had broken her heart. She had the feeling they weren't meant for her but for someone else.

Then his gaze had dropped to her lips, his eyes darkening to a deep jade.

Everything in her that was female knew he wanted to kiss her. And she'd wanted him to with an intensity that left her completely unmoored.

He was a dark, complicated man with secrets—secrets Admiral Dane was counting on her to expose. The more time she spent around him, the harder it was to believe he was a cold, unfeeling man who could sell weapons to the Taliban. He felt—maybe too much. She was sure of it.

She rose from her desk with a disgusted sigh. Maybe another hit of caffeine would get her brain back on work. She left her office and headed for the breakroom.

Jared stood at Penny's desk. He handed her a cream-colored envelope. "I forgot to RSVP to this art gallery event for tomorrow night. Can you do it for me?"

Art gallery event. "Is that the one at the Reston Art Gallery?" Sophia piped up. Her mind worked furiously. It was a shot in the dark that it was the same event Lachlan had gotten an invitation to. He'd avoided her all day and hadn't returned her email about the documents she needed for the government report. She needed to work faster to gain his trust.

Maybe he'd be more approachable in a social setting.

She stepped closer to Jared and tried not to appear desperate. "I heard the exhibit there now is fantastic." Whatever it was. She had no clue. Hopefully, he wouldn't ask her anything about it.

A smile hovered on Jared's lips. "I didn't know you were an art enthusiast. You want to come? The opening reception is tomorrow night. Invitation only."

"I'd love to." She bounced on her toes. Maybe her spy skills weren't so bad after all.

"Make the RSVP for two," Jared instructed Penny before turning back to Sophia. "Cocktail attire. I'll pick you up at six-thirty. Feel free to leave work a bit early to get ready."

She bit her lip, awkwardness creeping in as it occurred to her that her ingenious attempt to get closer to Lachlan meant she'd invited herself on a date with her boss.

You're overthinking this. Jared told her when she interviewed that part of her job responsibilities would be attending social functions with him to promote LAI. It was how business was done inside the Beltway. No one would think it improper for her to be seen with him. "I need to give you my address."

"Sophia," Jared's tone made her feel like she'd just asked a stupid question, "you work for me. I know where you live."

CHAPTER NINE

LACHLAN TOOK A SIP of Highland Park, its notes of heather, spice, and fruit warming the back of his throat. The art gallery occupied the bottom floor of a concrete and glass brick building in the historic part of Reston. Strategically lit paintings mounted on white demi-walls partitioned the vast open space while pedestals showcased three-dimensional pieces.

He spotted Lucas the second he arrived. The FBI AD still looked as fit as he had during his military days, simply trading his uniform for a charcoal pinstripe suit and conservative tie. He still sported a full head of short, black hair, although it looked to be graying at the temples.

When their gazes connected, Lachlan indicated a back corner of the gallery with a subtle tilt of his head. Tucked away behind the exhibits and near the gallery's administrative offices, it would afford them some privacy. Just two blokes attending the reception, taking a brief moment for a quiet chat about business.

Lucas appeared a few minutes later with a highball glass in hand. "They're serving up some decent Scotch." He gazed at his surroundings before his blue eyes came to rest on Lachlan. "How are you, Mackay?"

Lachlan understood the question behind the question. "Fine." He bit out the word in a tone that didn't invite further discussion. He hadn't invited Lucas to discuss his mental status.

He stepped closer to the AD and lowered his voice. "Mohammad Khan plans to use an upcoming wedding at his compound in Jalalabad as cover for a weapons auction."

"And you know this how?"

"One of my former SAS mates in Kabul training the Afghan military heard the rumor. The wedding is in two weeks."

Lucas took a sip of his whisky and stared at Lachlan over the rim of his glass. The back of Lachlan's neck tightened. He knew what was coming.

"Is there any evidence to back up this rumor?"

Lachlan frowned. "Khan may be getting his weapons from a US source. If I can find evidence, we could stop the auction and prove Khan is a threat to the Afghan national government and the Coalition. They'd have to move against him then."

"Jesus, Mackay." Lucas shook his head. "I know you have a hard-on for the warlord, but you have no legal authority here. None."

"Dammit, don't you think I know that? Why do ya think I've come to ya, man?" Lachlan could hear his accent thicken. He took another sip of his Scotch and struggled for control. His ghosts began to whisper in his ear. "At least look into the rumor of a US supplier."

If Lucas wouldn't help him, he'd continue on his own. Some shitty bastard out there was betraying his countrymen, and more innocent people would die.

More betrayal. More bloodshed.

Maybe this time, he could keep it from happening.

Sophia smiled her thanks as Jared handed her a glass of chardonnay he'd gotten from the event bar set up just past the entrance to the gallery. She peered around at the eclectic mix of well-to-do art patrons, corporate suits, and retired couples with both money and time on their hands. There was no sign of Lachlan.

"You look amazing." Jared's appreciative gaze had her glancing down at her black dress. It had three-quarter sleeves and an off-shoulder neckline and fell just above the knee.

A self-conscious laugh escaped her. She enjoyed dressing up and feeling sexy but stunk when it came to handling male attention. No wonder her sex life was non-existent. She bolted like a scared rabbit whenever a man made his interest known.

Deep down, she feared making herself vulnerable only to have her lover realize she wasn't all that interesting. It's not like her parents had gushed over her dance and piano recitals when she was young, her academic honors in high school, her acceptance into a prestigious college, or any other achievements in her life. She'd learned to be satisfied with her own sense of accomplishment.

"This exhibit is incredible." She turned the conversation away from her to a safer subject. The reception highlighted visiting Scottish artists, their pieces ranging from bold splashes of color in contemporary and abstract styles to more traditional still life and landscape pieces.

It made sense that Lachlan had received an invitation. Would he show?

Her wine glass halted on its way to her lips. If she was honest with herself, her reasons for inviting herself to the reception were only partly related to her business with Admiral Dane. Her body came alive in Lachlan's presence, yearned for his touch, responded to his scent. That heated stare he'd given her in the elevator had been predatory and all male. She hadn't wanted to bolt from Lachlan. He was the first drop on a roller coaster, both terrifying and exhilarating. And addictive.

She wanted more.

Jared's cell belted out a series of rings. He dug it out of his suit pocket and put it to his ear. "Jared Landry. Yes, Congressman Mitchell." Whatever the congressman said had Jared's forehead creasing. "One second, sir." He held the phone down by his hip and met Sophia's curious stare. "Sorry, I need to take this. Why don't you have a look around." He returned the phone to his ear, heading for the gallery entrance before she could reply.

"Well, okay then." She took another sip of her wine. Might as well enjoy the art and see if Lachlan was anywhere in the crowd.

She strolled in the direction of one of the Scottish artists, an older gentleman with a trim, white beard, a jaunty tartan square poking out of his jacket's breast pocket. Behind him hung oil landscapes of rocky shorelines and crashing waves, tiny cottages dotting the background.

Continuing further into the exhibit space, she browsed the art and scanned the growing crowd for familiar faces, finding none. She'd made it to the back wall when a painting grabbed her attention and drew her in as surely as if it was a giant magnet, pulling her irresistibly closer.

From its look, it was an oil painting of a historic battle—Scottish Highlanders versus British Redcoats. Vivid slashes of red, blue, green, and brown clothed the combatants. The pride and determination the artist had painted on the faces of the charging Highlanders was unmistakable.

Sophia's gaze fixed on the central figure, a Highlander with flowing black hair leading his men into battle, broadsword raised high in one hand, a shield in the other. A Spartan of his time. Four bright purple sprigs of heather sprouted from the top of the clan badge pinned to the tartan draping the Highlander's shoulder like a lover's token. But it was his face—those sharp cheekbones, firm jaw, and piercing eyes—that had her taking a huge gulp of her wine.

Forget Prince Charming on a white horse. Maybe what she needed was a Highlander in a kilt wielding a sword. He was breathtaking.

And he looked like Lachlan.

The wine went down the wrong way, seizing her lungs. Heads turned her way. Her face on fire, she moved to the edge of the exhibit to discreetly cough away the liquid she'd aspirated.

Movement in the back corner of the room caught her eye. Curiosity had her squinting to get a better look.

Was that? She practically leaped behind one of the demi-walls. She'd been thinking about Lachlan, and now she'd conjured him up during a wine-induced coughing fit. Once she could breathe without hacking up a lung, she peered around the wall for a better look.

It *was* him.

Lachlan spoke with another man almost as tall as he was, with neatly trimmed black hair. The other man looked older, maybe in his late forties or early fifties, but she couldn't tell from her vantage point.

She squinted some more. Lachlan's expression held an urgency to it as he spoke. The other man listened, his face giving nothing away. Whatever they were discussing, she seriously doubted it had anything to do with art.

As if sensing her stare, Lachlan glanced in her direction. She scrambled back behind the wall, her heart tripping. Had he seen her?

Her stomach churned. If Admiral Dane was right about Lachlan, this man might be his accomplice. She should try to sneak a photo of the two of them together and send it to the admiral.

What if Lachlan looked over again and caught her in the act? How would she explain herself?

She'd have to chance it. Even a blurry photo would be better than none.

Her phone vibrated with a text from Jared right as she opened her camera app.

Meet me up front.

The hair on the back of Lachlan's neck quivered. He glanced to his right. Had that been a flash of dark red hair next to one of the display walls?

A heavy hand landed on his shoulder, pulling his attention back to Lucas. The other man's concerned expression set Lachlan's teeth on edge. "I'll do some digging, see what I find out. But you need to stay out of it. You've got a good job here in the States, a fresh start. Don't let the past drag you under." Lucas drained his glass and left, moving into the exhibit space, and disappearing.

Lachlan finished his drink, the ice clinking against the empty glass. He'd love nothing more than to have another, but he needed to be clearheaded enough to drive home. That and experience had taught him that too much whisky opened the door for his nightmares to slip through. He spied one of the roving servers hovering on the edge of the exhibition and went to hand off his glass.

She'd have to snap off a quick shot. Sophia peered around the wall again, camera app open and ready.

Lachlan and the other man were gone.

Darn it. She'd lost her opportunity. And she would pretend she wasn't a tiny bit relieved that she hadn't snapped that photo and sent it to the admiral. Her brain kept shying away from the notion that Admiral Dane might be right about Lachlan. It didn't square with what she knew of him, which, admittedly, wasn't much. She was going off feelings, not proof.

Her shoulders drooped. She'd better not keep her boss waiting.

Jared stood near the front entrance, scanning the crowd with an impatient expression. When their gazes locked, he waved her over. "Congressman Mitchell has asked me to meet up with him. Would it be too much for you to get an Uber? I'll reimburse you for the trip."

"Don't you think I should go with you?" She was the director of legislative affairs, after all. Building relationships with members of Congress and their key staff was part of her job.

Jared gave her a bland smile. "The venue isn't one where I think you'd be comfortable and not one where the congressman would like to be seen."

Eeeww. Translation: the married congressman was at what was euphemistically called a "gentlemen's club" or something equally as tawdry. It was on the tip of her tongue to ask, but she chose discretion. "I'm happy to stay and enjoy the art, and I can get myself home."

"I knew you'd understand." Jared leaned in and kissed her cheek. The unexpected gesture caught her off guard, and she stiffened. Before she could recover, he was striding through the glass doors.

"Miss, would you care for another?" A black-clad server stared pointedly at her empty glass.

"Why not." A refill wouldn't hurt—she wasn't driving after all. She carefully placed her empty on the waiter's small round tray and picked a fresh one. She strolled around, her gaze frequently leaving the art to canvas the crowd, looking for a tall man with black hair. Lachlan was probably gone by now.

Or not.

There he stood, conversing with the Scottish artist in the tweed jacket.

Should she go over or pretend she didn't see him? Indecision kept her immobile.

This is ridiculous. She'd come tonight hoping he'd be here so she could get to know him better and gain his trust. *Remember the Afghan women and children.*

Taking another swig of wine for courage, she bobbed and weaved through the crowd, never taking her eyes off her prize. Lachlan's back was to her so she could catch him unawares. He wouldn't have time to school his expression. Would he look guilty, like someone who'd just had a clandestine meeting with his accomplice?

The Scottish artist conversing with Lachlan noticed her approach and sent her a warm smile before saying something to Lachlan. Suddenly, she found herself staring into a pair of emerald eyes that didn't look the slightest bit welcoming.

Lachlan was replying to MacLeod's question about living in the States when the artist's gaze veered past him, and a sunny smile broke out on his weathered face. He turned to see what had captured the older man's attention.

And met a pair of hazel eyes he recognized all too well.

Sophia. She *was* here. His shoulders tightened. Had she seen him with Lucas? If she had, she might ask questions he had no intention of answering.

Her hips swayed gently in a black dress that hugged the lines of her body, bared her shoulders, and gave him a tantalizing view of toned legs.

And those black and red heels.

Lust punched him in the gut and shot provocative images into his brain. His lips caressing the exposed skin of her neckline, his hands molding her curves. Her wearing nothing but those shoes. His mouth went dry. He shifted to try and accommodate the sudden bulge in his trousers.

The woman was a danger to his sanity and a distraction he could ill afford.

"Why are you here?" The question left his lips in a harsh rasp as he struggled to bring his unruly thoughts under control. He could feel MacLeod's frown of disapproval.

Sophia's steps faltered. She raised her chin and gave him a defiant stare that didn't hide the glimmer of hurt in her big eyes. Twin spots of color stained her cheeks. "Jared invited me."

"Jared's here?" Lachlan did a quick scan of the room. Had his boss seen him with Lucas?

"He was, he, ah, had to leave unexpectedly. I stayed to admire the art." She bit her lip, defiance giving way to uncertainty. "I guess I should call an Uber."

He tore his gaze from her mouth and frowned. "Jared brought you here and left you to get home on your own? That was a shitty move."

Surprise flared in her eyes at his tone. MacLeod's curious gaze flitted back and forth between him and Sophia.

Lachlan sucked in a lungful of air before he dug himself any deeper of a hole.

"Forgive me, Alan." He turned to the other Scot. "I'd like you to meet Sophia Russo, a colleague of mine. Sophia, this is Alan MacLeod, one of the artists exhibiting his work here this evening."

"A bonnie wee lassie, and a *ruadh*—a redhead." MacLeod bowed with a flourish and kissed the back of Sophia's hand.

A flush pinkened her skin at the artist's dramatic greeting. "It's nice to meet you—your paintings are lovely." She turned to Lachlan, her expression guarded. "I don't want to interrupt your conversation. I'm going to take one more peek at the exhibits and then leave."

"I'll take you home." The words tumbled out before he could stop them.

"You don't have to."

"I insist." He'd put that wary look on her face with his rudeness. "Jared should never have left you to fend for yourself." The thought of her getting into a car driven by a stranger didn't sit well with him when he could see her safely home.

She rolled her eyes, her lips pursing as if something he'd said amused her. "I'm more than capable of fending for myself, as you put it, but thank you. I accept your offer. Come find me when you're ready to leave."

"*Ach*," MacLeod cut in. "Any red-blooded Scot would rather spend time with you than continue to blether with an old man like me."

The flush in Sophia's cheeks deepened to a rosy hue. "I'm sure you are charming company. I'd love to know more about your beautiful paintings."

"Then stay," Lachlan found himself saying. *Stay with me.* He hadn't wanted her here, and now he couldn't seem to let her go.

"Okay." She gave him a shy smile.

His heart gave a strange stutter.

They broke eye contact when MacLeod cleared his throat and gave an amused chuckle.

Lachlan drank in Sophia's animated features as she peppered MacLeod with questions about the landscapes he'd painted. Once she'd finished, he took her around and introduced her to the other Scottish artists. They were all equally captivated by her, and Lachlan could see why. He was as well.

Sophia gave off an aura of sunshine, her wide smile and warm eyes focused on each artist as if they were the only person in the room when they answered her questions. Her passion was evident in her voice and delicate hands as they moved through the air like a conductor's, punctuating her speech.

Such a contradiction. Despite her professional prowess, she seemed oblivious to her feminine power. She'd held each of the artists in her thrall, and the gaze of every man at the reception had lingered when she passed by.

Lachlan's head hurt from gritting his teeth to throttle a snarl.

Was she like that when she made love? Her lover the singular focus of her attention. Her hands roving his skin, memorizing his body as she whispered words of seduction. Another wave of desire hit him, rolling through his veins and reviving his flagging erection. He shifted to stand just behind her and leaned down to whisper in her ear. "I'm going to get a drink. Would you like something?"

She shook her head with a smile and resumed her conversation.

Lachlan shouldered his way through the crowd to the nearest bar. "Water, please, with ice." His voice came out scratchy and a touch desperate. The bartender probably thought he was choking on something. "Thanks, pal." He grabbed the proffered glass of ice water and chugged, willing the cold liquid to take effect on his painfully hard cock.

"There you are." Sophia appeared next to him, her eyes twinkling with a touch of mischief. "I have something to show you." She grabbed his hand. The unexpected feel of her soft fingers twining around his callused ones left him short of air.

He didn't want to get involved with Sophia.

He didn't want to let her go.

She led him through the crowd to an exhibit along the far back wall.

"Look." Her hand swept up.

He followed its trajectory to the oil painting on the wall. Jacobites charged, broadswords and targes in hand, toward British redcoats. Fraser and Stuart plaids mingled with MacDonalds and Mackintoshes. The Battle of Culloden.

She pointed to the Highlander leading the charge. "He could be you."

Invisible bands squeezed his chest that her impish grin failed to loosen. A battle rife with betrayal and the beginning of the end for the Highland clans.

How fitting that she saw him in this scene.

Fitzy hadn't made it, then.

"We need to find out who gave Nadia that intel. They set us up."

Nathan's icy blue eyes turned arctic. "Yeah, about that. No one can find Nadia. Your guys conducted a base-wide search. Her things are gone from her housing unit."

"Lachlan?" A tug on his sleeve. He looked down at Sophia's faltering smile.

His hand lifted to trace the line marring the skin between her brows.

Her eyes softened, her tongue sneaking out to lick her full bottom lip.

What was he doing?

He dropped his hand. There was no changing the past. He was hardly the hero in the painting. "It's bonnie, as are you. Stand in front so I can take a picture of you both."

She stepped in front of the painting, posing with one hand on a cocked hip, the other pointing to the black-haired Highlander. "I think you should buy it."

Her cheeky smile amused him. "Maybe I will."

He snapped several photos, his good humor evaporating as he scrolled through them. Sophia saw him as a hero in a romanticized version of past glory. In reality, he was the aftermath of the battle, a broken version of the man in the painting.

"Are you ready to leave? I'll take you home now." He kept his tone light so as not to reflect the dark path his thoughts had taken.

If he let her get too close, she would see the real him.

The thought lingered like a slow poison in his system on the drive to Sophia's condo. When they arrived, he walked her to the entrance.

"Thank you for bringing me home. I had a nice time tonight." Her eyes were luminous beneath the glow of the building's exterior lighting, her hands clasped in front of her, fingers twisting around each other in a clear indication of nerves.

Before he could summon a polite acknowledgment and say good-bye, she stood on her toes and gave him a butterfly kiss. The touch of her lips sent an electric current to his groin and shorted out his sense of self-preservation. He hauled her into his body and seized her mouth, desperate for a taste.

Sophia melted into him. White wine and sugar. Heady and sweet. Her lush floral scent sank into his skin and embedded into his brain. Her breasts molded to the hardness of his chest. He wanted to yank down her dress, suck their rosy tips into his mouth, and grip them in his teeth. Wedging his hand between them, he covered one of the soft mounds, squeezing gently. Her answering moan jerked his hips forward, letting her know her power over him without words.

What did she see in a broken man like him?

"I don't trust her, Nadia." Thom's pale blue eyes met his, lines of tension carved in his face.

Lachlan frowned. "Why not? She's been a valuable asset to our team and the Americans."

"Maybe, maybe not." Thom paused, set his jaw, and met Lachlan's gaze with a steely resolve. "She might come off sweet and innocent, but something lurks behind her eyes that raises the hair on the back of my neck."

"Do you have any evidence that Nadia is lying? Anything at all?"

"No." Thom shifted on his feet, but he continued to hold Lachlan's stare. "Just my gut. It's served me well enough for fifteen years of military service."

Lachlan speared fingers through his hair and let out a frustrated sigh. "Gut instinct isn't sufficient to call off a mission as critical as this one. Nadia's a British citizen, here by her own choice, risking her life. You may not trust her, but I do."

Thom straightened, his posture stiff. "You asked for my opinion, and I gave it to you. Will there be anything else, Captain?"

Lachlan's jaw tightened. "Dismissed, Staff Sergeant Barnwell."

"Lachlan. Where did you go?"

His gaze focused to see confusion muddying the green flecks in Sophia's eyes. When had he stopped kissing her?

"Where did you go?" she repeated. Her fingers brushed his jaw.

To Hell.

"I'm sorry." Apologizing to her was becoming a habit. He took a halting step backward. "I shouldn't have done that." He owed it to Thom, Fitzy, and the others not to make the same mistake again.

"Goodnight." He took another step back.

She gave a hesitant nod, not meeting his eyes.

He stifled a curse. "By the way, thank you for the plant." He didn't want to leave things so awkward between them.

Her head lifted, and he was relieved to see a pleased smile curve her lips. "You're welcome. See you Monday."

He waited until she entered the building before leaving. The I-495 exit loomed on his right. His demons rode him hard. He hit the accelerator, and the Mercedes shot onto the Beltway as he tried to outrun them.

CHAPTER TEN

SOPHIA TRUDGED TO HER door, her body and emotions still reeling. One minute she and Lachlan had been sharing the hottest kiss she'd ever had in her life, and the next, he'd gone still, his mind somewhere else, and he'd pulled away from her like he had just found out she was Typhoid Mary.

The only thing that would make her feel better tonight was more wine, a romance novel, and her battery-operated boyfriend.

She jammed her key in the lock with a frustrated huff. What the heck was she doing, anyway? She was supposed to be discovering whether Lachlan was an arms trafficker, not throwing herself at him.

At least he liked the plant she'd picked out for his office. Her lips pursed. Or he was just being polite?

No, she decided. He'd genuinely thanked her. It was a small victory toward gaining his trust, but she'd take it.

She opened her door and tossed her purse on the foyer table. It bounced off a large Coach tote that hadn't been there when she left for the gallery reception.

"Finally." Emily Dane leaped from where she'd been sipping a glass of wine on Sophia's couch and raced over to envelope her in a hug. With her artfully styled, shoulder-length ash-blonde hair, periwinkle blue silk blouse, and cream tailored slacks, Emily looked like she had stepped off the pages of Marie Claire—classic and feminine.

Sophia's dismal mood evaporated as she returned her best friend's embrace. "You're supposed to be in Paris."

"I was. I've got some meetings at the State Department next week and thought I'd surprise you." Emily's changeable eyes were a deeper blue in the overhead light and almost matched her blue blouse. She leaned back to inspect Sophia's outfit. "Hot date?"

Sophia averted her gaze from her too-perceptive friend. "No, actually, I attended an art gallery reception for work."

"Uh-huh. You realize you have the worst poker face on the planet, right?" Emily gestured at Sophia's heels. "Take those off and have a seat on the couch. I'm going to get you a glass of sauvignon blanc, and you are going to tell me what man put that look on your face."

Sophia kicked off her pumps, breathing a sigh of relief on behalf of her toes. She padded into the living room. Long white drapes shut out the night, and a pair of lamps on her glass end tables bathed the room in a soft, warm glow.

Emily returned with a second wine glass and handed it to her before dropping onto the sofa and curling her long legs beneath her. Sophia took a sip of the crisp, pale yellow liquid to try and wash away Lachlan's imprint—whisky, a trace of mint, and the clean, masculine scent of a pine forest after a spring rain.

"Spill," Emily ordered.

Sophia let out a dispirited sigh. "I spent most of the evening with one of my new colleagues, Lachlan Mackay."

Emily's eyes twinkled over her wine glass. "Ooh, is he as sexy as his name implies?"

"He's Scottish." Sophia couldn't help her grin. "And, yes, he is. I secretly nicknamed him the Hot Scot."

"Do tell, girl."

"He's former British special forces and oversees LAI's security teams in Afghanistan."

Emily grimaced. "Ugh, which means he's probably an alphahole."

Sophia gave her friend a questioning look.

"You know the type," Emily said with a shrug, "bossy, overprotective, demanding." She took a sip of wine and arched a brow at Sophia over the rim of her glass. "Someone like my dad and brother."

Sophia huffed out a laugh. She could imagine Lachlan was all those things. "You are way too hard on your dad and Alex. Be grateful they care. You know what kind of family I grew up in."

She sobered. "Lachlan is suffering. I think something bad happened when he was in the military. We haven't known each other long, but we have a connection. One he's trying to fight."

She should be, too. It was becoming harder to remember that her need to gain his trust was so she could spy on him.

Emily would have a fit if she knew what her father had asked Sophia to do.

A huge yawn cracked open Emily's lips. She gave Sophia a bleary-eyed smile. "Still on Paris time. I need to hit the sack." She gave Sophia's hand a quick squeeze. "Be careful. You tend to think the best of people. Don't get your heart broken because you think you can save this guy."

Roshan Haider sat in the silver BMW he'd hired long after Lachlan Mackay's dark blue Mercedes drove off, the deep growl of its engine fading into the night.

What game was his contact playing that he'd sent Roshan to Afghanistan, to Khan, to learn the identity of Nadia's killer when he had to have already known it was Mackay?

His anger only increased after what he'd just witnessed, Mackay's passionate embrace with a petite red-haired woman. The bastard was going on with his life as if he hadn't murdered Roshan's sister in cold blood.

A rhythm of rage pounded Roshan's temple and pulsed behind his eyes.

Nadia had made mistakes, but she hadn't deserved to die. He and his father could have convinced the British government to drop the charges against his sister if she had lived.

They'd never gotten the chance because of Mackay, mad for revenge.

Roshan had planned to expose the former SAS soldier to the public as his sister's killer. Now his thoughts shifted, coalesced around a different objective. Did this woman matter to Mackay? What would he do to keep her safe?

He shoved the car into drive and backed out of the space. It had been a long two days of travel, and he needed sleep. For now, he'd head back to his hotel in Georgetown. Tomorrow morning he'd return and be back every morning until he learned this woman's routine.

Lachlan Mackay needed to know what it felt like to be afraid.

CHAPTER ELEVEN

"WHAT'S THIS PAINTING YOU need my truck for? Got a picture of it?"

Nathan's question had Lachlan's shoulders tightening Saturday morning as he climbed into the cab of his mate's pickup. "You'll see when we pick it up."

"Not if they packed it properly, I won't. It'll be wrapped up tighter than a tick." Nathan grinned and waggled his brows. "To quote Brad Paisley, loosely, is your priceless French painting a drunk, naked girl?"

"The painting is of a historic battle," Lachlan snapped, "it's Scottish, not French, and who the bloody hell is Brad Paisley?"

Nathan's grin widened until Lachlan thought he would go blind from all the perfectly straight, white teeth aimed in his direction. "Sounds boring, and I don't believe you for a minute. I must see proof."

Lachlan shot Nathan a dirty look and, after a moment's hesitation, pulled out his phone and swiped to the photos he'd taken Thursday evening. With an inward sigh, he braced for what was coming.

"Who's the hot little redhead?"

And there it was.

"Just a colleague." The words dragged reluctantly over his tongue. "She wasn't my date." They had left together, however. His body tightened at the memory of Sophia's soft lips and pliant curves when he'd given into temptation and kissed her.

"Uh-huh. You took several pictures of your sexy little 'just a coworker,' and from the look on your face, you've got an interesting slideshow running through your head. Wait," Nathan's brows drew together, "this isn't the same coworker that"—he made air quotes—"annoyed you, is it? Have you slept with her yet?"

"No, and I'm not going to." The last thing Lachlan needed was to be distracted by a woman and lose sight of his mission—find Khan's weapons supplier, knock the warlord from his lofty perch, and avenge the fallen.

Nathan chuckled. "No wonder your aim was crappy at the shooting range. You need to get laid."

Lachlan tossed his pal a one-fingered salute. "Piss off. Are you going to drive or not?"

His gesture only made Nathan laugh harder. "Don't get your panties in a wad, amigo." Still chuckling, Nathan turned out of Lachlan's apartment complex in Arlington and headed in the direction that would take them toward Reston's town center.

The gallery had packed his new acquisition in a wooden crate, making him grateful he'd corralled Nathan into lending his truck and his muscles to get it home and up to his eleventh-floor apartment.

After they'd hung the painting in his living room over his brown leather sofa, they stepped back to admire their work. The piece of art dominated the small space, the emotions of the men charging into battle leaping off the canvas with dramatic tension.

"It's quite the statement piece. Not bad." Nathan nodded his head in approval. "At least now you have something on the wall. I don't mean to be rude, amigo, but I've seen cheap roadside motels with more personality than your place."

Lachlan looked around his apartment. He had a bed to sleep in, a small table with four chairs to eat at in the small dining nook, and a couch to sit on in the living area. The sixty-five-inch flat-screen TV on the wall opposite the sofa had been an indulgence, though he hardly ever turned it on.

Viewing it through Nathan's eyes, he supposed it looked a bit sterile. "It's a rental," he offered, as if that was a valid reason when the truth was he didn't care what his living quarters looked like. Adding bits of fluff wouldn't keep his nightmares at bay or make him feel like he belonged in this city.

His job allowed him to return to Afghanistan. Once he'd taken care of his unfinished business there, he didn't know if he'd stay in the States, return to Scotland, or throw a dart at a map and see where it took him. He did enjoy working with his security teams, all former military men. It reminded him of what he'd lost when he'd left the SAS. Maybe he'd form his own security company somewhere. Start over.

For some reason, an image of Sophia popped into his head when he contemplated a normal existence.

"What brought that frown to your ugly mug?" Nathan's comment reminded him he wasn't alone.

"Nothing, pal. Dinner's on me. There's a decent steakhouse around the corner."

Nathan slapped him on the shoulder, humor brightening his icy eyes. "You know just how to woo me, you handsome stud."

Lachlan's lips tilted. "Arsehole."

CHAPTER TWELVE

A SILVER BMW.

Again.

Sophia double-checked the rearview mirror on her Prius. The man behind the wheel looked the same. Dark hair, mirrored sunglasses. She split her focus between the road ahead and the car behind. Her shoulders relaxed when she turned into the office parking garage, and the BMW continued past. Plenty of people made the same commute up Duke Street, she wasn't sure why she kept noticing this guy.

Maybe because the situation with Lachlan had her nerves on a tightrope. He definitely was hiding something.

Who was the man he'd met with at the art gallery reception? She should have snapped that photo and sent it to Admiral Dane.

And why, with all of Lachlan's secrets, did her brain keep replaying the kiss they'd shared that set her blood on fire? The kind you read about but didn't believe happened anywhere except in a novel or movie. Swoon-worthy.

Until whatever haunted him had taken over and he'd frozen, trapped in a memory.

She managed to banish thoughts of the silver car and Lachlan most of the morning and get her work done, but "the kiss" snuck back into her head during her walk to the Metro for her meetings on Capitol Hill. Lachlan's normal icy control hadn't just cracked, it had shattered.

His tongue had branded her, his hand on her breast possessive, his hard length pressed into her stomach, filling her with a heady sense of feminine power she'd never experienced before.

The sun shone brightly from a cloudless blue sky as she crossed over busy Duke Street and strolled down the brick sidewalk on Diagonal Road toward the King Street-Old Town Metro Station. Her mood upbeat, she donned her shades and sang the lyrics to a Rihanna song under her breath as it streamed through her earbuds.

Fingers of unease danced across her shoulders, whispering of a presence at her back. She glanced over her shoulder. A dark-haired man in black slacks, red shirt, and sunglasses, strolled behind her. Something about him jarred her senses like two discordant notes, but she couldn't put her finger on why.

She took out her ear buds and picked up her pace. The Metro station was only a couple of blocks away.

When she reached the station, she swiped her card and hurried up the escalator to the platform just as the yellow line pulled in. The doors hissed open, disgorging a few scattered passengers.

She made a beeline for the nearest train car and stepped in as the door chime sounded.

Her sigh of relief was short-lived. An arm thrust through the closing doors, and the stranger forced his way into the car.

The bass drum of her heart almost drowned out the train's automated scold.

Her fingers tightened around the strap of her shoulder bag.

He'd removed his glasses. His eyes were an unusual shade of aquamarine, creating a striking contrast to his olive skin, black hair, and heavy brows. His tight-lipped smile failed to warm cold features.

She cradled her bag to her chest, her muscles bunched, preparing for flight mode. The train wasn't crowded. Why had he been so determined to get into her car? And why did he seem familiar?

The man took a seat a few rows behind her. Maybe he'd get off at the next stop. He didn't, but more people got on, and she let out a quiet sigh of relief.

He didn't get off at the next four stops either. By the time the train pulled into L'Enfant-Plaza, Sophia was up and waiting for the doors to open. Without looking back, she bolted from the train, weaved through the crowd, and climbed the moving steps of the escalator rather than waiting for them to ferry her.

As she neared the top, she glanced back. A family with small children crowded onto the escalator, blocking the man.

The busy station's crowds and multiple exits might work to her advantage. She headed for the D Street exit and raced up the steep escalator that ferried passengers to surface level.

Finally, she reached the top and onto the street, her lungs on fire. She scanned the exiting crowd behind her for a brief second, then hurried down D, cut through the small park to 6th, then up to Maryland, and over to Independence Avenue. Only then did she stop to catch her breath and look around. There was no sign of the stranger amongst the pedestrians milling around her.

Above her head, tall banks of clouds cluttered what had been a cloudless, blue sky.

Her heart was still galloping like a racehorse. She dug her phone out of her bag and called Emily. "I just had the weirdest thing happen." She told her friend about the stranger while she walked the rest of the way to the Rayburn House Office Building at a more leisurely pace.

"You should call the police," Emily said.

"And tell them what? A creepy guy may have been following me? He didn't speak to me, didn't approach me." Sophia passed between the massive ionic columns of Rayburn's horseshoe entrance and through a set of glass and metal doors to the security checkpoint. "Maybe I imagined it."

"Be careful."

"I will," Sophia promised her friend. She hung up, texted her former boss, Tony, in Congressman Kellerman's office that she was downstairs waiting, and placed her bag on the screening table for inspection.

By the time two-thirty rolled around, Sophia had finished up her meetings. A dead calm had descended over the trees, disturbed only by gusts from passing cars. She cast a wary glance at the sky and picked up her pace back to the Metro. She descended into the station's bowels and took the shorter escalator to the yellow line track.

A flash of red drew her attention further down the platform. The air punched from her lungs, replaced by a sick feeling of dread.

It was a coincidence. Had to be.

The train pulled in, drawing crowds to the front of each car door.

It probably wasn't even him. She hadn't gotten a good look.

She sat through the next five stops, her stomach in knots, face pressed against the glass as she scanned disembarking passengers. Finally, the train decelerated into King Street Station. A humid gust of wind blew through the raised outdoor platform, tugging strands of hair from her twist as she stepped from the car. She peered up at the gathering storm clouds.

Her muscles twitched in warning. She scanned the platform and froze, her feet cemented to the hexagon tile floor.

That flash of red at L'Enfant Plaza hadn't been her imagination.

The stranger stood mere feet away, a malevolent amusement lighting his aquamarine eyes and twisting his lips. This close, it suddenly struck her where she'd seen him before.

In her rearview mirror.

"Why are you following me?" If only her voice had come out stronger instead of shaking with fear. Her gaze darted around the platform. Where was a police officer when you needed one?

"Tell Lachlan Mackay his day is coming," the man said in a crisp British accent. He turned and disappeared down the escalator to street level before she could take a full breath.

A rumble of thunder in the distance snapped her out of immobility.

How had he known she and Lachlan were colleagues? And why had he targeted her to deliver his message?

Whatever Lachlan was involved in, he was in danger. She needed to warn him.

Her shaking fingers could barely manage the rideshare app. Even if the weather didn't look menacing, there was no way she was walking back to the office. Fortunately, a driver was nearby with an ETA of two minutes. She stayed on the train platform for another minute, then took the escalator to the street and fast-walked to the rideshare zone, scanning the area for any sign of the British man.

After verifying the license plate and name of the driver, she jumped into the back of the vehicle. A fat drop of rain splattered against the windshield, then another. She glanced back at the station then up at a flash of lightning as the driver pulled into traffic.

Lachlan poured himself the last dregs of coffee and took a sip, grimacing at the burnt, ashy taste. He dumped the rest in the sink and glanced at the clock over the break room door. Too late to bother with a fresh pot.

Thoughts of Sophia had hounded him all weekend. He'd dreamed of her the night of the gallery reception after he exhausted himself circling the sixty-four-mile Beltway. Twice. Hot, steamy scenes of him licking her until she came hard, then thrusting into her until he found his own release and shattered the nightmares that usually haunted his sleep.

It was the first time in two years he hadn't dreamed of death.

Kissing her had been a mistake. He'd let his guard down. He had no right to want more, at least until he finished this business with Khan.

As if he'd conjured her, Sophia appeared in the doorway. Her frantic gaze met his. "There you are."

The anxiety in her voice and rigid set of her shoulders jacked every muscle in his body to attention. He straightened and took a step away from the sink, toward her. "What's wrong?"

"A man followed me today on the Metro. He's been following me."

"What man?" Lachlan's hands fisted. "Do you know his name?"

Her face was too pale. Was some cheeky twat harassing her because she'd refused his advances? Lachlan would have a talk with him. He'd be pissing his pants by the time Lachlan got done telling him in explicit detail what he'd do if the wank ever came near Sophia again.

"Some British guy. And he had a message for you. He said to tell you your day was coming."

The roar in his ears muffled her voice, but there was no mistaking her round eyes or the palms slapped against his chest. Lachlan blinked. When had he crossed the room? His gaze dropped to where his hands gripped her upper arms.

"Lachlan?" The tremble in her voice was a slap to his face. Spots of red colored her cheeks. "What is wrong with you?" She gave him a shove.

He released her at once, spearing trembling fingers through his hair to keep from touching her. *Fuck.* He wasn't a brute, at least not with women, but the thought of her alone, defenseless— "Did he hurt you?"

She flinched at the whip of fury in his voice. "No. He—"

"Come with me." The intensity of his reaction put him in unfamiliar emotional territory. He needed to regain control. He tamped his emotions and tried again, extending his palm. "Please."

After a moment's hesitation, she gave him her hand. His legs ate up the distance to his office, pulling her with him. He didn't give a damn who saw. He wasn't letting her go.

Someone had used Sophia to get to him. Given his previous career in special operations, the list of potential enemies was long.

They sat at the same table where they'd been working together only days before. He released her hand to trace her jaw, his rougher, tanned fingers a contrast to her delicate beauty. "Tell me everything. From the first moment you realized this man was following you."

She chewed at her lip, clearly marshaling her thoughts. "This morning, a silver BMW was behind me in traffic—one I've seen a lot the past few days," she added. "When I walked to the Metro earlier, I noticed a man following me. He looked familiar, but I couldn't place him. He gave off a creepy vibe, so when he got off at the same station as me, I tried to lose him in the crowd."

"And?" Lachlan tried to contain his impatience and let her get out her story.

"Well, I did lose him, or he didn't follow me. I thought maybe I'd imagined the whole thing. I went to my meetings on Capitol Hill and took the Metro back." Fear darkened the brown in her eyes to a deep chocolate, muting the green. "He was waiting in the subway and followed me back to King Street. That's when I realized where I recognized him from. The BMW. He delivered his message for you and then disappeared."

"What did he look like?"

Creases appeared between her neatly groomed brows. "Black hair. Tanned skin. Average height—definitely shorter than you. His features were kind of Middle Eastern."

She paused, her gaze focused inward. "He had unusual blue eyes."

Lachlan eased back in his chair and forced his muscles to relax to hide the fury that flowed like lava through his veins.

Ryder was right. Roshan Haider had come to DC. But why target Sophia? She had no ties to him or his life before he came to LAI.

Haider must have seen them together Friday night. Which meant Haider had been following *him*.

A sharp pain stabbed behind Lachlan's eyes. He'd been careless, let down his guard, and now this. He should have stayed away from Sophia.

"Do you know him?" She searched his face, worry and a hint of suspicion in her expression. "What are you involved in? Are you in danger?"

He hesitated to tell her the truth. His past was something he tried to keep in a box with a tight lid. "His name is Roshan Haider. He's angry because his sister joined the Taliban and died in a Coalition operation against a Taliban stronghold. He's gotten it into his head that British forces are to blame for her death."

That was the official story. The words were bile in his mouth. "He must have seen us together, maybe at the gallery reception on Friday, and assumed…" Lachlan didn't finish the sentence. If Haider had seen their kiss outside Sophia's condominium, it wasn't difficult to figure out what he assumed.

Sophia took up where he left off. "He assumed you and I are in a relationship."

He wanted to smooth the worry creasing her forehead, but he didn't trust himself to touch her again. Adrenaline and the need to protect her gripped him hard when what he needed was a clear head.

"Why is he angry with you?" Understanding lit her gaze. "British forces. You were involved somehow."

"She was our translator." Sophia didn't need to know the entire sordid story. He wouldn't be able to look her in the eyes again if she did.

"Should we call the police?" Her teeth captured her lower lip again. If she didn't stop, he would liberate the plump flesh with his own lips and nip it himself. Only he wouldn't stop with just a taste.

"Don't worry. I'll deal with Haider." His fingers curled into fists. He was going to track down the bastard and make him regret involving Sophia in his vendetta.

Her eyes widened. "Now I see it. In your eyes." Her voice was a hushed whisper.

"See what?"

"The SAS guy."

His throat tightened. "This is who I am, Sophia. Better you find out now. But I promise you, Roshan Haider will never get that close to you again."

His past wouldn't threaten her.

He'd make sure of it.

Lachlan pulled out his mobile the second Sophia left his office after promising him she wouldn't leave work without him.

Despite his best efforts, she had slipped beneath his skin and breached the outer wall of his defenses in a way no one else had in two years. He wouldn't let anyone hurt her.

Not even himself.

The realization sent a shard of pain to his chest, and he rubbed at the ache.

Roshan Haider was about to discover how dangerous it was to fuck with a former SAS man.

He pulled up Nathan's contact.

"Yo, amigo. Are you still up for me to embarrass you at the shooting range on Wednesday night?" Nathan's nasal twang and lazy vowels amplified the amusement threading his voice.

"I need your help."

"Name it." In a blink, his mate's tone shifted from good ol' boy to deadly operator.

"The woman I've mentioned, Sophia. I need you to keep an eye on her. Nadia's brother is in town, and he's sending me a message." Nathan's job as a white-hat hacker gave him the flexibility to shadow

Sophia, and for a big man, Nathan was unusually good at not being seen.

Nathan swore. "You need me to find out where Haider's staying?"

"Yes." Lachlan's fury morphed into an icy calm. "Then I'm going hunting."

"Roger that."

Nathan's response eased the knot in Lachlan's chest. The former SEAL wouldn't let anything happen to Sophia. "I'll text you her information."

He hung up and pulled up another contact. If he made this call, he was limiting his options regarding Haider. He'd just as soon bury pieces of the man beneath the Potomac River, but even in combat, there were rules of engagement.

Lucas Caldwell answered on the third ring. "I don't have any new information on Khan's weapons supplier, Mackay."

"I'm not calling about that," Lachlan growled. "Nadia Haider's brother is in town. He's stalking a colleague of mine, a woman."

"Call the police. That's not an FBI matter unless he kidnaps her and takes her across state lines."

Lachlan's back teeth ground together hard enough to crack. "He confronted her, told her to tell me my day is coming. Haider wants to expose me as the soldier who shot his sister. He wants revenge."

Lucas's weary sigh echoed in Lachlan's ear. "You know he'll get nowhere. How would he even know to go after you? JSOC doesn't let those mission details get into the public arena."

"Haider's been to Afghanistan." Lachlan let his news drop into silence. "Meeting with Mohammad Razul Khan." He stiffened, remembering the conversation he'd had with Ryder. "What if threatening me is a side benefit, and Haider is in DC meeting with Khan's supplier? He owns an import-export business. He could be acting as the middleman, which is why we haven't been able to pinpoint how the shipments are getting to Khan."

"I'll make some phone calls," Lucas replied. "In the meantime, watch your six, and don't do anything stupid. Has Haider made any threats to you or this woman?"

"Not yet, but if he goes near Sophia again, I make no promises." Lachlan didn't try to keep the menace from his voice.

"What's she to you?"

"Nothing. Haider has the wrong idea about her." The lie stumbled off his tongue. That damn ache in his chest returned.

"Hmmm. I'll be in touch." The Assistant Director hung up.

Lachlan sat motionless, the phone still held to his ear.

Dust and the stench of burn pits and latrines assaulted Lachlan's eyes and nose as he exited the hanger at Bagram where the SAS and SEAL teams had received their final briefing on the night's mission. Nathan walked with him.

The scowl on Nathan's face showed his thoughts about the SEALs being relegated to the support role.

Lachlan slapped him on the shoulder. "Cheer up, pal. You lads had lead last time."

Nathan grunted. "You'd better hope I don't have to sneeze or scratch an itch or something about the time some Taliban asshole has you in his crosshairs."

Lachlan laughed, then sobered as his mind returned to the mission. "Let's hope Nadia's intel and the aerial reconnaissance photos from this morning are accurate."

"Navy command staff thinks we're looking at a sixty percent success rate." Nathan slanted Lachlan a look filled with mischief. "I'll take those odds."

Lachlan nodded. "I'll take those odds as well. See you at zero dark thirty."

Lachlan's office phone buzzed, jolting him back to the present.

Nadia's betrayal had tainted every day of the past two years. His gut told him Sophia was different—her warm heart and trusting nature who she was, not how she presented herself. But his gut had been wrong before.

Maybe once Khan and Haider had been dealt with, and his debt to the dead paid.

Maybe then, he'd let her show him how to trust again.

Chapter Thirteen

THE SHARP STACCATO OF Sophia's heels echoed off the concrete floor of the parking garage beneath LAI's office building. She located her bright sea-glass-green car amidst the monochrome collection of gas guzzlers mid-way up the ramp to level one and held up her key fob. The locks disengaged with a click.

She had a feeling there was a lot more to this situation with Lachlan than he was admitting. Why did this guy, Haider, follow her if he was angry with Lachlan? And what role had Lachlan played, exactly, in Haider's sister's death?

And what kind of woman would defect to the Taliban?

Oh, sure, she'd seen the news stories of all the young women who'd left their home countries in the West and snuck over borders to marry Islamic fighters in Syria and Iraq, but that didn't mean she understood it.

A large hand shot out, covering her hand holding the car key.

She squeaked, pivoting to face her attacker, her other hand raised like a claw to go for the eyes like she'd learned in a self-defense class in college. Lachlan's familiar scent reached her brain at the same time her eyes registered his face.

He moved like a ghost.

"Geez, you scared me." She glared at him, hands on hips while her heartbeat slowly eased back to its normal rhythm.

"I told you to wait for me before you drove home."

"I did wait for you, then I went to your office, and you weren't there." She crossed her arms and waited for an explanation.

"I had something to take care of." Somehow, he'd ended up with her key fob in his hand. "Stay here."

He stalked to her car and crouched, running his hands around the bottom of the frame, then peered underneath. Straightening, he opened her door and inspected the inside before shutting the door and pressing the fob. The locks clicked into place.

"Let me drive you home."

Her stomach did a little flip. "Did you find something on my car? Like a bug?"

"Tracker, not bug, and no." He glanced down at her. "It was clean."

"If you're that worried about this Haider guy, maybe we should do what I suggested earlier and contact the police."

His hand curved beneath her elbow, gently tugging her forward to match his steps. She glanced back at her Prius. "What about my car?"

"It'll be safe here for one night. And as I told you earlier, I'll deal with Haider." His emerald gaze lasered in on her with an intensity that made her shiver, whether from nerves or desire, she wasn't sure.

"Fine," she huffed. "but we need to grab something to eat on the way. My friend, Emily, said she'd be home late, and I haven't had a chance to hit up the grocery store."

His only response was a brisk nod.

She followed him to his dark blue Mercedes, a sleek, sexy model that suited him more than the more familiar sedan styles she saw around town. He opened the passenger door for her, and she slid onto the black leather seat.

"Where do you want to get food?" Lachlan glanced her way before pulling onto the street. The afternoon storm had cleared out, leaving damp pavement and cooler temperatures as its parting gift.

"How about Snuffy's BBQ in Old Town? They have awesome shredded pork tacos, and I'm in the mood. We can grab some and take them to my place to eat."

"Snuffy's?" His dry tone paired nicely with the arrogantly arched brow.

She shook a finger at him. "Don't judge. I think the place is named after an old-timey cartoon character, but the food is delicious."

His lips tilted up, and his eyes warmed, causing her heart to stutter before regaining its normal rhythm. "Snuffy's it is. Tell me how to get there."

As they drove toward Old Town, the streets narrowed. Corporate office buildings gave way to tree-lined brick sidewalks and two-story colonial townhomes with painted brick façades in various cheery colors. They turned onto King Street, entering the historic district renowned for its eclectic boutiques and many independent restaurants reflecting cuisines as varied as the people who called the DC area home.

She noticed Lachlan's gaze frequently returned to his rear and side view mirrors. Was he looking for Haider? She shivered. There'd been no sign of the silver BMW since this morning.

Lachlan lucked into a metered parking space two blocks from the restaurant. Sophia soaked up his solid presence by her side as they strolled down the street. He stayed to her right, positioning her on the inside. His left hand hovered but didn't rest on her lower back.

The heat of his palm was an itch she couldn't scratch. They might have a dangerous man watching them even now, and all she could think about was how it would feel if Lachlan spread those long fingers over the curve of her rear in a possessive grip. Moisture pooled between her thighs.

Thank goodness his focus stayed on their surroundings and not on her. She was sure her face would give away the direction of her thoughts.

They passed a man seated on the red bricks beneath the covered entrance of an upscale women's boutique. He was young, maybe in his early thirties, dressed in worn jeans and a plaid flannel shirt, but when Sophia met his gaze, his eyes were bleary with addiction and knowledge of terrible things that couldn't be unseen. The cardboard sign beside his tan combat boots read *Homeless Vet, grateful for any help. God Bless*. A black plastic tarp lay beside him, still wet from the thunderstorm that had battered the area earlier.

He looked cold, damp, and hungry. And lost.

The last time she'd given money to someone on the street, a police officer advised her to donate to a charity instead. She understood the reason—don't feed an individual addiction—but it stabbed her heart every time. The least she could do was make eye contact and let the person know she saw them and recognized their humanity.

She tugged on Lachlan's jacket to get his attention. "We need to buy an extra meal."

He glanced down at her, then behind them.

What did he see when he looked at the young veteran? "Why did you join the military?" she asked.

His gaze swiveled back to her. "To serve my country. Because someone told me I'd make a good leader."

"And were you?"

Lachlan's jaw tensed.

She quickly changed the subject to keep him from clamming up. "Tell me about where you're from." She knew the basics from the file

Admiral Dane compiled but wanted Lachlan to choose to share the information with her.

"Thurso?" His face relaxed. "It's a seaport town in the far north of Scotland, in the Caithness region." His lips tilted, the shadows in his eyes receding. "People from all over the world come to Thurso to surf, did you know?"

"Surfing in Scotland?" She grinned. "I did not know. Did you surf growing up?"

"Aye. Though I haven't since I was a lad. My sister Fiona took it more seriously than I did. She just missed qualifying as an elite junior surfer on the UK pro tour."

"You have a sister? Younger or older?" The admiral hadn't included any information on Lachlan's family in his file.

"Younger. And a cheeky one at that." The warmth and affection in his voice revealed a different man than the one he usually presented at LAI. "She's a pharmacist now in Aberdeen."

He cocked a brow. "What about you? Any brothers or sisters?"

"Nope. Only child. One was more than enough for my parents." She injected a false note of humor into her tone.

Lachlan frowned. Before he could ask the question forming in his eyes, they'd reached the two-story painted brick building that housed Snuffy's. He held the door for her to enter. The first floor was all white brick, and above their heads, dark wood beams. Upholstered banquettes lined walls plastered with poster-size replicas of the 1930s comic strip that had introduced the restaurant's lovable hillbilly namesake to the world. Behind the order counter, the open kitchen design added to the lively vibe with the hustle and bustle of food preparations.

Lachlan ordered three plates of shredded taco meals to go and two bottles of water. He waved off the credit card in her hand with an offended glare.

She hid her smile. His old-fashioned manners were kind of charming. Most of her dates had never turned down her offer to split the bill.

Not that this was a date.

They headed back the way they came. When they reached the homeless vet, Lachlan set down the food bag and crouched. "Hey, pal." He pulled out one of the food containers, plastic cutlery, and the two water bottles and placed them next to the man. "Looks like you could use a meal. What's your name?"

"Thank you, sir." The man looked up and acknowledged Sophia, "ma'am," before turning back to Lachlan. "I'm Brady."

"Brady." Lachlan held out his hand, and after a moment's hesitation, the other man shook it. "Lachlan Mackay. You served?"

"Yessir, Army. Seventeenth Infantry. Three deployments to Afghanistan."

Lachlan stood from his crouch, a grimace chasing across his face. "Aye, I served there as well." He reached into his back pocket and withdrew his wallet, pulling out a white business card and a twenty. He handed them both to the younger man. "Here's the number to a local veteran's organization. When you're ready, give them a call. They can help."

Brady took the card and the money with a grateful smile. "Thanks, man. I will. And thanks for the meal." He looked at Sophia, and his wistful smile wrenched her soul. "And for seeing me."

She smiled back wordlessly, blinking away sudden moisture, not trusting her voice.

Lachlan's hand urged her forward. His touch was slight, but it grounded her. They walked the remaining distance to his car in silence.

"Thank you." She climbed into his Mercedes and accepted the bag of food, placing it in her lap.

"It was the right thing to do." There were undercurrents of emotion in his reply.

She'd give anything to understand them. Understand him.

Would a man who'd treated a homeless veteran the way Lachlan had sell weapons to the enemy? It didn't make sense.

They drove the short distance to her condo in guarded silence.

She waved at the guard on duty in the lobby before pointing to Lachlan. "Hi, Sal. He's my guest."

Sal nodded, his brown eyes narrowing suspiciously on Lachlan as they passed.

"I like him. He pays attention." Lachlan pressed the button for the elevator.

Sophia laughed. "He gives every new guy who comes into the building the stink eye."

They rode to the fifth floor. When they reached her door, Lachlan held out his hand and waggled his fingers.

She gave him a questioning stare. "I can open my door. You're carrying the food."

"Sophia, let me open the door." He kept his hand out, and judging from the stubborn glint in his eyes, she wouldn't win this one.

"Oh, for goodness sake." His manners were a bit too old school sometimes. She accepted the bag and dropped her keys into his waiting palm.

A flash of black drew her gaze to the gun in his other hand.

"What the heck?" She'd had no idea he was armed.

He unlocked her door and opened it a crack. "Your alarm isn't on. Is your friend home?"

"I never use my alarm." She checked her phone. According to her Find a Friend app, Emily was still in Foggy Bottom. "And Emily is still at work."

His glower had her raising her brows in return. "What? I'm on the fifth floor of a building with a security guard in the lobby."

"Stay here." He prowled into her home with soundless steps toward the two bedrooms down the hall and back to her living room before returning to scrutinize the alarm panel by the front door. The gun, thankfully, had disappeared.

Now that he was actually in her home, his commanding presence sucked all the air from the place, leaving her restless and aching. She was finding it harder and harder to believe Admiral Dane's suspicions about Lachlan. Her traitorous brain went right back to that scorcher of a kiss. Desire flushed her skin and heated her insides, dampening her panties. Once wasn't enough. She wanted more. Needed his mouth on her, his bare skin against hers.

Needed him to lose control because he wanted *her,* not just any woman.

If he looked at her now, there'd be no hiding the fact she was contemplating having him for dinner instead of the takeout from Snuffy's.

She hurried to the kitchen, took out the taco dinners, and arranged them on two plates, then poured herself a glass of wine and set the plates, silverware, and her glass on the dining table. "What do you want to drink? I have wine, sparkling and filtered tap water, and juice. Sorry, no beer. Emily and I aren't beer drinkers."

"Water's fine, thank you." He was still over by her door. "Do you have alarm contacts on your windows and sliding glass door?"

She squinted at him. "Who do you think is going to get in? Spider-Man?"

He scowled. She rolled her eyes, not caring if he saw. His sense of humor, if he even had one, was missing and presumed dead. "Come eat while the food's still warm."

He strolled with the grace of a big cat to the table and sat. "You're too naïve to the dangers in this world," he grumbled. The taco appeared tiny in his long fingers. One bite and half of it disappeared without a single piece of pork or a shred of cheese falling to the plate.

"And you're too jaded," she shot back. She bit down on her taco and watched in dismay as half the filling jumped from the tortilla like it was a sinking ship to land on her plate.

"I have reason to be." Lachlan didn't look at her as he polished off his meal.

Not ready for their evening to end, she moved the topic to more neutral ground. "We still need to finish getting the information together for the government report."

"We'll do it tomorrow morning." He pushed away his plate and leaned into the back of his chair. His direct, intense stare reminded her of a big cat homing in on its prey. It should have unnerved her instead of sending electricity zinging through her bloodstream to her core.

"Tell me more about your family. You're an only child."

His interest in her was more intoxicating than an entire bottle of chardonnay, even if she wasn't a fan of the subject matter. She wiped her mouth with her napkin and set it on the table. "My parents had me late in life."

She paused. How to explain her childhood? It hadn't been marred by dysfunction in the way one would expect. "I don't think they had planned to have children."

"So, you were a miracle baby?"

"I'm not sure they saw it that way. I think it was more them not knowing what to do with a child and not having the interest or energy to raise one." She glanced up, caught his frown, and added hastily, "Don't get me wrong. They weren't cruel or cold. Just...uninvolved. I didn't want for anything, and they paid for extracurricular activities, summer camps, Catholic school, and college. They bought me a car." She shrugged. She'd said too much.

"Money isn't love." Lachlan's big hand covered hers, enfolding her in his warmth. "I think they should be very proud of you, and if they aren't, that's their problem, not yours. You're a beautiful, intelligent, kindhearted woman."

His words cracked open a door to her heart. She returned his stare. He could probably read her face and see she was falling hard for him, but right now, she didn't care.

The air between them heated. Her skin beneath Lachlan's palm grew hypersensitive, her breasts heavy. His eyes darkened to jade. She licked lips that had gone as dry as the desert and waited for the storm raging in his eyes to push him in her direction.

Lachlan was at a crossroads. Sophia's eyes broadcast her every emotion, and right now, they were staring at him like he was the hero in the painting hanging in his living room. If he kissed her right now, it wouldn't end there. They'd be in her bed, his head and cock taking turns between her thighs as he made her scream while he slaked the hunger beating at him, testing his control.

For some reason, his thoughts went to his staff sergeant. What would Thom have thought of Sophia? Would he have approved, or would his pale blue eyes brim with disappointment and frustration that Lachlan had made the same mistake again?

I don't trust her, lad.

Fear struck swift and deep, like a bullet embedded in his chest. Nadia's beautiful, deceitful face hovered in his brain, taunting him. What if he fell for Sophia only to discover her open, trusting nature was a clever disguise, masking lies that would break him because he couldn't be betrayed by another woman he cared for and survive.

He snatched back his hand and shot to his feet, ignoring Sophia's startled expression. "I have to go. Make sure you keep your doors and windows locked and use the security system."

"Lachlan." His name tore from her lips to stab him in the chest. She ran, putting herself between him and the door. "Don't go, please."

"I'm no' your Prince Charming," he snarled. His ghosts rode him hard, even as hurt bloomed in Sophia's eyes. He was being irrational, and he knew it, but he couldn't seem to stop.

Her lips thinned, the pain in her eyes replaced with steel. "No, you definitely aren't Prince Charming." She stepped into his space despite her wee size and glared at him, her temper sparking. "This nutcase Haider followed me because of you." She poked him in the ribs. "Deal with *him*. I can take care of myself." A bleak look stole over her face that brought a protest to his throat he couldn't voice. "I've been doing it my whole life."

For a split second, he wavered. "Sophia, *mo leannan*, if I was another man, in another life."

"What's wrong with the man you are now?" She searched his face, seeking answers.

He responded with a kiss, pouring everything he couldn't say into her mouth with gentle strokes of his tongue. Not the burning desire he'd felt last time but something more profound that filled him with longing and a touch of melancholy.

Then he stepped away from her and opened her door. "I won't let anything happen to you. That's all I can give you right now." His voice sounded bleak to his ears. He couldn't help but think it matched his future. "Turn on your alarm."

CHAPTER FOURTEEN

LACHLAN GAZED BROODINGLY AT Sophia's back as she returned folders to his filing cabinet the next morning. The navy dress she wore clung lovingly to her body, and he allowed his stare to linger on the rounded curves of her bottom before moving on to her firm calves and matching heels.

Nathan had been waiting when her friend drove her to work. There'd been no sign of Haider.

As soon as Nathan tracked down where Nadia's brother was staying, Lachlan would be paying him a visit before the FBI did. The more he thought about it, the more he became convinced that Haider was involved in the weapons being trafficked to Khan. Maybe Nadia wasn't the only member of her family who'd sympathized with the Taliban.

He'd be able to get information out of Haider using methods the FBI would frown upon. His techniques might be unpleasant, but they wouldn't leave any evidence.

Sophia gathered the papers she'd assembled. "Well, I guess that's everything." She didn't look at him, and he cursed inwardly at the awkwardness between them after the way he'd left her home last night. It wasn't fair to touch her when he couldn't promise her anything. She wasn't the kind of woman who had sex for the sake of sport.

No, her emotions were involved, and he wouldn't take advantage of her attraction to him for his own physical gratification.

He didn't know if he was capable of offering her more.

How could he trust her when he couldn't even trust himself?

"That should keep Fred off both our backs, aye?" He mustered up a smile when she finally met his eyes. "Thank you."

"You're welcome." Her cheeks pinkened. She swept the papers into a manilla folder. "Thank you for your time."

He stood. "Sophia, I—" He needed to say something. He didn't like the stiff way she held herself.

"No, Lachlan, it's okay." Her sad smile bothered him more than he'd thought possible. "I understand." She sucked in a deep breath, her nose wrinkling in a way he could only describe as cute.

Cute? Nathan would laugh his arse off if Lachlan ever said it out loud.

"Besides, Emily went ballistic when she found out about my...stalker. She's not your biggest fan at the moment, I'm afraid."

"I'll pick you up from work and bring you home until I track down Haider. When I'm not available, my friend Nathan can escort you. He can also upgrade your sec—"

Her palm shot out like a stop sign, halting him mid-sentence. "No. Like I said last night, you deal with Haider. I'll be fine." She lifted her chin, determination mingling with the sadness he'd seen in her smile. "I think, after last night, you're right. It might be best if we kept our relationship on a strictly business level."

She whirled on her heels and marched out of his office, leaving him standing there with his hands in his pockets, feeling like a bloody fool.

Sophia might think she could keep herself safe, but until Lachlan located Haider, he wasn't taking any chances. As much as he loathed involving his boss in his personal affairs, another pair of eyes on her wouldn't hurt. He swallowed his distaste at the prospect of airing his dirty laundry and strode down the hall to Jared's office. Penny was away from her desk, so he went straight to Jared's door, gave it a firm rap, and turned the knob. "Got a minute?"

"A minute." Landry waved him toward the chairs in front of his desk.

Lachlan sat, indigestion burning behind his sternum as he contemplated what to reveal. "Did you ever come across Nadia Haider when you were in Afghanistan? She served as an interpreter for coalition troops out of Bagram."

Landry's brows knitted. "Maybe, I don't remember. We worked with several 'terps."

"You'd remember if you met her. She was one of the few female interpreters working with us. Her parents were Afghans who immigrated to London when she was a bairn."

"I think I know who you're talking about." Landry waved a hand in dismissal. "What about her?"

"Nadia's brother, Roshan Haider, is in town." Lachlan grimaced. "He's been stalking Sophia."

"Why the hell would he do that?"

"He blames British forces for his sister's death." Lachlan shifted in his chair. "I think he saw us together when I brought Sophia home from the gallery reception after you left her without a ride." *Arsehole.* He didn't say the word aloud, but his tone conveyed the message.

Jared's eyes cooled. "I was called away unexpectedly. You said he blames the British for his sister's death. Is Sophia in danger because of something you did?"

"I'm taking care of it." Lachlan rolled his shoulders to loosen the tension bunching them. "I wanted you to know so you could keep an eye on her, maybe make sure she has an escort if she has any meetings out of the office until I resolve the issue. I've made sure she can get to and from work safely." Thanks to Nathan.

"Jesus." Jared scrubbed a hand over his face. He picked up the pen on his desk and toyed with it before pointing it at Lachlan like a weapon. "I'll watch after her—but you'd better make damn sure this Haider doesn't pose a threat. And don't do anything illegal."

"I understand. As I said, I'm taking care of the situation." Landry's admonition hit too close to home. He stood, eager to end the conversation.

"Did you do it?"

Jared's question froze him in his tracks. "Do what?"

"Kill Nadia Haider. Is that why her brother is here?" Jared watched him with a curiously blank expression, hands steepled under his chin.

"You know better than anyone we can't talk about what we did on missions." He wasn't about to spill his deep dark secrets.

"Stay away from Sophia." The warning in Jared's voice was unmistakable.

"Is there a problem we need to discuss?" *Shite.* Lachlan had been going for neutral, not the challenge he'd just thrown out.

Landry threw up a palm. "Of course not. I'm not in the habit of concerning myself with relationships between my employees—unless it interferes with business. Or, apparently, their safety." His voice dripped with sarcasm.

Liar.

He saw the frost in Jared's eyes. He'd seen how Jared looked at Sophia when she wasn't paying attention. Landry was her boss. He'd better not cross that line.

Lachlan's hands fisted. Landry's gaze dropped to them before returning to meet Lachlan's, his brow arched.

Lachlan forced his fingers to relax. "You needn't worry. Sophia and I are strictly colleagues." *Now, who was the liar?* His words hung in the air while their stares fought for dominance.

Landry broke first. He gave a sharp nod. "She has a promising future with LAI. She's also innocent. Not your usual type, I assume. I would hate to see her hurt because she misunderstood your intentions."

"I won't hurt her." Lachlan couldn't promise that, though he wished he could. "I won't let anyone else hurt her either."

A vow he'd keep or die trying.

Sophia sat at her desk, chin in hand, getting nothing done as she stared blankly at her computer.

She was alone, and she knew why. It was her. She wasn't enough.

She was never enough.

When she'd first laid eyes on Lachlan, she knew she was out of her depth with a man like him. And that was before she'd seen the emotional baggage he carried around like a pack mule.

His rejection hurt, but she should have expected it. A few weekends sitting in her condo all weepy as she sipped wine, shoveled down Ben and Jerry's, and felt sorry for her miserable self, might be in order. Then she'd move on and find satisfaction in her accomplishments without needing anyone else's validation. Like she always did.

She sighed and pushed back from her desk to head to the break room for a fresh can of diet pop. As much as it saddened her, she'd done the right thing resetting the boundaries of her relationship with Lachlan back to a strictly business one.

At least she'd gotten her act together this morning to finish assembling the information for the Global Security division's part of the government compliance report, handing it off with a sigh of relief to Fred just after lunch. There had been nothing to warrant Admiral Dane's suspicions that Lachlan was involved in anything illegal, news she would happily convey to the admiral the next time they spoke.

She pulled out a can from the break room fridge and pulled back on the tab. It pressed through the thin aluminum barrier with a satisfying pop and fizz. Carbonated bubbles burst across her tongue and down her throat.

Lachlan might be many things. Complicated, stubborn, haunted. But he wasn't the type of man to profit off the misery of others. His care for the homeless vet only confirmed her gut instinct that he was a decent man. A man with secrets, yes. A man who struggled with his past, but not a criminal.

The snack basket on the counter teased her. Penny had restocked the candy bars, darn her. Eating an apple was so much easier when there weren't peanut butter cups around. Sophia grabbed an orange-wrapped treat and headed back to her office to enjoy this food of the gods.

Time to get back to work and focus on what she did well. Her job. Now that her spying days were over, she could put her full attention into promoting LAI's projects and securing additional funding.

"Sophia." The sound of her name coming from Fred's office halted her steps. She stuck her head in to see him sitting at his desk. "Did you call me?"

Irritation deepened the lines on Fred's face and colored his smoke-roughened voice. "I need to discuss the information you assembled from the Global Security division."

She stepped further into the room. "Now?" The data was all there. She'd double-checked.

"Now." The poor man looked like he wanted nothing more than to take a cigarette break and suck down a cancer stick. A slight sheen of sweat dotted his forehead, and his fingers drummed restlessly on his desk. "You must have missed something. The numbers don't add up."

She drew back with a frown. "I went over everything with Lachlan. What do you think is missing?"

"I decided to perform my own audit for each division so there are no unpleasant surprises if the government auditors find discrepancies. There are more payments for supplies for Mackay's security teams than there are invoices, export licenses, and shipping manifests." He glared at her from beneath bushy brows. "So, where is the rest of the documentation?"

"There must be a mistake." She winced at the stammer in her voice. "Maybe it's an accounting error?" There had to be a simple explanation.

Fred's gaze turned speculative. "Maybe. I'll take a closer look at it."

"I'll check with Lach—"

"No need," Fred cut her off. "I'll look into it. Finish getting the information from Meier's division. The paperwork for LAI's development projects is even more of a hassle than Mackay's security con-tracts."

Her neck warmed, the heat moving up to the tips of her ears. She prided herself on doing things right the first time. Had she overlooked something?

Or had Lachlan kept information from her?

CHAPTER FIFTEEN

LONG RED VELVET CURTAINS hung from the king-sized canopy bed, obscuring enough of the light from the bedside lamps that Sophia could imagine they were candles, and it was another century, the raven-haired man whose hands were secured to the brass columns at the head of the bed a gentleman pirate. She straddled him, raking red-tipped nails across his bare chest. He couldn't touch her, but his emerald gaze was a tangible caress, hot enough to soak her black lace teddy.

"Stop teasing and kiss me," he purred, his lilting accent brushing against her skin like raw silk.

She gave him her best seductive smile and arched her breasts in line with his mouth. "I'm getting there."

What was that annoying sound? She frowned. The Outlander theme song?

"Kiss me." Lachlan's molten gaze made her squirm. She ground her sex against the hard ridge of his erection and was rewarded by his deep-throated groan. The song fit him perfectly, her sexy, dangerous Highlander.

Darn it. Why was it playing in her head?

She came awake to pitch black darkness, her phone vibrating on her bedside table, the haunting notes of her ring tone filling her bedroom. The digital numbers on her clock told her it was one a.m.

A spike of adrenaline sent her pulse racing. Late-night phone calls never meant good news.

She stared at the lit screen. Why the heck was her boss calling her at this hour? "Hello?" Sleep muffled her greeting. She cleared her throat and tried again, "Jared?"

"Sophia, I'm sorry to wake you." The somber note in Jared's voice had her instantly on alert.

"What's wrong?"

"Fred was killed in the District tonight."

"What?" she gasped, fully awake now.

"The police said he was shot. A victim of armed robbery."

"What was he doing in DC?" She was pretty sure Fred had said he lived in Chantilly, in the Virginia suburbs. Why would he be in the city late in the evening on a weeknight?

"I have no idea. I'm calling to let everyone know, so they don't hear it on the morning news first. Tomorrow's going to be a rough day at the office. I'll need your help."

"Of course. I'll do anything I can."

"Thank you, Sophia. I know I can always count on you. You were the first person I called. I need to let the others know. Goodnight."

"Goodnight," she whispered, but Jared had already hung up.

Tears blurred her vision. *Poor Fred.* What a senseless, random act.

"Sophia?" Emily knocked, then cracked open Sophia's bedroom door. "Is everything okay? I got up for a drink of water and heard you talking to someone."

"That was my boss. One of my coworkers was killed tonight in the District."

"Oh my God." Emily entered the room and crawled onto Sophia's bed, settling beside her. "That's horrible. What is this world coming to?"

Sophia snuggled next to her friend, taking strength from her companionship. "I don't know." She'd always chosen to believe the best of people. It had given her the strength to believe in herself.

What if Lachlan was right, and what she thought of as a strength was, in fact, a weakness?

Maybe she was too naïve, too trusting. She trusted Lachlan. But Roshan Haider had stalked her because of Lachlan.

Admiral Dane suspected Lachlan of trafficking weapons to a warlord. She thought she'd discounted that theory, but after meeting with Fred earlier in the day, she couldn't help but wonder if she'd missed something.

Fred's personal audit of the Global Security division's financials might prove the admiral's suspicions were justified after all.

Only now, Fred was dead.

Everything kept circling back to Lachlan.

Was he the decent but troubled man she believed him to be?

Or was he a dangerous man with a hidden agenda?

Chapter Sixteen

Robbery Turns Deadly in Adams-Morgan

Sophia skimmed the online article in the local section of *The Washington Post*'s digital edition, then closed it with a click of her mouse. The few bites she'd taken of her bagel turned to lead in her stomach.

Outside the window, the hazy outline of the sun peeked through a blanket of dull, gray sky. A smatter of raindrops trailed down the glass, drawn by gravity to the pavement below.

The weather matched the mood of everyone at LAI this morning.

The division summary she'd compiled from Christian Meier sat open on her computer. Now what? The government report was due in two weeks. And she still had to find the discrepancies from Lachlan's division.

It felt almost sacrilegious to worry about it right now.

Her eyes were bleary from lack of sleep. She grabbed her mug and wandered to Penny's desk. "I'm going to get more coffee. You want some?"

"Another cup won't help." Penny's fingers stilled on her keyboard. "I'm not getting anything done. Poor Fred, I can't believe he's gone."

Sophia swallowed past the tightness in her throat. "Me either." She hesitated, hating even to bring up work. "Can we delay the report?"

Penny shook her head. "I don't think so. Why?"

"Fred and I were supposed to work on it today. I guess I should make sure everything has been assembled so Jared can decide what to do next."

Penny gave her a sympathetic look. "Why don't you see if you can find what you need in Fred's office? I'm sure Jared wouldn't mind. Goodness knows he has enough on his plate."

Sophia glanced at Fred's closed door and bit her lip.

The empty workspace sat silent as a tomb, the faint whiff of tobacco that lingered behind marking Fred's essence. She couldn't help feeling she was violating what was now a memorial to a dead man. Framed photographs of DC landmarks dotted his walls. No personal pictures or belongings in view. His space had a sterile, lonely feel. Like Lachlan's office.

She wiped away the moisture suddenly blurring her vision, and settled into his chair.

Where to begin?

Manilla file folders, labeled by project, hung on a metal frame in the bottom right drawer of his desk. Thank goodness Fred's perpetual dishevelment wasn't reflected in his organizational skills.

She pulled out the hanging file folder labeled *Government Report*. In it were individual folders containing the documentation for each LAI division that would be included in the report. She opened the file for the Global Security division. At the top were several sheets of paper bound by a paperclip. A spreadsheet of detailed expenditures made in the past year by Lachlan's division. Purchase orders for weapons, printed copies of export licenses, and bills of lading—ones she'd never seen. Her fingers stilled on the last sheet.

A photocopy of a Washington Post article about US weapons in the hands of the Taliban.

Highlighted in yellow were the specific types of weapons and equipment recently discovered during a joint US-Afghan raid. She compared the models to the purchase orders from the Global Security division.

Denial rose swiftly. Fred was wrong—there had to be another explanation. Her inner voice rattled its cage, mocking her.

A murmur of voices outside Fred's door sent her pulse into the stratosphere. She swept the papers back into their folder. The temperature in the room felt like it had gone up ten degrees. Sweat coated the small of her back. Clutching the folder, she crept to the door and peered out. Jared wasn't in sight, and Penny's desk chair sat empty. She made a beeline for her office and thrust the folder into her briefcase, her stomach in knots.

She needed to call Admiral Dane. But not here.

Lunchtime traffic had the elevators stopping at every floor. She bounced on her heels and mentally tried to will the cars into moving faster. *Finally.* A set of doors slid open with a ding. She leaped inside and jabbed the button repeatedly for her parking level, ignoring the stares from the other passengers. *Close, close, close.*

It took her a moment to locate her car, hidden between a black SUV and a gold minivan. She jumped in, locked her doors, and dug in her purse for her phone. Her finger hovered, trembling, over the screen. If she called the admiral and told him what she found, she'd unleash an investigation into LAI's activities that could end badly for Lachlan, maybe even for the company itself.

The wobble in her finger spread to her hand and up her arm. She dropped the phone back into her purse and leaned into the headrest, shutting her eyes against the harsh reality confronting her. She couldn't have misjudged Lachlan that badly. There had to be a different explanation.

Her phone call to the admiral could wait a day. She needed time to process what she'd found and plan her next move. Praying she was making the right decision, she headed back to the eighth floor.

"There you are. Jared's been looking for you." Penny's words halted Sophia's attempt to slip unnoticed back to her office.

"I went to grab some lunch." Her stomach chose that moment to loudly proclaim her a liar. She pressed her palm to her middle and gave Penny a weak smile. "Nothing looked good."

If Penny noticed, she didn't say anything. "He said to send you in as soon as you got back."

Sophia's hunger faded beneath an onslaught of nerves.

Jared was on the phone and beckoned her into his office with a wave.

She sat on the other side of his desk and fought to keep butterflies at bay. While waiting, she let her gaze wander to Jared's *me* wall. Jared and Lachlan were about the same age, but where Lachlan's aura projected a rough-around-the-edges kind of power, Jared's was smoother, more sophisticated, formed by wealth and privilege. Both men entered a room expecting to be in charge, which was probably why she'd picked up on the subtle tension between the two every time they were together, as if their magnetic polarities were so similar they repelled each other.

Her wandering gaze landed on the family portrait on Jared's credenza, and she shifted uneasily in her chair. The photograph unnerved her. Maybe it was the vacant stare on his mother's face or the firm grip Jared's father had on his wife's elbow, his cold features not softened by the elegant black tuxedo he wore. Then there was Jared, appearing bored by it all.

No. Sophia narrowed her eyes at the tableau. *Not bored. Disconnected.* As if he stood next to strangers.

She gave an internal shrug. Who was she to judge? Maybe Jared had grown up like her, seeking affirmation and affection from parents whose interests hadn't included their only child. At least her parents weren't cold or cruel. The elder Landry's eyes hinted he could be both.

Jared hung up. "Sorry, I had to take that."

"What do your parents do?" She wasn't sure why she was curious other than she wondered how a father with such cold eyes and a mother with such vacant ones could raise a caring, successful son.

Jared barely glanced at the photo behind him. "My father married the daughter of a wealthy man so he could take her money and her father's company and pretend he's a self-made millionaire. And my mother copes with marriage to my father by drinking herself into a stupor to the point where she's no longer allowed to attend social events lest she embarrass him." The undercurrent of contempt in his voice wasn't lost on her.

Sophia's face heated. "I'm sorry, I didn't mean to pry."

He waved away her apology. "I keep their picture to remind me that, unlike my father, I make my own destiny and will choose a woman who's an asset to me and my future rather than a liability."

Wow. And she thought she had issues with her parents.

Jared's expression was suddenly all business. "Where do we stand with the government report?"

The butterflies winged their way to her throat. "The division summaries are mostly complete, but there are a few pieces of information I still need to collect." *Some answers, actually.*

"You didn't find what you needed in Fred's office?"

She stared at her boss, her heart thudding so hard it was a miracle it didn't explode.

His gaze narrowed on her. "Penny told me you had gone through Fred's files."

"No." She forced herself to maintain eye contact. "I mean, yes, I did, but I still need some additional information from the Global Security division."

"Ask Lachlan for help." Jared's features softened. "I appreciate you taking on this extra work, Sophia. This week's been rough. Let's hope next week is better."

"Anything I can do." She stood on shaky legs. "I'm happy to review your briefing notes for the Senate subcommittee hearing next week."

He nodded. "I'll ask Penny to find a time in my schedule."

She spun toward the door. A few more feet and she'd be able to breathe.

"I made the right decision, hiring you." His words, spoken at her back, caught her off balance. "You're an asset to this company."

"Thank you." She fumbled for the doorknob. He wouldn't think so if he discovered what she kept from him.

There was a tentative knock on Lachlan's door before it opened partway, and Sophia stuck in her head. "I need to talk to you. It's important."

Her wary expression had him gritting his teeth. "Come in."

Instead of coming to stand next to him at his desk, she stopped just inside his door.

He pushed to his feet with an inward sigh, brushing past her to close the door. He shut the privacy blinds on the sidelights.

He stood so close he invaded her personal space, but he couldn't make himself move.

Need overrode caution. He lifted a lock of her hair, rubbed the silky strands between his fingers, and guided it to his nose to inhale her scent. The muscles in his shoulders loosened.

"Lachlan," she whispered, her tone both entreaty and warning that he was violating boundaries he'd been the one to set.

He let go of her hair and put some space between them. "What do you need?"

A manilla folder nailed him square in the chest. "I found these in Fred's office. They weren't in the files you and I went over."

Fred, the poor bugger. Lachlan took the folder, thumbed it open, and flipped through the pages, his muscles locking as his brain processed the information.

What the bloody hell? A litany of curses sizzled on his tongue. He'd been searching for Khan's supplier but never had he thought it would lead straight back to him.

"Are you trafficking weapons to Afghanistan?" Sophia's voice trembled, her eyes a mirror into her thoughts: anxiety, disbelief, and a wee bit of anger.

"Let me make one thing clear." Fury rolled over him like a tidal wave. "I may be many things, but I'm no' a criminal nor a liar."

"So you don't have anything to hide."

He had plenty of secrets but not this. "I'll repeat, I'm no' a criminal, and I won't lie to you. You either believe me, or you don't. Who else has seen this?"

"I...I don't know. I don't think anyone except Fred. He told me he'd discovered payments for weapons that weren't reflected in the division summary you and I prepared." Her lips thinned, the hints of green in her eyes becoming more pronounced. "I haven't shown this to Jared yet if that's what you're worried about. Don't make me regret my decision to bring it to you instead. My job is on the line now, not just yours."

His head tipped in acknowledgment and respect. She could have hung him out to dry. He might not have extended her the same courtesy if their positions were reversed. Given the circumstances, he owed her the truth. "When I was in Afghanistan a few weeks ago, one of my former SAS mates told me about a rumor that a warlord with known ties to the Taliban was holding a weapons auction. The warlord has ties to several prominent Afghan leaders, so the Coalition can't touch him unless we have proof he's trafficking weapons and selling them to groups whose intent is to bring down the national government."

He wheeled away, spearing his fingers through his hair. This was either a bad dream or the script for a bad movie. "I've been trying to unearth the identity of his weapons supplier so I could put a stop to the auction and expose Khan for the traitorous bastard he is."

"It looks like you're the weapons supplier."

He pivoted back to face her, willing her to see the truth in his eyes. "I swear to you, I don't know what's happening, but I will get to the bottom of this. And as soon as I do, I'll take it to Jared."

Sophia was all that stood between him and a ruined reputation, or worse, time in an American prison. "Trust me." The words sounded hesitant and rusty coming out of his mouth. He hadn't used them in over two years, and they left a bitter taste on his tongue.

"Let me help you."

"What?" He stared at her, not sure he'd heard correctly.

Her chin lifted. "I don't think you would traffic weapons to a warlord. I want to help you unmask the person who did and clear your name."

He'd just asked her to trust him, but could he trust her in return?

Not that he had much choice. If she took the information she'd found in Fred's office to Jared, he'd likely be in FBI custody by the end of the day. Maybe Lucas would be the one reading him his rights. After all, he'd asked the other man to help him find Khan's US supplier.

At least if Sophia betrayed him, it was only his life on the line and no one else's.

A bitter laugh formed in his throat. He throttled it so she wouldn't think he'd gone daft. He'd taken this job and brought Ryder on board so they could find a way to bring down Khan for his collaboration with the Taliban who'd ambushed their troop. Now someone was setting him up to look like an accomplice of the warlord instead. "Roshan Haider."

Sophia's forehead wrinkled. "What about him?"

"He runs an import-export business based in London but travels worldwide. He was just in Jalalabad, visiting Mohammad Razul Khan, the warlord holding the weapons auction." The more he thought about it, the more sense it made, except—

"How would he be able to make it look like you were the one supplying weapons to Khan?" Sophia asked the question that had been forming in his head.

"He couldn't." The familiar sting of betrayal lanced his gut. "Not without help."

"What are you going to do?" She bit her lip and sent him a wary look. Was she concerned for him or worried about what he might do next?

Before he could respond, his phone buzzed with an incoming text. He glanced at the message. Nathan had just sent him Haider's hotel information. "I'm going to pay someone a visit."

CHAPTER SEVENTEEN

ROSHAN EXITED THE ELEVATOR on the fourth floor of the Ritz-Carlton Georgetown and turned right, strolling down the gray geometric patterned carpet to his one-bedroom suite. When he reached his door, he withdrew the room key from his wallet and tapped it against the digital lock. A cold satisfaction filled him. The ginger-haired woman, Sophia Russo, had undoubtedly gone running to Mackay. He'd seen the fear in her eyes, the realization that Roshan wasn't a random stranger crossing her path.

Would Mackay be afraid?

Or would he not care?

He pushed open the hotel room door, his mind full of possibilities for his next move.

The scent of tobacco hit him first, a pungent, sharp odor in a room where smoking was prohibited. Shutting the door behind him, he ventured down the narrow hall to the living area in his suite and abruptly stopped, his heart pounding.

A black-haired man sat on the burgundy sofa, dressed in a navy suit with a pale blue patterned tie. He stubbed out his cigarette in a glass tumbler taken from the bar in the room, then placed the glass on the end table next to the lamp. His steely blue eyes met Roshan's. "Mr. Haider, what brings you to the United States?"

Roshan's stomach roiled. Whoever this man was, he was danger-ous. "Who are you? Why are you in my room? Get out before I call security." Maybe he could bluff his way out of this and get the man to leave. As soon as he did, Roshan would check out, find a new hotel, and figure out what to do next.

The man stood. He flashed a warrant card. "Assistant Director Lucas Caldwell, Federal Bureau of Investigation. Perhaps you've heard of us."

"Why are you here?" Sweat beaded Roshan's underarms and the small of his back. Surely his contact would have warned him if the American authorities had gotten wind of their business arrangement? "I'm a citizen of Great Britain. I've done nothing wrong." He eyed the FBI agent's jacket closely. These bloody Americans were all armed.

The man gave him a smile that reminded him of a shark. "I heard Jalalabad is nice this time of year. I imagine British intelligence would be surprised and a bit concerned to know you were the guest of Mo-hammad Razul Khan."

Roshan's heart galloped now, the pace of it making him lighthead-ed. "I was in Jalalabad on other business, and he invited me to tea. It would have been considered a grave offense to turn him down. He's a powerful man."

"I see." Was that a hint of condescension in the American's voice? "It had nothing to do with finding out who was involved in your sister's death."

Roshan could feel the blood drain from his head. He dropped into the brown leather accent chair across from the sofa.

"Here is what's going to happen." Assistant Director Caldwell's voice dropped in temperature and grew even more steely. "I'm going to escort you to Dulles. There's a flight to London leaving at five-thirty.

And," he stepped around the pedestal table between the couch and the chair to lean into Roshan's space.

Roshan couldn't help sinking into the back of the chair.

"I suggest you not return to the States for a while."

Caldwell straightened, then resumed his seat on the couch and crossed a leg over his knee. He glanced around the spacious room. "Nice place. I'll wait while you pack."

Roshan scurried through the French doors into the suite's bedroom. He took his suitcase out of the closet and threw it onto the king bed, then yanked clothes off hangers and scooped them from drawers, tossing them haphazardly into his luggage. He went into the spacious marble bathroom, closed the door, and pulled out a phone he only used under special circumstances. One that was prepaid and couldn't be traced to him.

He texted his contact. *An FBI agent is in my hotel room, threatening to report me to British intelligence if I don't return to London.*

How inconvenient, came the reply moments later.

Roshan gritted his teeth. *I have unfinished business here.*

You need to stay under the radar. Go back to London.

What about Mackay? He tapped his foot impatiently, waiting for a reply. The FBI agent was waiting. He'd get suspicious if Roshan was in the bathroom for too long.

The reply came several seconds later. *I'll deal with Mackay.*

Roshan's jaw tightened. He exited the bathroom and stuffed his toiletry bag into his suitcase before closing the lid and giving the zipper a vicious tug. If his contact didn't finish the job, he'd find a way to return and make sure Mackay spent the rest of his life regretting the day he'd shot down Nadia in cold blood.

Lachlan strode down the corridor of the Ritz-Carlton until he reached room four fifty-two. Nathan's hacking skills had produced both Haider's room number and a code to unlock the door, which Lachlan had on an app on his phone. He'd knock first to see if Roshan had the bollocks to open the door once he saw who waited on the other side.

He and Nadia's brother were connected by a dark moment in a past that didn't involve Sophia. Roshan might never accept that his sister had been a traitor, but if he threatened Sophia, Lachlan would make damn sure it would be the last thing he ever did.

The bastard wasn't clever enough to have orchestrated the weapons trafficking scheme. If Haider was involved, he wasn't the mastermind. But who was? Lachlan would choke it out of him if he had to.

He rapped on Haider's door and waited. Nothing. He pounded harder. When Haider didn't come to the door, he stepped closer, flattened his ear to gray-painted metal, and listened. No sounds were coming from inside that he could discern. He texted Nathan.

L: Where's Sophia?

N: Safe and sound at home.

L: Anyone follow her?

N: Only me.

He glanced in both directions before tugging on a thin pair of leather gloves, then held his mobile to the door's lock pad. The light flashed green, followed by a mechanical click.

Pocketing the phone, he lifted his pistol from the holster beneath his jacket and eased open the door. A short hall opened to a spacious living room. A burgundy couch and end tables sat in front of floor-to-ceiling windows covered in long, pearl-gray drapes. In front of the couch, a leather accent chair and round pedestal table completed the seating area. A credenza with a K-Cup style coffee machine on its mahogany surface and a mini-fridge beneath backed up to the entrance hall. The room smelled faintly of smoke from the cigarette stubbed out in a glass tumbler on one of the end tables. Glazed French doors led to what he assumed was the sleeping area. Using his left hand, he pushed open one of the doors and pivoted, weapon raised, into the room.

Pillows lay scattered across the mussed king bed. He proceeded into a marble and tile bathroom almost as spacious as his apartment living room. Towels lay in a damp pile on the floor. Used soap, hotel shampoo, and conditioner littered a glassed-in shower big enough to fit at least six people.

Lachlan surveyed his surroundings with disdain. Haider enjoyed his posh amenities—he wouldn't have lasted a day in the military.

He rifled through the drawers—no personal toiletries, no clothes, empty closet. Had Nathan gotten the room number wrong?

He stowed his gun and dialed the front desk on his mobile. "Good afternoon. I'm supposed to meet one of your guests this evening, Mr. Roshan Haider. Can you put me through to his room?"

"One moment, please." The woman who answered put him on hold.

Lachlan waited for the phone stationed by the bed to ring.

The desk clerk came back on the line. "I'm sorry, sir, but Mr. Haider checked out a short while ago."

Shite. Did Haider know they were onto him? He thanked her, then hung up and pulled up Lucas Caldwell's number.

"Mackay, I was about to call you."

"Haider checked out of his hotel." He paced over to the window and yanked open the drapes to peer down on the side parking area—no sign of a silver Beamer.

"He's on his way to London." Lucas's voice hardened. "I told you to stay away from him."

Lachlan stiffened in surprise. "How do you know he left the country?"

"I paid him a visit this afternoon." A car engine roared to life on the other end of the line. "I drove him to the airport myself, made sure he got on the damn plane."

"Why?" Relief and frustration warred for supremacy.

"Let's just say I had a feeling you weren't going to stay away. Looks like I was right."

"I wouldn't have hurt him."

Lucas snorted.

"I wouldn't have killed him," Lachlan amended.

"You owe me, Mackay. Stay out of trouble."

Lachlan hung up without making Lucas any promises he couldn't keep. At least Sophia was safe. But now, he'd have to find another way to prove Haider's involvement in the weapons shipments and find Haider's accomplice. Or boss.

As much as he respected Lucas, he wasn't letting the FBI in on the information Sophia had uncovered in Fred's office.

Not when it made him look guilty as sin.

Sophia dumped pasta into the colander to drain and waved away the steam. In the background, her kitchen smart speaker blasted a sad songs playlist. Her nice, orderly, if somewhat dull, life had been completely upended by Lachlan Mackay, and she deserved to wallow in her feelings if she wanted.

The small pot on the stove began to spit hot, red sauce, the smell of tomato and basil diffusing into the air like a culinary essential oil. She checked the garlic bread's oven timer and pulled the salad mix bag out of the fridge.

Before she could call Emily to dinner, her cell phone started dancing to the beat on the kitchen counter, its ring drowned out by Adele's building crescendo. She grabbed it on her way to the stove and silenced the music. "Hello?"

"Sophia."

Her stomach cramped. "Admiral Dane."

She looked furtively at Emily's closed bedroom door before shutting off the burner under the sauce and tiptoeing out to her balcony. "You want to know if I've discovered anything at LAI." She kept her tone as low as she could without whispering. If Emily knew she was on the phone with her father, there'd be questions she didn't want to answer. Emily still didn't know about their secret arrangement.

"Maybe I'm calling to find out how my bonus daughter is enjoying her new job."

The hint of warmth and humor in his voice made her smile. That wasn't why he'd called, but hearing it felt good anyway. "I've gotten involved in more than just my immediate responsibilities and have learned a lot."

"Good. What about Lachlan Mackay and his division? Have you come across anything interesting?"

She peered up at the sky, lit with a brilliant orange that transitioned to bright yellow at the center of the western horizon. The temperature was dropping with the sun, and she shivered as a cool breeze brought goosebumps to her arms.

If she was wrong about Lachlan, and Jared found out she'd known about the weapons shipments and hadn't brought the information to him, her reputation and future job prospects would tumble to the bottom of Capitol Hill. Withholding the intelligence from Admiral Dane felt even worse. He was like a father to her.

"Sophia? You're awfully quiet." Admiral Dane's voice sharpened. "Have you found something?"

She was in an impossible situation, dammit. A sudden spike of anger drove out her nerves. She wasn't ready to throw Lachlan to the wolves just yet. "I had an opportunity to access the Global Security and Global Development division files and found nothing unusual."

Truth. Sort of.

Judging from the beat of silence on the other end of the line, the admiral had picked up on her frosty delivery.

"What else is going on? Have you spoken to your parents lately?"

Thank God. He wasn't going to pursue the issue. For now. "No. They're in Italy, I think."

The admiral's harrumph of disapproval made her smile. "If they travel over the holidays again, you're always welcome at our home. Maybe we can convince Emily to fly in from Paris. And, if Alex's schedule allows, I'm sure he'd love to see you."

She rolled her eyes at the mention of his son. Emily's older brother was a Navy SEAL and, according to Emily, not the least interested in a relationship. If the admiral was scheming to match her up with Alex, he was out of luck. Sophia was his younger sister's best friend, and Alex had immediately placed her in the sister zone.

Lachlan's image popped into her head. Admiral Dane would like him. He was a warrior. Someone the admiral would understand.

Unless the admiral thought Lachlan was sending weapons to a warlord, then he would destroy him. A cold chill hunched her shoulders.

"Maybe Emily will come home for a visit in August when all the Parisians are on holiday. Sophia cast a nervous glance into her living room. "I'll bring it up next time I talk to her." Which could be any second, given that Emily was in her condo.

Another piece of information she was keeping from the admiral. Emily hadn't let her parents know she was in the States so she wouldn't feel obligated to pay a visit to their Connecticut estate in the short time she was here.

"You'll come with her, of course. The summers in Connecticut are much nicer than the swampy heat of DC."

"Of course." A flash of movement caught her attention. Emily had left her bedroom and wandered into the kitchen. "I have to go—my oven timer is dinging." She said goodbye and slipped back inside.

"There you are." Emily had pulled the garlic bread out of the oven and put the salad in a bowl. She glanced at the phone in Sophia's hand. "Everything ok?

"A charity soliciting donations. It's that time of year." Yet another fib to add to her growing collection.

For better or worse, she'd firmly put herself on Team Lachlan.

CHAPTER EIGHTEEN

THE MOOD WAS SOMBER in the conference room at LAI the following morning as everyone gathered to remember Fred and say a few words. When it was Sophia's turn, she stepped to the front of the room and tucked a strand of hair behind one ear.

"I haven't known Fred as long as most of you." Her voice wobbled. She still couldn't believe he was dead and in such a senseless manner. Her gaze sought out Lachlan, and he nodded, encouraging her to continue. "He was a bit gruff on the outside, as we all know. But inside, he was a sweet man. We need to keep his memory in our hearts and make sure he's not forgotten." Not knowing what else to say, she shrugged and returned to stand next to Lachlan.

"That was lovely, dear," Penny whispered.

When everyone had had a chance to speak, Jared wrapped up the memorial with an announcement that LAI would make a hefty donation in Fred's name to a local charity.

Jared approached her and Lachlan as the room began to clear. He greeted Sophia with a smile, but the look he sent Lachlan was decidedly cool. "Have you dealt with the issue we discussed the other day?"

"Aye. It's taken care of." Lachlan bit off, his brogue thickening.

Sophia's gaze bounced between the two men. The tension between them was thick enough to color the air.

One thing was certain—they didn't get along. Jared would never believe Lachlan if he got wind of those unexplained weapons shipments.

She could keep that from happening, or at least delay it.

"Do you have a minute?" She directed her question at Jared.

Lachlan stiffened next to her. She stepped closer, her hand grazing his back in a wordless attempt to communicate that she wasn't about to throw him under the bus.

"For you, always." Jared's smile was blinding. He squeezed her shoulder, his fingers lingering a touch too long.

She hadn't thought it possible for Lachlan to get any more rigid, his jaw so tight a tic formed.

Jared's smile held a hint of triumph.

Sophia quelled the annoyed sigh that wanted to break free. They were like two dogs trying to take a leak at the same fire hydrant. Which wasn't flattering because she had a feeling she was the fire hydrant, and this was more a pissing contest between two alpha males than a display of jealousy.

"Is there something else you need?" Jared directed a pointed stare at Lachlan.

For a minute, Sophia thought Lachlan might refuse to leave. Finally, he turned to her, his expression flat, revealing none of the turmoil he had to be feeling. He gave her a curt nod, then sent Jared an icy glare before exiting the room.

She didn't waste any time. "You should let me complete the government report," she told Jared. Her pulse fluttered wildly despite the confident tone she'd injected into her voice. "I've been working with Fred on it. I know what needs to be done, and I'd like to take the burden off you if I can."

Jared nodded approvingly. "Done. The report is yours. Penny can help you assemble it, and I'll take a look at it before it's finalized."

Her shoulders sagged in relief.

"Did Lachlan tell you about Roshan Haider?"

His question came from left field and had her rocking back on her heels. "How do you know about Roshan?"

"Lachlan told me." Jared's eyes darkened to charcoal. "You need to keep your distance from him. Lachlan's life is...messy."

The conversation felt like it was veering into personal territory. Hers and Lachlan's. "I appreciate your concern." She gave Jared a polite smile.

He was right, and he didn't even know the half of it. On paper, Lachlan was a lousy bet. He had emotional baggage that kept them apart, and he was smack in the middle of what looked to be an arms trafficking scheme. She should be running away as fast as her legs could carry her.

But he was a good man.

And she was emotionally invested.

She'd see this through and pray she wasn't making a huge mistake.

Jared lifted his wrist to glance at his Rolex. "I've got a lunch to go to, and I'll be out of the office most of tomorrow, but I'll pick you up at six-thirty for the reception."

"Reception?"

Jared was leap-frogging all over the place in this conversation, and she struggled to keep up.

Irritation cooled his eyes to the color of hematite. "Congressman Kellerman's event at his home in Great Falls tomorrow evening. Did you forget? Several legislators who sit on his appropriations subcommittee and their key aides will be there."

She *had* forgotten. "I just thought, with what happened to Fred—"

"Fred's death doesn't change the fact that we need funding from Congress to continue our work, and this is an opportunity to get in front of the right people. It's what I expected when I hired you."

A knot formed in her stomach at the hint of censure in his voice. "Of course, but if you don't mind, I'll meet you there." She'd already promised Emily they'd try the new Indian restaurant in Old Town. They'd have to eat earlier than planned, but she could still hang with her friend and then head to Great Falls.

"If that's what you want."

His curt reply irritated her. Why did it matter how she got there, as long as she showed up and did her job?

A job she'd better start paying more attention to. If indeed weapons *were* being shipped to the Afghan warlord from LAI, Jared would need all the help he could get to keep his company's reputation intact.

The knot in her stomach grew. Lachlan needed to find answers. Soon.

Lachlan made small talk with Penny at her desk, waiting for Sophia and Jared to exit the conference room.

When Sophia asked to speak with Landry, his first thought was that she'd decided to tell Jared about the unexplained weapons purchases. Then she'd brushed her hand along his back, a gesture he'd taken to mean she was still on his side.

Something Lachlan hadn't felt in a long time slipped through him, potent and possessive. He'd noticed the anger in Jared's eyes when Sophia had chosen to stand next to him during the gathering for Fred.

Landry's oblique reference to Roshan Haider in front of Sophia had been an implicit challenge.

He had no right to lay claim to Sophia, not with the situation he found himself in, but that hadn't stopped him from wanting to place his body between her and Jared and bare his teeth at the other man like he was some bloody troglodyte, and Sophia, his prize.

For reasons Lachlan didn't understand, she'd chosen to ally herself with him, despite the threat he'd brought to her door, despite his rejection, despite the evidence piling up that made him look like a traitor selling weapons to the enemy.

He wanted to believe she wasn't part of a larger game at play and he, the pawn to be sacrificed in the end.

The door to the conference room opened. He ducked around the corner as Sophia and Jared emerged and waited until Jared was out of sight before slipping into Sophia's office.

"Haider is gone. You needn't be worried about him anymore."

The relief in Sophia's expression twisted his gut. She should have never been in danger because of him. "Jared asked if you had told me about Roshan."

Lachlan barely held back his growl. "I thought Jared could help keep you safe, but it's over now."

She bit her lip. A tell she had when she was unsure or worried. "You didn't do anything inappropriate, did you?"

"I didn't even cross paths with him." If he had, he probably *would* have done something inappropriate, as Sophia put it. "I have it on good authority he boarded a plane to London yesterday afternoon."

"What about the other thing?" She gazed at him anxiously. "I'm not going to lie. It looks bad, Lachlan, and we won't be able to keep it from Jared much longer."

"I've asked my suppliers for complete listings of every purchase LAI has made in the past year. I've also contacted my shipper. I'm sure they think I've gone all doolally, asking for information I should already have."

She nodded. "I told Jared I'd finish the government report. That way, I can control the information flow and try to buy you some time."

"Well done." His shoulders relaxed. She'd done him a huge favor.

"What else can I do?"

"You've done enough," he assured her. "You've already put your career at risk for me. I can't ask you for more."

Sophia rounded her desk to stand in front of him. Her fingers, dainty and feminine with their polished nails, reached for his. He couldn't help but notice how smooth and pale her skin was next to his scars and calluses. She gazed up at him with an earnestness that warmed the cold, dark place beneath his sternum.

"Lachlan, you don't have to do this alone."

Sophia's words rang in Lachlan's head long after he'd returned to his own office. *You don't have to do this alone.* He didn't understand her faith in his innocence when the evidence said otherwise. It rocked him to his core.

His primary supplier had responded with the information he'd requested. He opened the email attachment and scanned the list of purchase orders. He'd need to cross-check it with the export license and shipping documents in his files, but he could already tell there were more orders than he remembered placing.

His attention snagged on the date on the latest order. He'd been in Afghanistan at the time. He checked the time. It was late, but his supplier was in a different time zone and should still be in the office.

"Hey buddy, did you get my email?" Chris Sullivan's thick Southern accent had taken Lachlan a while to understand when they'd started working together.

"Aye, thanks, pal. The most recent purchase order, how did you receive it?"

"Lemme check." Lachlan could hear the question in Chris's voice. "Looks like you emailed it to me."

Lachlan's shoulders jacked like they were on puppet strings. He rolled them to try and ease the tension. "Directly from my email address? Can you forward it back to me?"

"Sure, what's up?"

"Nothing, annual compliance bullshit." A new message notification popped up in the corner of his computer screen. He opened his email and found the forward from Chris. The original address was his, meaning whoever placed the order had direct access to his LAI credentials or somehow hacked into LAI's computer network.

"What's the status of that order?"

"Hold on." Chris came back on the line a few moments later. "It's in transit, in the hands of your shipper. Looks like it'll be in Kabul within the week."

Lachlan thanked him and hung up. Satisfaction and a grim determination surged through him. This might be the break he needed. He'd go to Kabul, be there personally to see who showed up to receive the shipment, then shut this operation down before those weapons ended up in Khan's hands.

He grabbed his suit coat from the hook on his office door and headed out. Most everyone had already left for the day, and a glance at Sophia's office confirmed she'd gone as well.

Once he'd reached his Mercedes, he drew out his mobile.

It took Ryder a few rings to pick up. "What's wrong?" Ryder's voice was husky with sleep.

Lachlan grimaced. A quick look at his watch confirmed it was the middle of the night for his team leader. "Sorry, pal. I didn't pay attention to the time. I'm coming to Kabul. Keep it to yourself." He gave Ryder the sitrep.

"Bloody hell," Ryder swore. "Sayed didn't find any information on LAI shipments coming through customs that I didn't already know about. Either someone's paid him to keep quiet, or the cargo is leaving customs under another name."

"Pull together everything you can on Josh's activity over the last six months." Lachlan trusted Ryder. Burkette, on the other hand, was a loose cannon. Someone in Kabul was receiving those shipments for Khan. Jared wouldn't appreciate Lachlan accusing his former Army Ranger teammate of weapons trafficking. If Burkette was involved, he needed proof.

He would go to Kabul and get answers. He refused to take the blame—again—for someone else's betrayal.

CHAPTER NINETEEN

THE NEXT MORNING, LACHLAN strolled into work and leveled his most charming smile at LAI's office manager. "Good morning, Penny. You're looking rather lovely today."

The older woman gave him an indulgent smile. "Pouring it on thick, aren't you?"

He grinned. "Jared in?"

Penny buzzed Jared's extension. "Lachlan is here to see you." She nodded at Lachlan to go in.

Sophia stood in her office doorway, wearing a dress that matched the green in his tie. She stared at him with wide, anxious eyes. He shot her a look meant to be reassuring before he stepped into his boss's office.

He wasn't planning to stay long, so he didn't bother to sit down. "I'm heading to Kabul on Monday to take care of some business with the teams."

Jared's fingers stilled on the computer keyboard. He'd continued doing whatever he'd been doing when Lachlan entered. Now, his narrow-eyed gaze connected with Lachlan's. "Is there a problem?"

Lachlan took note of his boss's rigid posture. "Some issues require a personal touch."

"You're not pursuing this weapons auction rumor, are you? I told you to leave it to the authorities—if it's even true."

Lachlan chose his next words carefully. "I can assure you my trip is strictly LAI business."

"Do you think you should go before we know whether any more people from your past plan to come out of the woodwork to threaten Sophia?" Jared picked up the silver pen on his desk blotter and spun it deftly around the fingers of one hand as he observed Lachlan.

The contempt in his voice had Lachlan's hands fisting. The bastard was baiting him, and he couldn't afford to bite, not now. "Haider is in the UK. Sophia is safe."

"We can only hope so." Jared's smile carried a trace of smugness. "She'll be spending the evening with me at Congressman Kellerman's reception. I'll take good care of her."

Lachlan responded with a brisk nod. He needed to leave before he said or did something that would get him fired. Landry had dropped the pretense and was openly declaring his intentions toward Sophia.

The bastard was going to have to stand in line.

Sophia wanted him. And he didn't share.

By this time next week, he should have his hands on the shipment destined for Khan and begin unraveling this entire fucking mess. He had a feeling Josh Burkette would be waiting to receive the weapons, and when he did, Lachlan would be ready.

"Have a safe trip."

Lachlan didn't bother to look back as he saw himself out.

Leave it to Landry to make a polite send-off sound like a threat.

The hair rose on the back of Sophia's neck. She looked up from the press release she was crafting for Congresswoman Chandler's office on LAI's school rehabilitation project outside of Kabul and nearly jumped a foot. "Geez! How does someone so big move so quietly?"

Lachlan had managed to slip into her office without her noticing.

"I'm going to Kabul on Monday." He closed the door behind him with a soft snick and perched himself on the edge of her desk, legs stretched out in front of him.

"What? Why?" She came out from behind her desk to stand between his ankles. He had on a navy suit today with a white button-down—she wasn't sure he owned any other color. His emerald and blue tie brought out the rich depths of green and gold in his eyes.

She glanced down at her dress. They matched. The color went well with her red hair, but that wasn't why she'd plucked it out of her closet. It reminded her of him.

Pretty wasn't the right word to describe someone so masculine and dominant, but God had blessed Lachlan in the looks department. She resisted the urge to take another step forward until she was between his thighs and could lick the thin white scar on his chin on her way to those firm lips.

Business only, she reminded herself firmly. She'd agreed to reset the boundaries of their relationship to protect her heart, and she'd do well to remember that.

"There's a new shipment of weapons arriving that I didn't order. I want to be there to see who picks it up."

"Are you sure that's safe? What did you tell Jared?" She tugged on her lip, worrying it between her teeth. Lachlan was planning to confront the people working with Mohammad Razul Khan in Afghanistan, where the warlord had the home-field advantage.

"Only that I need to visit my teams to take care of something. He didn't press for specifics," he replied.

Maybe now was the time to tell him about Admiral Dane. She could arrange a meeting between the two men, plead Lachlan's case, and convince the admiral to use his connections to prove Lachlan's innocence.

Her stomach gave a violent lurch. Lachlan would be furious when he realized he'd been under suspicion all along, and she'd not only known it, she'd been tasked to find evidence against him.

"Are you worried about me? I assure you I can take care of myself." Lachlan's gaze darkened to a deep jade as it fixed on her mouth. One long leg bent, and before she knew it, he'd stood, the movement bringing his body flush with hers.

She let go of her lip, her breaths turning shallow as his warmth soaked into her skin in tendrils of desire. This close, she couldn't help but breathe in his scent—lush pine forest and something uniquely male.

"In a week, this will be over, I promise." His palm lifted to cradle her face, the calluses on the pads of his fingers a reminder that he was much more than some white-collar executive who'd gotten his muscles in the gym.

With a simple touch, he left her aching and needy.

She met his eyes. Hunger and possession flared in their emerald depths, and something else that drove the air from her lungs. The emotional barrier Lachlan had placed between them was gone.

Her body responded with a burst of liquid heat. Her breasts grew heavy, needing to be touched.

"I—I hope so." She couldn't think straight with him this close. Her lips felt dry, and her tongue darted out to moisten them.

The hints of gold around his pupils sparked. "I'm sorry, *mo leannan*." He whispered the apology into her ear.

She didn't know what *mo-lannan* meant, but the sound rolling off his tongue in that Highland burr and his hot breath in her ear sent shivers of desire arrowing down her spine to gather between her thighs.

"For what?" The lack of oxygen in the room made her voice breathy. Her eyes drifted shut. She was edgy, restless, and could barely think. All she could do was feel.

"For not being the man you deserve." He took her mouth, hard and possessive, his lips and tongue demanding.

Strong arms wrapped her. Lachlan tasted of mint and coffee, sex and sin. His long fingers palmed her breast, molding her to his hands before they sought out the sensitive tip.

Electricity shot straight to her core at the contact. She moaned into the kiss and rubbed against him with wanton abandon, forgetting where she was.

More. She needed more.

His mouth lifted. "Sophia, look at me."

She gave a slight shake of her head in response. She didn't want to look—she wanted to feel. His hand dropped away from her breast, and she reluctantly forced her lashes apart.

"Tell me to stop." His features twisted as if in pain. "I'm not the kind of man you should want. If I don't find out who is sending weapons to Khan using my division as cover, there is a very real possibility I could go to prison."

Her heart gave a painful lurch at the torment in his voice. He might be right—he wasn't the kind of man she should want. Yet, she couldn't walk away. Beneath his veneer of control, a crack of vulnerability and pain in his eyes called to her.

She could sense they were about to cross a line that would smash any protective barriers around her heart where Lachlan Mackay was concerned.

His expression shuttered. He dropped his arms.

"No." She grabbed his suit coat, holding him to her before he could pull away. "Don't stop, please." Did that husky, wanton voice belong to her? She grabbed his hand and guided it back to her breast.

His answering growl was low and deep. He crushed her in his embrace and devoured her with the unleashed passion she'd remembered from their first kiss. His hand returned to caress one breast, then the other, before skimming over her dress to cup her bottom. He tilted his hips, and the evidence of his desire tore a gasp from her lips that ended on a moan.

She released the hand that had wound its way into his hair and brushed her fingers over the hard ridge.

He jerked at her touch and nipped her lower lip. "Careful Sophia, you're playing with fire."

Her hand lifted to cup his jaw so he was forced to see the truth in her eyes. "Maybe I want to get burned."

Lachlan's eyes blazed, melting away the last of his restraint. He captured her straying hand and joined it with her other one behind his neck. His fingers swept beneath the hem of her dress and blazed a trail up her inner thigh to the silken barrier between her legs. His foot nudged her shoe to widen her stance.

"You're already wet." The harsh rasp of his voice made her even wetter. His finger slid beneath the silk, sliding through her drenched sex to circle her most sensitive spot.

She jerked, crying out in shocked pleasure as her pelvic muscles spasmed, destroying any inhibitions she might have had left.

"More." She whispered the plea into his mouth as she tried to consume him. The world fell away until it was only the two of them and her desperate need for him to fill the hollow ache clawing at her insides.

His finger worked her clit, massaging slowly, then faster. "Do you want to come?"

She nipped at his lips and felt them curl.

He plunged one finger, then two, deep, and she exploded, spots dancing beneath her closed lids like fireworks, her body spasming around his thrusting fingers. His mouth swallowed her breathless scream until the delicious tension ebbed, leaving her boneless in his arms.

"Christ, you're beautiful." Lachlan kissed her forehead, his ragged breaths ruffling her hair. This close, she could feel his struggle to regain control.

Reason returned and brought with it a hefty dose of mortification. "Oh my God," she moaned into Lachlan's broad chest. "I can't believe we just did that. In my *office*." What if someone had walked in, or gotten a peek through the sidelight? "I've never done anything that...public before."

Lachlan's finger lifted her chin. His expression sobered. "Do you regret it?"

Regret it? The shadows were missing from his eyes. His normally guarded posture had relaxed. He'd pleasured her without asking the same in return. A wild, untamed hope filled her before she could rein it in. Maybe, for Lachlan, she could be enough.

"No regrets."

His lips quirked into a satisfied smile before brushing hers in a gentle caress. "I'm already looking forward to my return from Kabul."

As silently as he'd arrived, he slipped away, leaving her alone.

CHAPTER TWENTY

SOPHIA COULDN'T STOP THINKING about Lachlan and how she'd felt coming apart in his arms, even as she handed her keys to a waiting valet later that evening and stepped into Congressman Kellerman's Great Falls mansion.

The crystal chandelier above her gave off rainbow prisms of sparkling light from its two-story perch above the entrance foyer. She admired it as she passed her wrap to the waiting attendant and accepted a glass of white wine from a roving server.

She and Emily had managed to get in an early dinner at the new Indian restaurant they'd wanted to try, and now Emily was off to a DC United match with some of her colleagues at the State Department. She'd taken one look at Sophia's face and grilled her over dinner to spill until Sophia had given a sanitized accounting of what had taken place in her office.

Emily had burst out laughing and raised her glass of wine to salute Sophia for "getting her freak on," as Emily put it, in the workplace with the Hot Scot.

What Sophia hadn't admitted to her best friend was how hard she'd fallen for Lachlan or that he was caught up in an arms trafficking nightmare from which he might not escape unscathed. And Emily still didn't know about her agreement to spy on Lachlan for Admiral Dane.

Jared must be here by now. Her gaze meandered over the crowd of about thirty people. She spied him in the parlor to her right, conversing with Kellerman's chief of staff. When he glanced in her direction, she gave a brief wave to snag his attention.

His chin lifted in acknowledgment before he shook the other man's hand and worked his way through the room to where she waited. He'd changed into a tailored black suit, white dress shirt, and a silver paisley tie with a matching pocket square. She had to admit, he looked sharp.

"Breathtaking as always." His gaze lingered on her midnight blue silk sheath dress before coming to rest on her hair, which Emily had styled into a sleek chignon.

His blatant admiration flustered her. She focused on her navy pumps and fingered one of her diamond teardrop earrings—a graduation gift from her parents to make up for the fact they hadn't attended the actual ceremony. "Sorry I'm late. The Beltway was a mess."

He nodded in commiseration. "You should have let me pick you up. Road construction is a nightmare. Take Georgetown Pike home. It'll be faster."

To her relief, he switched into business mode. "I'll head across the hall, see who's there. You start here." He gave her a salute with his highball glass. "Let's do our thing."

She returned the gesture with her wine and drifted further into the parlor. *Time to get to work.* She scanned the partygoers for the legislators who sat on the congressional subcommittee responsible for funding LAI's projects. An electric buzz hummed in her veins as she worked the room, slipping LAI's successes into the natural flow of conversation when the opportunity arose.

Two hours later, she had canvassed all the principal players in attendance. A series of jaw-cracking yawns snuck up on her. The stress of the last few days had drained her energy reserves to zero.

It had felt good to focus on something other than Lachlan, the mess he was in, and her feelings for him.

She located Jared trying to escape a K Street lobbyist. "I'm sorry to interrupt." Her hand curled around Jared's sleeve as she flashed a bright smile at the lobbyist. "I need to borrow my boss for a moment."

Jared slanted a subtle look of gratitude at her before shaking the other man's hand. "Give me a call at the office, Ted. We'll get together for dinner soon."

He followed her lead into the foyer. "Thanks for saving me."

His exaggerated stage whisper made her smile. "If you don't mind, I'm going to head home. I'm tired, and I think we've spoken with everyone we needed to reach tonight." Some of the other guests were already gathering their coats from the wait staff.

"I agree. As usual, you were a hit." Jared drained the rest of the amber liquid in his glass, his gray gaze heating as it came to rest on her face. "It's not hard to see why. You know how to work a room. We make a great team."

A sudden tension gripped her shoulders. Jared's attention seemed more personal tonight. The foyer suddenly felt claustrophobic.

"Thank you for your confidence in me." She glanced longingly at the front door and sidestepped a congressman who'd had one too many bourbons as he was ushered outside by his visibly annoyed wife and a diligent staffer.

Jared cleared his throat. "Go on. It's been a long day. And take Georgetown Pike if you want to avoid all that messy construction."

With a murmured goodbye, she collected her wrap and clutch and stepped out into the crisp, black night.

The lack of streetlights and patches of dense forest formed a heavy curtain of obsidian over the two-lane section of Georgetown Pike between Great Falls and McLean. Sophia carefully navigated the winding curves with her high beams, scanning for any creatures that might choose the wrong moment to cross the road.

She turned on the radio for company.

The Beltway may have taken longer, but at least it was well-lit. All she wanted was to get home, take off her heels and sit down with a glass of wine. Between the situation with Lachlan and Jared's strange behavior this evening, she was on her last nerve.

The sudden glare of headlights in her rear-view mirror blinded her. The car narrowed the distance quickly, riding her back bumper.

"Jerk."

Where did he think he was going in such a hurry on a road like this? She signaled and moved as far to the right as the narrow shoulder permitted.

The car shot around in a flash of silver and disappeared around the bend.

Silver.

She shook off the dread trying to claw a foothold. Lachlan told her Roshan Haider was gone.

Around the curve, her beams landed on the tail end of the speed demon's car with its distinctive blue and white checkered logo. Her fingers tightened on the steering wheel.

Lots of people drove silver BMWs.

The car's brake lights flared bright red, its tires screeching on the asphalt. She jerked left on instinct into the oncoming lane to avoid a collision.

Her heart in her throat, she slammed the accelerator to the floor. The BMW kept pace, blocking her return to the right lane.

Alarm bells jangled in her head. She white-knuckled the wheel with sweaty palms. If she didn't get back over, she risked driving head-on into an oncoming car.

Thunk.

Sophia let out a terrified screech as the other car swerved, tapping her front bumper. The wheel jerked left, and her Prius skidded along the guardrail with a nails-on-chalkboard shriek of metal grinding against metal. Her senses narrowed to a slow-motion reel of her car's momentum as she wrenched the wheel to the right and pumped her brakes.

The Prius skidded to a stop back in the right lane.

She sat in stunned silence before her lungs screamed for air, and tension escaped through harsh, gasping breaths. She shoved her gear into Park with trembling fingers, her body quaking.

That had been too close.

Her gaze lifted to the windshield. The silver car was stopped a short distance ahead, the beams from its headlights illuminating the next curve. All of a sudden, its reverse lights came on, cold white malevolent orbs aimed at Sophia.

The contents of her clutch lay strewn in every direction. She unlatched her seatbelt and pawed through the items on the floorboard: lipstick, driver's license, tissues, business cards, ballpoint pen.

Where was her phone?

Lights glowed on the other side of the embankment through a steep thicket of pines, a beacon of civilization and safety. She'd probably break her ankle or worse, trying to navigate the heavily wooded, sloping terrain in the dark.

Her head shot up to peer over the dashboard. The Beamer continued its reverse course in her direction. Slowly, as if the driver were intentionally ramping up her fear.

She toed off her pumps and shoved at the driver's door.

It wouldn't budge.

Come on! Her mind flashed back to Lachlan, his mouth exploring hers, his caresses scorching her body, his skillful fingers bringing her to ecstasy.

Whatever happened, he would be the last image in her head.

The silver car was now directly in front of her. The driver's door swung open, and a jean-clad leg ending in a tan combat boot landed on the pavement.

The shivers wracking Sophia disappeared, replaced by a strange sort of calm. If this was the end, she wasn't going out without a fight. She snatched the ballpoint off the floormat and gripped it in her palm like an icepick. It might work as a weapon.

As long as her assailant didn't have a gun.

A sudden beam of light hit her rear windshield, lighting up the interior.

Car. Gripping her door handle, she threw her shoulder against her door until it finally gave way, dumping her onto the road.

Ignoring her stinging knees, she scrambled to her feet and waved her arms. "Help! Help me! Please!"

The approaching car's headlights blinded her, and she could only pray the driver saw her in time. She'd take her chances of getting hit rather than let the vehicle pass, leaving her alone with a man who probably meant to kill her.

Brakes screeched, echoing loudly against the surrounding trees. Sophia slammed her eyes shut and waited for impact. When none came, she cautiously opened one lid.

Behind her, the silver car's engine revved, its tires squealing as it fishtailed away. The sound nearly brought her to her knees as relief drained the last of her adrenaline.

"Sophia? What happened? Are you okay?"

Jared.

He exited his dark silver Lexus, mere feet from her back bumper.

"Thank God—that car—he wanted to hurt me." She stumbled into Jared's arms, her words a panicked jumble.

He held her, murmuring assurances until her ragged breaths evened enough for her to realize she was clinging to her boss's waist, her head on his chest, the scent in her nose a mix of citrus and spice rather than pine. She gently extricated herself and stepped back.

"Are you sure you're okay?" He stooped to peer into her eyes when she wouldn't look up, then glanced at her car.

"I am now." She twisted to stare at the space where the Beamer had been. "Whoever that was, I think he meant to hurt me." She took a deep inhale to steady the tremble in her voice.

"Another one of Lachlan's acquaintances, perhaps?" Jared snapped.

"I don't know."

Roshan Haider? Had he somehow gotten back into the country? A sudden chill iced her veins. If Haider had seen her and Lachlan together, then perhaps whoever was trying to frame Lachlan as a weapons trafficker had also seen them together.

Roshan's vendetta against Lachlan was personal. Was it possible that someone else held a very personal grudge against him?

And, like Haider, was willing to make her a pawn in their deadly game.

It wouldn't surprise her with all the secrets that shadowed Lachlan. Thank God Jared had come along when he did.

She frowned. "What are the odds you'd be the one to rescue me?"

"Pure dumb luck." Jared shrugged. "I left right after you did, and I live in McLean. I didn't want to deal with the Beltway construction either."

He took hold of her elbow. "Come on. Your teeth are chattering. Have a seat in my car while I look at yours." He guided her to the passenger seat of his Lexus and turned up the heat so it was blasting warm air before activating his flashers.

"Stay put and get warm." He closed the car door and went to her Prius, reaching in to turn on her car's hazards.

Circling her car, he examined her front right bumper, then traced the gouges along the driver's side before stooping to run his hands along the bottom of the frame and over the tires. The hazards from both vehicles bathed him in asynchronous flashes of amber, the discordance further jangling Sophia's already stretched nerves.

Jared's hands halted midway across her back bumper. He stood, depositing something in his jacket pocket before dusting off his hands and approaching the passenger side of his Lexus.

Sophia lowered the window.

"Who's had access to your car?" Jared reached into his pocket to show her a small, square black box.

"What is that?"

"A tracking device."

Sophia's body stilled as her mind raced. "Haider must have put it on my car. That's how he tracked me."

"Lachlan should have checked your car when he found out Haider was following you. That's what I would have done."

"He did." A part of her hadn't truly believed she was in danger before tonight. Roshan Haider had frightened her, but he'd delivered his message to Lachlan, and she hadn't seen him after that.

But getting run off the road, and a tracker on her car? Was it possible the real arms trafficker knew that she and Lachlan had discovered the illegal shipments and were working to expose them?

Who had the ability and the access to run an operation under Lachlan's nose and frame him for it? The audacity of the plan was breathtaking.

Jared. She stared at her lap to keep her thoughts hidden. As president of LAI, Jared could access anyone's computer. Get into anyone's files.

He had the ability, but what would be the motive? It was his company, his reputation on the line if LAI were ensnared in a weapons trafficking scandal.

And he wasn't the one who'd tried to run her off the road.

She needed to talk to Lachlan.

"I have to go home." Sophia gripped the door handle and pushed.

Jared blocked her exit, halting her escape. "We aren't far from my house, and we need to file a police report."

"I—"

"Please, Sophia. I'm concerned about you. I'll call a tow to collect your car, make sure it's drivable, and return it to your place." He gave her a sympathetic look. "You've had a traumatic evening."

She wanted to go home, but if the man in the BMW was lying in wait down the road? "O—okay." The heat blasting from the Lexus's vents had done little to chase away her chill. She rubbed her arms. "I need to get some things out of my car first."

She located her phone, wedged between the passenger seat and door, and scooped up the contents of her purse. Shoes in hand, she slid back into Jared's Lexus and pulled up Lachlan's number while Jared moved her car further onto the shoulder. After several rings that went unanswered, her call rolled over to voicemail.

Where was he? He said he wasn't leaving for Kabul until Monday.

Jared was heading back to his car, so she hung up without leaving a message. Given the tension between the two men, it was better if he didn't know she'd been trying to reach Lachlan.

The smooth hum of the Lexus's engine lulled her into a calmer state. Barely fifteen minutes passed before Jared drove up to a three-story stone and stucco home and into the middle bay of a three-car garage.

She followed him past a maroon sports car with an emblem she didn't recognize, through an expansive laundry room into a pristine white kitchen loaded with top-grade stainless-steel appliances a chef would envy. The décor was show-home perfect but had no trace of personality, and it was a massive home for one person.

"This way." He ushered her up a set of stairs to the second story and down a wide hallway, where he threw open double-paneled doors.

"My study. Have a seat." He gestured to a chair with wooden arms and a plaid fabric seat before he poured amber liquid from an ornate glass decanter into a matching tumbler and handed it to her. "This might help calm your nerves. I'll contact the police and see about filing a report."

She took a sip. The harsh burn of whisky seized her throat, making her cough. She set the drink aside and let her gaze wander the room as he settled behind his desk, phone in hand.

Jared's home office had more traditional furnishings than the modern design she'd glimpsed on the first floor. In front of her, moonlight peeked through a gap in the clouds to illuminate floor-to-ceiling windows. During a full moon, the entire room would be bathed in silver.

In the back of the room, two landscape paintings in antique frames flanked a grandfather clock, its somnolent, steady ticking almost hypnotic. Built-in cherry shelves took up the entire wall to her left. Rows of books lined the shelves, broken up by the strategic placement of niches containing objects d'art.

She wandered over to peruse the shelves, desperate for a distraction, while Jared dealt with the police. Her fingers trailed along a row of hardcover books while she scanned the titles—*Moby Dick, The Sun Also Rises, The Art of War, Playing to Win, The Prince.*

The row ended at a niche, bathed in the soft glow of lighting designed to highlight a piece of art or, in this case, a framed photograph of a clean-shaven Jared in desert fatigues and tan combat boots, his arms wrapped around a woman. They posed in front of a massive concrete wall in what Sophia assumed was a military base in Iraq or Afghanistan.

The woman wore a brightly patterned cobalt blue tunic and matching pants, her long dark hair cascading over one shoulder. Even from a distance, the camera's lens captured her striking blue eyes and sensual features. Something about her struck a chord of memory, almost as if Sophia had seen her before but couldn't place where.

Whoever she was, it was easy to see why Jared had been attracted to her. Was she still in his life? Or merely a fondly remembered wartime lover?

"An officer will contact you tomorrow to take your statement." Jared's voice, so close to her, had her whirling, her hand flying to her chest.

"I didn't hear you get off the phone." He was as quiet on his feet as Lachlan.

Jared glanced over her shoulder at the photo.

Her face burned at being caught snooping. She wanted to ask about the woman, but one look at his shuttered expression told her he wouldn't welcome her curiosity.

He held up the Lexus key fob. "I'll take you home now."

"Thank you. For everything." She followed him to his car, and they drove back to her condo in silence.

She gathered her clutch as Jared pulled up to the building's entrance. All she wanted to do was crawl into bed and pretend someone hadn't tried to hurt her tonight. That her life, her career, wasn't spiraling out of control.

First, she needed to talk to Lachlan.

Jared's eyes glinted in the semi-darkness. "I'll need your key. I've contacted Jeremy Powell, the kid who details cars at the surface lot next to our building. He's agreed to clean it up and buff out as many scratches as possible until you can get it into a body shop."

She dug the fob out of her clutch. "How much will I owe him?"

"It's taken care of. Let me walk you inside."

The lobby was only feet away, and Sal sat at the front desk—she could see him through the glass doors. Still, she scanned the cars parked nearby, searching for silver. "Thank you."

Jared escorted her inside, past Sal, to the elevators, and when the doors slid open, gripped her elbow, holding her in place. "Lachlan has brought nothing but danger to you, Sophia. Be careful."

A tremor wracked her, one he must have felt because his grip tightened before he released her. "Goodnight." He was still watching her when the doors slid shut.

She fumbled in her purse for her cell. She needed to hear Lachlan's voice. She needed him to tell her everything would be okay, but her call went to voicemail again. This time she left a message. "Lachlan, please call me. Someone in a silver BMW ran me off the road tonight. I—I think Roshan Haider is back."

Lachlan handed Nathan a bottle of beer he'd procured from the fridge and settled into a chair in the war room—Nathan's nickname for his home office.

The former SEAL had converted the formal dining room in his home into his workspace. Everything was state of the art, from the bullet-resistant polycarbonate windows and top-grade security system to the three monitors displaying feeds from cameras stationed around his wooded property and at the gated front entrance. Between some of the missions Nathan had been on, and his current work as a hacker, he couldn't be too careful about his security. His home had been the logical place for a secure video conference with Ryder in Kabul.

Lachlan glanced at his watch. "Ryder should be up and at his computer now."

Nathan tapped on his keyboard. Seconds later, Ryder Montague's face appeared on Nathan's center monitor.

"Rise and shine, pretty boy," Nathan greeted the other man with a grin.

Ryder returned the greeting with a slight smile half-hidden behind his white ceramic mug. "Scare any small children lately?"

Nathan slapped his chest. "Moi? I'm the epitome of charming and debonair."

As much as he enjoyed the banter, Lachlan brought his mates back to the matter at hand. "Were you able to install the tracker on Burkette's phone?" he asked Ryder.

"Yes, but it took some doing. He doesn't put it down often. I had to confide in Caleb Varella so he could create a distraction that gave me time to download the tracker."

Lachlan frowned. Caleb was Ryder's number two on his security team and a good man, a former Green Beret, but he wasn't comfortable with anyone else knowing their plans. "Will he keep quiet?"

"I trust him. He's not a fan of Josh either." Ryder took a sip from his mug before resuming. "I also did a bit of recon in Josh's living quarters when he was at the project site and came across another mobile. One that isn't registered to LAI."

"A burner, maybe," Nathan said. "Did you download the tracker on that one, too?"

Ryder nodded. "I'll send you the number."

Lachlan gave Ryder his flight information and arrival time into Kabul. "Stay on your contact at customs. I want to know when that shipment clears. You and I will be there waiting to see who picks it up. My working theory is Roshan Haider is using his import-export business to facilitate these shipments through customs and into Khan's hands. The question is, who is Haider working with? Either someone hacked into LAI's computer network to clone my system or..." He didn't want to think about the other alternative.

"Someone inside LAI helped Haider set you up," Nathan finished for him grimly.

Lachlan rubbed the back of his neck. He must have done something awful in a previous existence for his karma to be this bad. Other than Nathan and Ryder, was there anyone he could trust?

His phone vibrated. He turned it over. *Sophia.*

The urge to leave the room so he could answer and hear her voice surprised him and made him uneasy. Nothing was more important now than stopping Khan and clearing his name.

Nothing.

He'd get back to her later. She was out with Jared this evening at some Congressman's party. Even though he knew it was a work event, his blood heated with an emotion he refused to name.

He rechecked his phone. She hadn't left a message, so it must not have been important. He set the phone to do not disturb and slid it into his coat pocket so it wouldn't be a further distraction.

"Nathan, I need you to run background checks on everyone at LAI. See if anything unusual pops up."

Ryder piped up through the video feed. "What do we do if Josh is the one who shows up at customs to accept the weapons?"

"Part of me wants to record him accepting the shipment and then follow him to see where the weapons are delivered, but I can't let them fall into Khan's hands," Lachlan replied. "If it's Burkette, we'll pick him up, and—" he met his team leader's eyes across the thousands of miles separating them with a clear message, "—he will tell us what we need to know."

Burkette was a former Ranger and a hardened combat soldier. He didn't want to think too hard about what he and Ryder might have to do to get the information they needed from the other man, but he'd do what was necessary to find out who was setting him up as an arms trafficker.

"I always miss the fun part," Nathan grumbled.

"I can't clear my name until I prove I didn't place the orders for those extra weapons. Find me a lead on who at LAI is working with Haider." To Ryder, he added, "I'll see you in a couple of days." Lachlan levered himself out of his chair, ignoring the stab of pain in his left leg. "Right now, I've got a lot to do before I leave on Monday."

He said goodbye to his friends, grabbed his jacket, and let himself out of Nathan's home. Instead of heading to his apartment, he took the road that led to I-495 so the Mercedes could stretch her legs whilst he cleared his head.

He was in a fight for his life, his reputation, and his freedom. The only bright spot in his miserable fucking life was Sophia, but he should have listened to his instincts and avoided her. All he'd brought her was danger and a grave's worth of secrets.

Lights from the overhead streetlamps illuminated the Capital Beltway and washed over him in rhythmic intervals as he cruised the far-left lane with the faster traffic. At least Haider was no longer a threat to her. He kept driving, willing his brain to focus only on the road and the satisfying rumble of his engine until his muscles relaxed and tension slipped away. After an hour, he headed back toward his apartment in Arlington.

By the time he got home, it was close to midnight. He'd driven until he'd been tired enough to ensure he'd fall asleep as soon as his head hit the pillow. Maybe his ghosts would have mercy on him and let him sleep through the night. If he were really lucky, he'd dream of Sophia instead.

He tossed his coat, his phone still in the right pocket, onto the chair in his bedroom. It was too late to call Sophia back now. He'd do it tomorrow.

CHAPTER
TWENTY-ONE

LACHLAN, PLEASE CALL ME. Someone in a silver BMW ran me off the road tonight. I—I think Roshan Haider is back.

The lift was too fucking slow.

Lachlan shouldered his way past the opening doors, his gaze laser-focused on the end of the hall. He knocked on Sophia's door, rattling it in its frame. If he didn't calm down, he'd frighten her and alarm the neighbors. Why had he decided to sleep in this morning? Why had he put his mobile on do not disturb and left the bloody thing in his coat? Sophia called again last night and left a voicemail.

Christ. His blood had run cold when he'd listened to it.

The door opened right as he raised his hand to knock again.

Instead of Sophia, a tall woman with blonde shoulder-length hair dressed in jeans and a pink top stood blocking the entrance. She crossed her arms and tossed daggers at him with her light blue eyes. "Let me guess, the Hot Scot. You're a bit late to the party."

"Where is Sophia?"

The blonde dropped her arms, her hands curling into fists. "If you think—"

"Emily, it's okay. Let him in." Sophia's voice came from inside.

Lachlan peered around the blonde to see Sophia step out from the kitchen barefoot in a white t-shirt and short, flouncy skirt. Reddish-brown scrapes marred the skin on her knees.

"I just got your message." His voice was nothing more than a guttural rasp.

Her eyes flew wide.

Her friend's gaze bounced between him and Sophia. "I, ah, think I'll go run some errands. Unless you want me to stay?"

Sophia shook her head. "No, I'll be fine. Lachlan and I need to talk. Thanks, Em."

Emily grabbed a large handbag off the foyer table and gave Lachlan a warning glare before letting herself out.

"Sophia..." His gaze drank her in, alive and unhurt. A shudder wracked him. He took one step, then another, hauled her into his arms, holding her tight. Too tight, but he couldn't seem to let go. He'd been right. Without her shoes, she barely came to mid-chest. She felt tiny, fragile, and easily broken.

Her midnight floral scent enveloped him. He lifted his gaze to the ceiling, giving thanks to a God he'd turned his back on two years ago.

Sophia's death would be the one he wouldn't survive.

She squirmed in his hold. "Lachlan, let me breathe." Puffs of breath warmed his sternum through the cotton fabric of his shirt.

His grip loosened instantly, but he didn't release her.

She peered up at him, her eyes full of questions and a hint of anger that clawed at his insides. "How did you get past the security desk?"

"I accessed the elevator through the parking garage." He gave her a little shake. "Do you see how easy it is to breach your building security?" If he could do it, so could whoever had tried to harm her last night. "Tell me what happened."

She shoved against him with surprising strength, and he let go. "I tried to tell you last night, but you didn't answer your phone."

"I had the ringer off." It was a miracle she'd even let him through the door this morning. His fingers itched with the need to touch her. "Please, tell me."

"Someone ran me off the road last night. If Jared hadn't come along when he did, I don't know if I'd still be alive."

"How fucking convenient for Jared." The words flew out before he had a chance to rein them in. This strange, out-of-control feeling threatened to drown him. He reached for her again, needing to feel the beat of her heart, the soft exhale of her breath against his skin.

She batted his hands away and stepped back to put distance between them. "At least I know where Jared was last night—where were you?" She wielded the accusation like a Sheffield dagger, her hazel eyes glistening with hurt.

The blade sunk in with surgical precision, slicing his heart to ribbons. She'd needed him, and he'd failed her. *Like you failed Thom, Fitzy, and the rest of them.*

The dagger twisted as he watched a tear make its way down the side of her nose to balance precariously on her upper lip. She swiped at it with trembling fingers. "I thought I was going to die. And do you know what my biggest regret was? That I would never get to be with you." She gave a sad laugh. "Imagine that."

"Christ." Her confession sent a wrecking ball through the wall around his defenses and left him short of breath. He yanked her to him and crushed his lips to hers.

She gasped, giving him entrance to her mouth.

He took full advantage, sweeping in to taste her. So sweet. He drank her in like she was nectar of the gods, his tongue claiming every inch of her mouth as his.

Her hands flew to the back of his neck, and she kissed him hesitantly at first, then with equal ferocity.

Sliding his hands down her back, he cupped her bottom. He bent his knees to lift her, straightened, and spun toward the wall, trapping her body with his hips as her legs wrapped his waist. The words to express his feelings wouldn't come, but he could damn well show her. His hands shook as he pushed up her shirt. A flick of her fingers sent it to the floor.

The curves of her breasts were silk beneath his roving lips, the white lace and satin bra pretty but in his way. A quick twist of his fingers and it joined her shirt on the floor. He sucked one rosy tip into his mouth before gently biting down, then soothed it with his tongue before moving to her other breast, the sounds of pleasure she made urging him on.

Her fingers burrowed beneath his leather jacket, nudging it from his shoulders.

He shrugged it off, letting it fall to join her shirt and bra before moving his hand to her center.

"Ah, *mo leannan*, you're already wet for me." He pushed the satin aside and thrust a finger into her drenched sex.

"Lachlan." His name left her lips in a breathless gasp that threatened what little remained of his control. He added another finger and pumped in a lazy rhythm.

"I need..." Her head fell back, baring the smooth column of her throat.

He sank his teeth into the place where it met her shoulder and marked her as his. "What do you need? Tell me, and it's yours." *Anything.*

"Please..."

"Tell me." His fingers sped up. "What do you need, Sophia?"

"I need more." She punctuated her words with a sharp tug on his hair.

He reveled in the erotic sting and locked down the urge to yank open his zipper and plunge into her. Her needs came first, and if her pleasure was all she would allow him, he'd accept it gratefully. "Look at me."

The green around her pupils stood out against their brown background like shards of peridot, dazed with desire and need.

His thumb moved across her clit, back and forth, faster, harder until her eyes slammed shut and she let out a long, gasping moan, coming apart in his arms. Her inner walls squeezed his fingers in pulsing waves. He wanted to feel her grip his cock the same way.

He held her to him until her breathing returned to its normal rhythm, willing his balls not to explode before he could get inside her. Just this once, he would shut out the darkness and bury himself deep in her light.

Whether he deserved to or not.

Sophia caressed the side of Lachlan's face as she slowly came down off her high. Her breasts and neck were tender from the black stubble on his jaw, her lips and nipples swollen from his kisses. All the obstacles that stood in their path didn't matter. Right now, at this moment, he was hers, and she wasn't letting him go. "Make love to me."

The hunger that flared in his eyes made her lightheaded. Or maybe that was from Lachlan making her come so hard. Not only was he skilled with his mouth, but the man also had incredibly talented hands. She couldn't wait to see what he could do with the rest of his body.

He carried her down the hall to her bedroom and halted at the threshold, a laugh rumbling in his chest. "Plants."

She glanced at the Ficus tree in the corner, the out-of-control pothos trailing down the side of her dresser, and the cute mini-jade plant shaped like a bonsai tree on her nightstand. "Plants are soothing. They bring nature inside. Besides they—"

His tongue swallowed the rest of her sentence, exploring her mouth until she couldn't remember what she'd been saying.

The soft cushion of the lavender comforter on her queen bed met her back while his hard body draped her front. His hair slipped through her fingers like silk, in contrast to the rough texture of his jeans against her legs.

Firm lips closed around her nipple, heating her skin as he tugged and nipped, sending bolts of pleasure-pain straight to her womb and obliterating the boneless lethargy from her orgasm.

Lachlan took his time moving down her body, raining kisses across her ribs, over her stomach. She squirmed as his tongue rimmed her navel. Every touch of his lips and fingers was a fiery brand that sent spikes of need lancing through her. Her skirt and panties disappeared, leaving her completely bare before him.

He sat back on his heels and spread her knees to gaze at the most feminine part of her. Embarrassment pressed her thighs together. Neither of her previous boyfriends had stared at her in the way Lachlan was.

"Don't deny me the pleasure of knowing every part of you." He wedged his shoulders between her legs, and before she realized his intentions, he'd put his mouth on her. The shock of his tongue on her clit arched her back and made her gasp, the sensation overloading her mental circuits.

Neither of her boyfriends had ever done that, either.

His unshaven cheeks chafed her inner thighs. Clutching fistfuls of bedspread, she struggled to anchor herself under the relentless, sensual assault on her sanity. He drove her swiftly to another orgasm, continuing to lap at her even as she collapsed, unable to muster up more than a satisfied sigh.

She wanted more, needed to feel connected to him in the most intimate way. Gripping the material covering his shoulders, she yanked him up to her waiting mouth and kissed him hungrily, tasting herself on his lips. "You're overdressed."

Yanking his navy t-shirt from his waistband, her eager fingers found the warm skin beneath. She slid her palms greedily over the well-defined ridges of his abs.

He sat up and ripped the offending item of clothing over his head, sending it across the room, exposing a muscular chest with a light dusting of black hair and sculpted abs. A round metal tag hung around his neck on a silver ball chain.

Her fingers itched to explore the newly exposed expanse of territory. His skin was smooth yet firm, like velvet over iron. She welcomed the weight of his body as he covered her, the metal tag, warm from his skin, nestling between her breasts.

"I need you." She dug her nails into his shoulder blades and arched her back, telling him without words exactly where she needed him.

"You have me." Lachlan's reply was a promise, drenched in sex. She allowed herself to believe his words conveyed more than just his attention to their lovemaking.

He shed the remainder of his clothing with rapid efficiency. His erection, now freed from its confines, bobbed long and thick in front of him. He was not a small man, and it had been a long time since she'd had sex. Her gaze skittered away from the evidence of his desire to the round, puckered scar on his left thigh. A variety of other, lesser scars decorated his warrior's body.

He bent to pick up his jeans, giving her a prime shot of his spectacular backside. Another, jagged, pink scar line was visible on the back of his left leg. Removing a foil packet from his wallet, he tore it open and sheathed himself before kneeling between her legs.

His lips grazed her cheek, moving to her ear. "Ready?"

"Yes." She was more than ready. She'd been ready since seeing his photo in the file Admiral Dane sent her. Ready when she realized the shadows in his eyes masked pain that meant he cared too much. When she watched how he cared for a down-on-his-luck veteran. When she realized he possessed the same warrior spirit reflected in the painting of another Scot from long ago.

He thrust forward, entering her with slow, shallow strokes.

She sucked in a breath that had him stilling, a question in his eyes. She arched her hips. "Don't stop." She arched again, seating him deeper. Her initial discomfort dissipated, replaced by an erotic feeling of fullness that had her moaning with pleasure.

His hips moved in a steady rhythm. A light sheen of sweat coated his skin, marking her with his scent.

Digging her nails into his biceps, she met each thrust with her own. "Lachlan," she breathed, everything she felt but was too afraid to put into words echoing in her voice.

His emerald gaze bored into her, a window to his soul opening just enough for her to see fear before his control snapped. Slamming shut his lids, he threw back his head and surged into her, hips churning. Her headboard knocked against her bedroom wall with the force of his thrusts. She slid her arms around his back and hung on, reveling in his passion.

"Won't...lose...you...too." Each word seemed torn from between his clenched teeth.

He ground his pelvis against her, sending her straight into another orgasm before his thrusts became erratic, and he stilled, coming with a shout. His fingers dug into her hips, locking them together.

He was beautiful, powerful, and—for one unguarded moment—vulnerable.

Words that were tender but premature formed in her mouth. She held them back. It was too soon to speak them aloud. It would be too easy for her to dream that Lachlan could be the one to love her the way she'd never been loved before. To fill that empty hole in her heart.

He collapsed, chest heaving, on top of her, his hot breaths bathing her ear. "Did I hurt you?" Cool lips brushed her neck. "You made me lose my head."

She traced the muscles on his back, not caring that he was too heavy and she could barely breathe. "It was perfect."

He pulled out of her and disappeared into her bathroom. Dampness cooled her skin, pebbling her flesh. When he returned to the bed, she pulled him over her for warmth. She fingered the dog tag around his neck. *Barnwell, T.* Not his then, someone else's.

His hand covered hers, stilling her curious fingers. His mouth had flattened into a grim slash, and the shadows were back in his eyes.

"Tell me." She wanted to be there for him the way no one had been there for her.

Lachlan rolled to his back, his forearm shielding his expression.

"Tell me what put those shadows in your eyes." She caressed the side of his face. Would he open up to her?

He stayed silent, then stood, stepped into his jeans, and padded to her bedroom window. A remoteness had descended over him like an invisible shield, reflected in the stiff set of his shoulders, his straight spine, his fingers curled into fists.

Sophia gathered the pillow his head had been resting on against her chest, breathing in his scent to try and calm her nerves. "Tell me about Roshan Haider's sister. About that dog tag around your neck with someone else's name on it." She needed to know what had happened that continued to haunt him.

"We were in Afghanistan." Lachlan's voice was low, halting, the words ripped from him against his will. "My troop was assigned to hunt down and capture or kill leaders of the Taliban and Al-Qaeda."

He returned to the bed and sat, his jean-clad hip grazing her sheet-covered one. The ice creeping into his expression chilled her. His stare was unfocused—present, yet far away.

"Nadia served as an interpreter and liaison between the villagers and our teams. Her father had been a prominent physician in Kabul. When the Taliban took power in the mid-nineties, he brought his family to London, where Nadia was raised and educated. Most of the local Afghan men wouldn't deal directly with her, of course, but she could still interpret for us, and she picked up valuable intel from the women in the villages."

A brief, sad smile touched his lips. "She was beautiful and intelligent, and she had a way about her—I canna explain it. I think every man she met became a bit enamored with her."

Sophia's throat swelled until she could barely swallow. "She was important to you."

He grimaced, then his eyes lost focus again. "Nadia texted one afternoon, asked me to come to her base housing unit—that it was urgent. Once I got there, she told me a local man visiting relatives in a remote mountain village had seen three Westerners held prisoner nearby. Two months earlier, the Taliban had abducted three foreign aid workers from a village outside Kabul. Nadia said one of the hostages was a woman, and the Taliban planned to execute them as a political statement. She begged me to convince my superiors to mount a rescue mission, insisting the information she'd obtained was authentic. I trusted her."

He swallowed hard, his gaze darting around the room.

"I trusted her," he repeated, an echo spoken softly that reverberated throughout her bedroom.

His pain called to her, and she instinctively answered, reaching out. "Lachlan—"

He shot to his feet, his back unyielding, and her arms dropped, empty, back to the bed.

"I urged our commanders to green-light the mission." Lachlan paced back over to stare out her window.

This time, she followed, wrapping herself in the bedsheet. His back was warm against her cheek. He stiffened at her touch, then relaxed when she didn't let go.

"They knew we were coming. It was a disaster from the beginning. We'd just approached the village when we came under heavy fire. My team leader, Staff Sergeant Barnwell, was killed almost immediately, and the female hostage, Katherine, died in the crossfire trying to reach me."

Barnwell. The name on the tag around his neck. Her arms tightened around his waist as she fought back tears.

"Three of my other men were injured—Fitzy died soon after we returned to Bagram. Another group of insurgents on higher ground ambushed the SEALs supporting us, so they couldn't help. They lost a man as well. The helicopter providing fire support took an RPG and went down."

He turned from the window to face her. "It's a bloody miracle any of us made it out alive." The remoteness in his eyes and voice frightened her more than if he'd been raging. "Three good operators, a hostage, the crew in the Apache—all dead. Nadia betrayed us. I didn't want to believe it. She sent us into a trap, then ran off to join the Taliban with Mohammad Razul Khan's son."

His focus turned inward again. "Thom never trusted her. I thought he was being a crusty old bugger. But he was right, and he died because I didn't believe him." He swallowed hard, then again, visibly trying to hold back emotion now when before he'd been set in stone.

"How did Nadia die?" She had to know.

He stared out the window. "I took a bullet to the thigh during the mission. Busted my bollocks rehabbing and lied my arse off to the medical staff and my commanding officer so I could return to my troop. They were going after her. I needed to be there when they did."

Her throat ached from holding back tears. She should stop him right there. "And when you found her?"

His eyes turned cold, like a forest waterfall in winter. "I killed her."

She'd thought she was prepared.

His simple declaration, wrapped in ice, froze the breath in her lungs and pierced her heart.

He'd locked all his emotions back up in whatever box he'd constructed in his head. Nadia's betrayal had destroyed his ability to trust. Maybe he was too damaged to ever care for her the way she needed, but she wasn't giving up.

She grabbed his hands, willing him to look into her eyes. "No. You make it sound so simple. I don't believe that." Lachlan would never kill a woman he cared about in cold blood, even if she betrayed him the way Nadia did.

"It was—"

"Something happened." She cut him off, her voice strengthening with a certainty born of conviction. He was a man of honor. He *suffered* because he cared. The deaths of his men and Nadia's betrayal still haunted him.

"You killed her because you didn't have a choice." A cold-blooded killer didn't have nightmares.

Lachlan's jaw worked like he wanted to speak but couldn't form the words. Finally, he spoke, "She would have killed one of my men if I hadn't taken the shot." His voice was thick with remembered agony. And regret.

"That makes you a protector, not a murderer." She rested her palm against his bare chest, over his heart, and willed him to believe her. "You acted to save your teammate. Everything awful that happened, the ambush, the deaths—all of it—was Nadia's doing and the Taliban's. It wasn't your fault."

His shoulders slumped like the air had been let out of them. His eyes slammed tight. When they reopened, the emotion in them stopped her breath. "Pack a bag. I'm taking you to stay with my pal Nathan whilst I'm in Kabul. He's a former SEAL. Whoever tried to hurt you won't get past him. Better yet, go home to your parents in Cincinnati until I've settled this matter."

She frowned. "I can't just up and leave my job. If I don't handle the government report, someone else will, and they might discover what Fred did. Besides, I can help track those weapons purchases while you're in Kabul and figure out who authorized them."

Lachlan's jaw set. "This isn't your fight. I want you safe. What if the man who tried to hurt you last night comes after you again?" His gaze narrowed. "What if it's someone at LAI? I won't be around to protect you."

An involuntary shiver hunched Sophia's shoulders. "If it's someone at LAI, they'll know we're onto them if I suddenly disappear. They may start covering their tracks, and we could lose our best opportunity to prove you didn't authorize those shipments. I'll be safe at the office with Jared around."

Thunderclouds formed on Lachlan's face at the mention of Jared's name. "I'm sure he'll stick to you like a barnacle on a ship's hull," he muttered, his tone taking on a sarcastic edge. "You're most vulnerable when you're going to and from work. That's how Haider tracked you, and that's why your assailant last night waited until you were driving home."

The reminders sent her pulse skyrocketing, but it was too late to back down. She gentled her tone, trying to get Lachlan to see reason. "The only way we'll both be safe is to find out who the real trafficker is and stop them. Emily is here with me. She can bring me to work, and I won't go out and make myself a target until you get back. And I'm perfectly safe at home—mid-rise with a secure entrance, remember? I'll keep the door locked and the alarm on."

If it came down to it, one word to Admiral Dane, and she'd likely have an entire platoon of Navy SEALs at her door ready to escort her to the Danes' Connecticut estate for safekeeping.

Of course, then she'd have to tell the admiral the truth. That instead of searching for evidence to prove Lachlan Mackay was an arms trafficker, she was suppressing evidence in order to prove his innocence. Oh, and sleeping with him as well.

Her stomach cramped.

"If I got past your lobby guard, someone else can, too." Angry and frustrated, Lachlan was still hot, but this conversation was going nowhere.

She was saved from coming up with a counterargument when her front door slammed shut. Loudly.

"Hello? Do I need to find another errand to run?" Humor laced Emily's words.

"No, we'll be right out," Sophia yelled back.

She scrambled for her clothing. Where were her bra and shirt? Oh, right. In the foyer where Lachlan had stripped them off her. Her face felt hot enough to fry an egg. There was no way Emily wouldn't know what she and Lachlan had been doing.

By the time she'd pulled on a new top, Lachlan was fully dressed and still wearing an obstinate expression. On impulse, she threw her arms around him and pressed her lips to his. When she finally came up for air, she was breathless. "I'll be fine. You go to Kabul and do what you need to do."

Concern still shadowed his eyes. "Mind yourself, now. Don't do anything risky."

"I won't, I promise." She resisted an eye roll as Lachlan narrowed his gaze on her. "I mean it." *Stubborn man.*

She followed him to her front door. Emily had ducked into her bedroom and made herself scarce, for which Sophia was thankful.

Lachlan retrieved his jacket from the floor. "Lock the door, set the alarm, and don't let anyone in without checking to see who it is first."

"Yessir." She threw him a mock salute, hoping for at least a smile, but his scowl reminded her that he didn't seem to possess a sense of humor.

All of a sudden, the reality of what they'd done hit her. She'd made love with Lachlan. She searched his eyes, looking for something, she wasn't sure what. Reassurance? Affection?

His gaze softened. He brushed her lips in a gentle kiss. "I'll see you on Monday before I leave." His voice hardened. "Don't go anywhere alone."

She waited until he'd stepped into the elevator before locking her door and setting the alarm as promised.

Emily's heeled boots tapped across the floor behind her.

Sophia braced her back against the door and let out a drawn-out sigh. "Is it too early for a drink?" So much had happened, and it wasn't even lunchtime.

Emily snorted. "It's five o'clock somewhere." She cast a pointed look at Sophia's shirt and bra lying crumpled on the floor. "You forgot something." Then she marched to the kitchen, took down two champagne flutes from an upper cabinet, and grabbed orange juice from the fridge and a mini bottle of Prosecco from the bottom cabinet. "Sparkling wine first, a dash of juice for color, and voilà, breakfast of champions."

She handed a flute to Sophia, then gestured toward the sofa. "You were right. Lachlan is hot. But he also is definitely an alphahole."

Sophia took a sip of her drink before setting her glass on the coffee table.

Emily curled her long, jean-clad legs next to Sophia. She knocked back half her drink in one swallow. "So, miss prim and proper, any dirty little secrets you'd care to share with your best friend?"

"I've never seen him so rattled. One thing led to another...." Sophia trailed off, refusing to meet her friend's knowing gaze.

"It's obvious he cares for you." Emily leaned close, her eyes sparkling with curiosity and no small hint of mischievousness. "Come on, spill. How is he in bed?"

"*Emily.*" Why was it so hot in the room all of a sudden? Sophia tamped down the urge to fan herself. A satisfied smirk ruined her attempt to appear blasé.

"You're in love with him."

Sophia's startled gaze flew to meet her friend's knowing one. "What? No. I mean, it's too soon to be in love. Right?"

"Be careful, Soph." Emily's expression sobered. "A man like Lachlan could break your heart. Plus, he brought danger to your doorstep. I'm not sure I'd trust him just yet."

Sophia's body ached in pleasant ways. Lachlan's scent lingered on her skin. "I trust him." That didn't mean Emily wasn't right about Lachlan breaking her heart. She wanted something from him he might be unable to give her. Love. Commitment. A happily-ever-after found in sappy movies and romance novels.

"You said Lachlan told you your stalker was gone, but someone tried to hurt you last night." Emily's face puckered like she'd sucked a lemon. She drained the last of her mimosa. "Refill?"

Sophia shook her head.

Emily headed for the kitchen. "As much as I hate to say this, maybe we should call my dad."

Reality crashed in, filling Sophia with a weariness that went bone-deep. Emily still didn't know about her agreement with the admiral. Even worse, neither did Lachlan. And, she was keeping the truth about the weapons shipments from both Admiral Dane and Jared. Jared would probably fire her and Lachlan both, even if they managed to unmask the actual arms trafficker. The damage to his company's reputation would take time to repair and could cost LAI its government contracts.

Her stomach hurt from the sheer number of secrets she held. "Let's hold off on calling your dad." When Emily returned to the sofa with a fresh drink, Sophia gave her friend a smile to reassure her. "He'll go overboard and put me in witness protection."

After he got done telling her how disappointed in her he was.

"Since you started work at LAI, you've had a stalker, a co-worker's been murdered, and you've been run off the road. If your boss hadn't come along, who knows what that guy might have done." Emily's light blue gaze was as serious as Sophia had ever seen it. "What's really going on? What aren't you telling me?"

"I—" It killed Sophia that she couldn't confide the entire story to her best friend. "Look, it's got to do with some sensitive company information that's come to light. Lachlan's looking into it. He's going to Kabul on Monday, and when he returns, we'll be able to bring the information to Jared and find a solution that protects LAI and its employees."

One of Emily's manicured brows arched. "Lachlan's tripping off to Afghanistan and leaving you on your own at the office sitting on what sounds like a powder keg. Are you sure you're safe?"

"Perfectly," Sophia assured her. She crossed fingers on the hand sandwiched beneath her thigh. "I did agree to ask you to take me to work each day and not travel anywhere unaccompanied. And,"—she gave a little eye roll—"use the alarm system even when we're home."

Emily looked unconvinced. "We need to call my dad."

"One week, Emily. Give me one week. Once Lachlan returns, this will all get resolved."

"Fine." Emily harrumphed. "One week. But if anything else happens, the deal's off, and I'm siccing the admiral on you."

CHAPTER
TWENTY-TWO

LACHLAN GLANCED AT HIS watch as he left the office Monday afternoon for the airport. The numbers over the lift cycled past the lower floors as the car made its way to eight and opened. Before he stepped in, he looked in the direction of the empty executive suite. Maybe it was good Sophia wasn't around to say goodbye. He might be tempted to haul her into his office, close the door, and make love to her on his desk.

Store up more good memories as he headed back to a place where there were only bad ones.

His ghosts had stayed away from his dreams the past two nights. Instead, his brain thoughtfully played an endless loop of making love to Sophia, her expression when she came apart in his arms. He'd woken up in a sweat, hard as a tent pole, the shower and his hand a poor substitute for her soft skin and warm body. Blood rushed south even now at the memory, and he wrestled his wayward thoughts into submission before someone else joined him in the lift and got an eyeful.

He'd cracked open his dark soul to her in a way he'd never done with anyone else, leaving him feeling vulnerable and unmoored. She'd poured her light into him, stood her ground, and hadn't run even after he told her about how badly he'd failed the people who'd trusted him to watch their backs.

How he'd killed the woman he'd trusted more than his senior en-
listed man.

Sophia was important to him in a way no one else had ever been. He
wanted—no, needed—her in his life. When this was over, if he wasn't
in prison, he'd do whatever he had to do to get his head on straight, be
the kind of man she deserved.

The thought both excited and scared the piss out of him.

He pressed the button for his parking level, then delved into his
suit pocket for the Mercedes' fob. The familiar weight was missing.
Right—Jeremy Powell had asked him for it earlier.

He rang Jeremy's mobile. "Where's my car?"

"Hey, Mr. Mackay. It's done. I haven't taken it back to the garage.
Mr. Landry said not to bother 'cause you were leaving early today."
Crunching, likely from Doritos, Jeremy's favorite crisps, punctuated
his words.

Lachlan hit the button for the ground floor level. "I'm on my way
out. Keep your snack away from my upholstery," he teased the younger
man.

It was the kind of warm, late spring day he could have only imagined
growing up in Thurso, where the average temperature hovered around
nine degrees Celsius this time of year. A soft breeze rustled the leaves
on the trees planted along the street and swirled the remnants of
decaying cherry blossom petals scattered on the ground. It smelled of
new beginnings in the cycle of life.

Ach. He couldn't help a slight smile. Here he was, getting all fanciful. Even if he proved his innocence, Landry would probably eliminate
the entire Global Security division to try and salvage LAI's reputation.
He could start his own company—strongarm Ryder and Nathan into
joining him. Convince Sophia to come along. They could make a fresh
start.

Together.

Jeremy was already moving toward the Mercedes, tucked in the back corner of the surface lot away from the other cars. Lachlan put his fingers to his lips and gave a sharp whistle, then threw up a hand when Jeremy spun in his direction.

Jeremy waved. "I'll bring her to you, Mr. M."

The lad wanted one more opportunity to drive his car, and who would blame him? It was a braw ride. He strode in Jeremy's direction. As much as he'd like to let Jeremy take his time, he had a plane to catch.

A smooth rumble filled the air as the engine fired, and Lachlan smiled. *Listen to her purr li—*

Sophia took a bite of store-bought vanilla cake. The icing was an inch thick and a yard too sweet. *Poor Penny.* Everyone at LAI was doing their best to celebrate her birthday, despite the pall cast by Fred's death.

"Whoever he is, you look like you intend to rock his world."

She choked on her bite of cake and winced at Penny's knowing gaze. "What makes you so sure—"

A loud boom shuddered through the building, bringing conversation to an abrupt halt. Then everyone spoke at once.

"What was that?"

"—explosion."

"An accident—"

"Construction site, maybe."

"—plane—too low."

Tension suffocated the room.

They were only five miles from the Pentagon, and 9/11 was never far from anyone's thoughts.

The building fire alarms screeched to life.

Sophia tossed her cake into the garbage and hurried to collect her purse.

A tidal wave of heat and debris flung Lachlan through the air with a roar. He slammed into the asphalt and skidded several feet, shredding clothes and skin before his momentum halted. Deep, wheezing coughs wracked his lungs. He blinked his vision back into focus and found himself staring at sky.

Bomb. "Thom!" Where were his men?

Training kicked in. He felt around for his weapon. Where the bloody hell was it? Flipping to his stomach, the world spun.

When it stopped, he saw concrete and buildings, not mountains and dust. Virginia. He wasn't in Afghanistan. He was in Virginia.

Jeremy.

He stumbled to his feet, fighting off vertigo. Pieces of fiery debris littered the pavement. His ears were full of cotton, the world on mute. An inferno devoured what had been his Mercedes.

He shut down. Went into survival mode.

Need cover. Whoever blew his car might have stuck around. Lachlan limped toward the partially built skeleton of the office building going up next door. The construction crew was already gone for the day. Sweat dripped into his eyes and down the side of his face. He raised his arm to wipe it away. It came back with bright red smears on the tattered sleeve.

Not sweat.

A loud ringing in his ears signaled the return of sound. He patted crimson fingers over his body until he located his phone. *Thank Christ.* Other than a cracked screen, it was still in one piece. He blinked to clear his vision and pulled up Nathan's number.

"You're interrupting my siesta." The former SEAL sounded a thousand miles away.

Pain threatened to tow him under. *Don't bloody pass out.* He blinked some more, trying to clear the rivulets of blood. His knees gave out, and he dropped on his arse behind a concrete wall with a groan.

"Need help." Someone had sandblasted his tonsils. He couldn't suck in enough air to get out a sentence. "Car exploded."

"What the fuck? As in caught fire or hit an IED? Where are you?"

"What?" He shifted to peer around the wall. A crowd was forming. A security guard tried to use a fire extinguisher on the wreckage. The heat and flames drove him back. Lachlan's muddled hearing picked up the faint blare of sirens in the distance. He sank back behind his cover.

"Lachlan, are you there?" Nathan's voice grew louder, more strident. "Are you hurt?"

"Took some shrapnel." He drew in measured breaths, focused on staying lucid. *Jeremy, poor bastard.* Lachlan was supposed to be the one in the car. "I'm at the construction lot next to my office building. Hurry."

"Be there soon. Sit tight, brother."

Lachlan glanced at the sky and sent up a brief prayer for Jeremy's soul. There was nothing to be done for the lad now except avenge him.

Lachlan.

Sophia made a course correction away from her office as sirens blared outside, her trot slowed by her form-fitting skirt and heels.

Lachlan's office was empty, the lights off. Had he left without saying goodbye? Her shoulders slumped at the thought.

The blaring sirens and flashing strobes jangled her nerves, making her twitchy. She needed to get out. Lachlan wasn't here.

"What's going on?" Jared appeared at the end of the hall.

"Did you hear that sound? The building shook." She had to raise her voice to be heard. The muffled wail of multiple sirens from emergency vehicles added to the jarring symphony.

"You go. I'll make sure everyone has left." Jared jogged past her and began pounding on doors, calling for everyone to evacuate.

She hurried to her office and grabbed her things. Someone had propped open the exit stairwell door. She stepped into a sea of bodies and tried to descend as quickly as possible in her heels without stumbling.

Screw it. Kicking off her pumps at the next landing, she barefooted it the rest of the way, clinging to the handrail so she wouldn't get knocked over by someone in a panic and trampled to death.

In the lobby, she jammed her feet back into her heels as people schooled around her like fish, all on their cell phones, their voices combining into indistinct babble.

Two security guards directed the crowd through the lobby doors, away from the surface lot. She ignored them, a strange feeling of dread pulling her toward the chaos.

There were two fire engines, their rooftop lights still flashing though, thankfully, the sirens no longer blared. Firefighters unfurled hoses and shouted orders.

Acrid smoke stung her eyes. Burnt rubber, plastic, and oil coated her throat. She covered her mouth and nose with a tissue from her purse.

Angry flames wrapped in thick, black smoke devoured what was left of a car, licking the pavement beneath the twisted metal. Debris littered the area as if a belligerent toddler had flung them in a tantrum.

A mangled piece of dark blue metal lay no more than ten feet from where she stood.

Her feet moved. *It's not his.*

"Ma'am." A firefighter intercepted her. "You need to stay back."

"The car, what kind of car was it?" She raised her voice over the din, but no one responded. She plunged shaking hands into her purse, fumbled for her phone.

Please, please answer.

Lachlan's soft burr was music to her ears. "You've reached Lachlan Mackay—"

"Oh, thank God, Lach—"

"—leave a message, and I'll get back to you shortly."

Her relief evaporated at the beep.

"Sophia." Jared appeared next to her. "We need to stay out of the way." He took her by the elbow and urged her forward.

She resisted, her gaze glued to the burning car.

The smoke billowing from the wreckage turned gray as two firefighters drowned the flames with their hoses. One of them gestured, and two more firefighters returned with a large blue tarp. They unfurled it in front of the car, blocking her view.

"I can't get ahold of Lachlan." She couldn't get air into her lungs.

"Sophia." Jared tugged again on her arm.

"The car was dark blue."

"We should leave."

The smoke disappeared, and water formed a lake on the asphalt. The firefighters draped the tarp over what remained of the vehicle.

"There was someone in there." *Please, God, no.*

She pressed Lachlan's number again with a shaky finger. It rolled to voicemail. She tried again and again. The tremors expanded until her body quaked along with her hands.

Jared's hand closed over hers, trapping her frantic fingers. "Lachlan's probably already at the airport with his phone off."

Grief crashed into her in a violent wave before receding, leaving numbness in its wake. Jared's arm anchored her to his body. "Let me take you home."

She was too numb to argue.

He guided her from the surface lot and what remained of the car with its grim contents to his vehicle in the underground garage. The Lexus's interior was spotless and had that just-cleaned smell of cleaner and fragrance spray. She turned her cheek to the leather seat and inhaled through her nose, trying to banish the odors of burning chemicals.

As they pulled into the street, the flashing lights, the smell, the charred, water-soaked wreckage of a life faded into the distance.

Strange.

The sun still shone in the western arc of the sky. People bustled down the tree-lined sidewalks, leaving work, maybe stopping to buy dinner at one of the restaurants on the busy street. The man in the car next to her was singing to his radio at the stoplight. Was this just another day for him?

She closed her eyes, picturing Lachlan as they made love, cheeks flushed, green eyes burning, his arms holding her tight. She wouldn't cry. Not now. Not in front of Jared.

"I'm sorry." Jared gave her hand a gentle squeeze.

She didn't respond, directing her gaze back to the passing scenery. If she acknowledged his comment, it meant this nightmare was real.

When his car pulled up to the entrance of her building, it was all she could do not to leap out and race inside. Lachlan had turned off his phone. That was all. When he landed in Dubai to change flights, he'd turn it on, see all her desperate messages, and call.

"Do you want me to come up?"

"No, I'm fine." There was only one person she wanted to see.

Jared's fingers brushed wayward strands of hair behind her ear. "I'm going to tell everyone to take the day off tomorrow. Call me if you need anything."

"Thank you for driving me home," she managed to get out through numb lips.

She climbed from his car, her feet on autopilot taking her through the building lobby. The elevator hummed its way to the fifth floor while she stared at the closed doors, seeing only the burning car.

"Please be alive."

CHAPTER
TWENTY-THREE

LACHLAN TOSSED HIS NOW useless cell phone on Nathan's kitchen table. He'd discarded the battery at the construction site after his call. Anyone tracking his location would think the phone had been destroyed with the man.

His body ached like a Bushmaster had run over him. His face looked like he'd dragged it over broken glass. He scratched the tape securing the bandages on his face. Nathan had done a decent enough job stitching him up.

Yet another death on his conscience.

When the police figured out Jeremy had been in the car and not him, they'd have more questions than answers. And when they looked for those answers, the weapons shipments to Khan would surface. He was running out of time and ways to prove his innocence.

What was going through Sophia's head right now? He rubbed at the sudden ache in his chest. Maybe it would be safer for her if she believed he was dead.

"Here's the stuff you wanted from your apartment." Nathan dropped a duffle bag next to him and sauntered to the refrigerator to retrieve two beers. He handed one to Lachlan.

"Anyone see you?" Lachlan lowered himself with a wince onto one of the kitchen chairs.

Nathan snorted. "You offend me." He took a seat and eyeballed Lachlan over his bottle. "Now what?"

"I don't know."

"Someone didn't want you going to Kabul. Who at LAI could pull this off?"

Pain hammered Lachlan's skull. He took a sip of his beer and forced himself to assess his colleagues honestly. "Christian Meier, I suppose. He heads up the development projects and travels to Kabul more frequently than I do. He could have made a deal with Khan. Khan could have introduced him to Haider."

"I didn't find anything suspicious on the guy when I ran a background check on him," Nathan said. "But I can dig deeper."

"Rob Salas, our IT director. It's possible someone bribed or blackmailed him into gaining access to my online credentials so those weapons could be ordered and shipped from the Global Security division."

Nathan narrowed his eyes. "But from your tone, I'm thinking you don't believe either Meier or Salas is your guy."

Lachlan eased out of the chair and limped through the living room to the sliding doors that led to a back deck. The burnt-orange blackout drapes covering the glass provided privacy and cover in the unlikely event someone slipped past Nathan's security perimeter.

"I'm not sure I trust my judgment anymore when it comes to people's motives." The beer soured in the back of his throat. Nadia had taught him that harsh lesson. He'd allowed his feelings for Sophia to cloud his judgment as well. He had an enemy much closer to him than he'd realized. Someone put Sophia in danger to distract him, so he'd be more worried about protecting her than himself.

He pivoted back to face Nathan, still sitting at the kitchen table. The back of his neck tingled with growing suspicion, one he should have had before now, but he'd been too wrapped up in stopping the weapons auction and protecting Sophia from Haider.

"Sophia said Fred Biller, one of our coworkers, found the information on the weapons shipments during an audit he did on his own in preparation for the government report. What if he stumbled across those transactions, and he wasn't meant to?"

"Sounds plausible. Why don't you ask him?"

"He's dead. Murdered in a random street mugging in DC last week." Lachlan paused as the magnitude of his suspicion hit home. "Right after he found the information."

"Well, isn't that convenient." Nathan's grim response reflected the same conclusion Lachlan had just arrived at.

"Which leaves Jared Landry. If Burkette is the person receiving the shipments once they reach Kabul, he could be taking orders directly from his former Ranger captain." Lachlan rolled the beer bottle between his hands as the cold glass soothed the scrapes on his palms. "The question is, why would Landry risk his company and reputation to illegally traffic weapons to Khan, then murder to try and cover it up? What would be worth the risk?"

Nathan shrugged his massive shoulders. "Greed? The thrill of getting away with it? Something darker, maybe?"

"Like what?"

"I dunno. If Jared is behind this, he's taking an enormous risk and trying to frame you for it. Why? He'd have to have it in for you bad. Something beyond the fact you guys don't get along."

Lachlan took a sip of his beer while he marshaled his thoughts. "I'd ask you to touch base with Lucas, but I'm not ready for the FBI to know I'm alive."

"What about Sophia?"

Lachlan squeezed the bridge of his nose. The pain knocking around the back of his head joined the sting of shrapnel wounds and road rash from his skid across asphalt. The pieces to this puzzle didn't quite fit. What was he missing? "She's safe if she and whoever tried to kill me both believe I'm dead."

Nathan's heavy exhale resonated from the kitchen. He leveraged himself out of his chair and joined Lachlan in the living room. They stared at the drapes as if they held all the answers.

"Sophia has seen that information, too. Suppose someone at LAI is trying to cover their tracks and tie up any loose ends. Well, Sophia's a loose end." Nathan's words hung in the charged silence.

Fuck. Lachlan dropped his head back to stare aimlessly at Nathan's ceiling. He'd brought nothing but danger to Sophia's life.

He should have been the one who died.

"Can you check one more time," Sophia asked, twisting the hem of her shirt in her fingers as she stared out the balcony sliding glass door.

"I'm sorry, miss," the customer service rep for the airline said in a distinctly non-apologetic voice, "no one by that name checked into that flight, and he wasn't rebooked on another."

Flames, twisted metal, the stench of gasoline, burning plastic, and rubber. She gulped air but couldn't fill her lungs. Bile stung the back of her throat.

She'd watched Lachlan burn.

The cocoon of numbness she'd slipped into after Jared brought her home shattered like glass. Her living room tilted. She lunged for the couch before she ended up on the floor. A sob wrenched free, then another. For some crazy reason, she'd allowed herself to imagine a future with Lachlan. Someone to love and call her own. Someone who might have loved her the way she needed to be loved.

She thought of the painting at the art gallery, the one with the Highlander leading his men into battle. How she'd fantasized that it was Lachlan in the painting. The more she'd gotten to know Lachlan, the more she saw the same qualities in him that the artist had captured in oil. The fierce bravery in the face of death, the willingness to lead from the front, the protector of everything he valued.

Silly, maybe, but there'd been times she was tempted to return to the gallery to see if the painting was still there. Now, she didn't think she could bear looking at it. Her fantasy had been destroyed in an inferno of twisted metal.

Grief squeezed her chest and poured from her eyes. After what felt like hours, her breathing progressed from ragged hiccups to a steady rhythm. When Emily walked through the front door, she was too worn out even to summon a greeting.

"Sophia?" Emily bent over the back of the sofa, concern in her eyes. "Are you sick?"

"Lachlan's dead."

Emily's inhale was loud in the quiet condo, her mouth forming an almost perfect O. She rounded the sofa to sit next to Sophia and envelope her in a long hug. "What happened?"

"His car exploded." Sophia's weariness vanished on a spike of deep, burning fury. She vaulted off the couch, needing an outlet for the dark energy triggering her muscles and causing her heart to race. "Someone murdered him, Emily. I told Lachlan he was too distrustful once, and he told me I was too naïve." Tears—she hadn't thought she had any left to shed—blurred her vision. "He was right."

"You think the guy that ran you off the road..." Emily didn't finish the sentence.

"Maybe." How many enemies did Lachlan have? She sighed, swiping at the tears that leaked down her cheeks. "There's something I need to tell you."

Where did she begin? Might as well rip off the band-aid and start from the beginning.

"Your dad came for a visit before I started at LAI. He asked me to keep an eye out for any unusual activity, any shipments to Afghanistan that appeared out of the ordinary."

Emily exhaled long and slow. "He never stops with his scheming."

"He asked me to spy on Lachlan in particular, as head of the Global Security division."

"And then you met him and fell for him." Emily's brows lifted, then fell. "Awkward. Although, given the circumstances, maybe my dad had a good reason to suspect Lachlan was up to something."

"There's more." Sophia bit her lip. "Your dad asked me to look for evidence of illegal weapons shipments to Afghanistan, and after my coworker, Fred, was killed, I found it in Fred's office."

Fred.

He'd been the one to unearth evidence of the additional weapons purchases right before he was murdered. Had he told someone other than her what he'd found? Before today, she would have dismissed the idea of Fred's death as anything more than a tragedy of violence.

Now, she wasn't so sure.

"Did you tell my dad?"

"No, because it implicated Lachlan, and I know what you're thinking, but Lachlan is innocent. He was on his way to Kabul to confront the person accepting the shipments so he could discover who set him up."

Her lips trembled as the magnitude of the situation sank in. "Someone didn't want him to know the truth, and they killed him over it, which only proves he was innocent. Now, the actual criminal will get away with it, and Lachlan will always be known as an arms trafficker."

Emily stood to retrieve a box of tissues, handing several to Sophia. "Back up a minute. You said you found the information implicating Lachlan in your dead colleague's office. As in, the one who was murdered a few nights ago?"

"Yes." Sophia met her friend's concerned gaze. Emily was thinking the same thing she was thinking. The truth surrounding these weapons shipments to Afghanistan turned out to be more complex and deadly than she'd initially envisioned. "The police said Fred died in a random armed robbery." She offered up the explanation without any real conviction.

"I think it's enough of a coincidence to make me nervous. And now Lachlan is dead, meaning the only person left who's seen the information we know of is you." Emily grabbed Sophia's hands and squeezed. "You need to tell my dad."

A kernel of righteous anger slowly took shape in Sophia's gut. She reveled in it, nurtured it to replace the sorrow, guilt, and helplessness. She'd never gotten the chance to tell Lachlan the truth about her arrangement with Admiral Dane. In truth, even if she had, he might have seen it as a betrayal because of his experience with Nadia. Now Lachlan was dead, and the admiral was the only person she trusted to find out who killed him and, possibly, Fred.

Lachlan's enemies probably thought they were safe, their loose ends tied up.

Not if she could help it. Her fingers curled into fists, the bite of nails into flesh a welcome pain. Her tears dried.

"Bring me my phone."

The brisk knock on her door the following morning made her jump even though she'd expected it. Sophia glanced at Emily and uncurled her legs from the sofa cushion.

"Ready or not...." Emily's demeanor lacked its usual joie de vivre. She pushed herself off the couch and went to open the door. "Hi, Dad."

"Why didn't you tell your mother and me you were stateside?" The admiral stepped over the threshold and embraced his daughter.

Emily rolled her eyes, but not before Sophia caught the flash of guilt. "I've been busy. This is a business trip."

Butterflies attacked Sophia's insides, and her smile took effort. So did meeting the admiral's eyes. She rubbed sweaty palms on her jeans and stood. "You didn't have to fly down from Connecticut." It would have been easier to confess her sins over the phone than face-to-face, where she'd have to witness his disappointment.

He folded her into a warm embrace, and for a too-brief moment, she soaked up his strength and tried to make some of it her own. His gaze, when she finally met it, was steady and knowing. "This conversation needed to be in person."

"Would you like something to drink?" she offered.

"No, thank you." He settled into one of the club chairs while she sat on the couch and figured out how to begin.

"You asked me to help you find evidence that Lachlan Mackay was trafficking weapons in Afghanistan. And I did, but I didn't tell you before now because, well, things got complicated."

Other than a slight quirk of one salt and pepper brow, the admiral stayed silent while Sophia told him about Roshan Haider, what she'd found in Fred's office, and that she'd taken it to Lachlan, who'd professed his innocence and asked her to hold off on telling anyone until he could find out who set him up.

"And now, Lachlan's dead, and I wonder if Fred's death was really a random crime." The lump in her throat had grown to the point she could barely speak.

Admiral Dane regarded her steadily. "Why didn't you tell me earlier? You weren't supposed to get involved."

"I'm sorry. I didn't want to implicate an innocent person and thought I could help."

The admiral's piercing gunmetal gaze narrowed on her. "Who was Lachlan Mackay to you that you were willing to risk your career and your safety for him?"

The flush heating her entire face didn't go unnoticed. She stared at her clasped hands rather than meet the knowing eyes of a man who was a father figure to her.

"I'm sorry." He leaned forward to wrap her hands in his larger ones. "I should never have asked you to spy on your colleagues. You have a big heart, Sophia. Don't ever apologize for it, but now, you stay far away from this mess." His expression hardened. "Send me everything you've managed to dig up. I'll make some calls. We must ensure the weapons arriving in Kabul don't reach their intended destination."

Guilt stabbed her at the overwhelming sense of relief. "Lachlan was a decent, honorable man." Her throat swelled up. "We need to clear his name."

"We'll see." The admiral stood, looking every inch the respected and feared SEAL leader. "If Lachlan Mackay or anyone else at LAI has hidden skeletons, I'll unearth them."

Emily accompanied her father downstairs to see him off.

Sophia unlocked the sliding glass door and stepped onto the balcony. It was a beautiful day, the vast expanse of bird's egg blue sky marred only by wisps of cirrus clouds and streaks of jet contrails—the kind of day that normally lifted her spirits.

If she'd handed the information over to Admiral Dane earlier, would Lachlan still be alive? Or would he be in prison and hating her for betraying him? It was too late to what-if. Lachlan was dead, and she would do what she could to make sure he didn't end up the fall guy for someone else's crimes.

CHAPTER
TWENTY-FOUR

"I KNOW THE PAST two weeks have been hard on everyone." Jared's somber voice carried across the main conference room at LAI.

Sophia tuned out the rest of her boss's speech. Every time she closed her eyes, she saw Lachlan's car in flames, with him inside. She didn't want to hear empty platitudes about him. She wanted justice.

Her head snapped up at the sound of her name. Somehow, her colleagues had all filed out without her realizing it, leaving just her and Jared in the room.

Something, some expression she couldn't interpret, passed over his face and was gone in an instant, but it was enough to put up her guard.

"Could you come to my office?" He motioned for her to follow.

She had to walk fast to keep up with his long legs. He and Lachlan seemed to forget at times she was a short woman in high heels. A flash of grief hitched her stride, and she tamped it down with a firm press of her lips.

He motioned her toward the settee in the corner. "I'd offer you a drink, but it's a bit early."

She smoothed her olive knit dress and sat, the leather cool against the back of her knees. It creaked beneath Jared's weight when he settled next to her. "I'm fine. I need to be at work." The last part was true, at least. "Lachlan was murdered. We need to tell the police about Roshan Haider."

The look of pity on Jared's face stiffened her spine. "The police haven't released an official cause of the explosion yet. If it turns out to be a deliberate act, I'll tell them everything I know about Haider." He gave her hand a pat that made her teeth clench. "Trust me. There's nothing we can do for Lachlan. My concern now is for you and your safety."

Trust me. Lachlan had said the same thing. Now he was dead, and she was trapped in a web of lies. "What about Fred?"

Jared frowned. "What about Fred?"

"Why was he in DC late at night when he lives twenty-five miles away, in Chantilly? Aren't you the least bit concerned that two of your employees have died in mysterious circumstances in two weeks?"

"What are you implying? Maybe he was meeting someone for dinner or a drink. It's DC. Fred was in the wrong place at the wrong time. His death has nothing to do with Lachlan." Something shifted in Jared's eyes, like a shade had lowered, leaving them devoid of emotion in a way that made Sophia's neck shiver. "Unless you know something you aren't telling me?"

Her inner voice whispered at her to stop talking. No one could blame her for being paranoid, given everything that had happened, but she wasn't the only one at LAI keeping secrets. And until she knew who else was, no one, not even Jared, could be trusted.

"I don't know anything more than you do."

The need to escape flooded her muscles, vaulting her off the couch and toward the door. *Damn you for dying, Lachlan Mackay.* "And don't worry about me. Roshan, or whoever was behind Lachlan's death, got the revenge he wanted."

She fled to her office before saying anything more that might make Jared suspicious. Lachlan had kept the papers she'd gotten from Fred's office. Maybe Fred had made other copies.

There was only one way to find out. She dug her phone out of her purse in case she needed to take any photos to send to Admiral Dane, picked up her coffee mug, and pretended to head for the breakroom. Penny was typing away on her computer and didn't look up. Jared's door was closed. Christian and Rob's offices were further down the hall.

Fred's door was closed but thankfully, unlocked. She slipped inside after a furtive glance to ensure no one was watching.

She combed through his folders, scanning for anything relevant. If there was a smoking gun in all of this paperwork, she wasn't finding it.

Fred's computer. She booted it up, then searched every inch of his desk and beneath his keyboard for a clue to his login credentials. Her access code would get her nowhere. Rob set the system up to allow employees access to computer files related to their particular division and general corporate HR and IT files. She didn't have permission to access Fred's files, and with Fred gone, she wasn't sure who did other than Jared.

"Dammit." She wasn't big on cursing, out loud at least, but it fit the moment. Crossing her arms with an exasperated sigh, she glared at the computer. *Now what?*

Maybe Lachlan hadn't taken the information with him when he left for Kabul.

It was a slim hope but worth pursuing. She made sure Penny's back was turned before sneaking out of Fred's office and down the hall toward Lachlan's. When she passed the breakroom, the smell of coffee lit up her olfactory receptors.

Her gaze dropped to her hands. She had her phone but must have left her coffee mug in Fred's office. She'd get it later.

The brass nameplate on Lachlan's door brought another stab of grief. She traced the letters of his name, pretending she was touching him.

Glancing around to ensure she could get inside unnoticed, she snuck in and closed the door, making as little noise as possible. She opened Lachlan's cabinet drawers and brought a stack of folders to his desk.

A faint hint of his woodsy scent clung to his high-backed chair. She pressed her nose into the leather, her heart giving a painful lurch.

She thumbed through the folders. So far, she was coming up empty. Lachlan wouldn't have left damning evidence lying around for anyone to find. What was she thinking? The adrenaline and caffeine she'd been running on since arriving at work this morning washed away on an ebbing tide of disappointment. She needed a way into Lachlan's and Fred's computers.

The door opened without warning. She jumped, her heart taking off on a sprint.

Jared's narrowed gaze shifted from her to the files on Lachlan's desk and back. "What are you doing?"

Her pulse thumped like a bass drum, so loud in her ears she had to wonder if Jared could hear it. "I needed additional information for the government report." She returned the files to Lachlan's cabinet and palmed her phone. "I'm finished."

Jared's flat stare did nothing to calm her runaway pulse. He stepped aside, allowing her to slide past him into the corridor. She strolled toward her office with deliberate casualness, not looking back, but the twitch in her shoulders told her his gaze followed. Every day she kept the information on the weapons shipments from him, she dug herself a deeper hole.

Her phone vibrated against her sweaty palm. *Private caller.* Usually, she wouldn't answer, but desperate hope that it was Lachlan had her pressing the green button. "Hello?"

"Sophia?" The man had a deep voice she didn't recognize.

"Who's this?"

"I'm a friend of Lachlan's. Are you alone?"

The question froze her in her tracks. She looked around. Penny's desk sat empty, and Jared had been headed in the opposite direction. She whispered anyway. "Who are you? How did you get my number?"

"Nathan Long. I got it from Lachlan. In case something happened to him." She gasped, but he kept speaking. "I have information to give you. In person."

He had a drawl. *Southern, maybe Texan.* His name seemed vaguely familiar. Lachlan had wanted her to stay with his friend when he went to Kabul. "The SEAL?"

"Yes. Did he mention me? I'm flattered." A hint of humor coated the man's words.

Now that she thought about it, she remembered Lachlan mentioning a SEAL team involved in the hostage rescue mission. Nathan must have been there. "When can we meet and where?"

"My place, as soon as you can get here. I'll give you the address."

Her inner voice waved a big red flag. What if he wasn't who he said he was, and she was walking into a trap? If the past two weeks had taught her anything, it was that she couldn't be so trusting anymore. "Let's meet in a public place."

"What I have to show you can't happen in a public place. Look, I swear on my honor and Lachlan's memory, my sole intention is to protect you and find out who blew up our boy."

She flinched at his casual reference to Lachlan's death. And why did he think he needed to protect her? What did he know?

"How do I know for sure you're his friend?"

"The art gallery."

"Art gallery?" Now she sounded like a clueless parrot.

"You talked him into buying the painting that now hangs in his living room. He had a picture of you posing with it on his phone."

The Highlander charging into battle.

"He bought it?" She swallowed past the lump in her throat. "I didn't know."

"Why doesn't that surprise me," Nathan replied in a tone dry as the Sonoran desert.

He purchased the painting because she liked it. And yet, he hadn't told her. She cleared her throat to keep the tremble out of her voice. "Are...were you and Lachlan close?"

Did he trust you?

It took Nathan a moment to reply. "Yeah, we're pretty tight. Been through some shi—ah stuff together."

He can't use the past tense, either. If Nathan had also been through that terrible mission, she knew what "stuff" bonded the two men. She sighed. "Where do you live?"

It might be foolish, but she wasn't passing up the opportunity to meet someone who could tell her more about Lachlan. She wanted to know so many things about the man she'd been falling in love with and risked her career to avenge.

Nathan rattled off his address. "Come alone."

She hung up, entered his information into her phone, then called Emily.

"Did you get what you needed to send to my dad?" Emily asked.

"No." Sophia entered her office and closed the door. "Not yet. Listen, Emily, a man contacted me. Said he was Lachlan's friend. He has information about Lachlan, and he wants to meet. At his home."

"Have you ever met this guy?"

She knew where this was going and grimaced. "No, but Lachlan mentioned him once."

Emily snorted in her ear. "Tell him you'll only meet in a public place. I'll come with you."

"I tried that." She flopped into her chair and leaned back to stare at the ceiling. "He said he couldn't show me the information in public." Straightening, she opened her work calendar on her computer. "I'm leaving as soon as I think up a good excuse for being out of the office."

"Are you crazy?" Sophia moved the phone away from her ear at Emily's screech. "You're not going alone."

The calm Sophia forced into her voice didn't match the tightness in her chest. "I'm sure he's who he says he is. He knew something about Lachlan and me that only Lachlan could have told him."

"Sophia, I don't—"

"His name is Nathan Long. He's a SEAL, or at least was, which means your dad could run a check on him. I'll give you his address. Send in the cavalry if you don't hear from me in two hours."

"Sure, of course, you could be dead by then," Emily grumbled. "Be careful. Even though you believe Lachlan was set up, we don't know who's a good guy or a bad guy yet."

"I will." She recited Nathan's address to Emily and hung up. Her attempt to get more information from Fred and Lachlan's files had been a bust. Maybe Nathan knew something that would prove useful to clearing Lachlan's name and finding the person behind his murder.

An hour later, she veered onto Hampton Road in Fairfax Station, tapping out an anxious rhythm on the steering wheel.

Following Nathan's directions, she took a left at the second side street, then a right. Tall trees bordered a narrow gravel road. She braked to a stop in front of a steel security gate anchored between two brick columns flanking the driveway to what must be Nathan's home. Compound was more like it. A foreboding red light blinked like an omen from the security camera angled straight at her face.

No Trespassing signs dotted the tree line. These ones featured crosshairs with the words, *You are here,* in the center.

The trailer from every horror movie featuring a cabin in the woods flashed behind Sophia's eyes. Emily was right. This was a bad idea.

The steel gate rattled open.

If she was going to back out, now was the time. She swallowed hard and maneuvered her car forward. The gate shut behind her with a clang, like prison bars trapping her on the wrong side of freedom. Another sign posted around the bend warned her she was no longer a trespasser but a target. Trees lining the gravel road loomed overhead and blocked the sun.

The driveway ended at a tan, ranch-style brick home with a two-car garage that looked to be a later addition. A man seated in an Adirondack chair on a white-trimmed chair rail front porch rose to his feet and ambled down the steps toward her.

Her jaw dropped. The man was massive—even taller than Lachlan and more muscular. He had on a form-fitting black t-shirt with a skull graphic and the words *God Will Judge Our Enemies—We'll Arrange the Meeting*. The outfit, combined with his short, dirty-blond hair and the light brown stubble below his cheeks, made him look like a member of an outlaw biker gang.

She stepped reluctantly from the car, clutching the driver's door to her front like a shield even as her inner voice screamed to jump back in and lock the doors.

"Hello, darlin'." The scary stranger grinned, showing straight, white teeth. He plucked her fingers from their grip on the car door and kissed the back of her knuckles. Striking crystal blue eyes twinkled over their joined hands.

She forgot to breathe for a different reason now. The smile transformed his ruthless features, making him appear more like a Hemsworth brother—a taller, rougher version of Thor. He let go of her hand, and she sagged from the sudden letdown of adrenaline.

His eyes narrowed on her. "You all right?"

Her nod was a little too vigorous. "Fine, I'm fine." *Now that I'm pretty sure I'm not going to die.*

"I'm Nathan, by the way." He motioned her toward the house.

She preceded him up the four steps onto the porch and through a blue-gray front door into a surprisingly cozy if dated, kitchen and breakfast nook containing an oval-shaped table and four ladderback chairs beneath a bay window. The kitchen opened to a sunken living room with a brick fireplace and a sliding glass door that led to a back deck.

The oil painting over the mantle was striking—a lone cowboy on horseback, surrounded by cattle, facing the deep russet ball intersecting the distant horizon. She brushed past the leather sofa to get a closer look.

Between Nathan Long's accent and décor, she'd bet money he was a product of the Lone Star state.

"Can I get you something to drink?" Nathan called from the kitchen.

"Some water would be nice, thank you. Then you can tell me why you needed me to come here."

"*Leannan.*"

That one word, spoken by a ghost, stopped time. Sophia's heartbeat seemed to pause before it started again at a gallop.

It can't be.

She squeezed her eyes shut. She'd seen his car.

It wasn't possible.

Wild, untamed hope flooded her, one she strangled with a ruthless mental grip. If she turned around and Lachlan wasn't there, she'd break all over again.

Pivoting slowly, she kept her gaze directed at the floor until it collided with a pair of black boots. She stopped, inhaled a ragged breath, then continued up legs encased in crisp blue jeans, over a flat stomach and molded chest covered by a black, long-sleeved shirt, before coming to a stop on a familiar chiseled face. A face covered in cuts, scrapes, black stubble, and white bandages. Piercing emerald eyes stared back at her.

"You're dead," she whispered. "I saw—"

The room swayed.

Lachlan lunged and grabbed her by the elbows before her knees gave out. "Not yet."

She flattened her palms on his chest—soft cotton over warm, hard flesh—not a figment of her imagination. Sobs formed at the base of her spine and broke free, constricting her lungs. She threw her arms around him, clung to his muscular frame, and wrapped herself in his warm, familiar scent. His heart pounded a robust and steady rhythm beneath her cheek. "Oh, thank God."

Without warning, rage, visceral and hot, erupted like a volcano and flowed into her fingertips. She pushed against Lachlan's chest and stepped back, swinging.

Before it could make contact with his cheek, his hand captured hers in a firm grip. Regret shadowed his eyes. "It's not that I don't deserve it, but my face canna take any more damage at the moment."

"You let me think you were dead. I *mourned* you." Tears formed, spilling down her cheeks, of grief or anger, she wasn't sure.

Surprise flared in his eyes, fueling her anger. Did he not believe she'd be devastated by his death?

"I needed to regroup, figure out who to trust." He dropped her hand and left her to go to the kitchen. The hitch in his gait, noticeable when he grew fatigued, now was hard to ignore.

"And you didn't think you could trust me?" Pain bloomed in her chest.

Of course he didn't. He wouldn't have waited almost two days to tell her he was alive if he had. Dread unfurled in her stomach. And, thinking he was dead, she'd told Admiral Dane all of Lachlan's secrets.

She'd figure out how to tell Lachlan that news later. "The car. The police said it was yours. Someone was in it."

Lachlan fetched two glasses from an upper cabinet. He filled each glass with water from a pitcher in the fridge and shuffled back to her, handing her one. "Aye, it was my car. I was a lucky bastard. Jeremy Powell wasn't."

She gasped. *Poor Jeremy*. She'd just seen him when he returned her car to her.

Lachlan nodded, his expression carved in granite. She wanted to hold him, feel the life flowing through him, but his body language forbade it. The few inches separating them felt like miles.

"You must go to the police and tell them you're alive."

"And what do you think will happen?" His accent thickened on a tide of fury, his r's rolling like cresting waves. "They'll want tae ken why, and inevitably, the weapons shipments will come up. I have no way tae prove I'm no' an arms trafficker. I need to stop the shipment arriving in Kabul this week from getting ta Khan, and I canna do it if I'm in jail."

"I can help." She swallowed past a throat gone tight. Admiral Dane was Lachlan's only hope at this point. He couldn't expose himself.

She had to find a way into LAI's computers and send the admiral everything she could find that might help exonerate Lachlan.

"Sophia," Nathan spoke up, and she shifted her focus to the other dangerous man in the room. "Tell me about the documents you found in Fred Biller's office."

She frowned and glanced at Lachlan.

"They were in my car." He answered her unspoken question before gesturing toward the dining nook. "Go ahead."

Nathan grabbed a chair and held it out. She dropped onto the seat and gave him a smile of thanks. "I don't know anything more than what I already gave to Lachlan. And I looked, this morning, in fact." She bit her lip and sent Lachlan a hesitant glance. "In both Fred's and Lachlan's offices."

Nathan gave her an encouraging smile. "That's all right. I'd like to hear it from your perspective."

Her lips pursed. *Where to begin?* She leaned forward and braced her elbows on the table. "Fred Biller was responsible for the reports we submit to the government on our contracts in Afghanistan. He asked me to help gather data for the upcoming report, which I did, for both Lachlan's division and Christian Meier's Global Development division. Fred called me into his office to tell me there was missing documentation for Lachlan's division involving additional weapons shipments to Afghanistan. Before I could get more information regarding the discrepancy, Fred was killed." Her throat closed up. The more she thought about it, the more Fred's untimely death seemed like too much of a coincidence.

Nathan grunted. "Did Biller bring this to anyone else's attention?"

"I don't know—I don't think so. Once I found the papers in Fred's office and realized their significance, I took them to Lachlan and...." Her voice trailed off.

Metal scattered across the surface lot, the burning car, the blue tarp.

Lachlan squeezed her hand, but the touch was gone so quickly she might have imagined it.

"Sorry." She took a sip of water.

Lachlan stared into space, a tic along his jawline the only indication emotion simmered beneath his surface.

Nathan leaned back and stretched his arms over his head. Sophia got a quick glimpse of muscled abs but winced when his spine gave a snap, crackle, pop. "I thumbed through reports from the Metropolitan Police's homicide branch. Fred Biller was shot point-blank in the heart—a kill shot. The DC police have no leads on his killer, nor do they know why he was in Adams-Morgan alone, late on a Tuesday evening when he lived in Chantilly and had no known friends or acquaintances in the District."

Sophia eyed the big man curiously. "How did you access the report on Fred's death?"

Nathan smiled. "I have my ways."

"Don't ask. It's better if you don't know," Lachlan said. He and Nathan exchanged a look.

Sophia suppressed a shudder. It seemed she wasn't the only one who suspected Fred's death hadn't been random. Having those suspicions confirmed didn't make her feel any better.

Lachlan spoke up, directing his comments to Nathan. "I sent a back-channel message to Ryder to let him know I'm alive and to monitor Burkette's movements. He'll have to see who shows up to retrieve those weapons on his own. I told him he could let his number two, Caleb Varella, in on the plan, so he had back up. You and I need to focus on whoever set me up and tried to kill me. Haider may be involved, but he's not the mastermind."

She waved a hand to get both men's attention. "Hello? I can help."

The dismissive look Lachlan gave her set her teeth on edge. "I don't want you putting yourself in any more danger."

Her heart stopped, then restarted with a painful thumping rhythm. She had to tell Lachlan about her meeting with the admiral and convince him she'd done the right thing. "I need to find a way to access LAI's computers."

"Nathan can do that."

Nathan shifted in his seat and sent Lachlan a careful look. "I could get in faster if Sophia could access the main server and install a backdoor for me. I can tell her how to do it."

"No." Lachlan's tone brooked no argument. "It's not safe." He turned his attention to her, his brows drawn low over his eyes and his jaw set. "I'll have Nathan escort you to your condo to pack a bag. I don't want you going back to LAI."

"You don't tell me you're alive until now, and you snap your fingers and expect me to meekly do as I'm told? Really?" She narrowed her eyes at him. "You're a stubborn ass."

A strange gurgling sound came from Nathan. She glanced his way to see him coughing into his fist. "I'll rustle up some lunch. Sophia, you haven't lived until you've had the Long family's Hair-On-Fire Texas chili and homemade cornbread."

CHAPTER TWENTY-FIVE

LACHLAN SENT HIS BOOT into Nathan's shin. Again. The former SEAL needed to keep his eyes above Sophia's chin, cheeky bastard. Him and his bloody stories of his Texas childhood, flirting shamelessly with Sophia while Lachlan pretended to be fascinated with his lunch.

Nathan sent him a sly grin. Lachlan waited until Sophia's attention was on her bowl before using his middle finger—and only his middle finger—to scratch the itch on his forehead.

The snort from Nathan had Sophia looking up, her head swiveling between Lachlan and Nathan as if she realized she wasn't in on the joke.

Lachlan still was feeling a wee bit miffed at her refusal to see reason and had stayed quiet during the meal, despite both Sophia's and Nathan's efforts to draw him into the conversation. As the meal wore on, she got quiet. Her shoulders dipped. She didn't laugh as freely at Nathan's attempts to amuse her.

He sighed. He was being an arse.

"Lunch was yummy, Nathan. I'm impressed." Sophia gathered her plates and silverware from the table and carried them into the kitchen.

Nathan followed. "My mama told me with the way I throw back food, I needed to learn to cook." He gave Sophia a smile that made Lachlan's teeth grind. Throwing a casual salute in Lachlan's direction, he winked at Sophia. "I'm headed to my war room. Y'all play nice."

Nathan's office door clicking shut was overly loud in the strained silence. Sophia wandered into the living room and stood, staring out the sliding glass door to the deck.

The spicy chili sat uneasily in Lachlan's stomach. He stood, cleared his dishes, and started a pot of coffee. Bitterness dug its claws into him. Sophia had believed in him—thought he was a good man even though she knew he was damaged. With her, he'd allowed the tiniest glimmer of hope to penetrate his defenses, to let down his guard and trust again. Contemplate a future that wasn't all about penance and retribution.

Instead, betrayal found him again, and another dead soul haunted his dreams.

He'd hurt her by not telling her sooner he was alive.

When the coffee finished brewing, he poured her a cup and added cream, just as she liked—enough to create a pale tinge to the dark brew, but not enough to make it milky. The mug warmed his palm as he brought it to where she stood in the living room. Her posture was so rigid he thought it might shatter at the sound of his voice. He held the drink over her shoulder as a peace offering because he had no idea what to say.

For a moment, it seemed as if she would ignore his gesture. Then she turned, accepted the mug, and glanced at its contents. "You didn't add sugar, did you?"

"No sugar." He let his gaze wander over the olive-colored dress she wore. The soft fabric draped her curves and tied at the waist like she was a gift to be unwrapped. Despite his best intentions, he reached out a finger and brushed the delicate ridge of her collarbone, half-expecting her to slap his hand away.

But she didn't. Her breasts lifted on a sharp inhale, her cheeks turning a rosy pink, and he couldn't help the visceral surge of satisfaction. She might be angry with him, but she still wanted him.

"Nathan told me you bought the painting." Her eyes darkened with shadows, another black mark on his soul.

"I know."

"Why didn't you tell me?" The hurt in her voice twisted his insides.

He started to conjure up a suitable answer, but after everything he'd put her through, she deserved the truth, even if it left him exposed. "I bought it because I thought if I studied it long enough, I'd see myself the way you see me."

Her eyes grew moist at his confession. A tear escaped that he wiped away with the pad of his finger. "Please don't cry, *mo leannan*." He wasn't worth it.

"I thought you were dead," her anguished whisper was a dagger to his chest. She traced the bandage near his eye with a delicate touch before her lashes swept down, hiding from him.

He captured her hand, and his lips stroked her soft palm in a word-less apology. She was real. Flesh and blood. And for some mad reason, she cared about him. His fingers itched with the need to touch, to claim what he didn't deserve. More than ever, he needed her light to banish his darkness.

There was nothing sweet or gentle about the way he took her mouth. She tasted of coffee and spices, her mouth wet silk, and she kissed him back.

The mug she held needed to go. He broke the kiss long enough to place it on the fireplace mantle. Her hands slid up his chest to tangle in the hair at his nape. She raised herself onto her toes and yanked his head down to reclaim his lips.

Her assertiveness smashed any thoughts he'd held of restraint. He lifted her and pinned her to the wall next to the sliding door, her curves cushioning his hard angles. A wave of lust shot straight to his cock, hardening it to the point of pain. He reacted with an instinctive thrust.

The sound she made against his lips threatened to shred the last of his sanity.

What was it about this tiny slip of a female that vanquished the ugliness in his head to wrap around the heart he thought he no longer possessed? She made him want more from life.

"Lachlan." Her voice, breathless and needy, egged him on.

He slid his hand beneath her neckline to cup her breast and teased her nipple to a stiff peak. His mouth followed, nipping delicate skin, then laving the redness with his tongue. Her nails dug into his scalp, erotic pricks of pleasure/pain, her soft cries of pleasure his reward.

She was burning him alive, and he needed to be inside her. He set her on her feet and tore at the ties keeping her dress in place. The material fell open to expose creamy skin mottled with a rosy flush that spilled over her breasts and advanced to her cheeks.

Her wanton expression burned a hole in his brain. He dropped to his knees, ignoring the pain of new and old wounds, and brushed his mouth over the satin-covered juncture between her legs, breathing in her arousal. She was already wet for him, and he wanted a taste.

Lust tightened his muscles and fisted his cock. His need to put his mouth on her would have to wait. He eyed the hardwood floor, unsure if he could make it to the bedroom before he was so deep inside her that he wouldn't know where he ended and she began.

A loud rap on the kitchen wall brought him to his feet instantly. He ignored his throbbing leg, shielding Sophia with his body.

"Sorry to interrupt." There was no mistaking the amusement twinkling in Nathan's eyes.

Lachlan swallowed his irritation and ordered his body to stand down. "Give us a minute." Nathan gave a quick nod and disappeared back to his war room.

Behind him, Sophia's withdrawal was palpable. Lachlan faced her. He scrubbed his face with a sigh and winced at the sting of the cuts he'd forgotten about. If Nathan hadn't interrupted, he'd have taken her on the floor like an inconsiderate prick. He'd lost control, and he couldn't afford to lose it again until he dealt with his enemies.

She had re-tied her dress, her gaze directed somewhere over his left shoulder. "What are you planning to do next?"

He took in her flushed cheeks and subdued tone. Regret stabbed him. She was embarrassed, and it was his fault. "Find out who set me up. Call Jared and tell him you're taking time off. You'll stay here, where I can keep you safe."

She crossed her arms, the discomfort from a moment ago replaced by temper. "What excuse would I give Jared? Besides, like I already told you, I can access information at LAI that could prove your innocence." Dammit, if her big eyes didn't fill with tears again, pleading. "Why won't you let me help you?"

Her tears unmanned him. "*Leannan*, please. It's better if you disappear for a while. We don't know who the enemy is yet." Someone at LAI helped frame him. Here at least, he and Nathan could protect Sophia.

A disbelieving laugh tumbled from her lips. "What about you? You're dead, remember? And it won't be long before the police discover it wasn't you in the car. They'll be looking for you."

"Don't worry. I know how to blend."

She eyed him up and down. "Yeah, like no one will notice you." She turned away, mumbling, "Especially if they have two X chromosomes."

He couldn't help the grin. Leaning close, he let himself pretend they had the kind of relationship filled with lighthearted banter. "Do you think women find me attractive?"

She whirled on him with a huff. "At least your ego is still intact. Now, if you'll excuse me, I have to use the ladies' room." Her lips thinned. "Then I'm leaving."

Lachlan's amusement vanished. He gazed warily at the rigid set of her back as she marched away, her heels striking so hard he half expected to find dents in the wood.

Nathan reemerged and poured himself a cup of coffee. "How did she take your telling her to stay here, out of sight, for a while?"

He scowled, telling his friend without words how well the conversation had gone.

Nathan saluted with his mug. "Ah, redheads. They're something, aren't they?"

"They're stubborn and willful." He shouldered Nathan aside for the glass carafe and a clean cup.

"You're doomed, amigo." Nathan's grin was unrepentant. He slapped Lachlan on the shoulder and strolled back to his office.

Lachlan took a bracing sip of hot liquid and glared down the hall where Sophia had disappeared. A needle of pain stabbed his right eye, making it twitch.

He had a bad feeling Nathan was right.

"Hey, Lach," Nathan's voice from the war room carried a note of tension. "Heads up. We've got company."

Lachlan stalked into Nathan's office. The SEAL's big hands danced over his computer keyboard. A few keystrokes later, all three monitors displayed live camera feeds from around Nathan's property.

The center monitor showed the front gate, and the sporty red Lexus convertible parked at the entrance. A blonde in a khaki trench coat stabbed repeatedly at the intercom button as she peered at the camera above her head.

Nathan looked at him. "Any idea who our guest is? She looks vaguely familiar."

"Yes. Sophia's friend. Get rid of her." He didn't need anyone else knowing he was alive. Not yet. He'd have to convince Sophia to keep the fact that he was still breathing from her friend.

"Ah, the blonde who drove Sophia to work after her run-in with Roshan Haider." Nathan opened the connection on the intercom. "Yes?" His curt tone carried a distinct lack of welcome.

The blonde seemed undeterred. "Nathan Long? I need to speak to you. It's urgent."

"Ma'am, do you see all those 'No Trespassing' signs? Whatever you're selling, I'm not buying."

"I'm not selling anything, but let me tell you what I know." Emily inched closer to the intercom and lowered her voice. "I *know* you contacted Sophia Russo with information about Lachlan Mackay. I *know* she met you here this morning, and I *know* she hasn't been seen or heard from since."

Nathan unmuted the intercom. "Sorry, but I *know* I can't help you."

"Oh, this is ridiculous," Emily sputtered. She folded her arms across her chest and glared into the lens. "Sophia was supposed to contact me"—she made a show of raising her arm to check the elegant watch on her wrist—"an hour ago. Which she hasn't." Her light blue gaze swung back to the camera. "I swear to God, if you don't let me in, I will climb over this gate, march down your driveway, and pound on your door."

Lachlan bent over so he could whisper in his friend's ear. "Her name is Emily. She's a college friend of Sophia's. See if you can find out anything more about her."

"Easily done." Nathan's fingers danced over the computer keyboard. "Let's backdoor our way into a few government databases and see what pops up. Running a facial recognition scan—what the fuck?"

Nathan's exclamation drew Lachlan's gaze back to the center monitor. Emily was scaling Nathan's gate. She dropped to the other side and began to march up the driveway.

Nathan frantically disabled his security then stood and grabbed his Sig Sauer. He gestured Lachlan toward one of the monitors. "See if the computer spits out her details. I'll go welcome our guest."

Lachlan took Nathan's seat and scanned the information on the screen. *Emily Dane, political officer. Current station, US Embassy, Paris. Daughter of Admiral Porter Dane, former head of US Special Operations Command.*

He let the details the facial recognition software provided sink in. *Christ.* Emily Dane's father was none other than the former commander of Joint Special Operations Command in Afghanistan. The same bloody commander Lachlan had stood before and tried to explain how he'd been forced to kill the two people he'd been tasked to bring in alive.

This was a complication he didn't need. Wheeling out of the chair, he headed to the bathroom Sophia had sequestered herself in and rapped on the door.

"Sophia, open up. Please." The door cracked enough for him to shove his boot over the threshold. "Emily Dane is outside."

Her eyes flew wide. "Oh crap, I promised I'd call her by now. I completely forgot." She threw open the door and frowned when he blocked her attempt to get around him. "What's the problem? She's my best friend."

He leaned over and tried not to breathe in her scent or pay attention to the graceful whorls of her ear. "She doesn't know I'm alive. I think it's best if she remains ignorant of that fact for her safety and yours."

The green in Sophia's eyes sparked. "She knew I was meeting with Nathan this morning. Now you want me to lie to her?"

The look she shot him conveyed a bitterness that weighed on his conscience. "Why am I surprised? Distrust seems to be your default." She tried to elbow past him. "You may not trust her, but I do."

He continued to block her path. "And if she discovers I'm alive, it's not your life you're trusting her with—it's mine."

Guilt snagged him at her gasp, the hurt blooming in her eyes. "Until I know it's safe, I want you to stay out of sight. I mean it." He left her at the bathroom door, his neck tingling from the daggers her furious gaze was likely throwing at his back.

"You're a big jerk, you know that?" Before he could react, Sophia raced past him to the front door, threw it open, and stepped outside. "Emily."

Bloody Hell. Lachlan followed.

Nathan stood at the top of the steps with his back to the door, hands on hips, head bowed in defeat.

Lachlan speared his fingers through his hair to keep from wrapping an arm around Sophia and hauling her back into the house. He should have known she wouldn't listen. Emily was staring up at him open-mouthed.

"Why don't we invite Ms. Dane inside." Frustration knotted the back of his neck and colored his voice.

Emily marched up the stairs, brushed past Nathan like the six-foot-six SEAL was a minor inconvenience, and elbowed Lachlan aside to wrap Sophia in a hug. "Thank God, I was so worried." She gave Sophia a stern look. "You were supposed to check in."

"I know. I'm sorry." The guilt on Sophia's face found a home in Lachlan's chest.

The blonde released Sophia and turned on him with an accusing glare. "What kind of bastard lets people think he's dead?" She stabbed a finger at his chest. "You and your secrets have put Sophia in danger."

He bristled. "Which is why I had Nathan bring her here today. We'll make sure she stays safe. You should return to your job in Paris."

The woman's eyes narrowed, a dangerous flush staining her cheeks. "In other words, butt out?"

"Enough." Sophia's voice sliced through the room with a hard edge he'd never heard before. "Lachlan, I need to speak to Emily. Alone."

He glanced at Nathan, whose gaze was fixed on Emily Dane like he was trying to memorize every inch of her. Lachlan cleared his throat to break his mate from his trance.

The big man looked over at him and shrugged. Nathan grabbed a beer from the fridge and shuffled into the living room to settle into one of the leather armchairs in the living room.

Lachlan gritted his teeth and joined him, plopping his boots on the coffee table. Nathan took a long drag of his brew and grinned at him. He glared in return. Nothing was funny about this situation. Sophia needed to tell her friend to leave town, keep her mouth shut, and let him take care of everything.

"I cannot believe he didn't tell you he was alive sooner," Emily hissed. "What a jerk."

"Shh, keep your voice down." Sophia's gaze darted to the men seated in the living room and collided with Nathan's icy blue one. He winked before shifting his attention to linger on Emily. Lachlan sat stone-faced and didn't look her way.

When she turned back to Emily, she noticed Nathan wasn't the only one getting in some subtle scoping. "I haven't told Lachlan about my arrangement with your father yet. He'll think I betrayed him."

Emily whipped her head back toward Sophia. "You're trying to save him. Why would he think you betrayed him?"

"He has major trust issues. Remember what I told you the day he came to the condo and—" She paused, heat sweeping like a slow tide from her toes up to the tips of her ears at the memory of what had occurred after he arrived.

"You mean when you and he had S.E.X., Miss Prude?" Emily's lips pursed with an effort not to laugh.

"Yes." Sophia glared at her friend. "His female translator betrayed him and his team on a hostage rescue mission. People died, and Lachlan blames himself for trusting her." She paused, glancing again at the men in the living room. "He wants me to stay here so he can protect me, but I've got to find a way into LAI's computers. Your dad is the only one that can dig deep enough now to see through the trap someone laid to frame Lachlan for arms trafficking."

Emily's face pinched. "Maybe Lachlan is right. Whoever is behind this was willing to commit murder, possibly twice, if Fred Biller's death wasn't a crime of opportunity. Maybe you should lay low and let my dad handle this."

Sophia's head was already shaking before Emily finished. "What if the admiral stops at Lachlan and doesn't dig deeper? I know in my heart Lachlan is innocent. I need to find the information that will prove it."

"Are you sure he's innocent? Maybe he is involved and tried to double-cross his partner in crime, and that's why he was targeted." Sophia started to protest but stopped at Emily's raised palm. "I love you, but you tend always to think the best of people, even when it's not warranted."

Emily's comment stung. Sophia forced herself to assess the situation and her heart as realistically as possible. The evidence so far made Lachlan look guilty as hell. His past haunted him. He was a bad bet for a smart woman.

And she loved him anyway.

"What's the matter?" Emily whispered, "You just turned white as a sheet."

"Nothing." She needed time to process the revelation before telling anyone, even her best friend. "I understand your concerns, but I'm doing this. I have to."

Emily gave a pained sigh. "Okay." Her gaze slanted to the living room. "Let the fireworks begin."

The women huddled in the kitchen, their voices low. Lachlan's peripheral vision tracked their every twitch. When their heads lifted, he could tell they'd reached a decision. He and Nathan stood as they approached. Maybe Sophia's friend had talked some sense into her.

His gut twisted into a knot at the look in Sophia's eyes.

"I'm going home. And to work tomorrow."

Hell. No. "Sophia, that's not wise."

Her gaze turned steely. "Let me finish. I can help you more by showing up at LAI."

"It's not safe." His knuckles brushed the smooth skin of her cheek. "Stay here, just for a little while." He would fix everything.

"Trust that I'm trying to help you." Her eyes pleaded with him.

"I do trust you."

She gave him a sad smile. "If you trusted me, you would have told me you were alive sooner."

Her words put another arrow into his chest. He threw up his defenses, put his emotions in a box, and slammed the lid.

Fresh pain swamped Sophia's eyes. "I hate when you do that." Her chin lifted. "Emily and I are leaving."

What the hell did she want from him? He spun and gave everyone his back, stalking to the fireplace. Where had this stubborn streak come from? She didn't understand the danger. His fingers curled into fists. He felt like a grenade with a pulled pin. Pounding the bricks until his knuckles bled might release some of the pressure inside, but it would make everyone else question his mental status.

"Lachlan." Nathan's tone was careful. Lachlan knew he wouldn't like whatever his friend said next. "Whoever set you up and tried to kill you thinks they've succeeded. They probably don't consider Sophia much of a threat. Their guard will be down. Let Sophia go in and upload a backdoor into LAI's computer network so I can get in there. Give her one more day." Nathan's heavy hand landed on Lachlan's shoulders, his icy gaze somber. "It's the best chance you've got, amigo."

"Please." Sophia's soft plea pushed him over the edge.

"Fine," he snapped. "One day. Then I'll kidnap you myself if I have to and tie you to my bed if that's what it takes to keep you safe."

"Well, isn't that kinky," Emily drawled. Sophia blushed.

Nathan clapped his hands. "Everyone have a seat. Let's come up with a plan."

It didn't take long. Nathan downloaded a file from his computer to a thumb drive and gave it to Sophia. "Remember, you just need to log into the network, then download the file on the thumb drive. It'll do the rest."

Sophia's brows furrowed. "I'll need to use Jared or Rob's login credentials. They're the only ones with network-wide access to all the files on the system."

"No," Lachlan said. "It's too dangerous. I'll give you my login credentials. Nathan can access my files and breach the rest of the system from there."

"Actually," Nathan sent Lachlan an apologetic glance. "It'd be a lot faster if I got into the main network without having to break down firewalls, but I can do it."

"No," Lachlan repeated. His temple pounded, and the cuts on his face stung. He was knackered and pissed off. "I don't want Sophia doing anything that might call attention to herself. We don't know who's watching."

"I'll drive Sophia to and from work," Emily piped up. "We'll say her car is in the body shop getting repaired."

"Great, we have a plan." Sophia tucked the thumb drive into her purse and stood.

"Hold up, ladies. Until we get to the bottom of this, you need to watch your six." Nathan gestured at both women. "Give me your phones. I'll program in secure, untraceable numbers for Lachlan and me. If we don't hear all's well in your world by designated check-in times, we'll be coming after you weaponed up and with a bad attitude."

Lachlan hid a smile. *Crafty bastard.* It wasn't exactly what Lachlan was aiming for—he wanted Sophia to stay here and not return to her condo or LAI. But if Nathan planned to do what Lachlan thought, she wouldn't be completely unprotected.

Nathan held his hand out to Emily first, a clear challenge in his eyes. Lachlan knew what his mate was doing. Emily had grown up with a SEAL for a father, who was probably paranoid as hell, like Nathan. His request wouldn't seem out of the ordinary to her.

And if Emily agreed to Nathan's demands, Sophia would follow.

Emily gave Nathan a hard stare, then huffed out an irritated breath and slapped her phone into Nathan's waiting palm.

Lachlan held Sophia's gaze. *Make the right choice.* After a moment's hesitation, Sophia handed over her phone.

Bloody brilliant, mate. His friend had known just how to play it.

Nathan stood from the table, both phones engulfed in his massive palm. "Keep your daddy out of this, Miss Dane," he growled, "We don't need a retired Navy admiral sticking his nose into Lachlan's business."

Emily narrowed her eyes like she wanted to run her father's ceremonial sword through Nathan. "My *daddy*, as you put it in your charming colloquial way, does not need to protect Sophia or me." She glared at Lachlan. "And it's not my place to tell him about Lachlan's miraculous resurrection."

Her tone would shrivel most men's balls. It seemed to have the opposite effect on the big Texan. Nathan was fighting a grin.

Silence blanketed the room as Nathan excused himself to his war room. He returned a few minutes later and handed the women their phones. They gathered their coats and purses.

Pressure built behind Lachlan's eyes, and his lungs squeezed tight. He didn't like this plan. He was a damn prisoner in Nathan's home, relying on other people to prove his innocence.

If anything happened to Sophia...

"Lachlan?" A soft hand on his arm brought his gaze to Sophia's. "We're leaving now."

He nodded, not trusting himself to speak. He and Nathan followed the women out to Sophia's car.

Nathan, the tosser, leaned his forearms on Sophia's open window. "You can visit me anytime, sweetheart." The arsehole winked at her, then shot Lachlan a sly grin.

Lachlan made sure Nathan saw the fuck you in his eyes and ignored the other man's chuckle before bending down to peer in at Sophia. "I'll be seeing ya soon." It was both a warning and a promise. Sophia would not be collateral damage.

He stepped away, his gaze following her down the driveway until she rounded the bend, and Nathan's woodland buffer obscured his line of vision. "Did you put a tracker on their phones and Sophia's car?"

Nathan snorted. "I'm offended you had to ask."

CHAPTER
TWENTY-SIX

BILLIARDS WAS AN ANOMALY in the otherwise tony DC suburb of McLean, Virginia. True to its name, the dive bar boasted three pool tables down the center of the room, two dartboards on opposite sides of the bar, and mismatched worn wooden tables and chairs planted along the walls. A permanent haze of smoke fogged the air, clinging to the clothes and hair of anyone who passed through the doors.

Respectable people didn't come to Billiards. People who didn't want to be seen—or didn't fit the definition of polite society—did. It was one of Nathan's favorite places. Lachlan could see why. The former SEAL fit right in.

Tugging the bill of his ball cap lower, Lachlan followed Nathan through the haze to the bar. The bartender, a bloke with a crooked nose and cauliflower ears, took their orders and dropped two mugs of cold American brew on the sticky wooden surface before giving the counter a cursory wipe.

In the bar mirror, Lachlan sized up six members of a local motorcycle club shooting pool at the center table. Other than a slight tilt of their heads to Nathan when he walked in, they ignored them. The remaining occupants were a waitress with blonde hair, black roots and tired eyes and a sullen middle-aged man in a cheap suit perched on a stool at the rail. Neither gave him or Nathan more than a passing glance.

He threw down some cash for the beers. Nathan made his way to a table in the back corner, away from the activity at the billiard table, and sat, facing the door. He opened his laptop and began tapping away at the keys.

Lachlan joined him, his back to the side wall so he could view the bikers and the front door. "This is your office away from home?"

Nathan huffed out a laugh. "Hey, don't knock it. No one bothers me, and the food's pretty decent. Every once in a while, I need a change of scenery."

The waitress approached their table and gave Nathan a genuine smile. "Hey, handsome, I haven't seen you in a while."

Lachlan kept his head down and avoided eye contact. It was better that she not get a good look at him or the cuts and scrapes decorating his mug. Once the police discovered he hadn't been the one to die in his car, his face would likely be all over the evening news programs.

"Y'all gonna order food?"

Nathan flashed a broad smile, and Lachlan could almost see the waitress's knickers melt. "I'll have my usual, darlin', and so will my friend here."

"Sure thing, sugar."

After the waitress left, Lachlan asked, "What, exactly, am I being served?"

"Ribeye, medium rare, baked potato, and whatever veggie they're serving today." Nathan grinned. "Bikers like their meat and potatoes."

Lachlan took another glance around the poorly lit, smoky room. Like many pubs he'd been to in the UK, good food often came from the unlikeliest establishments.

Nathan's laptop dinged. "Ryder's coming online."

Lachlan scooted his chair closer to Nathan so he could see the monitor. Ryder's face appeared onscreen a moment later, his gaze focusing on Lachlan. "Mate, good to see you. That was a bloody close call."

"Aye, too close. You've kept it to yourself?"

"Everyone here thinks you're dead. Even Gilly and our SAS mates got wind of it." Ryder's lips turned down. "I felt like a tosser, not telling them, or my team, the truth. They've heard rumors. It stung a bit that they would even think you could be involved with Khan. Many of those men served with us."

Nathan swore.

Lachlan's snort had a caustic ring to it. "They've had to bribe, cajole, and threaten to get any scrap of actionable intelligence from the locals. If you spend too long in a place where corruption is as natural as breathing, it rubs off." He scowled into his beer. "I'll clear my name soon. Did you get what I asked for?"

Ryder held up a flash drive. "It took some doing. I didn't find anything connecting Burkette to Roshan Haider. However, he and Landry communicated a fair bit."

"That doesn't surprise me," Lachlan growled. "Anything interesting in those conversations?"

"Plenty of cryptic messages referencing an unnamed client. I wish I'd—" Ryder stopped mid-sentence when Nathan's forearm lifted from the table, his hand fisted in a modified tactical signal for stop.

Nathan lowered the lid on his laptop as the waitress approached the table with their food. Lachlan pulled on the brim of his cap and kept his head down.

"There you go. You boys let me know if y'all need another beer or something." After setting their plates in front of them, she trudged to the bikers at the billiards tables.

Nathan re-opened his laptop, and Lachlan gestured for Ryder to continue.

"Right, I wish I'd had access to Josh's phone earlier. The locational data we've collected is limited to the past several days, but if Nathan can decipher those messages and establish Khan as the client, and Josh's phone history shows he's been to Jalalabad...." Ryder's lips thinned.

Lachlan finished his team leader's sentence. "We may be able to prove Burkette delivered the weapons to Khan and took his orders directly from Jared Landry." *Shite.* He tilted his chair on its back legs until it met the wall behind him. "And given that it appears I authorized the shipments, Landry has a scapegoat if it all falls apart. Bastard."

He rubbed his chest absently. "Roshan Haider arrived in Afghanistan around the same time as the last shipment of weapons. Then he shows up and stalks Sophia. It's too much of a coincidence. I'm not ready to write off his involvement."

Nathan swallowed the piece of steak in his mouth and took another gulp of his beer. "How would Landry and Haider know each other?"

"I know Jared spent time in both Bagram and Kandahar like us. I asked him if he knew Nadia. He didn't seem familiar with her, so I'm not sure what his connection would be to Haider."

"If Jared's team ever used Nadia in the field, he would have remembered her." Ryder's gaze lost focus. "She was memorable."

Lachlan's front chair legs hit the floor with a loud thud, his response fast and furious. "She was a traitor who refused to surrender and almost killed you."

Ryder's brilliant blue eyes flashed with old pain even as his jaw hardened. "I remember."

One of the bikers peered over his pool cue in their direction as he lined up his shot. Lachlan stared back until the other man looked away.

He took a deep breath to calm himself. Silence hung as heavy in the air as tobacco smoke.

"I don't think I ever thanked you," Ryder said.

"For what?" Lachlan knew for what. He picked up his knife and fork and began sawing at his steak.

"She had me point-blank."

Lachlan gave a dismissive nod, looking anywhere but at the laptop screen and Ryder. "I did what I needed to do. Like you said to me before, it's time to let go."

Nathan broke up the silence that followed. "I think it's safe to assume if Jared Landry is behind this, he will regret hiring you."

A deadly calm filled Lachlan and iced his words. "If he is, he'll regret far more by the time I'm finished."

He directed his next words at Ryder. "Make sure you're there when that shipment is released to see who picks it up. Take Caleb with you. My money is on Burkette. Once you have proof, put a bug in Gilly's ear and see if our SAS mates and their Afghan counterparts can't intercept the shipment before it reaches Jalalabad. I don't want those guns and tactical gear ending up in Khan's hands."

He looked at Nathan. "As long as Landry believes I'm dead, I don't think he'll see Sophia as a threat." A slow burn started in his chest. "He's attracted to her, and he knows Sophia believes the best of everyone. He'll use that to his advantage, the bastard."

But if Landry found out Sophia was snooping in his business?

A cold sweat broke out on Lachlan's forehead.

Roshan's shoulders hunched as he glanced around him and quickened his steps. This section of East London was rough and the last place he wanted to be. Although he could fit in because of his ethnic background, his high-end clothing and expensive watch marked him as posh and not a resident of the area.

He located the pub, once frequented by the likes of Jack the Ripper. The Victorian-era establishment had its share of tourists during the day from all the tour companies capitalizing on its notoriety. This time of night, the pub was frequented mainly by East Enders or intrepid hipsters from West London.

Opening the double doors, he stepped in, glancing briefly at the blue and white Victorian-era tiling covering the walls floor to ceiling. The bloody Yank with his morbid sense of humor. His business partner's lackey made him nervous. The former soldier had dead eyes that Roshan didn't trust.

After his eyes adjusted to the dim lighting, he located the man he was supposed to meet in the far corner, seated at one of the small round tables.

Drawing a breath to steady himself, he approached and sat opposite the American. "What was so important we needed to meet tonight?"

The man regarded him lazily over the rim of his beer glass, his soulless black gaze eliciting a shiver that skittered across Roshan's neck. "Our operation has been compromised. My boss is shutting it down. We won't be needing your services any longer."

Tension knotted Roshan's shoulders. "Who knows?" His agreement with this man's employer had been lucrative but risky. If the UK or US governments had gotten wind of his involvement, he would lose his business, even if he had built in plausible deniability as to the contents of the shipments he'd facilitated from the US to Afghanistan.

"Relax. Everything will point to Mackay."

Blood rushed to Roshan's head. He forgot his fear of the American, stabbing with his finger to make his point. "And I told your...employer that putting Mackay in prison was no longer sufficient to avenge my sister. I thought he agreed."

The other man's lips lifted beneath his full brown beard in an expression that was more sneer than smile. "Didn't you hear? Mackay died the other day when his car exploded." He made a tutting sound. "Such a shame."

Shock had Roshan's hand dropping to the table. On its heels, a surge of primal satisfaction. "So it is done. My sister has been avenged."

The American's shoulders lifted. "Whatever. Mackay's dead, and our business arrangement is over. My boss is tying up loose ends as we speak. He wishes to extend his appreciation for your services. Did you bring the phone?"

"Yes." Roshan dug out the mobile he'd used exclusively with his contact in the States and with this man on occasion. He slid it across the table.

The man palmed it and stuffed it into an interior pocket in his jacket. He drained the last of his beer and stood. "It was a pleasure doing business with you." He brushed past Roshan and strolled through the bar.

Roshan watched him exit onto the street and disappear around the corner.

His shoulders drooped from the release of tension. As lucrative as this arrangement had been, he was glad it was over. The American business partner was ambitious and had taken risks he'd found surprising, given the man's desire to acquire power through the US political system.

He closed his eyes and absorbed the indistinct babble of other conversations around him, the smell of spilled ale, and the loud music. He couldn't wait to tell his father that the man who murdered Nadia was dead. The final step in restoring his family's honor would be to find someone in the British media willing to research Mackay's background and expose him as Nadia's killer. The tabloids wouldn't hesitate to investigate a former SAS soldier once news broke about his role in trafficking weapons to the Taliban.

Maybe he should have a celebratory drink as long as he was here. His parents, as observant Muslims, disapproved of alcohol consumption, but he occasionally allowed himself the indulgence. Perhaps a glass of champagne. After reviewing the menu, he dismissed the idea. Champagne here was only bottle service, and he had no interest in drinking an entire bottle alone in a part of town he'd rather not be in.

Besides, he had to be in the office early tomorrow.

Exiting the pub, he started in the direction of Liverpool Street Station before coming to a stop at the corner. Something crunched beneath his feet. Shattered glass covered the pavement. He tipped his head to examine the streetlight overhead. No wonder it was out, no doubt the casualty of neighborhood hooligans. He'd done as the American had asked and took the tube to get here, but he could bloody well take a cab back.

"Haider." The voice came from the side of the building to Roshan's left, making him jump. He could just make out the American's tall form.

Roshan licked his lips, his pulse skyrocketing. He should have called the cab at the bar and had it pick him up there. "I thought you left."

"My boss wanted me to give you one more thing. You know, tying up all those loose ends." The American's arm lifted.

Roshan saw the gun in the other man's hand a fraction too late.

CHAPTER
TWENTY-SEVEN

"WISH ME LUCK," SOPHIA said as she grabbed her purse and briefcase and opened the door of Emily's car. She'd figured out a plan to access LAI's computers, and luck was on her side—when she'd checked in with Penny yesterday after leaving Nathan's, she'd learned Jared was due to be out of the office all day. Today might be her only chance.

"Be careful." Emily shot her a worried look from the driver's seat. "You don't have to do this."

"I do. It might be the only way to prove Lachlan's innocence." She gave Emily's hand a reassuring squeeze. "Have a good last day of work in Foggy Bottom before you head back to Paris tomorrow. I'll see you later."

Penny was already at her desk when Sophia pushed open the glass doors leading to LAI's executive suite. She set down her briefcase in her office and looked around for her coffee mug. It wasn't in its usual spot on her desk. Had she left it in the break room?

Then she remembered she'd left it in Fred's office. After receiving Nathan's phone call, she'd completely forgotten about it. She bit her lip and glanced out her open door at LAI's office manager. Coffee could wait until she'd finished what she planned. Her stomach was a bundle of nerves anyway. Adding caffeine on top probably wasn't the smartest thing to do.

Best to get started. This entire plan would fall apart if she couldn't get Rob Salas to agree to her request.

"Sophia." Penny stopped her as she passed by. "A detective from the Fairfax County police phoned this morning." The cautious note in Penny's voice had Sophia stiffening. "He wants to interview LAI employees about Lachlan. He said the body in the car may not have been Lachlan's. The young man who details cars in the surface lot has been reported missing by his family."

Sophia squeezed her eyes shut to keep Penny from seeing the truth and forced out yet another lie. "That makes no sense. If Lachlan were alive, he would have told us." She didn't have to fake the tears brimming beneath her lashes. Her nerves were at the breaking point.

"That's what I told him. Lachlan wasn't the kind of man to just disappear." Penny stood and enveloped Sophia in a hug. "I'm sorry I upset you, dear. I wanted to make sure you knew before the detective contacted you."

"Thanks. I just—the best thing for me right now is to work." She politely waved off Penny's mothering with an excuse about needing coffee. Down the hall, out of sight, she slumped against the wall. If she was going to pull off what she had to do next, she needed to get herself together. Breathing in determination, she squared her shoulders and headed to the IT director's office.

Rob's door was open and his light was on, but he was nowhere to be found. Sophia passed Christian in the hall. "Have you seen Rob?"

Christian swallowed his bite of croissant. "He's in my office. My computer keeps shutting down on me. Piece of crap. We need to put upgrading office equipment into the next funding request."

"I'll get right on that." She liked Christian, so she refrained from pointing out that his penchant for eating and drinking over his keyboard probably wasn't doing his technology any favors. She'd seen him spill his coffee on it twice when she'd met with him to gather the information needed from his division for the government report.

She found Rob on his knees beneath Christian's desk, messing with cables. She took a deep breath for courage and belted out yet another falsehood. "Hey Rob, Jared called in and wants me to get some information off his computer. Can you give me his login credentials? He needs the data right away."

Please, God, let Rob not hear the tremble in her voice or how hard her heart thumped.

The look Rob sent her from his position beneath Christian's desk spoke volumes about his frame of mind. She smiled and shrugged. "Sorry. I know you're busy. He said to hurry."

With an exaggerated sigh, Rob levered himself upright and searched Christian's desk for a notepad and pen. He pulled a sticky note off its pad and scribbled a series of numbers and letters on it. "Here."

She accepted the paper, willing her fingers not to shake. "Thanks."

He waved her off. "It sounds like the boss might need a reminder about security protocols."

Guilt threatened to suffocate her at deceiving yet another one of her coworkers. If Rob mentioned her request to Jared, her lie would be exposed.

There was no going back now. Her career at LAI was over once her role in helping Lachlan became known. It would be for nothing if she didn't find information proving Lachlan's innocence.

She headed to Lachlan's office first. After closing the blinds, she locked the door, booted up the computer, and typed in Jared's access code. She fished two thumb drives from her pocket and stared at the one Nathan had given her.

That one could wait.

She inserted her other thumb drive into the machine and down-loaded every file and email she could find relevant to LAI's security teams in Afghanistan, including Lachlan's communications with his team leaders. When she finished, she made her way down the hall to Fred's office.

This time, there was no stopping to mourn Fred. She headed straight to his computer and copied every electronic file pertaining to the government report, including the information she'd gathered from both Lachlan's and Christian's divisions.

Where was Fred's audit? The audit had been how he found the discrepancies in the weapons shipments. She searched his files. Her fingers halted over an Excel file, *FBAuditAPR*.

"Bingo." She went to click on it, her finger freezing over the mouse. "Date last modified was yesterday?" That didn't make any sense. Fred had been gone for a week. No one except her had been in his office. At least, not that she knew of. Her gaze went to her coffee mug, still sitting where she left it yesterday morning, what now felt like a lifetime ago.

She right-clicked on the file and opened up version history on a whim. Someone modified the spreadsheet yesterday. She clicked on the previous version dated the day Fred died and saved it to her flash drive, along with the newer version.

Eleven forty-five. Penny usually ate her lunch from noon to one outside if the weather was nice. Today was a clear, sunny day.

Penny was lifting a small cooler bag from her bottom desk drawer when Sophia passed by. "Going to lunch?" Sophia winced at the ea-gerness in her voice.

"Yes. Would you care to join me? It's beautiful outside."

"I'd love to, but I think I'll eat at my desk today. I've got tons to catch up on."

"Don't work too hard," Penny tsked. "You've had a rough time of it lately."

"I won't." Sophia slow-walked in the direction of her office until Penny was out of sight, then made a beeline for Jared's door.

She eased behind Jared's massive desk and logged into the computer. Most files related to LAI's operations or Jared's networking with DC's powerful elite. She downloaded LAI's financial spreadsheets and several other documents that pertained to LAI's operations in Afghanistan, then she performed a search for folders with Global Security or Lachlan Mackay in the file name.

Mackay.

Sophia's pulse kicked as she clicked on the folder and a second password screen popped up. Jared's credentials didn't work on this one. Why was this folder password protected? Dragging it to her USB drive, she breathed a sigh of relief when it created a duplicate file.

She removed the thumb drive and replaced it with the second one Nathan had given her, then uploaded the file it contained as Nathan had instructed. Once she was finished, she removed Nathan's USB drive and pocketed both drives before leaving Jared's office.

She grabbed her things and wrote Penny a brief note saying she had a migraine and was going home for the day. Emily might get angry with her for not following the plan, but her friend was in meetings most of the day and didn't have the time to pick her up and drive her the short distance to the condo. She pulled up her rideshare app and took an Uber home.

Once she was safely inside her home with the alarm dutifully set, Sophia changed into her favorite yoga pants and a loose-fitting t-shirt before sitting down at her dining room table. She inserted the flash drive she'd used to download the files from Lachlan's, Fred's, and Jared's computers into the USB port on her laptop.

There were a couple of hundred files, all obtained illegally.

The first file she opened would cement her status as a thief, no matter how well-intentioned. Her hand shook as the curser arrow hovered over each document, inviting her to click on the mouse and make a discovery.

By the time she'd skimmed the last file, spots danced around the screen, she was pretty sure her vision was no longer 20/20, and the sick, gnawing feeling in her stomach wasn't because she'd forgotten to eat lunch. Too many questions swirled in her brain with no clear-cut answers.

Lachlan had swept into her life with all the impact of a tornado. Her ability to be subjective about his guilt or innocence had gone out the door with him after they'd made love and he'd told her of Nadia's treachery.

Before she lost her courage, she connected to the secure online cloud storage site Admiral Dane had set up and logged in using the password he'd provided. She began uploading the files from the flash drive, her heart sinking as the percentage ticked upward on the green progress bar. "Please let me be doing the right thing."

When the file transfer was completed, she picked up her phone and called Admiral Dane. "I've uploaded the information."

"Good, now stand down, Sophia. I'll handle it from here."

"I know what it looks like," she bit her lip at the tremble in her voice, "but I know Lachlan. He didn't do this. There was a mission in Afghanistan."

She paused. How many more of Lachlan's secrets should she divulge? "Bad things happened. I think someone is framing him, and it's related to that mission. Do you know what I'm talking about?" The admiral had been head of US Special Operations Command. Surely he knew about the mission or could find out.

"I know." A grim knowledge underscored the admiral's curt reply.

There was one thing she wouldn't divulge, even to her best friend's father. That Lachlan was alive. He was safe as long as people believed he was dead, and it was the least she could do.

When Lachlan found out she was working with Admiral Dane and had been from the beginning, he'd never forgive her.

CHAPTER TWENTY-EIGHT

LACHLAN MASSAGED THE TIGHT muscles in his thigh as Nathan finished his phone conversation with the Fairfax County Police detective.

The police were looking for him. He was running out of time. The walls of Nathan's war room closed in on him. He needed to be out tracking people down, not hiding in his mate's home, waiting for information to fall into his lap.

Nathan tossed his phone onto the desk and rubbed his hand over his short, spiky hair. He let out a long, tired sigh. "The police ID'd the body in the car. This detective is contacting everyone who knows you to try and generate any leads on your location. He wants to come here to interview me in person even though, as you probably heard, I told him I had no idea where you could be."

"I should leave. If the detective finds out you lied, he'll charge you with aiding and abetting a fugitive."

Nathan's eyes narrowed, lit with an icy fire. "If he wants to have a look around, let him get a fucking warrant. And this conversation is over."

Lachlan moved to stare out the window so Nathan wouldn't see him tear up like a wee bairn. After everything that happened, Nathan and Ryder still had his back. Sophia had his back.

Just for a moment, he'd like to block out the nightmare his life had become.

Again.

He closed his eyes. An unwanted montage of images crept into his internal vision. The whine of bullets flying in the wrong direction. The screams of agony from the wounded, the silence of the dead, the weight of disbelief, the bitter taste of betrayal.

"Stop thinking about it."

Nathan's barked command jerked his lids up and had him whipping around to stare at his friend. "How do you know what I was thinking?"

"Hitched breath. Your back got so rigid you looked like a corpse in rigor. Wasn't hard to guess." Nathan's eyes lost focus. "We all have our nightmares."

Aye, they did. Lachlan breathed in, held it, breathed out, as he had in that sodding meditation class the counselor forced him into whilst rehabbing his leg. He'd done what he'd needed to get back to his troop.

He returned to the chair next to Nathan's desk. This time, when he shut his eyes, he pictured Sophia the way she'd looked after they'd made love, her red hair spread out in waves over her pillow, the shocked pleasure in her eyes as she climaxed. His nostrils flared as if her scent was in the room. His muscles tightened for a different reason now.

"For fuck's sake, I said think of something else, but if you start jacking off in front of me, I'm going to have to kill you." Lachlan lifted his lids in time to catch Nathan's smirk. "Thinking of a certain redhead?"

He acknowledged the truth of Nathan's words with a tilt of his lips. "It's a helluva lot better than looking at your ugly mug."

Nathan slapped a big paw to his chest in mock indignation. "I have it on good authority from several women that my mug is quite pleasing, thank you very much."

"No one likes a braggart, but I guess we can't expect much from a SEAL."

"We brag because we can, amigo."

Their brief moment of banter was interrupted by a beep from Nathan's computer signaling an incoming video transmission. A touch of a key from Nathan and Ryder's face appeared on the monitor.

"Burkette left Afghanistan." Ryder's brilliant blue eyes betrayed a hint of frustration. "His work phone is still in Kabul, but his other phone pinged in the UK."

"Bloody hell." The back of Lachlan's neck tingled. "He must be going to meet with Haider."

"Locational data put him in east London last evening, Greenwich Mean Time. His last known location this morning was Heathrow."

Nathan grunted. "He's on the move again. I'll find out where Haider's cell phone pinged last night. If we can place Burkette and Haider in the same part of London, we can show a connection between them."

"Search for his flight reservations. I want to know where he's headed next." Lachlan tilted his chin at the monitor. "Ryder, find out what Burkette's team members know about him going AWOL. I still want you there when that weapons shipment releases from customs. We need to know who picks it up if it isn't going to be Josh."

Somewhere on Ryder's side of the world, the sharp, military staccato of a knock sounded. Ryder's head jerked toward something off-screen. "Right. I've got to go. I'll let you know when Burkette's new location pops up." The screen went dark.

"We need to get into Landry's computers. At LAI and his home." Lachlan grabbed the laptop Nathan had loaned him. He opened

Google Earth, typed in Jared's address, and selected the 3D projection, zooming in on Landry's spacious residence.

"I'm still waiting on a text from Sophia to see if she was able to install my back door into LAI's network. As for Landry's home computer, give me thirty minutes." Nathan grinned. "Although it might be worth a peek inside his house to see what's hiding in a filing cabinet. What's a little B&E amongst friends?"

Lachlan shook his head. "There is no *we*. You've already put yourself on the line sheltering me. This part, I do alone."

"Come on." A hint of excitement shone in Nathan's eyes. "It's been a while since I've infiltrated an enemy stronghold."

Lachlan suppressed a smile at Nathan's enthusiasm. "This isn't a government-sanctioned operation, pal. If we're caught, you go down with me."

Nathan shrugged, his demeanor sobering. "Then, you need to contact Lucas Caldwell."

"Not until I have more proof I've been set up."

Nathan's face telegraphed disagreement, but he didn't argue. Next to his keyboard, his mobile danced and hummed like a honeybee who'd just discovered a secret cache of pollen. Nathan picked it up and looked at the number. "Speak of the devil. It's Lucas. Should I take the call?"

"Put him on speaker."

Nathan jacked up the volume and hit the speaker button. "Colonel, what's up?" he said, calling Lucas by his former military rank rather than his current FBI title.

"Where's Mackay?" Caldwell's voice snapped with authority and a sense of urgency that had both Lachlan and Nathan jerking to attention.

Nathan shot Lachlan a questioning look.

Lachlan shook his head. He wasn't ready for anyone to know he was alive. Not yet.

Nathan grimaced. "Dead, last time I checked. Why are you asking?"

"Cut the shit, Lieutenant. The police know it wasn't Mackay in the car. He's now a person of interest. And I got a call this morning from my contact in Scotland Yard. I put Roshan Haider on a plane to London as a favor to our SAS friend. Last night, the London Metropolitan Police found Haider with a bullet in his head."

Nathan mouthed a string of silent curses.

Surprise rooted Lachlan in his chair. Burkette had gone to the UK to clean up loose ends. He grabbed a piece of paper and wrote in rapid strokes before shoving it across the desk. *Tell him I've been framed.*

Nathan blew out a heavy breath. "Look, it wasn't Lachlan, I swear. Someone set our boy up to make it look like he was funneling weapons to Mohammad Razul Khan and then tried to end him before he could get to Kabul to rattle cages."

"Whatever's going on, Mackay is in a heap of trouble. I just got off the phone with Admiral Dane. Somehow he got his hands on a whole bunch of files from LAI, and none of it looks good for Lachlan. He's asked me to open an official investigation."

A strange roaring filled Lachlan's ears. His breath gusted from his lungs like he'd taken a 50-caliber bullet to the chest. He glanced down, half expecting to see his insides exposed to the elements, his heart in a million jagged pieces.

Nathan watched him as if he were an unexploded grenade. He muted the phone. "Breathe, brother. I know what you're thinking."

"Admiral Dane is her best friend's father." Sophia had betrayed him. She'd gone behind his back and given the admiral information that would send him to prison.

Once this arms trafficking nightmare was over, he'd been ready to bury his past and learn how to banish his ghosts for good so he could live a normal life again.

For her.

He rubbed a hand over his face as the gravity of fatigue pushed his weary bones closer to the earth.

You bloody fool. Thom's Brummie accent whispered from the beyond into his ear. *You let a pretty face turn your head again.*

Lucas continued. "The body in Lachlan's car belonged to some kid who owned an auto detailing business. The police are treating it as a homicide. Whatever you two are up to, Mackay needs to come out of hiding and turn himself in. Now."

Lachlan scribbled more words. *Give me two more days. Then I'll surrender.*

Nathan held his stare, his mouth set in a grim line. Lachlan nodded and pointed at the paper.

Nathan swore. "If we haven't come up with proof of Lachlan's innocence by the end of the week, he'll turn himself in."

"This isn't Afghanistan, Nathan. I may be unable to keep Lachlan from taking the fall this time." Lucas hung up without saying goodbye.

Lachlan slammed his fist into his left thigh, the throbbing ache a welcome distraction from the pain in his chest. He limped to the kitchen and the burner phone Nathan had given him.

"Hello?" Sophia's answer was tentative, as if she wasn't sure who was on the other end. Nathan had programmed the number into her phone but put it under the name James Fraser, after some Scottish character in a TV show that women apparently wet their knickers over. Any other time, he'd appreciate the arsehole's warped sense of humor.

"I need to see you. Meet me at my apartment." He rattled off the address, struggling to keep his voice calm and his tone neutral to not alert her to anything amiss.

When he told her he knew of her betrayal, he wanted to see her face.

"Are you sure it's safe?" Her voice dropped to a whisper. "The police are looking for you."

Would she bring the police with her when they met? Was he baiting his own trap? Another reason not to meet at Nathan's home. He wouldn't put Nathan any more at risk than he already had. "I'll be careful."

"When do you want to meet?"

"One hour." That would give him time to get there, recon his place in case the police had it staked out, and be waiting when she arrived. "I...miss you." Emotion leached into his voice despite his iron control. *Bloody Hell.* Even knowing what she'd done, he wanted to see her, touch her, one more time.

"Lachlan." The way she said his name, as if he meant something to her, twisted the knife she'd already embedded in his chest. "I miss you, too. I'll be there."

He turned to find Nathan leaning against the wall, heavy arms crossed and a scowl on his face.

"What are you planning?"

"I'm going to go see about a girl." Instead of being humorous, the words fell bitterly off his tongue.

"I'm going with you."

"No, I need to do this alone. Can I borrow your bike? It'll be faster and less noticeable than your truck."

Nathan's scowl deepened. "I'll drive. If you don't want me in the room, fine, but I can monitor the building and warn you if the police arrive."

Lachlan gave up. He wasn't going to change the stubborn SEAL's mind, and they were wasting time he didn't have.

"You need to hear her out, amigo. Don't do anything stupid."

"I'm no gonnae hurt her." Rage deepened his voice to a guttural snarl. He might have been willing to shoot Nadia to save Ryder's life, but he couldn't bring himself to harm Sophia, no matter what she'd done.

Maybe, when he was sitting in his prison cell, he'd eventually learn to hate her.

Nathan got in his face. The big man lowered his head, anger glazing his eyes and curling his lip. "I know you won't, asshole. You killed Nadia to save Ryder, not because you wanted to."

"I wanted to." The confession burst out of him. He let Nathan see the truth in his eyes.

Nathan's eyes flashed with remembered pain. "We all wanted to, but you wouldn't have pulled the trigger if she'd surrendered. You're not that kind of guy."

His heavy hand landed on Lachlan's shoulder. "Sophia matters to you. I think you should trust her. If she's the one who gave the files to Admiral Dane, she did it for the right reasons."

Sophia's betrayal paled compared to Nadia's, yet it had his heart in a vise, squeezing the air from his lungs, inflicting a pain worse than the bullet that had ripped through his leg.

He *had* trusted her. She'd cracked open the dark place in his soul and let in the light.

And the whole time, she'd been handing over information that could end his career and his freedom. Even now, his heart refused to accept his brain's conclusion.

Lachlan stepped back to let Nathan's hand fall, breaking their connection. "Let's go."

CHAPTER
TWENTY-NINE

THE POLISHED BRASS AND mahogany paneling in the elevator at Lachlan's apartment complex reminded Sophia of the country club her parents belonged to—sophisticated, masculine, and timeless. A modulated feminine voice announced her arrival on the eleventh floor.

The corridor curved in a gentle slope along the architectural lines of the building. She followed the numbers, stopping in front of the door marked 1118, and pressed the doorbell. A muted chime came from inside, and she strained to hear the muffled voice telling her to enter.

Lachlan? She twisted the doorknob, heart tripping.

Something had been off in his voice when he'd called her earlier. Until he told her he missed her. Then his voice filled with a longing she felt deep in her soul.

"Hello?" She glanced at the galley kitchen to her right with its dark cabinets and granite countertops. To her left sat a round wooden table with four chairs. The pale cream walls were bare. She took a few more steps, letting the door close behind her.

No mail, magazines, or personal clutter anywhere. Her heart ached for everything the space didn't say about the man who lived there.

"Lachlan?"

Where was he?

Her shoulders twitched. The energy in the room felt off, but she couldn't put her finger on why. She passed by a hallway into the living room and halted, transfixed.

Lachlan's walls weren't completely bare. Highlanders charged into battle over a brown leather sofa. She moved closer, admiring the painting that still took her breath away. The Highlander leading the charge could have been Lachlan's ancestor. Fierce. A leader. A protector of all he held dear.

Just how she saw Lachlan.

How she wanted him to see himself.

"The Battle of Culloden. The Highlanders were doomed from the beginning. Fitting, isn't it?" Lachlan's tone was flat.

She spun at the sound of his voice, and when she met his eyes, they were equally devoid of emotion. Dread roiled her stomach. "What's wrong?"

"How long have you been funneling information to Admiral Dane?"

Her breath left her with a whoosh at his verbal punch to the stomach. She swallowed hard, past a throat suddenly thick with an unnamed fear. She'd been right. He believed she betrayed him.

"The evidence against you is too strong. Admiral Dane is the only one who can save you. Please—"

"How long?"

His stillness unnerved her.

"Right before I started at LAI, he told me the government suspected a US contractor was selling weapons to an Afghan warlord—weapons that might end up in the hands of the Taliban or ISIS. He asked me to keep my eyes and ears open. He asked me to," she stumbled over her next words, knowing how they sounded, "he asked me to start with you."

There was a flash of pain in his eyes as his hands fisted at his sides. "So, from the instant we met, you were helping the admiral build a case against me," he snarled. "You knew my division was being used as a front for arms trafficking before we met."

His emotionless façade dropped away, the look he sent her so full of bitterness, she nearly fell to her knees.

"It wasn't like that." She stretched her hand into the vast gulf between them. "Once I got to know you, I never believed you were guilty. I've been trying to help prove your innocence. You have to believe me."

"Believe you?" He took a step toward her, and it took everything in her not to retreat from the fury emanating from him in waves. "Why should I believe you? You've been lying to me from the very beginning. And to think I bared my soul to you."

His lip curled. "You're a bloody good actress, Sophia. I thought you cared. I actually believed we might have a future together."

"I love you." The words burst from her on a sob. "Admiral Dane will help." Tears slid down her cheeks. "Don't give up." Her lips trembled. "Don't give up on us."

Lachlan's finger brushed her cheek. He contemplated the moisture he'd gathered on the pad of his finger, almost clinically, as if to discern its chemical properties. "Unless new evidence emerges to exonerate me, I'm probably going to prison for a very long time." He stepped back, putting both physical and emotional distance between them. "There is no future. There is no us."

She bit her lip hard to keep from crying out in protest.

"Goodbye, Sophia." He strode to his apartment door, holding it open.

Every painful moment in her life that had tried to chip away at her self-worth paled compared to how her heart shattered now, into a million little pieces.

She reached the door and forced herself to meet his gaze.

He'd sequestered every hint of emotion behind an iron wall of control. She envied his ability to hide his feelings even as she resented it.

"I love you," she repeated, "even if you don't believe me right now. Maybe you will one day."

She wouldn't say goodbye.

It felt too final.

His door clicked shut at her back. She almost wished he'd slammed it. At least it would have shown he felt something. When the brass elevator doors slid open, she sagged in relief at the sight of the empty car. The doors had barely closed before the first sob tore from her chest.

Sophia drove blindly, not caring if people noticed her sobbing her heart out at the stoplights. Lachlan had accused her of being a good actress. She needed to prove him right and convince Emily nothing was wrong. Once Emily left for Paris tomorrow, she could crawl into her bed, curl up in a ball, and spend the weekend waiting for the next shoe to drop.

The police were hunting for Lachlan.

Soon, LAI would be embroiled in a federal investigation.

Jared would find out she'd kept the weapons shipments a secret, then stole company files and gave them to an outsider. He'd fire her for sure.

Then again, if Jared were involved, everyone at LAI would be out of a job, and it would be more evidence that she was too trusting.

She laughed, the sound bitter, and wiped her face and nose with a crumpled tissue from her center console. How naïve of her to think she'd finally have the kind of life she'd always dreamed of. A man to love her unconditionally in a way she'd never experienced growing up. A home. Children.

The pretty picture she'd painted of the world as she wanted it to be went up in flames, floating away in delicate pieces of black ash to disappear into the wind.

She parked in her designated space in the condo's garage and stepped out of the car, so wrapped up inside her head, she nearly came out of her shoes at her name.

"Sophia."

Her head whipped around. "Jared?" Lachlan wasn't the only one who knew how to gain access to unauthorized places. Icy fingers crawled down her spine. "What are you doing here?"

Her boss stood a short distance away, between her and the elevators, dressed in a charcoal gray suit, his navy and silver tie still in its neat Windsor knot despite it being mid-afternoon.

"Trying to keep you from making a mistake." His knowing gaze made her think of a hawk circling its prey. "Lachlan is alive. But you already knew, didn't you."

Her heart thumped against her chest, trying to escape while the rest of her was frozen in place. "Penny told me the news yesterday."

"Hmmm." He didn't call her out for her lie of omission, but she knew she'd be wasting her time denying she'd seen Lachlan. "I'm sure he's convinced you of his innocence. I know about the weapons he trafficked to an Afghan warlord." His look of regret was unconvincing. "I'm going to have to turn him in to the FBI. You'll cooperate and tell them where he is if you're smart."

"Why do you think Lachlan would do such a thing?"

Maybe one of her neighbors would show up if she stalled, and she'd have a witness and an excuse to move her conversation with Jared to the lobby, where Sal or one of the other security guards would be watching. There was no way she was inviting Jared up to her condo.

His answer was an arched brow and a mocking smile. "What do you know about Lachlan? Other than what he wants you to know?"

What did she know?

Everything that matters.

Not knowing what to say, she kept silent. She could jump into her car and lock the doors, in which case Jared would realize she was hiding something, or she could bluff her way past him to the elevators and the safety of her condo.

Right about now, she'd welcome that platoon of SEALs Admiral Dane would send if she sent out an SOS.

She edged further from her car toward the elevators, keeping her distance from Jared.

"He's a trained killer. And he's good at it." Jared's casual, offhand delivery chilled her blood, making her second-guess her decision to go for the elevators. He smiled, but it wasn't a kind smile. "I know what he's capable of better than you." The subtle change in his demeanor dropped the temperature around them ten degrees.

"You have, too," she whispered the realization. Her inner voice screamed to run, but she was exhausted by the web of lies and wanted the truth.

"Have what?"

"Killed people."

And he'd been good at it. She didn't have to guess—she just knew. The urbane businessman was gone, leaving only the deadly special operations soldier and a criminal.

She'd gone this far. She wasn't stopping now. "Did you frame Lachlan?"

His mocking laugh set her teeth on edge. "I *am* Landry Associates International, sweetheart. Why would I jeopardize my career and company by getting involved in weapons trafficking?"

It was a valid question.

Why risk everything he'd worked for trafficking weapons and God knows what else? What kind of man did that?

There was more to Jared than what he presented to the world.

The unsettling photo of Jared and his parents should have clued her in. That, and his achievements, framed and highlighted on his walls for the world to see. He was narcissistic enough to take on the challenge and egotistical enough to believe he'd get away with it.

Make more money than he could with his legitimate business.

Best a man who was his equal.

But there had to be more.

His effort to frame Lachlan seemed too personal. Her mind scrambled to fit together pieces of the puzzle. What was she missing? They'd both served in Afghanistan. Was there a connection? She thought back to Jared's medals and commendations. There had been no photos of him with his unit, only ones with famous people and politicians taken after he'd gotten out and started LAI.

In fact, the only photo she'd seen of him in the military was the one in his home with his lover.

His Afghan lover with the striking blue eyes.

Eyes she'd seen on someone else—Roshan Haider.

Nadia.

Nadia Haider had been Jared's lover. Sophia stared at Jared wide-eyed as all the pieces slid into place. Jared and Roshan Haider had worked together to get revenge against Lachlan for Nadia's death.

She needed to get away from Jared. Call Lachlan, warn him.

"I don't know what I'm saying. I didn't mean to accuse you. This is all so confusing." She clutched her purse tighter to her shoulder and cast a longing glance at the bank of elevators. "I have to go. My friend's waiting for me upstairs. Take your evidence to the FBI—I'll tell them everything I know."

One step, then two.

She kept her gaze locked on the elevators.

"I know you accessed LAI's computers, Sophia." Jared's words halted her steps. "It didn't paint a pretty picture of Lachlan, did it? What did he say when he saw all the evidence against him?"

Her knees trembled.

Rob must have told him about her asking for Jared's login credentials. There was no point in denying it.

"I didn't show it to him. I sent it to someone with more power and connections than you." Hopefully, Admiral Dane would piece together the truth before it was too late.

Just a few more steps.

A flash of anger melted the frost in Jared's eyes before they chilled again. "Then that makes what I have to do so much easier."

Sophia took another step forward, her heart hammering in her throat.

A stranger stepped out of the shadows. Muscular, a bit shorter than Jared, he had a full, dark brown beard, a high and tight haircut, and black eyes that stared at her with a total absence of emotion.

She pressed her lips together to suppress a scream. Black spots danced in her vision. *Breathe.* Passing out now wouldn't save her. She had to think her way out of this. Letting her shoulders droop, she did her best to look deflated and teary. "I have to agree that the evidence against Lachlan is pretty damning."

Jared had closed the gap and now stood directly in front of her, the ruthless-looking man at his back. Fear cemented her feet to the floor. His hand lifted, caressed her cheek. "You're a terrible liar."

She recoiled.

"It's a shame it's come to this. I had plans for us." His gray gaze turned to dirty ice. "Do you know why I hired you? It wasn't your high-powered references. You're smart and capable, but you lack the experience of older, more seasoned professionals."

He fingered a lock of her hair, raised it to his nose, and inhaled.

Bile rose to the back of her throat.

"It was the potential I saw to mold you into the kind of wife who would be an asset to my political ambitions."

His wife?

Someone he thought he could control.

Someone who wouldn't embarrass him at the high-powered cocktail parties where Washington elites made backroom deals and anointed future politicians.

If Jared had had his way, she would have ended up like his mother, a beautifully dressed tragedy in a gilded prison.

Jared hooked his finger beneath her chin. The charming, supportive boss was gone. The man in front of her was cold, ruthless, and without an ounce of mercy.

He shook his head with a disappointed tsk of his tongue. "Unfortunately, your allegiance to Mackay leaves me no choice but to end our relationship."

"If something happens to me, Lachlan will come for you." She notched her chin up and shot Jared a look of defiance, even if her words wobbled as much as the rest of her.

"Oh, I'm counting on it." His smile twisted. He took out his cell and tapped on the screen. Inside her purse, her text tone dinged. "Take out your phone."

What game was he playing? She fumbled around her purse until her fingers latched onto her phone. Her lungs shriveled when she saw the photo Jared texted her.

He took the cell from her nerveless fingers. "Ah, here's a call from earlier today. James Fraser. With a masked number. How clever." He held up the phone. "I'm assuming this is Lachlan?"

She dropped her gaze to his expensive Italian leather shoes rather than answer.

"Let's send him this photo, shall we?" Jared's thumbs moved over her phone, then he strolled to her car and placed the phone on her windshield. "He placed a tracker on your Prius, so I have no doubt he can trace your phone."

Her head flew up to see his amused expression.

"My friend here found it just now." Jared held up a small black box for her inspection, his grin sending shivers across her neck. "So trusting, Sophia. So naïve."

Jared turned to the man with the dead eyes, his nod a signal that sent adrenaline flooding through Sophia's muscles. "Josh."

Jared's henchman reached for her. She wheeled around and ran for the ramp leading up to the garage exit. She hadn't taken more than three steps when a powerful arm jerked her back into a hard body. Something sharp stung her neck. She opened her mouth to scream. A big hand clamped her mouth.

She slumped against her captor as the world went dark.

CHAPTER THIRTY

LACHLAN GLANCED AROUND HIS apartment.

Nothing had changed in the short time Sophia had been here, yet he'd never noticed before how sterile and empty his home was. He'd done the right thing severing ties with her, even if his stomach ached and his chest felt like he was buried beneath the rubble of a four-story building after a Coalition air strike.

She'd told him she loved him, and as badly as he wanted to believe her, he couldn't wrap his head around the fact she'd been spying on him from the very beginning.

His ghosts found him, whispering in his ear, mocking him for thinking he'd escape the darkness.

There was a single rap on his door. He opened it to find Nathan, his face grim. Was it his imagination, or was that a look of disappointment in his mate's eyes? "We should go."

Lachlan nodded. He took one last look at his apartment. Who knows when he'd be back. If he went to prison, he'd have to rely on Nathan to pack up his few belongings and store them. His gaze lingered on the painting over the couch. "Did you see Sophia leave?"

"Yep. Cried all the way to her car." Nathan left off *arsehole,* but it was written on his face.

They made their way to the exit stairs. Lachlan had climbed eleven floors to avoid being recognized, and his bum leg was feeling the strain of overexertion. If he weren't careful, the damn thing would give out on him, and he would need to lean on Nathan to make it the rest of the way down.

"Was it worth it?" Nathan kept his voice low. The stairwell, with its walls of concrete, was an echo chamber.

"She's been spying on me since she started at LAI." Renewed anger sizzled through his veins. "Admiral Dane knew before I did that someone was using my division to traffic weapons to Khan."

"Jesus," Nathan swore, "the admiral's a scary son-of-a-bitch, but he's solid. If we can get him evidence showing you've been set up, he'll follow it."

Lachlan kept silent as they made their way into the underground garage.

Nathan had used Lachlan's access card to keep his truck out of sight. While Nathan drove them back to his home, Lachlan leaned back against the headrest and shut his eyes. *Christ*. He was properly scunnered. Maybe he should turn himself in and let the chips fall where they may. What did he have to look forward to?

All his plans—to bring down Khan, start his own security company, and have a life with Sophia—were so far out of reach that they might as well be on the other side of the universe. He was sick of finding a reason to get out of bed each morning.

"You're a fool if you think Sophia doesn't have feelings for you." Nathan's voice cut through the silence like a blade.

"She lied to me. I can't trust her."

"Bullshit. Admiral Dane tasked her to spy before she ever met you. And when she found information that incriminated you, who did she bring it to? You. And you saw how she reacted when she found out you were alive."

Nathan took his eyes off the road long enough to glare at him. "You think a classy woman like that would have let you practically fuck her in my living room if she wasn't emotionally invested?"

Bollocks.

Nathan wasn't going to let this go. Lachlan's mobile vibrated, pre-empting his retort. A text from Sophia. Maybe she'd gotten home and decided to let him know what a prick he was for the way he'd treated her. He braced himself and opened the message.

Time stood still as he stared at the beautiful, treacherous face of his nightmares wrapped in Jared Landry's arms.

"*Bloody. Hell.*" He pressed the call button and held a shaking hand to his ear.

"What's wrong?" Nathan's hands tightened on the steering wheel.

"Come on, *leannan*, answer your phone." Lachlan counted each unanswered ring. "Can you track Sophia's phone on your mobile?"

Nathan made an abrupt turn into the strip mall on their right and parked. "Yeah. Tell me what the hell is happening."

Lachlan held up his mobile. "This was sent from Sophia's phone." Jared had lied about knowing Nadia. One glance at the photo confirmed they'd not only known each other, they'd been lovers. The pieces of the puzzle came together.

"Son of a bitch." Nathan's lips flattened in a grim line. He opened his mobile and tapped on it. "She's at her condo."

"Head there." Lachlan tried calling again and got no answer. "Do you have Emily's number?"

Nathan handed Lachlan his phone. "Here, her number is listed under Princess."

He'd ask Nathan later about the reason behind the nickname. Right now, all he cared about was making sure Sophia was safe.

"If you're calling, Frogman, it had better be good news." Emily's voice came through on the speakers in Nathan's truck.

Nathan snorted.

"Emily, it's Lachlan Mackay. Is Sophia with you?"

"No, I'm at the State Department. I just got out of a meeting." Her voice tightened. "What's wrong?"

"Sophia's not answering her phone. Nathan and I are headed to the condo."

"Hold on, let me try her." Emily returned to the line several seconds later. "She's not responding to me either. I swear to God if anything happens to her—" The steady stream of highly creative, incredibly vulgar threats Emily lobbed at Lachlan singed his ears.

He deserved every one of them.

"You can tell she grew up around SEALs," was all Nathan muttered after she had hung up.

"Park over there, in one of the visitor's spots," Lachlan directed once they reached Sophia's condo. "We need to get to the elevators through the garage to avoid security in the lobby." If the guard named Sal was on duty, no amount of charm or threats would get them past the man.

They slipped around the barrier arm and into the garage. Lachlan spotted Sophia's Prius. "There's her car." They went over and peered inside.

"And here's her phone." Nathan held up a mobile enclosed in a sparkly pink case.

Cold sweat dampened Lachlan's forehead. He should have trusted her. He should have tried harder to protect her. If Landry laid a finger on her, Lachlan would take him apart, piece by piece, until nothing was left.

"Come look at this." Nathan had headed in the direction of the elevators. He'd stopped halfway and was crouched down, examining something. He pulled a small, white square of cloth from his mission pants, plucked the object of his curiosity off the concrete floor, and held it up for inspection. "Syringe cap. I think Jared drugged her." He stood. "Question is, where did he take her?"

Ice formed in Lachlan's lungs and spread to his chest. "Someplace easy for me to find, where he has the advantage. He knows I'll come," he ground out, his voice feral with suppressed violence.

So was Nathan's answering grin. "Then let's not keep the man waiting."

Sophia's eyelids stuck together. Her tongue felt thick, fuzzy, her stomach queasy. A metronome swung in the background, every tick reminding her of endless hours of childhood piano lessons.

Needles stabbed her back and shoulders, and she couldn't feel her fingers. She tried to stretch her arms over her head to alleviate the discomfort, only her body didn't obey. The fog lifted enough to realize she was sitting down, arms pulled behind her. Something held her wrists together. Her chin rested on her collarbone.

It took a few tries, but she managed to pry her lashes apart to see her jean-clad thighs, the fabric between them some kind of green and red plaid upholstery. The rug beneath the chair looked Persian.

Expensive.

Familiar.

Where had she seen it before?

Jared's study. The ticking sound must be the grandfather clock.
At least it's not a bomb.

Fear, sickly sweet and overwhelming, replaced her brief spurt of morbid humor. Jared had been in her parking garage with some creepy guy. They must have drugged her.

"You're awake."

Jared's voice.

Her heart leaped to her throat and stayed there. She kept her head down.

A chair creaked. The tips of Jared's brown leather shoes brushed against her sneakers.

He lifted her chin, forcing her head up. "I was afraid Josh gave you too much sedative." The brush of his thumb across her cheek sent shivers through her body. "Would you care for some tea? It might help you feel better."

She throttled the urge to tell him to go to Hell. Antagonizing him wouldn't help. "Yes." Her voice emerged as a dry croak.

He smiled kindly, the personification of a benevolent host. He'd changed clothes. Dressed in a white golf shirt and tan slacks, he was the corporate executive on his way to the country club for a quick nine holes and drinks. Not a kidnapper, arms trafficker.

Murderer.

"I'll get you a cup. Then we can loosen those restraints." He left the room, closing the double-paneled doors behind him.

She twisted her body as far as her bound arms permitted and surveyed the room. The movement sent a dizzying wave of nausea through her. She faced forward, dropped her chin, and breathed deep to calm her stomach.

The bonds around her wrists stuck to her skin but didn't dig in as rope would. Duct tape? Maybe she could rip or loosen her bindings.

Get free. She glanced at Jared's desk near the double doors. She could break free and call the police before he returned. Find a letter opener, something, anything to use as a weapon.

Her desperate optimism fizzled.

Even if she could get away from Jared, where was his sidekick? She'd rather take her chances with her boss than be at the mercy of that monster.

The doors opened. Jared carried a delicate china teacup and saucer on a small silver tray. A paper tag dangled from a string draped over the rim. The tableau looked so out of place that she had to bite back a semi-hysterical laugh.

He set the cup and saucer down on his desk and rummaged through one of the drawers. "Ah, here it is."

She zeroed in on the wickedly sharp knife he held up. He brought it with him, along with the tea.

Her lungs wouldn't inflate, turning her scream into a squeak. She shrank in the seat as far as her bound arms permitted. Pain ripped through her shoulders.

Jared gave a short laugh. "Relax, I'm freeing your arms." He crouched behind her. There was a tug on her wrists before they sprang apart.

Pins and needles shot from shoulder to fingertip. Her teeth drew blood trying to keep in a moan. She carefully peeled the remaining tape from her wrists and rubbed the skin briskly to get the blood circulating.

Jared shifted to her front. The knife had disappeared, and in its place was the cup of tea. He handed it to her, and she balanced it on her lap. He fetched his desk chair and positioned himself in front of her. Propping his chin in his hand, he assessed her like he was deciding her fate.

The tea's warmth tempted her sore, parched throat. Still, she hesitated.

"It isn't drugged." Jared's voice held a touch of amusement at her expense.

She took a tentative sip. The hot liquid soothed her throat but did little to warm her cold insides. "Why am I here?"

"Mackay will come for you. I need him to cooperate. He will, with you as leverage."

The teacup rattled on its saucer. She set it on the floor next to her chair and clutched her ice-cold fingers. "Don't do this, Jared. I'm begging you. You don't need to hurt Lachlan. You still can walk away." There had to be something she could do or say to make him see reason.

He cocked his head, the gentle smile on his lips a stark contrast to the coldness in his eyes. "Don't be naïve, Sophia."

He stood and returned his chair to the desk. "Besides, Lachlan took something from me. I'm returning the favor."

Nadia.

Sophia shuddered, another bout of nausea cramping her stomach.

She wasn't going to make it out of here alive.

CHAPTER
THIRTY-ONE

LACHLAN'S FINGER CARESSED THE smooth surface of the Sig Sauer in his lap. A cold, primal fury took root. If anything happened to Sophia—

"Drive faster."

"If I go any faster, we'll attract the attention of every cop in this vicinity. We're almost there." Nathan's gaze dropped briefly to Lachlan's hands before returning to the road. "How 'bout you put the weapon away until we've reached the target site."

The confines of Nathan's truck grew claustrophobic. The band around Lachlan's chest grew tighter with every second that passed. He had failed to protect his men and Katherine Purcell. He'd failed Nathan's man and the helicopter crew.

He wouldn't survive if he failed Sophia as well.

"I don't think Jared will hurt her," Nathan answered Lachlan's unspoken question. His voice hardened to steel. "At least, not until you're standing in front of him."

Lachlan's mobile rang. Ryder calling from Kabul. "What did you find out?" Lachlan asked without preamble.

"Burkette arrived in DC a few hours ago."

Rage lowered Lachlan's voice to a growl. "Keep tracking him. I need an exact location. Landry has Sophia. Nathan and I are headed to his place now."

"Be careful, mate. Burkette is probably there with him."

What kind of game was Landry playing? If he planned to use Sophia as bait to force Lachlan to reveal himself, it had worked.

Nathan pulled to the side of the road a quarter-mile from Landry's home in McLean. "How do you want to do this? We're going in blind into a hostage situation." He sat back, scrubbing his face with a deep sigh. "History has a bad habit of repeating itself."

Lachlan's teeth hurt from the effort to keep his wits together and not go off like Rambo into the trees. "This won't end the same way."

It can't.

He clamped a hand on his friend's shoulder. "I'm going to get Sophia. If Landry and Burkette have to die, I'll accept the consequences. You don't have to, *mo bhràthair*."

Nathan's glare was fierce. "Fuck you. How many times do I have to tell you I've got your six for you to believe it?" He held up his fist. "The only easy day was yesterday. We do this together."

Lachlan gave a close-lipped smile as Nathan spouted the SEAL motto. He bumped Nathan's fist with his own. "Who dares wins." The motto of the British SAS.

His eyes stung with unexpected tears. He'd been prepared to go it alone if necessary but wasn't sure he'd succeed. Landry and Burkette weren't unskilled insurgents or poorly equipped militia. They were well-trained, combat-hardened, former Rangers.

He stared out the side window. "Thank you."

Nathan coughed into the silence that followed. "I'm gonna shoot Emily a text and let her know what's up." He threw open the driver's door. "Let's gear up and go get your woman."

The late afternoon sun gave way to encroaching shadows of twilight. Landry's home backed up to a woodland buffer. Lachlan scanned the exterior of the stately stone and stucco three-story. The security cameras they could get around. Motion lights, too, and it wasn't dark enough yet to make night vision useful.

However, if the men waiting inside had thermal imaging devices, he and Nathan might as well walk up and ring the doorbell.

"I've got eyes on Burkette," Nathan's voice whispered through Lachlan's earpiece. "First floor—northwest corner. No sign of Landry or Sophia."

Light shone from a bank of windows on the second story. "I'm headed to the second floor, southeast corner."

Jared would be waiting for him. "Wait for my signal."

"Roger that—out."

A stone-wrapped chimney ran up the side of the house. Lachlan raced to it in a low crouch. He holstered his gun, felt for anchor points, and scaled the chimney to the roof.

He crawled to the darkened window of a third-floor dormer. Separating the pane from the window frame with his tactical knife, he placed it carefully on the shingles before slipping into what looked to be Landry's home gym.

Gun in hand, Lachlan moved with soundless steps down a set of stairs to the second floor. At the end of the hall, a warm glow leached from the bottom of a set of double doors.

He crept forward and flattened his ear to one panel. Inside, there was the murmur of a man's voice, followed by a woman's.

Sophia.

She was alive.

He swallowed hard, corralled his wayward emotions, and refocused.

They weren't out of the woods yet. Landry would be armed. If Lachlan charged through the door, Sophia might get hit in the crossfire. His best option was to balls up knock and hope Jared assumed it was Burkette.

If he could catch Landry off guard, it might give him enough time to take the other man out without endangering Sophia. Nathan would neutralize Josh.

Decision made, he sent Nathan a pre-arranged series of clicks on the mic as a non-verbal *go* signal.

Control. Training. Sophia's life depended on it.

He lifted his knuckles and rapped on the door.

"Come in."

Definitely Jared.

Lachlan lifted his weapon into position and gripped the doorknob. On an internal count of three, he burst through the door, his gaze and gun sweeping the room and stopping dead center.

Sophia sat in a chair.

Jared stood behind her, the 9mm in his grip too close to her head.

"Are ye all right, *leannan*?" Lachlan kept his gun pointed at the space between Jared's brows. *Steady.* He'd get Sophia killed if he didn't shut down his emotions.

The muzzle of Jared's gun dug into Sophia's temple. Fear, stark and raw, flooded her eyes.

Lachlan's hands tightened around the pistol grip.

"Right on schedule." A hint of triumph infiltrated Jared's smooth cadence. "You should have stayed dead—it would have been better for Sophia." His free hand caressed the side of her face, sliding down her neck and collarbone to graze her breast.

The bastard was trying to provoke him.

Lachlan let the air leave his lungs in a smooth flow, as he'd been trained to do in special forces selection.

To her credit, Sophia stayed composed, her gaze locked on him. He could sense the message in her eyes, and his chest tightened. *Trust.*

She trusted him. Even after the way he'd treated her.

"You can't think you'll get away with this, Landry. Cut your losses. Let her go, and you can walk out of here."

Jared's amused laugh tightened the back of Lachlan's neck. "I'm holding all the cards, Mackay. I know you SAS operators think you're the best, but do you think you can shoot me before I put a bullet into sweet Sophia's brain?"

Jared's expression hardened. "Weapon on the desk—remove the magazine and clear the chamber first." He dug his pistol deeper into Sophia's skin for emphasis.

Bloody Hell. Lachlan had no choice. His gaze trained on Landry, he ejected the magazine from his gun, retracted the slide, and tilted his weapon. The shiny copper and lead projectile bounced off the wood floor and landed at the edge of the rug. He placed the gun and magazine on the desk.

Jared nodded approvingly. "Now, your coat. And your other weapons. Slowly. My trigger finger is itchy."

Lachlan grimaced. He shrugged out of the leather jacket. It landed with a *thunk* next to his gun.

Jared's free hand gestured to Lachlan's mission pants.

He dug into the various pockets and removed his folding knife, multitool, and Maglite. His shoulder holster came off next. He yanked up his right pant leg, unfastened the fixed blade holstered above his boot, and added it to the growing pile. When he finished, he held his arms away from his body.

Jared's eyes narrowed. "Your other gun."

Shite. Lachlan hesitated, then withdrew the compact pistol from the small of his back, unloaded it, and tossed it with his other gear.

"Move away from the desk."

Lachlan sidestepped in the direction of a pedestal displaying a Murano vase. Not close enough to touch it. Not yet. He breathed a shallow sigh of relief as Jared lifted the gun from Sophia's temple.

Lines bracketed her mouth and forehead, but she remained calm. He diverted his attention from Jared long enough to lock gazes with her. What he saw threw him off balance. It wasn't fear. It looked like...

Love.

He stopped breathing. No matter what happened to him, Sophia would survive.

His focus returned to Jared. "What now? Are you going to shoot me where I stand? I wouldn't want to mess up your wood floor or that fancy rug you're standing on."

"I loved her, you know. We were kindred spirits."

Lachlan frowned. "Loved who?" The bastard couldn't mean Sophia, even though he was clearly attracted to her.

"Nadia." Jared was too calm. His fingers brushed Sophia's hair. "Beautiful like our Sophia and intelligent."

Lachlan's jaw clenched. "You're not capable of love."

"Who do you think introduced me to Khan? We weren't just lovers—we were business partners." The hand in Sophia's hair clenched.

She winced.

Lachlan stifled a step forward.

"Until Khan's son, Sharif, the little prick, ruined everything." A thread of anger showed in Jared's voice for the first time.

"She betrayed us." Lachlan's rage bubbled up, cold and deadly. "An innocent hostage and five soldiers dead. Lives ruined. All because of her."

Jared released his grip on Sophia's hair, waving his hand in a careless gesture. "People die all the time. How many civilians did we kill in Iraq and Afghanistan? You could have taken out Sharif and the others without killing her."

Lachlan smothered the anger roiling in his gut and softened his tone. Maybe he could appeal to the bastard's sense of duty—if he had ever had any. "She refused to surrender. Had her gun trained on Ryder. You would have done the same to protect one of your own."

Jared shrugged. "I would have let Nadia kill my men if it kept her alive."

The man had gone stark raving mad.

"My business association with Khan resulted in a tidy profit, but I knew it couldn't go on forever," Jared continued in the same conversational tone. "I hadn't planned to kill you. Ruining your reputation and knowing you'd spend twenty years behind bars seemed enough. At first."

Jared's grip on the gun relaxed, but it was still too damn close to Sophia's head. "Roshan Haider helped facilitate the shipments to Khan. When you heard the rumor about the weapons and started getting nosy, I told Haider that Khan knew the identity of the man responsible for killing his sister. Haider came to the States to confront you, but then he saw you with Sophia and decided exposing you as his sister's killer wasn't enough." Jared caressed Sophia's cheek.

Lachlan's hands fisted. *Control.*

"I would never have let Roshan hurt her. I simply wanted her to understand the danger you were to her. Like the night of Congressman Kellerman's reception." Jared's smile mocked Lachlan. "I was her savior. Where were you?"

"You bastard—she could have been killed." Lachlan lurched forward. He would wrap his hands around Landry's neck and laugh when the life drained out of the other man's eyes.

Jared's gun jerked back to Sophia's temple.

Her whimper froze Lachlan in place. He forced himself to stand down and step back, another inch closer to the vase.

Buy Nathan more time.

"Why kill Fred?" It was a shot in the dark.

The arrow hit home. "Ah, Fred." Jared's lips pursed. His gun hand relaxed again. "He pieced together enough financial information to expose my business dealings with Khan. He suspected you, but I knew if he kept digging, he'd figure it out."

Hate turned Jared's eyes the color of New York snow. "You lead a charmed life, don't you, Mackay? Jeremy Powell died in your place. Sophia gave her loyalty to you instead of me. Now she'll die, like Nadia. You took from me. I take from you."

He shifted the gun from Sophia to point it at Lachlan. "A former soldier with PTSD finds his lover with their boss and kills her. I'm forced to shoot you in self-defense. Such a tragedy."

For the first time, a trickle of unease filtered through Lachlan. If he didn't find a way to distract Jared, he'd be dead, and so would Sophia.

He slid his boot another inch closer to the vase.

His gaze found Sophia's and held. He let everything he felt for her show in his eyes. Despite what she'd done, he regretted he wouldn't be around to love her.

Love. He loved her. *Too late.*

Sophia's eyes flew wide, her face growing slack.

Lachlan shifted his weight and prepared to act.

Her gaze broadcast a silent plea that shocked him to his core. *Trust me.*

What was she thinking? He throttled the instinct to shake his head and reject whatever plan she had formed. He owed her his trust. With the barest blink of his lashes, he signaled his acknowledgment.

The smile she gave him made his heart stutter.

Whatever happened, they were in this together.

Without warning, Sophia threw herself sideways into Jared's arm. The gun flew from his grip to land on the floor with a clatter.

Lachlan lunged for the vase.

CHAPTER
THIRTY-TWO

SOPHIA HIT THE RUG and rolled. She scrambled for the gun, her shaking fingers wrapping around the grip.

The Murano vase flew from Lachlan's hand like a missile toward Jared's head. Jared ducked, the vase shattering harmlessly against the wall of shelves.

Head down, Sophia army-crawled to the wall of windows as Jared grabbed the chair she'd been sitting in and threw it at Lachlan.

Lachlan snatched it from the air. The two former soldiers faced off, hatred bleeding from their pores. The china cup and saucer shattered beneath their feet, Sophia's remaining tea soaking a brown stain into the expensive rug.

Lachlan parried, and Jared retreated in a deadly circle.

A well-timed roundhouse kick from Jared knocked the chair from Lachlan's grip, sending it skidding across the floor out of reach.

A flash of silver drew Sophia's gaze to Jared's right hand.

The knife he'd used to cut her bindings.

She lifted the gun. It was heavy in her hand. Aiming wasn't possible—not with the tremors shaking her body. What if she hit Lachlan? She'd never even fired a gun before.

The men continued their deadly dance.

Sweat glistened on their skin. They didn't speak or curse, their combat silent other than the sound of flesh hitting flesh and grunts when a blow hit its mark.

Jared thrust and slashed. Lachlan parried with kicks and blocks, but the effort to avoid Jared's wicked blade showed in the flare of his nostrils and the trickle of sweat along his temple.

Finally, Lachlan got in a solid leg kick that drove the air from Jared's lungs. He doubled over but recovered quickly. He delivered a vicious kick to Lachlan's left thigh that collapsed Lachlan's leg.

Lachlan crumpled with a groan.

"How's the old combat injury?" Jared taunted. He stood over Lachlan. The knife in his hand glinted in the overhead light.

Sophia's heart stopped. *Get up! Get up!* She scrambled to her feet and raised the gun between sweaty palms.

A wave of dizziness assaulted her. She sucked in as much air as her frozen lungs would allow. *Now! Shoot him.*

Her finger crept to the trigger.

Lachlan struck out with his foot, connected with Jared's knee, and sent him to the floor.

She'd lost her opportunity.

The men grappled. Lachlan's face creased in pain, his lips peeling back to expose clenched teeth.

He was weakening. She could see it. When Jared flipped him on his back and straddled him, she shrieked. She couldn't help it.

The tip of Jared's blade grazed Lachlan's neck. Droplets of crimson appeared.

Sophia pulled the trigger.

Her shoulders jerked at the recoil, and her ears rang from the deafening noise. Wood splintered from one of the ornate landscape frames on the opposite wall.

Both men froze, their heads turning in her direction.

Lachlan recovered first. He thrust his hips, flipping Jared to his back. He and Jared battled to control the knife.

Lachlan slowly forced the blade toward Jared. He raised his upper body and threw it down. The blade sunk partway into Jared's chest.

Lachlan lifted, threw down his weight again. The knife sunk in the rest of the way, exposing only the hilt.

Sophia forgot to breathe.

Silence wrapped around the room.

Lachlan's labored breaths grew loud to her ears.

Jared's wheezing gasps.

The ticking of the clock.

The faint screech of sirens.

She glanced at the gun in her white-knuckled grip, then set it carefully on the floor.

Lachlan stumbled to his feet with a snarl. He swiped the side of his neck and examined the smear of blood.

A crimson stain ebbed slowly around the blade's hilt, spreading across the white fabric of Jared's shirt.

Sophia couldn't tear her gaze from the gruesome tableau as Jared's breath rattled, then stilled.

Church bells rang from the clock, followed by six sonorous chimes.

She spun toward the windows. It didn't help. Storm clouds had rolled in, darkening the sky. The glass reflected the horror at her like a funhouse mirror. The sirens in the distance grew louder. Blue and red flashes streaked through the gloom, then scattered in the nearby trees. One, then two police cars raced up the driveway.

Lachlan's reflection approached her in the glass.

She turned to the flesh and blood man. Lines of pain bracketed his mouth and the corners of his eyes. His lips were a grim slash, his gaze somber. He raised bloody fingers to her cheek.

Were they trembling?

Or was she the one shaking?

Maybe they both were.

"I'm sorry you had tae see that, but I'm no' sorry he's dead."

The room spun.

Lachlan grabbed hold of her before her knees could buckle. "Sophia, I—"

"Lachlan." Nathan's voice came from the doorway. He glanced at Jared's body, then at Lachlan and Sophia. "The police are here. And so is—"

Before he could say more, a tall, dark-haired man in a suit brushed past him into the room.

The man stopped short when he caught sight of Jared. He knelt, placed his fingers on Jared's neck, then turned piercing blue eyes on Lachlan in a glare. "Jesus, Mackay."

Sophia's eyes widened in recognition. It was the man Lachlan had met with the night of the art gallery reception.

"It was self-defense, Lucas." Aggression still colored Lachlan's voice. "The bastard kidnapped Sophia and tried to kill us both. He murdered at least two people that we know."

Nathan chimed in. "We're pretty sure the guy downstairs murdered Roshan Haider. He was in London when Haider ate that bullet."

Two uniformed police officers entered the room and stopped short. They looked at the body on the floor, at the living occupants, then at the man Lachlan had called Lucas before one mumbled words Sophia couldn't make out into his shoulder mic.

Lucas stood and approached her and Lachlan. She caught the faint whiff of tobacco. "Miss Russo, I'm Assistant Director Lucas Caldwell with the FBI. Are you all right?"

FBI? She leaned into Lachlan's broad chest and tried not to fidget under the AD's scrutiny. "If by okay you mean alive and unharmed, then yes. I was drugged but not injured."

The fact her life had been turned upside down, her boss was dead, and she was feeling exposed and vulnerable? By that measure, she definitely was not all right.

AD Caldwell gestured to one of the officers who'd now stepped into the room and was examining Jared's body. "Take Miss Russo to the hospital and have her checked out. Detective Johnson can interview her there and then see that she gets home."

He scowled at Lachlan, then at Nathan, still hovering by the open doors. "You two are with me."

"Hold up a minute." A man who looked to be in his fifties joined the group. He had thinning brown hair, a brown sport coat that did little to obscure his middle-aged paunch, and a harassed expression that looked so at home Sophia suspected it was his resting face. "We got a guy downstairs who needs medical attention and—" his gaze traveled the room before landing on Jared. "Nice office." He pointed at Jared while looking at the FBI agent for confirmation. "Dead?"

At Caldwell's nod, the detective heaved a weary sigh, then withdrew a small, spiral-bound notebook and pen from his breast pocket. "This is a crime scene. No one goes anywhere other than Fairfax County PD Headquarters."

"These people are involved in an active federal investigation, Detective. I'll need to be present when you interview them." The Assistant Director gestured toward Sophia. "Miss Russo was forcibly abducted by the deceased. I suggest you get an officer to take her to get medically cleared before you interview her."

The detective's mouth turned down at the corners. "Fine." He motioned to one of the uniformed officers. "Escort Miss Russo to Fairfax Hospital."

Sophia turned in Lachlan's arms, digging her fingers into his biceps to anchor herself to him. "I don't want to leave you." Why did she feel if he left here without her, she might never see him again?

"Go, *mo chridhe*. Everything will be all right." He brushed his lips over hers before gently setting her away from him, leaving her bereft of his warmth.

The detective pointed at Lachlan and Nathan. "You two are under arrest." He glared at Lucas Caldwell. "The crime scene techs and the guy from the coroner's office need to get in here."

"Wait!" Sophia objected. "Why are they under arrest?" Lachlan and Nathan had come to save her. Now they stood with their hands behind their backs while an officer handcuffed them and read them their rights. She wanted to scream at the injustice of it all.

The detective ignored her and continued down the hall.

"How did you know to come here?" Lachlan's question to AD Caldwell turned her attention back to the men in the room.

The man gave Sophia a measured look before responding. "Admiral Dane's daughter called him and told him Jared Landry had abducted Sophia." His face twisted in a look of disgust. "I'm almost surprised a SEAL team didn't beat us to the scene. When the admiral says jump, everyone in this town asks how high."

Sophia's heart stopped, then started again, pounding a furious rhythm. Lachlan's face had turned to stone. *Look at me, please*, she begged him silently.

"Miss." Sophia glanced into the face of a young dark-haired police officer, not much older than her. "We need to go."

"Lachlan." *I love you. I was trying to help.* She wanted to scream the words.

He stood there, handcuffed, grim-faced. When he met her eyes, he'd tucked his emotions back into himself. "Go." His gaze hardened as he directed it to the officer gripping her arm. "Make sure she gets home safely."

That was it?

After everything they'd been through, that was all he was going to say?

Her body went numb, her mind finally reacting to the trauma she'd just experienced by wrapping itself in a cocoon of protection, dulling her emotions.

Nathan sent her a sympathetic glance as the policeman ushered her from the room.

Raindrops began to fall, gently at first, then with greater intensity as the officer assisted Sophia into the back seat of one of the squad cars. Leaning her head against the window, she watched through fogging glass as Lachlan and Nathan were escorted from Jared's home amidst a growing swarm of law enforcement and placed into the back of another vehicle.

She shut her eyes and pictured Lachlan's face when he'd decided to trust her before she launched herself at Jared. The emotion in his eyes had been real.

It had given her hope.

If this was the last time she ever saw him, that was what she wanted to remember.

CHAPTER
THIRTY-THREE

Two Weeks Later

The deep-throated roar of a passenger jet taking off from Dulles rattled the windows of Nathan's pickup as Lachlan climbed into the passenger seat and slammed the door. "You don't understand."

"Don't understand what, amigo." Nathan backed out of the space in daily parking and headed for the ticket booth. "That you haven't bothered to contact Sophia since we were arrested?" He scowled at Lachlan. "Two fucking weeks ago?"

He lowered his window and jammed the parking ticket into the machine. "She helped save your sorry ass and almost died because of it." The bar lifted, and he exited airport parking toward Dulles Toll Road.

"Exactly." Lachlan's temper ignited, as did his guilt. "She almost died because of me and my past. And it's no' like I've been lounging around. I haven't even had the chance to get a new phone." He'd been held in detention, then sent to Kabul to help the FBI uncover and dismantle Landry's trafficking operation along with Ryder.

Once Burkette learned Landry was dead, he'd spilled his guts in return for leniency on the trafficking and kidnapping charges. It hadn't stopped the Metropolitan Police in London from taking a hard look at his time in the UK, and it was likely they would charge him with Haider's murder.

Even with Josh's confession, Lachlan wasn't sure he would walk away with his freedom. Jared had done a damn good job stacking evidence against him.

He might have succeeded if it hadn't been for Sophia and the files she'd turned over to Admiral Dane. A sharp-eyed forensic accountant at the FBI identified minute discrepancies between the financial spreadsheet on Fred Biller's computer and the one from Jared's. They were able to piece together the money trail and locate the accounts where Jared laundered his dirty money.

Then there was the encrypted folder with Lachlan's name on it.

Landry had been gathering information on him since before he left the SAS, tracking his movements even after he came to work at LAI. All circumstantial evidence, but with Jared's connection to Nadia, enough to lend credibility to Lachlan's claim he'd been framed and wasn't a co-conspirator.

Sophia had told him she loved him, but after everything that had happened, what if she'd decided he carried too much baggage? With Jared's death and LAI under federal investigation, he was unemployed.

Christ. Until yesterday, he hadn't been certain he wasn't going to be indicted for arms trafficking.

For the past two weeks, he'd given Sophia the time and space to sort out her feelings.

Nathan took one hand off the wheel to dig into his jeans pocket. His phone landed in Lachlan's lap. "Here."

Lachlan stared at the device. "I'm not sure what to say." He shifted uneasily on the seat and rubbed at the ache in his chest.

"How about this? Hi, Sophia. I'm an ass. Please forgive me because I will never find another woman as incredible as you for as long as I live." Nathan glanced at him and arched a brow. "See? Easy."

"Piss off. It's more complex than that. Maybe she doesn't want to be with me after all the shite I put her through. Did ya ever think of that, ya *bawbag*?" Lachlan glared at his friend. His heart pounded in a furious rhythm. "And turn the heat down." He wiped the sweat from his hairline.

Nathan gave a derisive snort. "The heat isn't on. You coward. You don't deserve her." The look he sent Lachlan was calculating. "Maybe I'll give her a ring, offer to comfort her."

A snarl burst from Lachlan's throat. Red colored the edges of his vision. All the shite he'd dealt with in the last month and the fear that Sophia might walk away simmered below his skin. He'd love nothing more than to release it through his fists. "If you weren't driving, I'd have a go at ye."

Nathan's jaw went rigid. "If there were a place to pull over on this damn road, I'd let you try so I could beat some sense into that thick Scottish skull."

Tension, impenetrable as a dense fog, hung between them for the rest of the drive.

Nathan pulled to a stop in front of Lachlan's apartment building. He leaned his head back against the headrest and let out a deep sigh. "Give Sophia some credit. She's stronger than you believe. You've been given a huge gift, my man, your freedom and the chance to start over with a woman who loves you."

He turned to meet Lachlan's eyes, and his crystal blue gaze wouldn't let Lachlan look away. "It's time to bury the past and live your life."

Lachlan's throat was too tight to get out any words. He grabbed his bag and climbed from Nathan's truck, lifting his hand in a brief wave as his mate drove off.

Thankfully, he made it to his apartment without encountering any other residents.

He might no longer be front-page news, but that wouldn't stop some of his nosier neighbors from trying to corral him into conversation. He breathed in stale air and shuffled down the hall with a weary sigh before tossing his duffel on the bed and heading to the bathroom.

A splash of cold water on his face snapped him into focus. *Christ.* His reflection mocked him. He hadn't looked this haggard on the worst days of deployment. Pasty skin, dark circles, misery lurking in his eyes. He needed a shave.

There hadn't been a minute of the past two weeks he hadn't thought about Sophia. At first, he'd tried to convince himself that he couldn't entrust his heart to a woman who might betray him, but the excuse rang hollow. Sophia was a decent woman to her marrow. She wasn't Nadia. Her only thought had been to try and help.

She wasn't the problem.

His fears were.

He wiped his face with a towel and headed to the kitchen, straight for the bottle of Scotch.

After blowing the dust off a highball glass, he gave himself a generous pour and added a splash of water. A taste of home.

He stared into the amber liquid. Was Scotland his home anymore?

His apartment's barren, beige walls were proof he hadn't made the States his home, either. He'd been too caught up in his past to realize there were people in his present who cared about him. People who wanted him to have a future.

Nathan and Ryder had never wavered in their support. Lucas Caldwell kept his agents digging until they found evidence against Jared. Sophia had believed in him enough to risk her life and career.

It was time he returned the favor.

Once the FBI publicly exonerated him, he could start again. Admiral Dane had promised to pull considerable strings to salvage his reputation. When Lachlan asked why, the admiral said simply, "Sophia believes in you."

He wandered into his living room, the one place in his apartment where his walls weren't so empty. His finger traced the figure of the black-haired Highlander.

What if he stayed here, built a business and a life where his heart lived?

Mo Chridhe. My heart.

Would she give him a chance to show her that a life with her meant more to him than his past? In her presence, his ghosts had ceased to be ghosts and instead had become memories he could put into perspective and move on from.

DC's monuments glowed in the distance, a view that made his eleventh-floor perch worth the hefty sum of rent he paid. The setting sun had taken what was left of his energy with it.

He'd get some sleep, plan out what he needed to say because she might only give him one chance.

He was damaged and battle-scarred, but he would find a way to prove worthy of Sophia's love. Nathan was right.

It was time to put his past behind him and look to the future.

Fourteen days. Two long and agonizing weeks since the nightmare at Jared's home. Her boss was dead, his company shuttered, and Lachlan had been taken away by the police and FBI.

Sophia twisted the faucet knob closed and dumped fresh water into the reservoir of her coffeemaker, the morning sun streaming into her condo doing little to brighten her dismal mood.

A glance at her phone confirmed Lachlan still hadn't tried to contact her.

No texts. No voicemails. No emails. Heck, she even checked her mailbox every day for an old-fashioned letter. Pride kept her from reaching out to Nathan or Admiral Dane.

If Lachlan didn't want to speak to her, she wouldn't beg for scraps of information.

She poured coffee grounds into the paper basket and jabbed the start button.

After a few seconds, the machine hissed. Coffee dripped in a steady stream into the glass carafe. Maybe Lachlan was still in jail.

What if, after all her efforts, the FBI didn't believe he was innocent?

The last bit of water sputtered into the pot.

She took out a mug and poured herself some of the hot brew, adding a splash of half and half. Emily called every day from Paris to check on her. There were times Sophia was tempted not to answer the phone so she could mope in peace. She didn't need her friend's pity, no matter how well-intentioned. Her career was up in smoke. The man she loved hadn't loved her back.

At least not enough to overcome his demons.

She sat on the sofa and skimmed through her emails. The only new one was from Barclays, letting her know her credit card statement was available. Non-essential purchases were out for the time being. Her savings would get her through the next couple of months, but not much more.

Her parents had offered to pay her bills until she could find a new job.

After they learned her boss had tried to kill her, they'd even volunteered to fly out to see her—which she'd politely declined. All those years spent trying to be the perfect daughter, the high achiever to get her parents to notice her when all she'd needed was to torch her career, almost end up dead, and get her heart broken. They meant well, in their way, but she wasn't up for the awkward visit.

A sniff of her pajamas told her in no uncertain terms she'd wallowed long enough. Her mug landed on the coffee table with a thud, sending a wave of hot brew over the rim onto the glass. It was time to shower, get dressed, re-do the resume, and search for a new job.

Maybe sell her condo and leave DC.

Start fresh somewhere else.

Meet a nice, non-threatening guy who supported her career and wanted at least two kids, a dog, and a house in the suburbs. Or maybe, she'd live a carefree, single life in a big city somewhere and stop worrying about finding someone to love her.

After she got a paper towel and wiped up the mess she'd just made.

After she cleaned up her spill, she took a nice, long hot shower. It was just what she needed. That, and the lectures under the hot spray and shampoo lather, using every psychology trick she knew about self-efficacy and positive affirmations. She blew her hair dry until it was straight and glossy, then applied makeup.

Start as you mean to go on.

Blah, blah, blah.

Lachlan wasn't going to return. She needed to get on with her life. It hurt, but she'd keep up the internal pep talks for as long as necessary. There were some promising legislative affairs positions at the state level in Colorado, Kentucky, and Michigan and several in corporate government relations. A fresh start in a new town might be just what the doctor ordered.

As for her heart, it would mend. She breathed into the pain blossoming in the hollow space in her chest.

Padding to the kitchen in her comfy socks, she grabbed a bottle of sparkling water and took a swig. Now, about that resume.

A sudden burst of three forceful knocks rattled her door. Her hand jerked, spilling water down the front of her t-shirt. She grimaced as the liquid soaked into the cotton fabric. At least it wasn't wine.

Would this ever be over? Another round of police or FBI with more questions and no answers about Lachlan and his whereabouts. Active federal investigation, they said. The security guards downstairs had stopped calling her for permission to let them up.

She yanked open the door and froze.

"I told you to always look through the peephole first." The admonition was flavored in aged whisky with a hint of the sea—a melody of Scotland that drew her in like a piper's flute.

Her fingers tightened around the water bottle hard enough to send liquid over the rim to wet her fingers.

Shadows bruised Lachlan's eyes, the lines bracketing them more pronounced. His skin had a sallow tinge, and he looked like he hadn't slept in days.

She drank him in, waiting for a burst of joy to engulf her.

It didn't come.

Anger, then—she'd be struck by fury any second.

That didn't happen either.

Numbness.

Bingo.

"How did you get past security?"

"The security in your building is a farce." Lachlan strode past her to her living room. He rubbed the back of his neck, then shoved his hands into the back pockets of his jeans.

She tried not to notice how the action stretched his forest green t-shirt across his sculpted chest or how the color matched his eyes.

"I was afraid you wouldn't let me come up if you knew I was here." He eyed her carefully. "You're angry with me."

She arched her brows. "Why would I be angry?"

"Sophia, I—"

"Would it be because you disappeared for two weeks, and you couldn't manage to pick up the phone?"

"I—"

"Not to let me know if you were alive, where you were? Because I wasn't important enough for you to bother?" So much for numbness.

The fear and grief she'd been mired in for two weeks rose like a tidal wave to swamp her. Her vision hazed, and her muscles twitched with the need to release the pent-up emotions.

She stomped over and jabbed a finger into his hard chest. "You suck."

"I know."

Jab. "Everything I did, I did to help you."

"I realize that now."

Another jab. "You don't deserve a minute of my time."

"I ken."

"You don't deserve *me*." Her voice broke. She poked him again.

This time, he trapped her hand to his chest and wouldn't give it back. "I know that better than anyone, *mo chridhe*, but I'm asking you to give me a chance to explain."

This close, his familiar scent reached her nose. His body heat warmed her palm, the thud of his heart echoing beneath her fingers. His eyes willed her to listen.

God. She loved him, despite everything. And he cared for her, maybe not enough, but she'd seen it on his face when he showed up at her door after her attack, when they'd made love, and when he realized they might not make it out of Jared's alive.

He'd run toward the battle when her life was at stake, *knowing* Jared planned to kill him.

Her Highlander. Just like the one in the painting.

Then he'd left her without a word for two weeks because he didn't trust her.

What was love, or whatever he felt for her, if there was no trust?

She yanked free her hand and gave him her back so he wouldn't see her lips tremble. "Fine. Explain." Now that she'd spent her fury, she needed to sit down before she fell.

He sat next to her on the couch. Too close.

Her traitorous body loosened, every cell reaching for him. She twined her fingers together to keep from not so accidentally brushing his muscular thigh and forgetting she was angry with him.

"After the police got your statement and took mine and Nathan's, they ruled we'd acted in self-defense, so I won't be going to prison for killing Jared."

Thank you. Sophia's eyes shut before opening to spear Lachlan with an arch look. "The police wouldn't let you call me?"

Lachlan's Adam's apple bobbed on a hard swallow.

Her heart gave a painful lurch. "You didn't want to."

His fingers crept to the back of his neck. "The police released Nathan, but Lucas Caldwell placed me into federal custody. The next thing I knew, I was on a plane to Afghanistan with Lucas and his agents to comb through LAI's Kabul office for information that would help unravel Landry's business arrangements with Mohammad Razul Khan."

"Did you get what you wanted?" At his puzzled look, she continued. "To bring down the warlord and avenge your teammates." Maybe now he could finally bury his ghosts.

"Did I?" He pursed his lips. "I guess so. Afghan special forces raided Khan's compound before the weapons auction could take place. Confiscated dozens of weapons. Khan disappeared somewhere into the Hindu Kush. He may avoid capture, but he'll no longer enjoy the protection of the Afghan government."

He turned his head, his gaze capturing hers with an intensity that did not allow her to look away. "And all I could think about was you."

"And yet you didn't try to contact me. Because you didn't know if you could ever bring yourself to trust me again."

"I'm sorry." Regret shadowed his features.

Sorry for what? she thought. Was this where he tried to let her down easy? The *I care about you, but we can't be together because I can never trust you* speech?

She stood, hugging her arms to her body, and put some distance between them. She ought to give him credit for breaking her heart in person but ghosting her might have made this easier.

He rose from the couch and stood there, watching her like she was a bomb he didn't know how to defuse.

She may not have much, but she still had her dignity. Faking a smile, she injected a light, breezy tone into her voice. "So, now what? You're free and out of a job. Will you go back to Scotland?"

He frowned. His shrug was stilted, not his normal fluid movement. "I guess that depends on you. I'd planned to stay here. Nathan, Ryder, and I have discussed forming our own company. With our backgrounds and contacts, I think we could make a go of it."

Okay, now he'd lost her. "Why does it depend on me?"

"Because *mo chridhe*, if you're no' part of my life, I'll no' stay." His voice had roughened, his Highland accent more pronounced.

When he closed the gap between them, she didn't back away.

"I don't understand. What are you saying?"

"I didn't contact you because I convinced myself you needed time to decide if you could overcome everything my bloody past had put you through. In truth, I was afraid you'd come to regret loving me."

A rogue kernel of hope found its way to her heart, her natural optimism rebounding. "I will never regret loving you. What does *mo-chree-eh* mean?"

Lachlan's arms came around her. He lowered his head until the only thing she could see was the truth in his emerald eyes. The shadows had disappeared. In their place was an apology mixed with tenderness and something more profound. "It means my heart. I love you, Sophia. I'm sorry I didn't trust your love. You make me a better man—a more hopeful one. For the first time in years, I can see a future instead of simply existing. Please say you'll forgive me."

Her doubts evaporated, leaving her twenty pounds lighter. Of course she forgave him, but after everything he put her through, she wouldn't make this easy. "I need a job."

He blinked. "That's not the response I was expecting."

"I'm not finished. I want to be part of your new company."

She had to bite her lip to keep from laughing at the confused look on his face. "Of course. People would much rather deal with you than me any—"

"And an ownership stake."

Lachlan's brows winged upward. "My rose grew thorns whilst I was away."

"Do you want me or not?" Her mouth went dry when his expression turned grave. Had she pushed too hard, too soon?

"On one condition. We seal our business arrangement with a marital one."

"A—a what?" Now that she hadn't been expecting. She had to blink rapidly to clear her vision.

"Please don't cry, *leannan*. Tell me you love me—that it's not too late for us." His words were issued as a command, tinged with desperation.

She gave a watery laugh as a burst of happiness flooded her. "That sounded like an order, Captain Mackay."

The corners of his mouth lifted. His eyes glistened, which did her in. "I love you, Sophia."

"I love you, too. And I accept. Both offers." She kissed her Highland warrior.

He wouldn't be an easy man to love, but he *saw* her.

She didn't have to prove she was worth loving, that she deserved respect.

And she saw him. He *was* the man in the painting.

She would make sure he never doubted it and that the ghosts from his past stayed banished forever.

EPILOGUE

Lachlan crouched, running his palm over white limestone. Memories and the scent of freshly mowed grass filled the air. His fingers traced the engraved winged dagger insignia of the SAS. Beneath it, *25068743* Troop Staff Sergeant Thomas Barnwell, 22 Special Air Service Regiment, Age 34.

His fiancée's hand rested on his shoulder, her gentle touch grounding him. In a week, Sophia would be his wife. First, however, he was here in Herefordshire to say goodbye to an old friend.

"*Mo charaid*, it's been a long time." His throat closed up. *I'm sorry.* He glanced at the woman next to him before returning his gaze to the stone. "You should see her, Thom. She makes life worth living."

He looked to the clouds, the religion of his youth telling him his friend was more likely to be found in that direction than beneath the cold earth at his feet.

"I have my own company now. Dìleas. It means faithful. And I will be."

Lachlan dug beneath his shirt and lifted the metal ID disc over his head. He draped the tag over the grave marker. "This belongs to you, pal. I've kept it long enough."

Rising to his feet, he rendered a crisp salute.

He and Sophia stood for a moment in silence. The row of markers glistened against the backdrop of the green manicured lawn. Beams of sunlight fought through the overcast sky above them, dappling the gravestones.

The sound of a child's laughter drew their gazes to the path on their right. A young mother pushed a pram while the man with her chased down a giggling toddler.

Life amid death.

"You deserve happiness." Sophia twined her fingers in his.

"I have it." He raised their joined hands to kiss her knuckles. "I have you."

THE END

If you loved Lachlan and Sophia's story, please consider leaving a review on Amazon and/or Goodreads. Reviews help other readers find my stories!

Excerpt from Missing in Action

Dìleas Security Agency, Book Two

Prologue

Nathan Long set down his mug and propped his boots on the corner of the desk in his Fairfax Station, Virginia, home office, which he'd affectionately nicknamed the "war room." Burnt-orange blackout drapes covered his polycarbonate bulletproof windows, shutting out any prying eyes and the afternoon sun that had just begun to peek through the clouds.

Leaning back in his chair, he banged away on the game controller in his lap, waiting for his buddy Lachlan to deal with the pretty little redhead who'd sequestered herself in Nathan's hall bathroom. The first time he'd headed to the kitchen for coffee, he got an eyeful of Lachlan and Sophia Russo getting up close and personal in his living room.

Hell, he would have stayed for the show, but he didn't think Sophia was the kind of woman to appreciate voyeurs. Instead, he'd retreated back to the war room and waited until the sound of the bathroom door slamming served as his cue to grab a cup and beat feet during the temporary lull.

A well-timed virtual grenade toss lit up his monitor.

Damn, I'm good. Another bad guy down.

He'd hang out and kill time and video game enemies until Lachlan let him know it was safe to come out. He never thought he'd see the day Mackay would have his balls twisted in a knot over a woman.

Not after Nadia.

A loud buzz came through his computer speakers.

Visitor at the gate.

Which was a problem.

He dropped his feet to the floor with a thud and tossed the game controller aside. "Hey, Lach, heads up. We've got company."

A few keyboard clicks later, all three of his monitors displayed live camera feeds from around his property.

Lachlan Mackay appeared over his shoulder, green eyes narrowed on the screen.

The center monitor showed his front steel security gate, the cameras giving him a high-def image of the sporty red Lexus convertible parked at the entrance. The persistent buzz came courtesy of a blonde in a khaki trench coat stabbing the intercom button on his brick-clad gate pillar. She scowled at the camera above her head.

Nathan's curiosity spiked along with his libido.

Shoulder-length light blonde hair surrounded a heart-shaped face and pale blue eyes. The woman had a slight cleft in her chin beneath full lips glossed in a peach color. Her nose tilted upward, just a touch at the end, giving her a perky quality that kept her overall appearance of sophistication from seeming too snobbish. She cocked a hip and gave the camera a look that told him she didn't plan to go anywhere.

He twisted his head around to look at Lachlan. "Any idea who our guest is? She looks vaguely familiar."

"Yes." Irritation thickened Lachlan's Scottish burr. "Sophia's friend. Get rid of her."

"Ah, the blonde who drove Sophia to work after her run-in with Roshan Haider." Nathan opened the connection on the intercom. "Yes?" Not his friendliest tone, but he didn't take kindly to uninvited guests. Especially now, with the predicament his former SAS buddy was in.

"Nathan Long? I need to speak to you. It's urgent."

"Ma'am, do you see all those 'No Trespassing' signs? Whatever you're selling, I'm not buying."

Well, not entirely true. If she'd shown up any other time, he might have let her in. She looked like a classy, intelligent woman who'd turn her cute little nose up at his faded jeans and concert t-shirts.

But if there was one thing he liked, it was a challenge.

"I'm not selling anything, but let me tell you what I know." The woman's gaze somehow found him through the camera even though the video feed wasn't two-way. She inched closer to the intercom and lowered her voice. "I *know* you contacted Sophia Russo with information about Lachlan Mackay. I *know* she met you here this morning, and I *know* she hasn't been seen or heard from since."

He unmuted the intercom. "Sorry, but I *know* I can't help you." He had a sinking feeling it would take more than a verbal brush-off to send Blondie on her way.

"Oh, this is ridiculous," Blondie sputtered. She folded her arms across her chest and glared into the lens. "Sophia was supposed to contact me—" she made a show of raising her arm to check the elegant watch on her wrist, "an hour ago. Which she hasn't." Her baby blues swung back to the camera. "I swear to God, if you don't let me in, I will climb over this gate, march down your driveway, and pound on your door!"

"Her name is Emily. She's a college friend of Sophia's. See if you can find out anything more about her," Lachlan murmured in his ear.

"Easily done." Nathan's fingers flew across his keyboard as he opened up some of his favorite software toys on his left monitor. "Let's backdoor our way into a few government databases and see what pops up. Running a facial recognition scan—what the fuck?" His gaze narrowed on his center monitor.

The woman was scaling his damn fence.

She dropped down on the other side and began to march up his driveway.

He frantically disabled laser tripwires between the gate and the house. Then he spun out of his chair and palmed his Sig Sauer P226 before waving Lachlan toward one of the monitors. "See if the computer spits out her details. I'll go welcome our guest." The oak floorboards creaked beneath his weight as he hoofed it out of his war room down the hall to his front door.

Emily rounded the curve of his driveway right as he stepped out onto the porch. He watched her gracefully navigate puddle-filled potholes from the early morning rain shower. As she got closer, she raised her head and came to an abrupt halt at the sight of Sophia's car.

Nathan grimaced. He should have had Sophia park in the garage. *My bad.*

Too late now.

Her gaze traveled past the vehicle to land on his face before dropping to the pistol in his left hand. She stiffened, then squared her shoulders and kept advancing. He let nothing show on his face, even as his body flared to life. This woman had a set of brass ones—he'd give her that.

The security camera hadn't lied. She was a looker. Her eyes had appeared blue in the live feed. They looked greener in person, although it was hard to tell where he stood.

She stopped at the base of the stairs and peered up at him with a wary expression. "Where is Sophia?"

Emily Dane sucked in a breath for courage and faced the giant with the short, spiky blond hair glaring down at her from a cute front porch with white posts and picket railing fronting a tan brick seventies-style ranch. The door behind him was painted a blue-gray to match the shutters framing the white paned windows.

Her father and brother were both a few inches over six feet. This guy was even taller.

And built.

A lefty. He made no move to conceal the handgun in his giant palm—as if everyone greeted people at their front door in such a manner. Her heart beat triple time. She was pretty sure it wasn't exertion or even fear. Which left...

Damn.

Icy blue eyes regarded her suspiciously over a straight-edged nose. She let her gaze drift over the muscles stretching the fabric of his black graphic t-shirt and noted the tattoos peeking out from under the short sleeves. Faded blue jeans rested low on his hips. His long, muscled legs ended at a pair of tan combat boots that looked almost twice as big as her size nines.

Her hormones shivered in delight. And didn't that just tick her off.

She'd done some digging on Nathan Long. He was a former Navy SEAL, which was both good and bad. Good, in that she knew SEALs, and most of them only killed when they had to, during an op. Bad, in that SEALs possessed deadly skills, and if she was wrong about this particular SEAL, she and her best friend Sophia were in a crapload of danger.

She would have pegged him as an operator even without her research. This guy had the warrior vibe she recognized, having grown up around Team Guys.

The paranoia, too, if his home security was any indication.

"You're big for a SEAL." She almost slapped a hand over her mouth after the words escaped. Where had *that* come from?

Apparently, her ability to intimidate men with her infamous 'take no prisoners' demeanor had taken a vacay and left her stranded on Ditzy Island.

A startled look crossed his face. Then his lips twisted as if he were trying not to laugh.

"It made BUD/S and SQT more challenging," he said in the distinctive Texas drawl she'd picked up through the intercom. "But I got by."

His voice was as deep and rumbly in person as it had been through the speaker at the front gate and reverberated through her body.

His amusement fled as quickly as it arrived. "You know who I am, but I know nothing about you." He didn't stir from his position at the top of the steps, nor did he put his gun away.

"My name is Emily Dane. I already told you. I'm here because my friend Sophia was supposed to meet with you this morning, and I haven't heard from her."

Judging by how his eyes widened a fraction when she told him her name, he'd put two and two together and come up with Admiral's Daughter.

Her father was highly respected in the SEAL community. Maybe she could leverage that in her favor.

She gestured in the direction of Sophia's car. "Where is she?"

Nathan didn't answer, observing her in silence. Was he going to deny Sophia was in his home when they were both staring at her *freaking* car? And he really needed to come down to her level before she developed a crick in her neck.

She blew out a hard breath. As much as she was enjoying the staring contest—*not*—it was time for a new approach. "Look, I know Sophia came to you looking for answers about Lachlan Mackay. I'm afraid she's in danger."

There. *Danger*. A nice keyword a SEAL could focus on. If she couldn't rouse his sense of propriety, she would appeal to the part of him that had made him want to serve his country. If he was like the rest of his SEAL brethren, he had an alphahole protective streak a mile wide.

"We could use some help." She resisted the urge to do the whole "damsel in distress" thing and bat her eyes.

The blue-gray door behind Nathan flew open.

Sophia stood in the doorway. "Emily."

Nathan Long let out a defeated sigh that seemed to come from the tips of his massive boots.

Emily cocked her brow and gave the big SEAL a victorious smirk. Poor man, he'd actually thought he stood a chance of winning this standoff. He didn't know her.

She'd learned from the best.

Missing in Action *(Dìleas Security Agency, Book 2), Available on Amazon*

Bonus Freebie

Want to know how it all began for the men of Dìleas Security Agency?

Sign up for my newsletter at cssmithauthor.com and I'll send you the prequel novella, The Mission, for free!

Also By C.S. Smith

Acknowledgments

Near Miss is my debut romantic suspense novel and I don't know where to begin to thank everyone who has helped me get Lachlan and Sophia's story out into the world.

I first would like to thank my husband and children. You've been the best cheerleading team anyone could imagine. I love you all to the moon and back.

So many amazing writers have critiqued endless pages, I will inevitably miss some of you, and for that, I apologize:

Charlotte Lit's Authors Lab: Kim, Paul, and Kathy. My Author's Lab coach, Rick.

My awesome Killer Writers: Nancy, Vicki, and Tina. You ladies have made me a stronger writer. I don't know what I would do without you!

My Charlotte Writers Club Womens Fiction critique group gave me valuable beta reader feedback.

My fellow romance author, Tracy in the early stages of this story told me it didn't start in the right place and critiqued it until I got it right.

My editor, Liana dragged me kicking and screaming into changes that made this story so much stronger. My copyeditor, April ran a fine-tooth comb over the results.

My Sensei, Louis who helped me choreograph the fight scene.

Mairibeth graciously agreed to read my book to make sure Lachlan sounded like a proper Scot.

Writing is a solitary endeavor, and yet, it requires a village to birth a book.

Thank you to my village. I hope I make you proud.

Any and all mistakes are mine alone.

About the Author
Heat, Heart, and Heroes -- Steamy Romantic Suspense

C.S. Smith parlayed her degrees in government and national security studies into various careers as a policy analyst, export manager, and director of a city government committee on global connectivity. Her love of spine-tingling romantic suspense can be traced to her formative years in Washington, DC, surrounded by intrigue and good-looking men in uniform—including the one she married.

A native New Englander who has spent over half her life in North Carolina, she has joined the ranks of empty nesters, leaving only her husband and "faux" Golden Retriever at her mercy.

For more information, please visit cssmithauthor.com or connect with her on any of these platforms:

Made in United States
North Haven, CT
26 September 2023

42004832R10198